The Patchwork Players

Also by Jennifer Chiaverini

Canary Girls
Switchboard Soldiers
The Women's March
Mrs. Lincoln's Sisters
Resistance Women
Enchantress of Numbers
Fates and Traitors
Christmas Bells
Mrs. Grant and Madame Jule
Mrs. Lincoln's Rival
The Spymistress
Mrs. Lincoln's Dressmaker

The Elm Creek Quilts Novels

The Quilter's Apprentice
Round Robin
The Cross-Country Quilters
The Runaway Quilt
The Quilter's Legacy
The Master Quilter
The Sugar Camp Quilt
The Christmas Quilt
Circle of Quilters
The Quilter's Homecoming
The New Year's Quilt
The Winding Ways Quilt
The Quilter's Kitchen
The Lost Quilter
A Quilter's Holiday
The Aloha Quilt
The Union Quilters
The Wedding Quilt
Sonoma Rose
The Giving Quilt
The Christmas Boutique
The Museum of Lost Quilts
The World's Fair Quilt

The Patchwork Players

An Elm Creek Quilts Novel

JENNIFER
CHIAVERINI

wm
WILLIAM MORROW
An Imprint of HarperCollins*Publishers*

This is a work of fiction. Names, characters, places, and incidents are products of the author's imagination or are used fictitiously and are not to be construed as real. Any resemblance to actual events, locales, organizations, or persons, living or dead, is entirely coincidental.

HarperCollins books may be purchased for educational, business, or sales promotional use. For information, please email the Special Markets Department at SPsales@harpercollins.com.

hc.com

FIRST EDITION

Designed by Nancy Singer

Library of Congress Cataloging-in-Publication Data has been applied for.

ISBN 978-0-06-338180-3

26 27 28 29 30 LBC 6 5 4 3 2

To my family, with all my love

The Patchwork Players

1

Julia adored launch parties, especially when she not only starred onscreen but also played the role of hostess, entertaining dear friends and colleagues at her hillside mansion in Malibu. The mood was festive and full of anticipation that September evening, the air humming with conversation and laughter as about four dozen members of the cast and production crew, their plus-ones, and a select few members of the press mingled in her elegantly appointed great room, a paradigm of California Coastal design in warm earth tones, clean lines, and simple silhouettes. The two sets of glass doors to the broad balcony had been thrown open, the gossamer drapes gracefully drawn back, the soft ocean breezes beckoning guests outside to admire the breathtaking panoramas of the Pacific and stunning views of the Santa Monica Mountains.

Sipping champagne as she mingled among her guests, Julia graciously accepted air-kisses and congratulations and offered plenty of the same. She paused by the Steinway baby grand in the corner to murmur her thanks to the handsome young assistant from set design who had claimed the bench upon arrival and had been enchanting everyone with deft renditions of jazz classics ever since. Uniformed catering staff circulated with trays of enticing canapés, the savory aromas vying with the fragrance of lush flowers artfully arranged in the elegant earthenware vases Julia had collected on her world travels. A few subtle yet intriguing contemporary artworks adorned the walls—oil paintings, watercolors, and one antique Prairie Rose quilt she had acquired while filming on location in Kansas the previous winter. Photos and memorabilia from her decades-long performing career were displayed on the shelves flanking the fireplace on one end of the room, but she kept her Emmys and Golden Globe out of sight on a discreet shelf in the master suite. Anyone who might visit her already knew she had won the awards. Flaunting them would suggest a desperate craving for approval that really should be beneath her.

Yet her deliberate modesty didn't extend to her late husband's honors. Her gaze traveled to the bespoke art nook in the archway between the great room and the foyer, where Charles's two golden Oscars gleamed softly beneath the museum-quality lights she'd had installed a few months after his death in 1993. At the time, she had been debating whether to leave the home they had shared for most of their marriage, suddenly achingly empty without him. Now, eleven years and a few months later, she was thankful she had stayed. The sharp anguish of mourning had receded over time, and fond memories of Charles lingered in every room, bringing a smile to her lips at unexpected moments throughout the day.

"Seems to me there's room on that shelf for your own statuettes," a familiar, gravelly voice rumbled just behind her.

Drawn from her reverie, Julia turned to find her longtime agent at her side, his wife smiling beside him. Maury's face had grown wizened through the years, his shoulders stooped, his nearly bald pate fringed by thin wisps of gray hair, but his eyes were as knowing and kind as ever. Belying the stereotypes of his profession, Maury was honest and straightforward rather than ruthless, one of Hollywood's last true gentlemen. He and Evelyn had seen Julia through the bleak aftermath of Charles's death and the two foolish, utterly regrettable, mercifully swift marriages and bitter divorces that had followed. Maury had unraveled hundreds of management snarls and eased countless disappointments on her behalf throughout the years. Although he had officially retired five years before, he had resumed representing Julia, his sole remaining client, after a disastrous experience with his replacement proved that she couldn't manage without him.

"Don't tempt me to brag about myself," Julia scolded him playfully. "You know excessive pride is my fatal flaw."

Evelyn, lovely with her upswept silvery hair, fine features, and effortless grace that recalled her years as a dancer and choreographer, regarded Julia fondly. "But you should be proud of yourself, tonight of all nights," she said. "The fifth season premiere of any television series is a remarkable milestone, but *A Patchwork Life* is that elusive dream, both critically acclaimed and exceptionally popular. Enjoy your success, Julia. You've earned it."

"Oh, Evelyn, stop before you make me blush." Raising her glass, Julia inclined her head toward Maury. "You're very kind, but we both know I owe it all to your husband."

"Hardly," Maury demurred.

"You brought *A Patchwork Life* to me," Julia pointed out. "When I rolled my eyes at the title and scoffed at the premise, you insisted I take the part anyway."

"No, I merely urged you to read the script before you rejected the role," said Maury. "But that script was for the movie. Need I remind you that was an utter disaster?"

Evelyn shuddered dramatically. "As if we could forget. But that wasn't your fault, dear, nor yours, Julia. Who could have foreseen that Stephen Deneford would transform your feminist historical drama into a preposterous action flick? *Prairie Vengeance*, indeed."

"You stood by me when I quit the film with no notice," Julia reminded Maury. She had never stormed out of a director's office like that before, but the ludicrous changes to the script and the humiliating reduction of her role had become intolerable. "You got me out of my contract with a minimum of fuss and no lasting damage to my reputation or my finances. That was no small feat."

"Fair enough," Maury conceded. "I did that much."

"Everything worked out for the best," said Julia, as Evelyn patted her husband's arm and smiled up at him affectionately. "If the movie hadn't failed, Ellen wouldn't have reworked her movie script into a television series. I wouldn't have been invited to reprise my role as Sadie Henderson, and we wouldn't be gathering here tonight to celebrate our fifth season premiere." Pausing to sip her champagne, Julia couldn't resist adding, "An episode, by the way, I not only starred in but also directed."

"All the more reason to celebrate such a tremendous achievement," Evelyn declared, clinking her glass lightly against Julia's.

"It certainly isn't my achievement alone. Ellen's writing has been consistently brilliant, and I couldn't have asked for a better cast or crew. We're more than colleagues. I know people say this all the time without meaning it, but I sincerely believe we've become a family."

Maury and Evelyn looked so happy for her that Julia felt a catch in her throat. They had known her too long not to be well aware that she hadn't always been so generous, sharing praise rather than claiming all the credit for herself. Once she would have hoarded every compliment, but she had learned humility from late-career disappointment, and wise friends had taught her empathy. She knew now, mere days away from her seventieth birthday, something most people learned at a much younger age: Everyone deserved respect and kindness, and she would find no joy in achievements won by clawing her way to the top and kicking those below her to keep them down.

It chagrined her, looking back, to realize how much time she had wasted in the absolute conviction that she could win only if someone else lost. This very party was a sign of how much she had changed since the Cross-Country Quilters had befriended her at Elm Creek Quilt Camp. The old Julia would have supplemented the guest list with several carefully chosen, perpetually envious frenemies, but not as an overture to reconciliation. Instead she would have wanted the doubters and the haters to see for themselves how gloriously she had thrived after they had dismissed her as a faded, irrelevant has-been, with nothing to contribute to the industry except the occasional unflattering photo in the tabloids or the scandal of yet another failed marriage. Her rivals' barely concealed envy would have added a deliciously exciting spice to the gathering, and oh, how she would have savored it.

But that wasn't who she was anymore. If she had any frenemies, she couldn't name them, and she hadn't issued a spite invitation in years. She genuinely liked and admired every person she had welcomed into her home that evening, and she had every reason to believe the feeling was mutual. She remained a work in progress, but she had come a long way.

She sighed, momentarily wistful. Her party would be absolutely perfect if only the other Cross-Country Quilters were there. She owed so much of her recent success to her generous friends, who, five years before, had helped her learn to quilt to play Sadie Henderson, a role she'd desperately hoped would resuscitate her faltering career. She had won the lead in *A Patchwork Life* only because Maury had implied that she was an experienced quilter, which the director insisted was essential for convincingly portraying a woman homesteader on the Kansas frontier. After the contracts were safely signed, Maury had enrolled Julia at Elm Creek Quilt Camp in rural central Pennsylvania, far from the paparazzi and gossip columnists who might have exposed her deception. The camp's excellent faculty had taught her well, and after the surprisingly wonderful week ended, the new friends she had made had tutored her and offered long-distance encouragement through frequent letters, emails, and phone calls. Their friendship had sustained her as *A Patchwork Life* morphed into *Prairie Vengeance* and Julia found herself diligently perfecting her quilting skills for a role that no longer resembled what she had signed up for. The whole dreadful movie had fallen apart by the time the Cross-Country Quilters had reunited at quilt camp the following summer, but as Julia had told Maury and Evelyn, its failure had been a blessing in disguise.

As she raised her champagne flute to her lips in a silent toast to her absent friends, her assistant director appeared in the archway to the foyer and waved discreetly. At twenty-five, Lindsay Jorgenson was young for such an important post, but she had graduated summa cum laude from USC's film school, she'd proven herself exceptionally capable as a production assistant in the show's early years, and she absolutely deserved a promotion. She was also the eldest daughter of Cross-Country Quilter Donna Jorgenson, which made her all the more qualified as far as Julia was concerned. Wasn't one of the perks of being an executive director to be empowered to make executive decisions that happened to benefit a friend's daughter?

When Julia raised her eyebrows in a question, Lindsay smiled and nodded, her loosely braided, long blond hair slipping over one shoulder. It was time.

Julia tapped her glass with a fingernail, taking care not to damage her flawless manicure. "If I may have your attention, please, friends," she called, projecting her voice as conversations hushed and her guests' smiling faces turned her way. "Lindsay has the show queued up, so as soon as we take our seats, we can begin."

"This way, everybody," said Lindsay, beckoning. Murmuring with anticipation, the guests followed her through the archway into the hall and downstairs.

Julia gestured graciously for her friends and colleagues to precede her to the theater room, a feature that even more than the spectacular views had convinced her and Charles to purchase the house so many years before. Built deep into the cliffside foundation, windowless and cool even when the Santa Ana winds blew mercilessly, the theater could comfortably seat forty-eight people in the plush leather seats arranged before the large screen in six rows of eight, and a dozen more on the tall stools along the back wall. Julia had always been the first audience for Charles's documentaries, aside from his cinematographers and editors, who saw dailies and rough cuts throughout production. After Charles passed, Julia had remodeled the adjacent cutting room into a yoga studio, but she hadn't changed a thing in the theater, except to update the projector after her second husband made off with the original. After serving him with divorce papers, she had allowed him a day alone in the house to clear out his things, but he had taken other random pieces out of pure spite. Ironically, he could have well afforded to buy a new state-of-the-art projector with what he'd been paid for their honeymoon snapshots, which he'd sold to the *National Enquirer* without her permission, setting off a chain of revelations that compelled her to divorce him less than a year after the wedding. She had taken care not to repeat that mistake when she divorced husband number three. That time she had changed the locks before the papers were served, and her assistant had kept watch during her soon-to-be-ex's move-out.

Shoving the ugly reminiscences aside, Julia followed the last straggler into the theater and shut the door behind them. Searching for an unoccupied seat, she spied Ellen gesturing to her from the front row. After making her way down the aisle, Julia settled in between Ellen, on her left, and Nigel Crawford, her leading man, on her right. She glanced over her shoulder to smile at the two young actors who played her grandsons: Noah, age twenty, and Chance, sixteen. The young men paused long enough to flash her a pair of impressively photogenic grins, but they quickly resumed their conversation, apparently debating the merits of what sounded like a horrifically violent video game with philosophical pretensions.

Julia and Noah were the only actors from the movie version of *A Patchwork Life* who had been offered roles in the television series. Nigel's character hadn't existed in the ill-fated film, and Chance had been cast only after the original actor's agent had flatly declined the television reboot, dismissing the failed film as a "toxic train wreck" and the series as "probably cursed." This turned out to be yet another blessing in disguise, since Chance proved himself a fine actor and an excellent addition to the company of players. In recent years he had also become something of a teen heartthrob, but with any luck he wouldn't let the flattery go to his head, ruining his craft and turning him into a miserable Hollywood cliché. His real name was Eugene Durchdenwald, but he'd changed it when his agent warned him he'd never make it in Hollywood burdened with such a clunky moniker. So he adopted Chance for the roles he hoped casting directors would give him, and he picked Boxty after seeing it on a menu during a family trip to Ireland. By the time he realized "boxty" was not the chef's name but a type of potato pancake, the name Chance Boxty had become so well-known that he'd had no choice but to keep it.

Turning back around, Julia fixed her gaze on the screen, heart beating a bit faster in anticipation. She and Ellen exchanged quick, reassuring smiles. They had spent hours conferring with the editor and they were very pleased with the final cut, but they wanted their colleagues, the critics, and their fans to love it as much as they did.

"'Once more unto the breach, dear friends, once more,'" Nigel proclaimed, regarding the screen expectantly, his rich baritone no doubt reaching all corners of the room. At sixty-four, Nigel was as ruggedly handsome as when he had first played Henry V for the Royal Shakespeare Company in his native London four decades earlier. An avid swimmer and longtime vegan, he was as fit as a man twenty years younger, and the few lines around his hazel eyes and threads of silver in his gingery-brown hair made him appear all the more distinguished. Julia, who knew the same adjective was almost never used to compliment a woman, took care to keep her own hair the same lovely shade of honey blond she'd favored since the early 1980s. Her vigilant stylist had vowed that no gossip columnist would ever have cause to snark that Julia looked too old to play Nigel's love interest, not on her watch.

"Our fifth season," Ellen marveled, shaking her head, then reaching up to adjust her glasses. She had been a rather awkward and mousy twentysomething when she and Julia had first met, but after a few years in Los Angeles, and with Julia's tactful guidance, she had acquired a fine sense of style. That evening, Ellen's tan slacks, white scoop-neck top, and blue blazer were well tailored, and her thick, light brown hair was cut in a chic layered bob. "Honestly, who could have imagined it, when we shot the pilot?"

"I could have, and I did." Julia smoothed her linen slacks as she settled more comfortably into her seat. "I knew we were on the cusp of something glorious and groundbreaking."

"Really? Even after the movie version imploded so spectacularly?"

"The concept was excellent. The film didn't implode until after you and I resigned." Julia tossed Nigel a smile that might have been mistaken as flirtatious by anyone who didn't know them well. "If this dashing fellow had been cast in the movie, it might have succeeded even without us."

"Doubt it," said Ellen flatly. "Stephen Deneford ruined my script beyond redemption with the ridiculous changes he demanded. As long as he was directing, not even the second coming of Laurence Olivier could have saved that movie. No offense, Nigel."

"None taken, darling." Nigel waved a hand dismissively. "We all suffer in comparison to Olivier."

Julia patted his shoulder fondly. "I'd rather have you as my scene partner any day."

She would have gone on, but the house lights were dimming. A moment later, the familiar hammered dulcimer, guitar, and fiddle tune of their theme song flowed from the surround sound speakers, though the music was nearly drowned out by applause and cheers. Julia too applauded enthusiastically as the opening credits rolled, and she breathed a happy sigh when the title in its familiar vintage font appeared, superimposed over a crane shot of a sweeping prairie landscape.

That title hadn't always inspired such delight.

Years before, when Julia had been searching for a new project after her previous series had been abruptly canceled, Maury had shown her the script for a movie he promised was the project they had been searching for. "It has heart, it has warmth, and it has a fantastic part for you," he had said, placing the script in her lap and closing her hands around it. "Trust me."

"*A Patchwork Life*," Julia had read the cover page aloud, testing the sound of it. She had winced so forcibly she could've pulled a muscle. She wanted *Masterpiece Theatre*, and Maury had given her something so corny it could have been freshly harvested from a Midwestern farm. But Maury had represented her throughout her career and she trusted his judgment, so, shaking her head and expecting the worst, she had turned to the first page and had begun to read.

Within moments, she had forgotten everything else troubling her—the lamentable demise of *Family Tree*, the humiliating dearth of new offers, the patronizing responses of the few industry execs who owed Maury too much to avoid returning his phone calls. Sadie Henderson and her life in pioneer-era Kansas drew Julia in entirely. She could almost smell the prairie grasses and tilled soil as the script transported her to the small prairie homestead Sadie struggled to build with her husband, Augustus. When Augustus died in a tragic accident, leaving Sadie with two young sons to raise alone, she persisted despite grasshopper plagues and drought even when other settlers gave up and returned back east. Impoverished but ever resourceful, Sadie sold off cherished family quilts and took in sewing from her more successful neighbors to make ends meet, running the farm by day and stitching her neighbors' quilts late into the night. Sadie's quilting kept her family alive until at last, years later, the farm flourished.

After she finished the final page, Julia had held the script to her chest, lost in the details of Sadie's hardship and triumph. If only she could meet Sadie and learn her secrets for persevering when all hope was lost. That was impossible, sadly, but Maury had introduced her to Ellen, Sadie's great-granddaughter, a promising young director and screenwriter. Julia was thrilled to learn that Sadie Henderson was not just a fictional character, and that Ellen's wonderfully immersive script had been inspired by her diaries. When Ellen confessed that there was no one in the world she would rather have portray her great-grandmother than Julia, Ellen's sincere admiration and remarkable familiarity with Julia's repertoire had compelled her to accept the role on the spot.

After that lovely beginning, they couldn't have imagined that *A Patchwork Life*, the movie, would crash and burn less than a year later. Julia and Ellen had bailed out before then, increasingly disillusioned with the film's jarring departure from their original vision. First, the studio had replaced Ellen as director, dismissing her as too young and inexperienced to helm a major feature film even though she had written it, even though her previous movie had won an honorable mention at Sundance. Next, Stephen Deneford had cast as Augustus the up-and-coming action star Rick Rowan, lead in the blockbuster movie *Jungle Vengeance*, despite his limited range and the fact that he was more than twenty-five years younger than Julia, and thus rather implausible in the role of her husband. Then Rick's agent persuaded Deneford not to kill off Augustus but to keep him around in the role of heroic provider and protector. Otherwise, Rick warned, Augustus's absence would "turn it into a chick movie."

"Chick movie?" Ellen had bristled at the script meeting. "This is a movie about women—strong, intelligent women going about the difficult business of life in nearly impossible circumstances."

Rick had shrugged, puzzled. "Right. A chick movie." He had flipped through the script, shaking his head. "It should be Augustus, not Sadie, who keeps the farm from going up in flames. He should be the one to scare off the claim jumpers. I mean, come on, who's going to believe a woman did all that?"

Ellen had fixed him with a blistering look. "That's how it really happened."

"How it really happened doesn't matter," Deneford had said, rubbing his forehead as if warding off a headache. "What matters is that it's believable."

"I fail to see what's so unbelievable about a woman performing heroic acts, especially to protect her children," Julia had said. "Women were widowed all the time on the frontier. They could hardly afford to wait around for a man to rescue them."

Ellen had thrown her a look of sheer gratitude. Julia had given her a small nod in return, but her conscience had pricked her annoyingly. She had spoken up to protect her role, not the integrity of Ellen's script. The scene where Sadie faced down the unscrupulous cattle ranchers with nothing more than an unloaded rifle and a pitchfork contained one of the film's best monologues. Julia wasn't about to graciously hand over such an Oscar-worthy scene to a pompous, over-muscled Rambo wannabe.

But Julia and Ellen had lost that battle, and soon thereafter, the men had conspired to entirely reimagine the film, now retitled *Prairie Vengeance*, as a vehicle for Rick. Dismayed, Ellen had nonetheless revised the script as ordered rather than lose what little creative input she still possessed. Julia too had persevered as her most compelling scenes were rewritten and turned over to the beautiful ingenue cast as Young Sadie. But when Deneford had decided to remove all of the quilting from the picture and to have Sadie save her farm not by taking *in* sewing but by taking *on* shifts at the local bordello, Ellen had resigned, unable to bear the insult to her great-grandmother's memory. Julia had followed her out the door, certain she was extinguishing the embers of her career by doing so.

She had never been so happy to be so wrong. As filming continued without her, *Prairie Vengeance* went so far over budget that Deneford had been obliged to forgo his salary in exchange for back-end compensation, so he would be paid only if the movie made a profit. He had boasted in the trades that he was certain to benefit from the deal, but his confidence had been wildly unwarranted. When a final cut was ready, screening audiences panned it so vehemently that the studio sent the movie straight to video, where it quietly slipped into obscurity.

Through it all Ellen had retained the rights to her great-grandmother's diaries, and with *Prairie Vengeance* gone and mostly forgotten, she had rewritten her original screenplay as a television series. When Ellen offered Julia the role, she explained that in this new version, Sadie Henderson would be Augustus's mother, not his wife, summoned to Kansas to keep house and raise her grandsons after their mother's death. Augustus would still perish, right on schedule, leaving Sadie in charge of the homestead.

Julia appreciated that Ellen had tactfully refrained from pointing out that the changes were a pragmatic concession to Julia's age. "But this isn't how it really happened," Julia felt obliged to remind her. "I know how important it is to you to be faithful to your great-grandmother's diaries."

"It's more important that the role is a perfect fit for you," Ellen had replied. "As I've said from the beginning, there's no one in the world I'd rather have portray my great-grandmother than you."

Her heart full, Julia had accepted the role gladly, gratefully. PBS had immediately green-lit the pilot, and almost before she could catch her breath, Julia was once again donning Sadie's corset and calico dresses. Coming to work every day on a much friendlier, motivated, competent set was a pleasure, and every risk she and Ellen had taken was validated when the show premiered to excellent ratings and glowing reviews. Though it lacked the vast budget and reach of programs on the Big Four networks, by the end of the second season, *A Patchwork Life* had become a cultural phenomenon, first in the US and then, after the BBC picked it up, abroad. Season after season it became, indisputably, one of the few shows considered appointment television. Millions of viewers gathered around their TVs every week at the appointed hour—setting their VCRs and DVRs if they had inescapable conflicts—and obsessively discussed every plot point and character revelation around watercoolers and in blog posts the next day. Three different Kansas towns hosted annual *Patchwork Life* festivals, earning millions of dollars in tourist revenue, and one small city near the ranch where most of the exteriors were filmed transformed a long-shuttered storefront into a *Patchwork Life* museum, revitalizing their downtown. As for the cast, the relative unknowns were catapulted into fame and success, while Julia found her career rejuvenated beyond her most ambitious hopes.

To her astonishment, one of the first fan letters she received—on elegant stationery in impeccable penmanship—was from Deneford's mother, Lillian, who declared *A Patchwork Life* her favorite program and praised Julia's performance in particular. Julia promptly wrote back to thank her for her kind words, and a cordial, intermittent correspondence blossomed. Occasionally their paths crossed at awards programs and charitable events, where they always enjoyed a pleasant chat. They were mutually delighted to discover they were both members of the same women's fraternity, Pi Beta Phi, making a sincere friendship inevitable. They never spoke about Stephen or *Prairie Vengeance*, which probably helped them remain on such cordial terms.

The first two seasons of *A Patchwork Life* covered nearly everything in Sadie Henderson's diaries, so after that, the show departed from the original source material. Ellen seamlessly introduced new plotlines inspired by actual historical events, as well as new, entirely fictional characters. Nigel had joined the cast in the middle of season two to play Benjamin Atherton, a ruggedly handsome cattleman and will-they-or-won't-they love interest for Sadie. Julia and Nigel had made the most of their sparkling on-screen chemistry, delighting viewers with scenes of heated conflict, smoldering anger, grudging respect, secret longing, and steadfast but wistful friendship. Mutually admiring but competitive, Julia and Nigel pushed each other to perform ever more brilliantly, which inspired the rest of the cast to rise to meet them. No wonder the show had garnered numerous awards through the years, although Nigel's much-wished-for second BAFTA still eluded him.

An expectant hush settled over the theater as the recap sequence played, punctuated by quick smatterings of applause as various actors made their first appearance on-screen for a line or a reaction shot. When Julia appeared as Sadie, eyes flashing as she delivered a withering rebuke to Nigel as Ben, Noah reached over the back of her seat to clasp her shoulder. "You tell him, Sadie," he murmured.

Smothering a laugh, Julia patted his hand and threw him a quick smile before returning her gaze to the screen.

Soon she found herself riveted, even though she had seen the episode a dozen times before in the studio cutting room. The previous season had ended on a cliff-hanger, with the main characters confronting a torrential rainstorm, lost cattle, conniving railroad barons, and complications to numerous friendships and romantic entanglements.

Just as Sadie and Ben were about to acknowledge the deepening affection they had long denied, a misunderstanding fomented by a jealous rival sparked a terrible, very public argument outside the dry goods store where Sadie sold her beautiful quilts on consignment. They parted ways angrily just as the towering thunderclouds billowed into view in the west. By the time Sadie arrived home, the rain was pouring down, but the farmhouse was empty. After a quick search, she found a note her grandsons had left on the kitchen table: The livestock, terrified by the lightning and thunder, had bolted the barn, and the boys had gone off to fetch them back. As Sadie gazed pensively out the window at the worsening storm, Ben arrived at his ranch only to learn that some of his cattle were missing. Ben ordered the hands to move the rest of the herd to safer ground while he and his trusty border collie, Buck, went after the strays, who had fled the west pasture for the river bottoms, the worse possible place for them to seek shelter in a storm. Meanwhile, back at the Henderson farm, Sadie was drawn outside by the sound of an approaching horse. She halted on the front porch, drawing her shawl tighter, wind whipping her hair loose from the heavy knot at the nape of her neck, only to discover not her beloved grandsons but a neighbor returning her wayward goat. She invited him in to wait out the storm, but he was on his way into town to warn folks that the dam on the North Stone River was in danger of bursting. Sadie gasped in horror. Ben's ranch was on the river below the dam, and he might unwittingly be heading straight into a flash flood. She faced a terrible choice: to find her grandsons and the livestock and bring all safely home, or to race off to save the man she loved—for yes, she did love that stubborn, infuriating man, and it had taken the threat of losing him forever to make her realize that.

That was where the season finale had ended, a breathtaking cliffhanger that, to Ellen's great satisfaction, had sparked avid speculation in the press and fan websites all summer long.

The season five premiere began as most fans predicted it would, with Sadie pulling on her sturdy waders and Augustus's old vulcanized rubber mackintosh and heading out into the storm after her grandsons.

Although Julia had agreed with Ellen's choice, not everyone in the cast had. At the table read in January, Noah had pointed out that Sadie's grandsons were old enough to look after themselves. "They've probably already found the livestock and are heading back to the barn," he pointed out. "Ben is on his own, unaware of his impending doom. Maybe Sadie should race off to warn him instead."

"Plus, Jesse and Frank had to be rescued in the season four premiere," Chance had chimed in. "Can't someone else need saving for a change?"

"Exactly," said Noah, raising his fist to Chance, who bumped it.

"Nope," Ellen had said firmly. "Confronted with a choice like this, obviously Sadie would help her grandchildren."

"Perhaps Sadie's warning should arrive too late," mused Nigel, stroking his chin. "Ben can be swept downstream, defy certain death, and yet survive. I'd certainly relish those scenes."

"Would you all please read the whole script before you ask for rewrites?" Ellen had implored. "After that, if you're not happy, we can talk."

They agreed, and when the table read was finished, they all declared that it was brilliant. Ellen had given each of the leads scenes that played to their strengths and set up their characters for interesting arcs in future episodes. Sadie chose her grandsons over her beloved, which meant that the legions of viewers who conflated character and performer wouldn't conclude that Julia was a terrible person and that they ought to hate her. Jesse and Frank rescued the missing livestock on their own and made their way back to the farm safely, not encountering their grandmother until they were nearly home. The unwitting Ben was indeed swept away by floodwaters, but in a thrilling sequence that required a stunt double, a helicopter, and a special observer from the ASPCA, he was hauled from turbulent waters by his faithful companion, Buck the border collie. Everyone congratulated Ellen on this especially clever plot twist, for fans adored Buck and persistently wrote in to demand more screen time for him.

Still, Julia wasn't sure how fans would react to the final scenes. After dragging Ben to the safety of the riverbank, Buck raced off to find help, but as fate would have it, the nearest homestead was where Sadie's jealous rival, Charity, lived with her family. Meanwhile, Sadie had spent a sleepless night worrying about Ben, lamenting their foolish misunderstanding, berating herself for not telling him she loved him when she had the chance. As soon as it was safe to venture out, she raced on horseback to his ranch, fearing she would be informed of his untimely death. Instead, when she knocked frantically on the door, who should answer but her jealous rival. Smiling with vicious sweetness, Charity explained that Ben had been so concerned with her welfare that he had waited out the storm at home with her family, and so she was repaying his kindness by fixing dinner for him and his hired hands. There was no mistaking her implication that they were now courting. Stunned, Sadie turned away and rode home, the misery in her expression eventually giving way to resolve. She did not know that Ben had heard her voice and had staggered from his sickbed to the window, where he had watched her riding away, his expression full of longing.

Fade to black. As the end credits rolled and the closing theme played, raucous cheers and applause filled the room. Someone shouted, "*Bravi*!" and someone else called out, "Encore! From the top!" Everyone laughed as they rose from their seats and began filing out of the theater, eager to return to Julia's great room, where they knew coffee and dessert awaited them.

"Your last scene, the way you conveyed everything through your shifting expressions?" Ellen said to Julia as they made their way up the aisle. "Wow. Just wow. That was so much more effective than any line I could have written for you."

"Don't sell yourself short." Lowering her voice confidentially, Julia asked, "You don't think the fans will be disappointed that it didn't end with Sadie and Ben in a sweeping, emotional embrace?"

"No, not at all." Ellen waved that off. "They'll get that scene soon enough, in episode six. It'll be all the sweeter for the delay."

Julia nodded. That was what she had thought too, but it was good to have Ellen confirm it.

"And that look Ben gives Sadie as she rides off?" Ellen threw Nigel a grin over her shoulder. "That's why so many people are convinced you two are a couple in real life, no matter how many times Nigel and Alistair are photographed hand in hand on the red carpet."

"What can I say?" Julia paused in the doorway to allow Nigel to catch up, then linked her elbow through his. "Fans want to believe we're in love. If it doesn't bother Alistair, it doesn't bother me."

"Alistair finds it all rather amusing," Nigel said as they climbed the stairs, a wry twist to his mouth. "He has no reason to question my devotion, however much I try his patience by spending far too much time away from London."

"He should move here," said Julia, as she had many times before, and probably would many times again. "We have museums and charitable causes in Los Angeles. Any one of them would be grateful for his expertise."

"He's quite content where he is, darling, and he's not one to abandon any project unfinished." As they entered the foyer and passed the art nook, Julia thought she saw Nigel's gaze linger wistfully on Charles's Oscars. He would never say it aloud, but she knew he longed for one of his own. "Besides, it would hardly make sense for Alistair to find work here when I'll be returning to London soon enough."

"For the holidays, you mean?" Julia asked. They had reached the great room, where their friends and colleagues were helping themselves to refreshments and exchanging rave reviews about the premiere. Julia hoped the invited members of the press were equally impressed.

"Yes, of course, the holidays." Nigel glanced around, distracted, but his expression brightened when he spotted the tea service. As if she would ever forget to have tea for him. "He's flying in for the Emmys first, but we'll spend Christmas and New Year's together in London, when we aren't gathering with his family on the ancestral estate in Derbyshire. I'll return in January in time for our season six table reads. Those few weeks together will have to do until our more permanent reunion."

As a server passed with a tray of sweets, Ellen helped herself to a chocolate cannoli. "We'll keep you so busy with rehearsals and filming that you won't have time to be lonely," she promised Nigel. "The months will fly by. You'll see."

"Months?" Julia echoed. Surely Ellen meant years. Nigel was a lead and had to be on set nearly as often as Julia herself. He could hardly do that from the other side of the Atlantic.

"Thank you, Ellen. I confess we're counting the weeks." Nigel's rueful grimace softened as he turned his gaze to Julia. "You can count on me to return for your sixth season premiere gala. And when I tell Alistair what a joy this penultimate celebration was, he'll insist upon accompanying me."

"I'll be here too, no matter what," Ellen declared. "Julia's launch parties have become a cherished tradition. I wouldn't miss the grand finale."

"Grand finale? Penultimate?" Bewildered, Julia looked from one to the other and back again. "What are you two talking about?"

For a moment her friends studied her, puzzled, as if they thought she was telling a joke and they were awaiting the punch line. When she said nothing more, they exchanged a look of mild alarm.

Her heart sank.

"What are you two talking about?" she repeated, bracing herself for the answer.

2

Penultimate means 'last but one,'" said Ellen carefully. "Some people think it means something like 'even better than the best,' but—"

"I know what the word means," Julia said, a note of panic sharpening her voice. She turned back to Nigel. "Why are you using it in this context?"

"Why?" he echoed, puzzled. "You know our contracts end after season six."

"Yes, but then we'll renew the series for another two years, as always."

Nigel put an arm around her shoulders and pulled her closer. "I told you at the Christmas party that I thought it was time to move on," he said in an undertone, his gaze darting to the nearest guests, who were not quite out of earshot. "I said then, as I have before, that we owe it to our audience and ourselves to bring the series to a satisfying conclusion rather than let it run on endlessly, with the inevitable decline in quality."

"Yes, but you weren't serious." Julia lowered her voice too. No need to ruin a fabulous party with a ghastly emotional scene. "You made that speech right in front of all those studio execs. Obviously it was a ploy to scare them into giving you more money when you renew your contract."

"It wasn't a ploy, darling. I was in earnest. It didn't matter whether the execs overheard because they already knew how I felt. Perhaps they even agreed with me."

Julia forced a laugh and gave Nigel a playful push. "Okay, enough. This joke isn't funny anymore."

He took her hands, raised them to his chin, and held her gaze with his own, sympathetic but firm. "I wouldn't play such a cruel joke on you of all people. The next season of *A Patchwork Life* will be our last. Although I've enjoyed every moment, for me the conclusion can't come soon enough. You know Alistair and I loathe spending most of the year apart. I'm returning to London so we can be together."

"But your *career*, Nigel. You haven't peaked yet. You can't seriously intend to retire."

"Who said anything about retiring? I'm leaving Hollywood, not my profession." He squeezed her hands and released them. "I'm not supposed to reveal this yet, so you mustn't breathe a word. I've been cast in the next Harry Potter movie. We begin shooting in June."

"Wow, Nigel, that's fantastic!" said Ellen. "I didn't realize you had a role lined up already. I assume you'll be a wizard. Hero or villain? Can you tell us?"

He shook his head and raised a finger to his lips. "I've said too much already."

"Wait. Wait." Julia held up her hands, closed her eyes for a moment, and took a deep, steadying breath. On the exhale, she fixed Nigel with an accusing look. "You said next season would be *our* last. You meant *your* last."

His brow furrowed. "No, as we discussed at the full-cast meeting—" Then awareness dawned. "But you missed that meeting. You were traveling . . . in Pennsylvania, I believe. Something about a quilt exhibit."

"Lindsay sent the notes around afterward," said Ellen. "You mean you didn't read them? I know you have an aversion to opening attachments—"

"My assistant checks my work email for me when I'm on vacation." Julia never wanted work to intrude on her tranquil, restorative visits to the Elm Creek Valley. Her trip in August hadn't been for quilt camp, but she had toured a quilt exhibit and had spent time with quilting friends, so it qualified. "She always brings important matters to my attention when I return. Did she miss something?"

Or had Julia herself missed something? She vaguely recalled her assistant emphasizing an important file she'd received, but Julia had been wildly busy as their season premiere date approached. She'd only skimmed the subject lines in her inbox, opening the emails that sounded important and saving the rest for later.

She had eventually read everything, hadn't she?

"Oh, Julia." Nigel shook his head. "No wonder you look so bewildered. I confess I've wondered why you haven't spoken up. I thought perhaps you were in denial."

Julia felt her heart drop. "What does *that* mean?" She turned to Ellen. "What does he mean? In denial about what?"

Ellen threw Nigel a helpless look, but he only gestured to indicate that she should proceed. "Well, Nigel isn't the only one of us who's lined up a new job. I was going to tell you after the party—"

"Tell me what?"

"I'm going to be the lead writer for a new scripted drama series for HBO," Ellen blurted, the concern in her eyes lingering even as a smile brightened her face. "I helped write the pilot when we were on hiatus last year, and HBO ordered a full season. As soon as *A Patchwork Life* wraps in the spring, I'm moving to New York."

"Wow, Ellen," said Julia, overcome. She was thrilled for her younger friend, and so proud of her, and yet— "That's simply wonderful. But—well, doesn't it seem rather risky to you, to leave an established network for a cable channel?"

Ellen shrugged, her smile dimming. "I think it's a risk worth taking. There's so much potential for growth with cable, and HBO in particular is creating very compelling programs. *Angels in America*,

The Sopranos, *Sex in the City*—they're giving our traditional networks a lot of competition for Emmys, and for viewers."

"I suppose that's a fair point." Julia forced a smile that took in Nigel too. "Congratulations to you both. I'm so happy for you. I hope you'll invite me to your premieres."

"Of course," said Nigel. "In fact, I insist that you come."

"I was actually thinking about writing a guest-starring role for you midseason," said Ellen.

"Oh? That would be fun." Momentarily intrigued, Julia nonetheless felt the frisson of anticipation quickly dissipate. "Well, maybe I can look forward to reuniting with you on a set somewhere in New York, sometime next year." She attempted a carefree laugh. "It won't be the same around here without you two, but when we begin shooting season seven, you should visit us on location in Kansas for old times' sake. I know how much you two love the frigid air and knee-deep snow."

Nigel and Ellen exchanged a wary look that made Julia's heart sink further. Honestly, how much lower could it go? "Maybe . . . maybe you should talk with Noah and Chance," said Ellen.

Julia scanned the room and spotted the two young men out on the balcony, chatting animatedly with a lovely, dark-haired young woman who had joined the cast late in season five, appearing only in the final episode. Julia had met her briefly at the table read, but they had not shared any scenes together and Julia couldn't remember her name. Pamela? Paula? Something like that. Julia scarcely knew her but, mindful of everything the Cross-Country Quilters had taught her about inclusivity, she had made sure to add the newcomer to the group email inviting everyone to tonight's party. They would have plenty of time to get to know each other while filming season six.

At the moment, though, the young woman was gazing so admiringly at Noah that Julia was reluctant to interrupt. "No, let's just cut to the chase," she said, turning back to Ellen and Nigel. "Spill it."

"Noah intends to go to university," said Nigel, "and Chance—"

"What?" Julia exclaimed. A few guests turned curious glances their way before resuming their own conversations. "Why would Noah want to do a silly thing like that? What can he learn in a classroom that he can't learn on the set?"

"A great many things," said Nigel patiently. "Perhaps he doesn't plan to study theater."

"That would be a massive waste of his talent."

"You majored in theater in college," Ellen pointed out.

"Yes, but that was to get the training so I could get the career. Noah already has the career."

"Maybe he wants something more, or just something else." Ellen paused to murmur her thanks to a passing server as he refreshed her coffee. When he approached Julia, she smiled tightly and shook her head. Only after he had moved off did Ellen add, "As for Chance, he's in negotiations to star in a new live-action fantasy series, something about brothers who hunt supernatural creatures."

Julia felt lightheaded. A series might survive the loss of the head writer and a single lead actor, but the departure of the showrunner and three stars in a single season usually heralded the beginning of the end. Without Ellen, Nigel, Noah, and Chance, *A Patchwork Life* wouldn't be the same show. It would surely suffer the same fate as *Happy Days* after Richie Cunningham left, or *All in the Family* without Mike and Gloria.

But why hadn't Julia heard anything from the rest of the cast, those who would be left behind to carry on? Where were the anxious emails from the actors in supporting roles, worried about the future of their show? For that matter, where were the phone calls from their ambitious agents hoping to get their clients promoted to a lead?

Why was everyone else okay with this? Either they too hadn't read the email attachment or—

"Who else—" Julia cleared her throat and tried again. "Who else is planning to leave?"

"Everyone else," said Ellen, as gently as anyone could. "We're all making plans, moving on. I'm so sorry. I thought you knew."

"It's not your fault. I should have known. I should have been checking my email more vigilantly." Julia shook her head slowly. None of this felt real. "I don't understand why you—why anyone—would want to leave a successful show so abruptly, at the height of its popularity."

"It's hardly abrupt, darling," said Nigel, pulling her into a comforting hug. "We still have season six to film. We'll be together for months yet."

Julia clung to him, overwhelmed. She might have sobbed into his shoulder except she didn't want to ruin his very fine shirt with tears and makeup. Instead, she pulled away and managed a tremulous smile. "I know I'm being ridiculous," she said, giving her head a little shake. "I'm just not ready to say goodbye."

"We don't have to, yet," said Nigel. "The series finale is almost two years away."

"And it's not like we'll never see one another again," said Ellen, a furrow deepening between her eyebrows. She knew Julia too well to be fooled by a little self-deprecating humor. She would understand that Julia's heart was aching even if she pretended otherwise.

The rest of the evening passed in a blur. Though Julia had been dealt a staggering blow, she was too accomplished a performer to let anyone other than Nigel and Ellen see it. She chatted and smiled, laughed on cue, and whispered a different, enticing, behind-the-scenes detail to each member of the press. If she didn't appear perfectly at ease, her unexplained distress would become the evening's story and tomorrow's headlines. She couldn't allow anything to steal the spotlight from *A Patchwork Life*.

Only once did her mask of composure nearly slip and shatter. She had gone out to the balcony for a respite in the fresh air only to find Noah alone, possibly for the first time all evening. He was slouching a bit, his forearms on the railing as he gazed out at the distant ocean, his handsome features in the characteristic brood that made the girls swoon, and probably a good many of the boys too.

"So, I hear college is in your future?" Julia greeted him, eyebrows raised, pleasant smile firmly in place, voice scrubbed of any hint of accusation.

"Yeah, that's the plan." Straightening, Noah ran a hand through his thick, dark hair and threw her a wry grin. "I figured it's now or never."

"Never sounds good," said Julia brightly, planting an elbow on the railing as she smiled up at him. It seemed not so long ago that he barely came up to her shoulder, and now look at him. Where had the time gone? "Seriously, though, why college? And why now?"

"College was always my plan, and I don't want to put it off much longer. If I start school next fall, I'll be twenty-one, three years older than your average freshmen. I've had on-set tutors since fourth grade, so I never had a normal school experience. I don't want to miss out on college too."

"But what would you be missing, really?"

"Oh, nothing much, just an education," he replied, amused. "You know, the opportunity to develop my critical thinking skills and broaden my horizons?"

"Oh, *that*," she said, waving a hand dismissively. "I suppose some people might consider that important."

"Yeah, and I'm one of them. Acting can't be my whole life."

"Why not? You're an excellent actor with a promising future. Everyone says so."

"Not everyone."

She gave him a playful shove. "Knock off the false modesty, kid. Everyone."

"Maybe everyone here tonight," he conceded. "Julia, don't get me wrong. I love acting, but I've been doing this forever. I never really had the chance to explore other interests, to see what else I might be good at."

She regarded him, skeptical. "You mean you might prefer to be an accountant or an archaeologist?"

"I don't know. Maybe. But I'll never know if I don't give it a shot." He leaned forward to rest his forearms on the rail again, his gaze turned to the ocean. "To be honest, I'll probably come back to acting in the end. I do love it, and I'd like to direct someday. But even if I don't major in acting, going to college, taking the time to satisfy my intellectual curiosity, will make me a better, more thoughtful, more daring actor. Art is all about taking risks, right?"

"I suppose," Julia said reluctantly. "Yes, of course it is."

"So what kind of artist would I be—ten years from now, or twenty—if I just stuck with everything that's safe and familiar rather than putting myself out there, finding out how little I really know about the world, and the people in it, and myself?"

For a moment Julia could only blink at him, impressed—and a bit ashamed of herself for hoping he'd change his mind. "You make a good argument," she admitted. "Maybe you should study law. You definitely should write college recruiting brochures."

He rolled his eyes. "Very funny."

"I do hope you'll find your way back to acting eventually," she said, entirely sincere for the first time since the conversation began. "You have so much to offer. It would be a great loss to the profession if you left forever."

"Forever? I wouldn't even be leaving it now if *Patchwork* wasn't ending after season six." He shrugged. "It seems like a good time to take a leave of absence for college, between gigs."

Julia felt a spark of hope. "So if the series were extended another season or two—"

"I'd stick around to see it through to the end, obviously. I wouldn't want them to recast my role."

"Never. Ellen would kill off Jesse before she'd allow that."

"Oh, good." His brow furrowed. "I guess that's good?"

"Of course that's good. It means she can't imagine the show

without you." She felt tears threatening and forced them back. "And neither can I."

"Not that it matters. It's already settled, right? One more season and it's a wrap." He held up a fist, and after a moment of confusion, she realized she was meant to bump it. "Here's to Jesse and Sadie surviving to the series finale."

"Hear, hear," said Julia, wishing with all her heart that the finale wouldn't have to come so soon.

The party wrapped up soon after that. Maury and Evelyn were among the first to leave, but Julia followed the couple outside for a quick word where no one else could overhear. "Can we meet tomorrow?" she asked, tears choking her voice. "It's urgent."

"The gala," Evelyn murmured to her husband, with an apologetic smile for Julia.

"Right." Maury grimaced. "Sorry, Julia, but Evelyn's annual fundraiser for the children's hospital is on Sunday, and we have a lot to prepare before then. How about Monday? Can it wait until then? You can come for lunch."

Monday seemed ages away, but Julia nodded. "Sure. Monday would work."

He peered at her. "Are you sure? Is everything all right?"

Everything was definitely *not* all right, but Maury would be enjoying retirement already if not for her, and she couldn't bear to become a burden. "I'll explain on Monday," she said, kissing each of them on the cheek and seeing them off with a smile.

The intervening days offered her time—too much, perhaps—to fret and strategize. She tried to distract herself with yoga, script reads, and quilting, but her thoughts returned again and again to the apparently impending and very premature conclusion to her beloved series. As she had suspected, it was her own fault that she had been caught off guard at the launch party. When she reviewed her inbox the next morning, the meeting notes and the email chain they had sparked made the unhappy truth painfully clear. But even if she had read the attachment promptly, she still would have been stunned by the news, just not in such a dramatic and public fashion. She hadn't seen this coming, and why should she have? Everything had been going so splendidly that she'd assumed *A Patchwork Life* would continue forever, or at least until she decided it was time to bring the story to a glorious, satisfying, unforgettable end. But now was not that time.

On Monday, she drove her BMW down the winding road through the Malibu hills and south on Pacific Coast Highway to Maury and Evelyn's gracious Brentwood residence. Over iced teas and decadent sandwiches of turkey, Brie, caramelized onion, and green apple chutney on brioche, they chatted about the glowing reviews the season premiere had received, what the Benowitzes' grandchildren were up to, and what Julia and Evelyn planned to wear to the upcoming Emmys, where Julia expected to lose graciously to Jennifer Garner. After the meal, Evelyn declined Julia's offer to help tidy up and shooed her and Maury off to his study. There Julia settled down on the soft, tapestry-covered sofa in front of the fireplace, the scene of so many crucial deliberations about her career and countless other conversations of a more personal nature. Maury had been Charles's oldest and dearest friend, and although he hadn't intended to play matchmaker, he had brought them together by landing her a role as a narrator on one of Charles's documentaries. In that sense Julia owed Maury both her career and the happiest years of her life.

"So what's on your mind?" Maury asked as he took his usual seat in the adjacent armchair. "You seemed a little distracted at the launch party. Did you see something in the episode you wished you'd done differently?"

"Don't I always, but that's not the problem." She leaned forward, bracing her hands on her knees. "Were you aware that everyone but me expects *Patchwork* to end after season six?"

His brow furrowed. "Who's 'everyone'? No one at the network has said a word to me suggesting they want to cancel."

"This isn't from the network. It's from Ellen and Nigel. They're leaving for other roles, and they say Noah and Chance are out too. Ellen's exact words were 'Everyone else'—everyone but me—'is moving on.'" Julia lifted her hands and let them fall to her lap. "Even if Ellen's exaggerating and only she, Nigel, Noah, and Chance are leaving, what would *A Patchwork Life* be without them?"

"It would be an entirely different show."

"You're almost right. It would be the *end* of the show."

"Not necessarily." Maury rubbed his jaw, thinking. "The network hasn't officially canceled the series. I would have heard from them, since your new contract is pending. Maybe they plan to hire a new showrunner, write the actors who are leaving out of the story—"

"I don't want a new showrunner and I don't want new castmates," Julia said, emphatic. "Why prepare to fix what isn't broken when you can hold it together and keep it from breaking?"

"I'm sorry, Julia, but it doesn't sound like you can hold this together. If Ellen and the others have decided it's time to leave the show, you have to let them go."

"Not if I can persuade them to stay. And that's where you come in."

Maury sat back, grimacing. "I'm not sure I like the sound of this."

"I've had all weekend to think about it, and I know what to do." She inhaled deeply, pausing for dramatic effect. "You agents all know one another. You talk all the time. I think you need to get on the phone with each of their agents, or meet for drinks if you think that would be better, and through some subtle questioning, find out what it would take to convince Nigel, Noah, and Chance to stay on for another two seasons. Ellen and I have a history, so I'll work on her. I'm sure their asks will be reasonable, and I will personally deliver them to the network. The network owes me. Ellen and I brought them a hit, right?"

"Julia—"

"After these four commit, I'm confident 'everyone else' will decide to stay too." She studied him, expectant. "What do you say? Are you in?"

He shook his head. "I know you mean well, but this is a terrible idea."

"Why?" she protested. "You said yourself that the show isn't officially canceled. Why not offer them an incentive to stay?"

"It's probably already too late. Since they're leaving for other roles, they've surely signed binding contracts."

"That only applies to Nigel and Ellen. Chance is still negotiating, and Noah wants to go to college." Julia waved a hand dismissively. "Anyway, as the old saying goes, contracts are made to be broken."

"That's not how the old saying goes." Maury heaved a sigh. "Julia, think this through before you do anything you'll regret later. Your castmates wouldn't have made these decisions lightly. I'm sure deep down you're happy for them, that you want them to succeed and thrive."

She shifted uncomfortably. "Of course I do, but they can succeed and thrive on *Patchwork*."

"Would you really want them to stay if they're no longer passionate about the show? Surely you wouldn't want *Patchwork* to limp along with performances from a half-hearted cast, the diminished quality tarnishing the memory of a once-acclaimed program."

She frowned. "You sound like Nigel but without the accent."

"I'll fake the accent if that's what it takes to convince you. Look, Julia. Your friends are moving on to exciting new opportunities. You could do the same. The end of *Patchwork* would give you time to pursue other interests. A passion project. A return to live theater. More directing. Say the word and I'll start making inquiries."

For a moment intrigue kindled, but the thought of hanging up Sadie's bonnet permanently was so alarming that the small spark was promptly extinguished. "Thanks, Maury," Julia said, without a hint of actual gratitude, "but I'm much too busy preparing for season six to even consider any other long-term plans."

He shrugged and spread his hands, conceding defeat. "As long as you know that you have options, if you want them. Let me know when you're ready."

She managed a tight smile as she thanked him for his counsel, which was lamentably less helpful than she had expected. Obviously she *could* move on, but she didn't *want* new opportunities. She wanted to keep what she already had, a successful series and the best cast and crew she'd ever worked with. Was that really so wrong? And if Maury wouldn't help her convince her friends to stick around for another season or two, or even more, to whom could she turn?

At least she knew the answer to the second question—the Cross-Country Quilters.

3

Although Maury hadn't agreed to help Julia quite the way she had hoped, she still left the Benowitz residence no less determined to persuade the cast and crew not to abandon *A Patchwork Life*. The Cross-Country Quilters didn't have Maury's connections, but they were her dearest friends, each of them wise in her own, unique way. They would surely come up with some creative solutions together.

As it happened, Julia never would have met her far-flung friends if Maury hadn't sent her to quilt camp, so she owed him for that too. At the time, though, she had felt so injured and abandoned that gratitude was the last thing on her mind, despite the countless ways he had helped her throughout her career.

She had always known he intended to retire eventually. Most people eventually retired, and he and Evelyn had dropped delicate hints about their retirement plans for several years before he made it official. And yet Julia had sailed along in blissful denial, certain he would change his mind when he remembered how much he loved his work and how much his clients needed him. And yet, somehow, on an otherwise lovely evening in June 1999, she found herself sipping champagne at his retirement party, tempted to seize a bottle and find a secluded corner in which to sulk and drown her sorrows alone.

She might have gone home early, except Maury took her aside for a private conversation in his study. "A little farewell present," he said, placing the script for *A Patchwork Life* in her hands. "You didn't think I'd leave you without one last great project, did you?"

That was precisely what she had thought, but she wouldn't spoil the evening by saying so aloud. She had assumed her next project would come through her new agent, a rising star in the business whom she knew only by reputation. Maury had recommended a different colleague, but Julia had instead chosen someone famed for his ruthless determination to do whatever it took to get his clients the roles they sought. The fact that he was the nephew of one of Hollywood's most powerful directors also weighed in his favor.

But when they finally met in person one week after Maury's retirement party, she began to suspect that she had made a serious mistake.

"I'm Ares," he announced when she joined him for a getting-acquainted lunch at a bistro on Sunset Boulevard not far from the agency. After she took her seat, he reached across the table and offered her his hand and a flash of white teeth. Maury would have stood as she approached, and he would have pulled out her chair for her and not returned to his own until he was sure she was comfortable.

"Aries the Ram?" she asked, shaking the younger man's hand.

"No." His grin suddenly became almost feral. "Ares, the Greek god of war."

"How interesting," Julia had replied, gingerly releasing his hand, realizing that she couldn't have picked an agent less like Maury if she had tried. Still, perhaps Maury's approach, a gentleman bargaining honorably on the strength of his word, was too old-fashioned for these crueler, modern times. As the conversation turned to business, Julia resolved to give Ares a chance, despite the casual insults he tossed off about her previous series in his eagerness to praise the forthcoming movie.

It was Maury who enrolled her in Elm Creek Quilt Camp, but it was Ares who made her go through with it rather than arranging for private quilting lessons at her home, as she would have preferred. "The Elm Creek Quilters are supposed to be the best of the best," he noted, "and you can't cancel a lesson if you're stuck in the middle of nowhere."

"I wouldn't cancel," Julia said, knowing she had already lost the argument. "I want to learn."

"You have to learn. Your entire career depends on it."

Julia refrained from pointing out that if she *did* lose this role and Ares couldn't find her another, he was rather useless as an agent. She needed him on her side.

On an August day a few weeks after their first meeting, Ares escorted her to the secluded, nineteenth-century manor in rural central Pennsylvania where her clandestine quilt training would take place. Maury had wanted a place far from the scrutiny of gossip columnists and paparazzi, and from her airplane window, the Elm Creek Valley certainly seemed to be hundreds of miles from anything resembling a city. Julia marveled that the agency's chartered jet managed to locate the tiny airport at all, much less come to a halt before speeding off the end of the runway. Except for the control tower and a small one-story building she assumed was the terminal, the view through her window revealed only trees and sky.

"I've kept your arrival a secret, but don't be surprised if there's a crowd gathered around," Ares warned as the plane taxied to the terminal. "They probably get a limo in this backwater only once every twenty years."

Julia shot him a look of sharp disapproval. The last thing she needed was an agent who scorned her target demographic. "People in towns like these watch movies. They also kept *Family Tree* at the top of the Nielsen ratings for many years."

"Near the top, anyway," Ares allowed. "The top of the middle, at least."

Stung, Julia unfastened her seat belt and held back a retort, reminding herself that she didn't have to like him to work with him.

Contrary to Ares's snarky prediction, no crowd had gathered by the limo parked on the tarmac, but it did attract a few curious glances from other travelers climbing ramp stairs into tiny prop planes or collecting their gate-checked bags from oversized carts. As the driver loaded Julia's luggage into the limo's trunk and opened the rear passenger door for her, she noticed four women near the terminal entrance greeting one another with shrieks of laughter and warm embraces. As the limo drove through the parking lot, Julia lowered her sunglasses to take a better look, curious. Judging by their eclectic patchwork clothing, pieced and appliquéd like wearable quilts, surely they were quilt campers too.

Suddenly the tinted window began to rise. With a start, she turned in her seat to find Ares with his finger on the button of his armrest. "We can't have the locals gawking at you," he said.

Julia thought the women seemed too preoccupied to spare the limo a second glance, but she settled back into her seat, resigned.

For more than an hour they drove in silence past picturesque farms and rolling, forested hills. Julia felt her tension ease as she admired the scenery, but trepidation stirred when, although they still appeared to be in the middle of nowhere, they came upon a large, rustic wooden road sign with beautifully engraved, freshly painted lettering announcing that they had reached the Elm Creek estate.

The driver skillfully managed the sharp turn off the state highway onto a narrow gravel road that plunged into a dense, leafy forest. Even so, Julia instinctively clutched her armrest when she realized that the narrow road had no shoulder. If an oncoming car approached, one of them would have to pull off into the trees to avoid a collision.

"Sorry, it's a bit rough here," the driver warned, slowing the limo to compensate.

"The least they could have done was pave the road," Ares grumbled.

"Not your fault," Julia replied to the driver, ignoring Ares, raising her voice to be heard over the crunch of tires on gravel. "We're fine."

When the road forked, the driver took the slightly wider road on the right. They crossed a narrow bridge over a creek so clear Julia could see stones at the bottom, and soon thereafter, the leafy wood gave way to a vast expanse of sun-splashed wildflower meadow. The road smoothed, and at the end of it Julia spotted a gray stone mansion with tall, white columns supporting the high roof of a broad veranda. As the limo drew closer, Julia spied two stone staircases descending in mirror-image arcs to the curved driveway, which encircled a fountain in the shape of a rearing horse. At least a dozen people were unloading luggage or helping others carry their bags up the stairs and through the tall double doors of the front entrance. With a pang, Julia suddenly remembered how much she had always hated the first day of school. Where would she sit in the classroom? Would she eat lunch alone every day? As lovely as this Elm Creek Manor appeared to be, her heart sank at the thought of spending an entire week there, alone in a crowd.

Instinctively she slipped on her sunglasses again, bracing herself as the other guests broke off their conversations to watch as the limousine slowed to a halt in front of the manor. When the driver opened her passenger door, Ares quickly raced around from his side and offered his hand to assist Julia out. She accepted ungratefully, suspecting he was performing gallantry for the crowd, who watched and whispered to one another as he escorted her up one of the semicircular staircases. The driver followed behind carrying Julia's suitcases and her favorite Louis Vuitton Neverfull MM tote.

A tall, silver-haired woman who looked to be about a dozen years older than Julia met them at the entrance. "Miss Merchaud?" she inquired pleasantly, studying Julia over the rims of her glasses, which were attached to a fine silver chain draped gracefully around her neck. "I'm Sylvia Bergstrom Compson. Welcome to Elm Creek Manor."

"Thank you." Julia followed the woman inside to a splendid foyer with a gleaming black marble floor and a high ceiling open to the third story. Camp registration appeared to be taking place in the center of the room, judging by the long folding tables arranged there and the three name-tagged women assisting new arrivals with various forms, maps, and room keys. Beyond the busy scene, Julia spotted a pair of closed doors on the far wall, but to her left, an open doorway revealed glimpses of what appeared to be a large, elegant room divided into smaller spaces by movable partitions. A grand oak staircase in the corner climbed gracefully to the second story, which, like the floor above it, was open to the foyer below. Colorful quilts in an assortment of patterns and styles hung from the high balustrades, offering an enchanting display of antique and modern pieces intermingled. It was all so artistically striking and yet warm and comfortable that Julia felt anxiety slipping off her shoulders as easily as removing a heavy wool coat in fair weather.

"You must be tired after such a long trip," said Sylvia. "Let's take care of your registration and show you to your room. Matthew will help you with your bags." She signaled to a young man with curly blond hair, who smiled as he approached and reached to take Julia's luggage from the driver.

Ares put out an arm to stop him. "It's under control, thanks." In an undertone, he added to Sylvia, "We don't need the entire staff knowing where Miss Merchaud will be staying. Security. You understand." He shrugged at Matthew. "No hard feelings, buddy."

"Sure," the other man replied. Julia had the distinct impression he was trying hard not to laugh.

"Matthew is our caretaker," said Sylvia. "I assure you, he's quite harmless."

Julia removed her sunglasses and pretended not to notice the hush that had fallen over the other guests, who were no doubt astonished to see wise Grandma Wilson from *Family Tree* going full prima donna. "Give him the bags," she murmured to the driver. He looked from her to Ares, uncertain. "I said, give him the bags." At last the driver complied, and she smiled an apology to Matthew.

To her relief, the registration process went quickly, and soon she, Ares, and the caretaker with her bags were following Sylvia upstairs. "Your suite is in the west wing," Sylvia said as they reached the second-floor landing. "You'll have your own bath. I trust you'll be quite comfortable."

"Thank you," Julia said, watching as other women went from room to room introducing themselves, as excited and happy as children at summer camp. A few greeted Julia as she passed. She smiled guardedly in response, wondering if they recognized her out of costume, and without all the makeup and flattering lighting.

Sylvia ushered them into a large suite with a four-poster bed covered with a blue-and-red quilt pieced of homespun plaids. "It's lovely," Julia said. "Thank you, Sylvia."

"You're quite welcome. Now, I'll let you settle in while I welcome our other guests."

Ares held up a hand. "Before you go, let's establish some ground rules."

The older woman's eyebrows rose.

"Miss Merchaud's status may cause some excitement," Ares went on. "Ordinarily Miss Merchaud goes out of her way to please her fans, but this week, we can't allow her to be disturbed. To that end, she'll take her meals in her room rather than the common dining area, and she won't participate in any of the camp activities other than classroom instruction."

Sylvia folded her hands. "All of our activities are voluntary, Mr. Ares."

"Just Ares. Also, is there any way Miss Merchaud could have private instruction rather than attending classes?"

"I'm afraid that's not possible."

"Then at the very least, she'll need a table to herself at the front of the classroom."

"I'm sure that can be arranged."

"Ares," Julia interjected, "I don't think—"

"You'll also inform your staff and other guests that they are not to address Miss Merchaud or trouble her in any way."

Sylvia regarded him, bemused. "Do I understand you correctly? You wish me to announce that no one may speak with her?"

"Unless she speaks to them first, yes."

"That's absurd, and I won't do it." Sylvia fixed Julia with a level gaze. "And I'm tired of talking about you as if you aren't in the room. If you wish to ignore people who speak to you, that's your decision, but I won't offend my other guests by clamping muzzles on them."

"I never wanted that," Julia protested. "This wasn't my idea."

"I'm pleased to hear that, because otherwise you'll have a dreadful time this week. What an idea—to come to quilt camp and refuse to make any new friends." Sylvia shook her head in disapproval and frowned at Ares. "You see, I have a few ground rules of my own. If they don't suit you, I'd be happy to return your agency's check."

"That won't be necessary," Ares said tightly. "I'm sure Miss Merchaud will be able to adapt to the circumstances."

"Good." Sylvia returned her attention to Julia, her voice noticeably warmer. "Please inform someone on the staff if there's anything we can do to make your stay more enjoyable." Her eyes flicked to Ares as if getting rid of him would be a step in the right direction. With that, she and the caretaker left the room, closing the door behind them.

"What a crazy old bat," Ares muttered.

"I found her quite pleasant," Julia said. "And I do wish you had consulted me before deciding I should isolate myself in my room all week. Maybe I would have enjoyed—"

"You're not here to enjoy yourself. You're here to work."

"Observing quilters would help me prepare for my role."

"You can observe them during your classes. The less you interact with these quilters, the less likely you'll reveal the truth. The press releases for the film will promote you as an expert quilter. Do you want these old biddies running to the media with the real story?"

"I doubt the tabloids would be interested," Julia retorted, scornful. "As secrets go, it's not very sexy."

"You can't afford the risk. Maury didn't want to tell you, but Deneford agreed to give you this part only because he thinks you already know how to quilt. If he discovers Maury misled him, you're out of a job, and I don't think I need to tell you how difficult it will be to find you another role this good."

"I appreciate your honesty," she said crisply, though she would have preferred a bit more tact.

It was a relief when Ares finally left her to settle into her suite, although the room felt oddly still when she was alone, the silence broken only by the little noises she made unfastening her suitcases and opening and closing bureau drawers. From the hallway came the sounds of the other women talking and laughing, and of quick footsteps going from room to room. Why did all the other guests seem to know one another already, though quilt camp had barely begun?

Julia had just finished unpacking when she was startled by a knock on her own door. When she answered, a young woman with shoulder-length reddish-brown hair smiled tentatively and introduced herself as Sarah McClure, one of the founding Elm Creek Quilters. "The Welcome Banquet will begin in fifteen minutes," she said. "I understand you'd prefer your meal to be brought to your room?"

It was Ares's preference, not hers, but Julia nodded anyway. "Yes, please."

"Are you sure? The Welcome Banquet is one of our most beloved traditions. Aside from the delicious food and beautiful ambiance, it's also a chance to get to know your fellow campers before classes begin. Our Candlelight welcome ceremony will take place afterward, outside on the cornerstone patio." Sarah gestured to one of the windows. "It's almost directly below your room. If you've looked outside, you may have noticed the gray flagstones surrounded by evergreens and lilac bushes. The lilacs aren't blooming now, of course, but the late summer flowers are, and the weather this evening should be lovely."

For a moment Julia was tempted, but then she remembered the other campers staring while Ares made a scene at registration. "Thanks, but it's been a long day. I'd rather have dinner in my room and turn in early, if that won't inconvenience anyone."

"It's no trouble at all," Sarah assured her, but something in her voice made Julia suspect that no one in the history of Elm Creek Quilt Camp had ever willingly skipped the Welcome Banquet and Candlelight ceremony.

After asking if Julia had any dietary restrictions or preferences, Sarah left and returned about twenty minutes later with a sturdy wooden tray, which she placed on the small desk in the corner. "I'll come back for the tray later," she said, regarding Julia hopefully, "unless you'd like to bring it down on your way to the Candlelight ceremony?"

But Julia declined a second time, pleading fatigue. Sarah smiled understandingly and wished her a good evening.

Julia had expected a club sandwich on a paper plate, but she was pleasantly surprised to discover that the chicken piccata was perfectly seasoned, the rosemary roll flaky and warm, the mixed greens salad crisp and flavorful. The delicious food was enhanced by the elegant china, delicate antiques Julia wouldn't have wanted to carry up that grand oak staircase. In the center of the plate was an emblem of a rearing horse, reminiscent of the fountain in front of the manor. Julia couldn't help wondering what other unexpected pleasures she had missed by not attending the banquet.

When she finished eating, Julia set her tray in the hallway outside her door, freshened up, and changed into more comfortable clothing. Then she stretched out on the bed, idly paging through the issue of *Variety* she had brought to read on the plane. It couldn't hold her interest for long, so she soon tossed it aside and rummaged through her tote for the movie script and a notepad. Ares didn't want her to waste time memorizing lines that would probably change in the rewrite, but that didn't mean Julia couldn't work ahead in other ways. She returned to the small desk in the corner and began reading through the script, noting each quilting technique that Sadie had used and that Julia would need to learn. By the time darkness fell, she had gone through the first four scenes and had listed several unfamiliar terms on her notepad: "basting," "piecing," "binding." Pleased with herself, she stood up to stretch, but the distant murmur of voices broke her concentration.

Curiosity drew her to the window. On the gray stone patio below, the other campers were seated in a circle of chairs, their attentive gazes fixed on a red-haired woman whose cupped hands held a lit candle in a spherical crystal holder. "That's when I realized that if I only ever attempted things I could do perfectly, I'd never experience anything new—and what a waste that would be of the life I'd reclaimed after my divorce," she was saying, her voice low and solemn. "So, since I finally have a place of my own and no one to complain about how I spend my hours, I've decided to learn to quilt."

A soft chorus of approval went up from the circle as she passed the candle to the woman on her left, who gazed at the dancing flame for a long moment in silence. She had luminous brown skin, strong cheekbones, and natural, black-and-gray hair worn in a crown of spiral curls. "I'm Grace Daniels, from San Francisco," she said. "I'm an old friend of Sylvia's. She's been after me to visit her camp for years now, and I finally decided to indulge her." She smiled at Sylvia as the others laughed softly. But then her smile faded. "What do I hope to gain this week? Some inspiration. I feel like I've run out of ideas, and . . . and I hope to discover some here." With that, she handed the candle to the next woman in the circle, who cleared her throat nervously before introducing herself.

For more than an hour, Julia sat at her window, spellbound, listening as one by one the women shared the deepest secrets of their hearts with perfect strangers. If she were seated among them, what would she have shared when it was her turn to hold the candle? She had come to Elm Creek Manor to learn how to quilt so that she could keep a movie role. She had to keep the movie role to breathe life into a stalled career. She had to revitalize her career or fade away into obscurity before she had ever truly made a difference, before she had ever participated in something worthwhile, something worth remembering.

If only she could be as open and trusting as the women gathered in the circle beneath her window. But none of them feared that someone would race to the tabloids with her deepest secrets. None of them worried that her failures would become fodder for late-night talk-show comedians. They could afford to trust one another.

Suddenly aware that she was intruding on an intimacy she did not deserve, she let the curtain fall back and withdrew from the window.

ON THE FIRST FULL DAY OF QUILT CAMP, JULIA OVERSLEPT.

She had forgotten to set the alarm clock and woke with a start, groggy from jet lag, at the sound of a knock on her door. "Miss Merchaud?" a woman called. "Breakfast."

Julia scrambled out of bed and snatched up her robe. "Just a minute." Hastily she finger-combed her hair as she went to the door, hoping the woman in the hallway didn't have a camera. The tabloids would pay big for a shot of her with bedhead and no makeup. Drawing her robe closed at the neck, she opened the door a crack, enough to glimpse Sarah holding a covered tray and peering back at her inquisitively.

Julia invited the younger woman to place the tray on the desk and ushered her out again as quickly as possible. She wasn't hungry, but she nibbled on an English muffin and ate most of the fruit, leaving the omelet untouched. The coffee was suitably strong, though she missed her cinnamon cappuccino.

She showered quickly, got dressed, put her long blond hair up in a French twist, and applied her makeup with care. In the hallway, the muffled sounds of other campers making their way downstairs had faded, and a glance at the clock told her she would have to hurry. She grabbed a pen, the script notes she had compiled the previous night, and the papers she had received at registration, which included a map of the manor. She quickly followed the directions downstairs to the ballroom, which had been partitioned into classrooms with folding screens decorated in patchwork. She found Quick Piecing with barely a moment to spare, the last of eleven students to arrive.

The instructor—Sarah, who was proving to be remarkably versatile and never idle—had already begun class when Julia slipped into a seat at the back of the room, grateful that she had a table to herself. She would have been mortified if another camper were asked to trade places to accommodate Ares's demands.

When Sarah passed out the first lesson, Julia scanned the title and discovered that they would be learning how to quick-piece quarter-square triangles that morning, whatever that meant. "First, you'll need to pick a light fabric and a medium or dark," Sarah said. "Cut a six-inch-by-twelve-inch rectangle from each fabric using your rotary cutter, and then lay the two fabrics with right sides facing, the light piece on top."

Julia watched with alarm as the other ten students reached into their bags and brought out folded bundles of fabric, plastic rulers, and odd-shaped tools that resembled pizza cutters. Should she have brought her own fabric? She glanced around her workstation—a sewing machine, a gridded plastic mat, no fabric—and felt heat rise in her face. Everyone else had come prepared with fabric and other supplies, so apparently she alone hadn't received the memo. Dismayed, she looked to the front of the classroom for help, but Sarah was already walking around the room observing her students as they layered fabric on their mats and happily sliced away at it with the pizza cutters.

"Is everyone ready to go on?" Sarah called out. Julia's meek no was lost in the chorus of affirmatives. "Okay, then next, I want you to take your pencil and, using your ruler, draw a grid of two-inch squares on the back of your light fabric."

A ruler. Julia snatched up her notebook and quickly tore out a sheet of paper. The pages were eight and a half by eleven inches; she could fold it into sections and estimate an inch. Then she remembered the gridded plastic mat and scooted her chair closer to it. To her relief, she saw that the grid was marked in eighth-inch increments along two edges. Folding her paper to strengthen it, she lined it up against the edge of the mat and began marking off inches. By the time her makeshift ruler was completed, the rest of the class had already proceeded to the next step. Racing to catch up, Julia tore two more sheets of paper from her notebook and wrote "Dark" on one and "Light" on the other. She drew a wobbly edged grid as the other students moved on to their sewing machines. She was too far behind to ever catch up, but she persevered grimly. Ares had shipped her off to camp with none of the proper materials, but she needed that role and she was going to learn to quilt if it killed her. When she thought of the many, many times her mother had wanted to teach her when she was a girl, and how vehemently she had refused—

A shadow fell over her table. "Is everything okay back here?"

Julia looked up to find Sarah regarding her with concern. "I . . . Yes, everything's fine," she said. "Please continue."

"Did you leave your things in your room? You have time to run upstairs and get them."

"No, thank you." Julia was mindful of the other students pausing in their work to watch. "Please, I don't want to hold up the rest of the class."

"Wasn't there a supply list in the course confirmation packet mailed to your home?"

A supply list. Of course, there must have been a supply list, and it must have been sent to the agency. "There probably was," Julia said, picturing her hands closing around Ares's throat, "but I didn't get it."

"I see," Sarah said, with a puzzled frown that said she didn't see at all.

"I have some extra fabric," sang out an older woman with a cloud of shockingly bright white hair. "What do you like? Red or blue?"

"Oh, no, that's quite all right," Julia demurred.

The woman was already making her way down the center aisle, a bundle of fabric in her arms. "Nonsense. I always bring plenty." She placed the bundle on Julia's table and held up a piece of bright green fabric with wide red lines zigzagging across it. "Here's a nice one. Or do you prefer calico?"

"Calico," Julia said quickly, recognizing one of the unfamiliar terms from Ellen's script. The older woman smiled indulgently and handed her a piece of dark blue fabric sprinkled with tiny white flowers.

"Here's something you can use for the light fabric," another woman called out, waving a cream-colored piece over her head like a banner. Sarah supplied her with one of the pizza-cutter tools, and soon everyone had joined in, showering Julia with extra rulers and needles and pins and so much extra fabric she wasn't sure how she'd carry everything back upstairs to her room. Mortified, she accepted their gifts and stammered out her thanks.

"I'm sorry you didn't get a list," said Sarah. "After class, why don't you show me your course schedule and I'll send into town for the rest of the supplies you'll need."

"Thank you. I'd appreciate that." Julia couldn't bear for her to think that an experienced quilter would be so ignorant. "I'm sorry for the disruption, but I've never quilted before."

The white-haired woman's eyebrows rose. "This is your first quilting class? Ever? My goodness, you're ambitious, skipping the basics and going straight to this high-tech stuff."

"Skipping . . ." Julia looked from the white-haired woman to Sarah. "This isn't a beginner's course?"

"Most new quilters start out in Beginning Piecing," Sarah said. "You've really never quilted before?"

Julia shook her head. Wasn't it obvious?

"Then . . ." Sarah hesitated. "I don't mean to question your judgment, but why did you sign up for Quick Piecing?"

Julia had never even seen a course description. Ares had signed her up for this course, and suddenly she understood why. "Because I need to learn quickly."

The white-haired woman laughed as if Julia had made a joke, but Sarah smiled kindly. "I think tomorrow morning we should switch you to Diane's Beginning Piecing class, okay?"

Julia managed a smile. "That would be lovely, thank you."

As the class resumed, the white-haired woman settled into an empty workspace at Julia's table and did what she could to help her keep up, but Julia was in over her head and she knew it. When Sarah called for a fifteen-minute break, while the other students rose to stretch and strike up conversations with their neighbors, Julia thanked her would-be tutor, gathered her things, and headed for the exit, murmuring a hasty apology to Sarah in passing.

"Miss Merchaud, wait," Sarah called after her.

Julia halted, muffling a sigh. "Julia," she said, turning around. "Just Julia is fine."

"Julia," Sarah said. "Please don't feel embarrassed. You did well for your first-ever quilting lesson."

"Oh, don't worry about me," Julia said, clutching her hand-me-down supplies awkwardly. "I've bombed in front of live audiences before and survived."

"You didn't bomb." Sarah gestured to Julia's gifted supplies. "Do you need a bag for all that?"

"Yes, please, if you have one."

"One sec." Sarah darted back into the classroom and returned moments later with a paper grocery sack that had seen better days. "Sorry," she said, holding it open so Julia could fill it. "Best I could do on short notice."

"It's fine." Julia took the bag, holding it carefully from the bottom. "Thank you."

"Lunch will be a picnic buffet on the verandah at noon," Sarah said as Julia turned to go. "Or, if you really prefer solitude, you can stop by the kitchen and take a tray up to your room."

Julia thanked her with a nod. If those were her only options, a tray in her solitary room would have to do.

JULIA APPROACHED HER AFTERNOON CLASS, APPLIQUÉ WORKSHOP, with the same purposeful energy that had seen her through many a difficult audition. She arrived precisely on time and chose a place in the back row, determined to avoid repeating the morning's spectacle by drawing as little attention to herself as possible. Another student was already seated at the table, but her gaze was riveted on the teacher, a petite, white-haired woman whose blue eyes shone warmly behind pink-tinted glasses as she introduced herself as Agnes Emberly and welcomed them to class. Next she distributed pattern sheets, one stack for each row. "Take one and pass the rest down," she chirped, smiling.

Julia's table partner sat on the aisle, so she took a page from the top of the stack and turned to pass the rest to Julia. She gasped, her eyes widening in recognition. Julia smiled grimly and tried to take the papers, but the other woman was so astonished that she forgot to release her grip. "I have them, thanks," Julia said, tugging at the pages in vain.

The other woman released the pages as if they were on fire. "Sorry." She was about fifty years old and a bit stout, with long, straight blond hair swept back into a loose bun and held in place with a pink plastic claw clip.

Julia nodded in reply and turned to face front, but she felt the woman's eyes on her even after Agnes began the lesson. She was used to brief stares from a stranger, but when it went on much too long, she gave the woman a sidelong glance. The other woman blushed, snatched her gaze away, and pretended she had been studying the pattern sheet.

Muffling a sigh, Julia focused her attention on Agnes's instructions, which were mercifully easier to follow than those in Quick Piecing. When Agnes announced that someone from each table needed to come to the front of the room for a roll of freezer paper,

Julia's table partner bolted up from her chair. "I'll get it," she said, smiling. Julia gave the barest of nods without looking her way. "Here we go," the woman said brightly when she returned, placing the long blue box on the table between them.

"Thanks," Julia murmured. The woman was trying to make up for her starstruck moment by treating her like any other student. That was actually rather nice.

Following Agnes's instructions, Julia tore off a sheet of freezer paper from the roll, placed it on top of the pattern sheet, and began tracing the first design. Uncertain, she glanced over at her table partner, who had deftly completed her first tracing and moved on to the second. Julia promptly decided to follow along, and between Agnes's instructions and her unwitting table partner's demonstration, she managed to stumble through the making of several stylized flower buds and leaves. But perhaps the woman wasn't as unwitting as Julia believed, for soon it seemed as if she was deliberately slowing her movements and taking care not to block Julia's view of her work.

Julia managed well enough until she attempted to sew the appliqué to the background fabric. She couldn't quite make the needle slip through both pieces so that they aligned correctly, and she struggled to make small stitches that didn't create little corners where a smooth curve should be.

"Do you want some help?" her table partner murmured, in a distinct Upper Midwest accent.

Julia nodded, wishing she had concealed her frustration better. The woman quietly explained the steps again, demonstrating each one. When Julia tried again, she managed to complete a shaky but perfectly respectable appliqué stitch. "Thank you," she said, offering the woman a tentative smile. "I think I have it now."

"I think you do too," the woman said, beaming like a proud teacher.

They both soon became engrossed in their own work. Agnes continued to offer instructions to the group, and when she made her rounds of the classroom, she gave Julia specific advice and much-welcome encouragement. For the first time, Julia felt confident that given enough practice, she should be able to master the skills required for the role.

But sufficient time to practice was precisely what she didn't have. She needed a crash course, a quilting boot camp. At the very least, she needed a quilting consultant, a technical adviser.

"Excuse me," she murmured to her table partner as the class was drawing to a close. "I don't mean to interrupt you, but you seem to know more about this than I."

"Just a little, maybe," the woman replied diplomatically.

"I wondered . . ." Julia hesitated. "Is this the same method as needle-turned appliqué, just using a different name?"

"No, they're two different styles. Agnes probably picked freezer paper because many people think it's easier."

"I see. But this technique has been around just as long, I suppose?"

The woman shook her head. "I don't think so. As far as I know, freezer paper appliqué is fairly modern."

"Oh, dear." Julia set down her needle and sank back into her chair, her fledging hopes vanishing. "I have to learn needle-turned appliqué."

"Your Whig Rose block will look exactly the same," the other woman assured her. "It doesn't matter what technique you use."

"It does matter." Julia took her notebook from the paper bag and opened it to the first page. "I have to learn certain quilting techniques for a movie role. But this morning I found out I was in the wrong piecing class, and now I'm in the wrong appliqué class—"

"Don't worry. It'll be all right." She patted Julia's shoulder consolingly and picked up the notebook. "Let's take a look at this list. Okay. All of these terms have to do with piecing. Are you taking Beginning Piecing?"

"I'm transferring to it tomorrow."

"Then you'll definitely cover the first half of the list." The woman pointed to the next few lines. "These steps here have to do with quilting a finished top. Did you sign up for a class on quilting?"

Julia nodded.

"Hand or machine?"

"Hand."

"Then you're all set there too. The only problem seems to be needle-turned appliqué." As the woman returned the notebook, her face brightened. "If you like, I could teach you during free time."

For a moment Julia was rendered speechless. "You would do that for me?"

"Sure. I've never won any ribbons for my appliqué, but I can at least give you a crash course in the basics."

Julia gratefully accepted. She could hardly believe her good luck when the woman, who introduced herself as Donna, offered to begin tutoring her right after class. And although she looked puzzled when Julia asked her not to reveal to anyone that she wasn't already an expert quilter, she barely even flinched when Julia asked her to sign a confidentiality agreement to make certain of it.

Five years later, Donna still enjoyed teasing her about that confidentiality agreement, and Julia was still embarrassed that she had asked. It was hard to imagine now why a binding agreement had seemed so necessary then.

Because although she didn't realize it, she and Donna were poised at the beginning of a beautiful friendship. Donna's appliqué tutorials were the first step. Then, the next day, the friendly white-haired quilter from Quick Piecing knocked on Julia's door by mistake while searching for another camper, Megan, whom Vinnie hoped to introduce to her newly single grandson. When Vinnie learned that Julia planned to eat lunch alone in her room, she insisted that Julia accompany her to the banquet hall for the legendary, absolutely-not-to-be-missed made-to-order pasta buffet. Julia soon found herself enjoying a surprisingly excellent dish of al dente penne with sun-dried tomatoes, fresh basil, and extra-virgin olive oil with

Vinnie; Megan, the camper Vinnie had been searching for when she knocked on Julia's door; Vinnie's other new friend, Grace, who had riveted Julia with her moving confession at Candlelight about longing for creative inspiration; and Donna herself, who looked just as surprised to see Julia pulling up a chair at their table as Julia was to find herself there.

As the days passed and they shared confidences and encouragement in quilting lessons and late-night chats, the new acquaintances stitched together a friendship unlike any Julia had ever known. They had all come to Elm Creek Quilt Camp seeking an escape from problems back home, and they had found in one another the mutual support and understanding they needed to return to their daily lives with renewed confidence to overcome whatever troubled them. On the last day of camp, the thought of bidding one another farewell and scattering across the country never to meet again was so heartbreaking that they vowed to return the same time the following year to enjoy another magical week of quilting and friendship together.

And so they had done, every year since.

The Cross-Country Quilters had become Julia's most cherished friends, her most trusted confidantes. Julia knew she could safely confess the secrets of her heart to them, for they would listen without judgment and offer whatever comfort or insight or counsel they could.

If the Cross-Country Quilters couldn't help her figure out a way to keep her cast and crew together and save *A Patchwork Life*, then it simply wasn't possible—and Julia refused to believe that was so.

4

On the last day of quilt camp in August 1999, the Cross-Country Quilters had lingered on the cornerstone patio after the Farewell Breakfast and show-and-tell, reluctant to say goodbye. Soon Julia would be returning to Southern California, Grace to San Francisco, Vinnie to Cincinnati, Megan to Dayton, and Donna to Silver Pines, Minnesota, a small town about an hour north of the Twin Cities. Their only consolation was their promise to one another that they would reunite the following year. In the meantime, they would stay close through regular phone calls, letters, and emails.

But Donna's smile suddenly turned crestfallen. "People always say they'll keep in touch, but they usually don't."

"We'll be different," Vinnie declared.

Julia wanted to believe them both, but experience had taught her skepticism. They might leave Elm Creek Manor with the best of intentions, but as the weeks passed and they fell into the patterns of ordinary life, they might forget how special their week together had been. If they failed to nurture their friendship, it might become nothing more than a fond memory, something to reflect upon and cherish when leafing through an old scrapbook rather than something vibrant and alive.

"We need a symbol, something to remind us of our promise," Donna mused aloud.

"I know," Vinnie exclaimed. "Let's make a challenge quilt."

"A what?" Julia asked. As far as she was concerned, every quilt was a challenge.

"A challenge quilt," Vinnie repeated emphatically. "We'll take a piece of fabric and divide it into equal shares. We'll each piece a block of our choice from it, and next year, we'll meet at camp and sew our blocks together to make a sampler."

"The challenge comes from being required to use a particular fabric rather than being free to choose whatever you like," Grace explained for Julia's sake. "But sometimes there are other restrictions. Should we have any?"

"How about this?" said Megan. "We can't begin our block until we take steps to solve our problems back home. That will keep us from procrastinating."

In the months that followed, the challenge quilt spurred them to persevere even when confronting their personal issues proved easier said than done. When they reunited at quilt camp the following August, they were so pleased with their first challenge quilt that they promptly began another, but without the requirement that they resolve major life crises before beginning their blocks. The next year, Vinnie and Donna proposed making an elaborate Twelve Days of Christmas appliqué quilt, but Julia and Megan balked, so they decided to make a holiday-themed row round robin instead, using red, green, gold, and white fabrics and a variety of star patterns and other blocks suited to the festive season. For this style of quilt, which Julia particularly enjoyed, one quilter began by sewing a row of blocks of her choice, which she then passed along to the next quilter. The second quilter would add a row and pass it along, and so on, until every quilter in the group had added as many rows as they needed to make a finished top.

By this time, the Cross-Country Quilters had discovered that sharing custody of the finished pieces was rather complicated, so the following year, they switched to creating their own interpretations of the same pattern rather than working together on a single quilt. Currently they were working on their most challenging project by far, reproductions of an exquisite antique sampler called Harriet's Journey.

The story behind the quilt was as fascinating as the quilt itself was beautiful.

In 1987, future Elm Creek Quilter Maggie Flynn was walking home from the bus stop after work when she passed a garage sale and discovered a sampler quilt being used as a tablecloth for a glassware display. Although she was no expert, one look told her that this quilt, despite its dusty, disheveled appearance, was a remarkable find. The homeowner was astonished by Maggie's interest in the bedraggled old sampler, which she had kept in her garage since moving to the neighborhood twenty-six years before. Her mother-in-law had bought it at an estate auction, and when she tired of it, she had given it to her son to keep dog hair off the car seats when he took his German shepherds to the park.

"We were just using it to hide an ugly table," the homeowner said, bemused. "If you're sure you want it, I guess I'll take five bucks for it."

Maggie gladly paid.

She took the quilt home, where she examined it carefully and discovered that despite the years of ill treatment, the sampler of one hundred unique blocks was free of holes, tears, and stains. More than that, the quilt was unquestionably a masterpiece, completed in 1854 by a woman named Harriet Findley Birch, or so several lines of embroidery on the back revealed.

With the help of the Courtyard Quilters, a quilting bee at the Sacramento retirement home where Maggie worked, she relearned her long-forgotten sewing skills and made a replica of the fragile antique. Fellow customers of her favorite local quilt shop admired her sampler so much that the proprietor invited her to teach a class so they could make their own versions. The success of that class led to several more, which soon brought Maggie to the attention of local guilds, who invited her to lecture and teach at their monthly meetings, shows, and retreats.

Her students' questions about the identity of Harriet Findley Birch and Maggie's own enduring curiosity inspired her to find answers. She delved into research that took her from the De Young Museum in San Francisco—where she consulted with none other than future Cross-Country Quilter Grace Daniels, in a bit of serendipity that astonished them both when they reunited at Elm Creek Manor years later—to the New England Quilt Museum in Lowell, Massachusetts. Eventually Maggie discovered that Harriet had worked as a mill girl in Lowell in the 1840s. Later, as a newlywed bride, she had traveled west with her husband along the Oregon Trail, eventually settling in Salem, Oregon. Maggie theorized that Harriet had collected quilt patterns from friends and family before setting out on the journey west. Perhaps the sampler was intended as a sort of quilt block library she could draw upon throughout her life as a wife, mother, and homesteader.

As Maggie's fame in the quilting world had spread, she had written a pattern book, *My Journey with Harriet*, which quickly sold out of its first edition and went into its third printing within a month. The success of her book and her outstanding reputation as an instructor eventually led to a faculty position at Elm Creek Quilt Camp, where she taught beginning hand-piecing and quilting classes and led workshops dedicated to mastering Harriet's Journey.

At the Cross-Country Quilters' most recent annual quilt camp reunion, Donna and Megan had taken Maggie's Harriet's Journey workshop. Julia hadn't enrolled because she found the project too daunting, Grace because she preferred more improvisational styles, and Vinnie because she had become thoroughly enamored with jelly roll quilts, quilts made from bundles of two-and-a-half-inch-wide strips of coordinating fabric. She had packed her schedule with jelly roll design and sewing classes as well as something called "jelly roll race training," the concept of which still bewildered Julia despite Vinnie's frequent, animated descriptions.

But even Vinnie had been willing to set her new obsession aside for Harriet's Journey when Donna suggested it as their new group project. "I don't know if I'm up to it," Julia had demurred, studying the photo on the cover of Maggie's copy of *My Journey with Harriet* with trepidation.

"Of course you are," Vinnie had protested. "You're perfectly capable of anything if you put your mind to it."

"You're not a novice quilter anymore," Grace had reminded her. "Don't let the sampler's complexity intimidate you. It might not be obvious at first glance, but you already know all the techniques required to make each of these blocks."

"It can be daunting when you take in the whole quilt at once," Donna had added, sympathetic. "But try not to think of it that way. Break it down into its parts, and just enjoy making one block at a time without worrying about the rest."

"And whenever you need help, all you have to do is ask," Megan had assured her. "We're here for you."

Heartened by their confidence, Julia had agreed to the plan, and she had taken great pleasure in shopping for an assortment of rich earth-tone fabrics with sky blue and peach as bright accent hues. After further discussion, the friends decided to work on one block a week, with the new block announcement falling on Monday and the deadline to finish on Sunday. Every Thursday evening they would have a conference call to note their progress, share tips, and offer encouragement. Emails were welcome anytime. At that rate they would need more than two years to complete all one hundred blocks, and perhaps several weeks more to sew the blocks together with sashing strips and borders, and more time yet to quilt and bind the top. But the leisurely pace would allow them time to work on other projects too, without turning the weekly block assignments into a burden.

Then came the matter of how they would choose the block of

the week. Julia wanted to start with the easiest patterns and work up to the more difficult ones. As the least experienced quilter of the group, she figured she would benefit from time to perfect her sewing skills so she would be better prepared to tackle the trickier patterns later. Grace preferred the exact opposite approach, most difficult patterns to least. Her long-standing habit was to complete a day's most difficult tasks first, when she was freshest, and to enjoy how her workload became easier as the day went on. Donna, who always sought fairness and consensus, suggested that they take turns choosing the week's block, each according to her preferences. Megan, a methodical engineer, wanted to make the blocks in the order in which they appeared in the quilt: left to right, top row to bottom. As for Vinnie, "I don't care which blocks we make or when," she declared, "as long as we all work on the same block each week and have fun doing it."

In the end they decided that Megan's plan would be best. That way, patterns of different degrees of difficulty would be dispersed over time rather than concentrated at the beginning or the end. Also, if someone finished a block early, she would already know the next week's assignment and could work ahead, if that suited her. And if Julia—or anyone—encountered a particularly challenging block before she felt up to the task, the other Cross-Country Quilters would guide her through it, step by step.

The week after Julia's season premiere party, the Cross-Country Quilters began working on the fourth block of the second row. Churn Dash was one of the simpler blocks, with all straight seams and no set-in pieces or curves, so their weekly check-in conference call quickly turned from noting their progress to catching up on their personal news. Julia's friends were especially eager to discuss the upcoming Emmy Awards ceremony, which they planned to watch on television. They couldn't wait to see her walk the red carpet in her strapless Versace gown of champagne silk chiffon with a small train and a matching shawl, and they teasingly declared that they expected her to mention them by name in her acceptance speech when she collected yet another golden statuette.

"Please don't place any bets," Julia begged them. "Everyone says this is Jennifer Garner's year. *Alias* is one of the most popular shows on television, and Jennifer has never won. I'm not even writing an acceptance speech."

The chorus of protests made her glad she had her friends on speakerphone rather than directly in her ear. "But you performed so well all season long," said Vinnie. "You had so many wonderful scenes. I know you personally, but you almost made me forget I was watching my friend. I saw only Sadie Henderson."

As ever, Julia was grateful for the effusive praise, although after so many years in the industry, she wished she didn't crave so much reassurance. "Thank you, Vinnie. That means a lot to me."

"And I *did* bet on you to win, so there."

Julia's heart sank as she envisioned the elderly woman's life savings disappearing in a puff of smoke. "Please tell me you're kidding."

"Not at all. We shook on it and everything."

"Vinnie," said Megan warily. Almost three years earlier, thanks to Vinnie's persistent matchmaking, Megan had married Vinnie's favorite grandson, Adam. Vinnie often fondly referred to Megan as her granddaughter-in-law. "How much did you bet and with whom?"

"And since when are bookies allowed to prowl the halls of your retirement community?" asked Grace.

Vinnie trilled a laugh. "Oh, relax, girls. The bet is with Ethel from across the hall. The winner has to treat the loser to a piece of pie and a cup of coffee at the café down the block. That's all."

Julia heaved a sigh of relief, one she heard echoed over the speakerphone. "I appreciate your optimism, Vinnie, but you're going to owe Ethel dessert."

"We'll see about that," said Vinnie. "We'll be watching Sunday night on the big-screen TV in the lounge, and I'll be the one laughing when you have to make up a speech on the spot when you win."

"Lindsay is absolutely thrilled that you're taking her as your plus-one, Julia," Donna said. "That's so generous of you."

"Not at all. It's my pleasure, and she deserves to be there. Lindsay inherited your work ethic and she's exceptionally good at her job. She's also delightful company." Besides, many other members of the cast and production team would be attending the ceremony, as nominees in other categories. It wouldn't be right to leave Lindsay out, and it wasn't as if Julia were dating anyone.

Vinnie sighed, comically forlorn. "Well, if it couldn't be me in the seat beside you, I'm glad it's Lindsay."

"You were my date last year," Julia reminded her. "Not to mention that I escorted you to the gala grand opening of the Union Hall quilt exhibit just last month."

"So you did," Vinnie admitted.

"Dibs on the Emmys next year," Megan sang out.

"I call season six," Grace chimed in.

"If I'm nominated," Julia said, laughing, warmed by her friends' absolute, unshakable belief that she deserved all the awards. "Don't go buying your gowns and booking your flights just yet."

"You will be nominated, if the voters have any sense," Vinnie said emphatically, "so put me down for season seven."

"Don't budge the line," Donna teased, feigning indignation. "I'll be Julia's plus-one for season seven."

"If there is a season seven," Julia said.

One of her friends gasped; she couldn't tell who. "Why wouldn't there be?" asked Megan.

"I've been dying to tell you for days. To be honest, I'm desperate for your advice."

"My goodness," said Vinnie. "How foreboding."

Taking a deep, steadying breath, Julia confided the miserable tale, tearing up as she remembered how happy and proud she had been at the premiere party until her friends' revelations had blindsided her. "If Ellen and most of the leads quit, that would mean the end of the show," she lamented. "I honestly don't see how *A Patchwork Life* could continue without them."

"Oh, Julia, dear, that's simply awful," said Vinnie. "I don't understand why anyone would want to leave such a charming series."

"I don't either. We haven't even peaked yet. We have so much more of Sadie's story to tell."

As Megan and Grace murmured sympathetically, Donna was curiously silent. "Hold on," she eventually said. "Is the show officially canceled? Has everyone been fired? Lindsay hasn't mentioned it, but it would be just like her not to worry me until she knew for sure."

Too late, Julia realized the implications of her news for Donna. "It isn't officially canceled yet, and we still have season six to film," she hastened to assure her friend. "Don't worry about Lindsay. She already works on other programs when we're on hiatus. Whenever *Patchwork* eventually ends, I'm confident she'll move on to bigger and better things."

"The same could be said for you, Julia," said Grace.

"Thanks, but there *isn't* anything bigger or better for me than *A Patchwork Life*."

"You don't know that," said Megan. "You were an acclaimed actress before the series began and you're even more popular now. I'm sure your agent will find you a new show, or maybe a movie. There must be dozens of directors who would be thrilled to cast a five-time Emmy Award–winning actress in a starring role."

"Six-time, after Sunday evening," Vinnie declared. "But that's not the point. Julia doesn't want a new show. She has a perfectly good show right now."

"And a perfectly lovely cast and crew I'd hate to see go our separate ways," Julia added, glad that Vinnie, at least, understood. It was unsettling to hear Grace and Megan echoing Maury's talking points. "I'm touched by your confidence in my ability to land another part, but trust me, there isn't exactly a wild abundance of compelling roles for women my age."

"Or any guarantee that a new series would last more than a single season," Donna said. "Some series get canceled after a few episodes if the ratings are too low. *A Patchwork Life* is a sure thing. It's popular and the critics love it. I can't imagine it would be in any danger of cancellation if not for those irresponsible, reckless people who've suddenly decide to bail."

"Networks rarely cancel their most successful shows," Julia noted, although she winced to hear her friends described in such terms.

"All good things come to an end," said Grace.

"That doesn't mean they should," Vinnie countered.

"Maybe not," Grace replied, "but when change is forced upon us, we honor ourselves best by adapting and moving forward with dignity and hope."

"Or," said Vinnie, "we fight like the dickens to hold on to what we have for as long as we can."

"I know a little something about how well *that* works," said Megan. "If I learned anything from my divorce, it's that—"

"Your first husband was a louse?" Donna finished for her.

Megan laughed. "Well, yes, but what I was going to say is that when someone decides they no longer want to stay, you have to let them go. You'll only demean yourself by clinging desperately to something that to them is over and done with. What's worse, you'll never know what wonderful future you're denying yourself by refusing to move on."

"Like your marriage to my grandson Adam," Vinnie exclaimed, delighted. "Wait. Wait. Scratch that. I'm not agreeing with you, dear. I mean, I am, but only about your marriage. Not about Julia's series. She absolutely should cling desperately to it if that's what she wants."

"Thanks, Vinnie," Julia said wryly. "Is that really how I seem? Desperate?"

"Not at all," said Donna.

"Yes, but in a good way," said Vinnie brightly.

"Maybe a little," said Megan.

"'Desperate' has unflattering connotations," said Grace. "Maybe 'anxious' is a better word."

"Well, maybe I *am* anxious about the future," said Julia, a bit defiant. "I just found out that I'm going to lose a job I love, working with people I absolutely adore, with no guarantee that anything else will come along."

"Something will," Grace said. "You have an entire year to find it."

"I'd rather put off that search quite a bit longer." Inhaling deeply, Julia managed a shaky laugh. "You know, I wasn't only looking for sympathy when I spilled the tea. I was hoping you could help me figure out how to convince Ellen and the others to stay with the show."

Her friends were silent so long that Julia prompted, "Are you still there?"

"Forgive me," Grace ventured, "but I'm not convinced that would be the best use of your time and creative energy."

"I'm with Grace," said Megan. "They're adults, and they're free to make their own decisions. I think you should focus on searching for your own fantastic new series or movie or whatever."

"Yes, and with deciding what to do in season six so you can resolve all the storylines and give the audience a satisfying conclusion," said Grace.

"That will definitely be important when we finally wrap up the series," Julia said patiently, "but again, as I said, I'd like to postpone that a few years. Vinnie? Donna? Any thoughts?"

"Would a raise persuade them?" asked Donna. "If the studio or the network could outbid those other offers, that would be a good incentive to stay, wouldn't it?"

"I thought of that too," said Julia. "Unfortunately, I can't imagine that the network could match what Nigel is likely getting from Warner Brothers. Then there's Noah. He's willingly forgoing any pay to attend college. I don't think money will motivate him."

"Have you tried simply asking your friends to stay?" Vinnie asked.

"Maybe if they knew how much it means to you, they'd stick around for another season or two, as a special favor to you."

"They know how I feel," said Julia, remembering the scene at the party. "And I can't ask them to make major life and career decisions simply as a favor to me. They have to choose to stay not because it's what *I* want, but because it's what's best for them too."

"But what if staying *isn't* what's best for them?" asked Grace.

"I honestly believe that it is."

"I'm sure you do," said Megan, "but you're not exactly an objective observer."

Julia laughed, forlorn. "No, I'm definitely not."

"Then I think you have your answer, even though you may not like it," said Grace. "They have to decide on their own that it's in their best interest to stay with the show—*if* that is, in fact, true."

"You could remind them what they'd miss if they left," said Donna.

"But if they do decide that they should move on, you should let them go, willingly and with love," said Megan. "Don't let your personal disappointment ruin the friendship."

"Oh, I wouldn't dream of it," exclaimed Julia.

"Then tread carefully," Grace warned. "To be honest, I can imagine many ways this could backfire on you spectacularly."

"I won't let that happen. If I have to choose between saving the show and preserving the friendship, I'll always put the friendship first, front, and center."

Her friends murmured approvingly, then fell into a contemplative silence. Julia thought she heard the snip of scissors through fabric.

"Well, I don't feel like we've been especially helpful here," Vinnie grumbled.

"That's not so," said Julia. "I'm feeling much better."

"I don't see why. You still don't know what to do."

"Maybe not, but you all were willing to listen to my tale of woe, and you offered me sympathy and your honest opinions. I can work with that."

"I'm glad you're feeling less anxious," said Donna, "but as soon as we hang up, I feel like I should call Lindsay and tell her to start polishing her résumé."

"Please don't do that," Julia begged. "It's too soon. The show hasn't been canceled yet—and if I have my way, it won't be."

"But if my daughter's job is in jeopardy—"

"It isn't. We have an entire season yet to shoot. Lindsay still has a year's worth of paychecks coming." Julia thought quickly. "Obviously Lindsay isn't worried or she would have called you, right?"

"Well . . ." Donna hesitated. "I suppose that's true."

"Then why stress her out about something that might be nothing, especially with the Emmys coming up?"

"Oh, I wouldn't want to do that," said Donna. "Okay, I won't say anything. Lindsay should enjoy the ceremony and the parties without worrying about unemployment looming on the horizon."

"It isn't looming," Julia insisted, but she doubted Donna believed her.

Three days later, when her phone rang on the morning of the Emmys and she glimpsed Lindsay's number in the caller ID, she felt a frisson of dread. What if Donna's worries had gotten the better of her, and she had passed on her anxiety to her daughter? But to Julia's relief, her young friend greeted her cheerfully, thanking her again for the invitation and chatting happily about her gown, the expensive jewelry she had borrowed from a friend, and her upcoming appointment at the salon so she would look red carpet ready. "Anyway," Lindsay eventually said, "I'm actually calling about a work thing."

"The Emmys *are* a work thing when your show is nominated," Julia reminded her.

"True. But this question comes from production design. In episode four, when Sadie is stuck overnight at Ben's ranch, he offers her his bed while he takes a quilt on the floor in front of the fireplace in the other room—"

"And neither Sadie nor Ben can sleep, kept awake by longing. Yes, I remember the scene."

"The question is about Ben's quilt. It isn't vintage. The prop master had it made using reproduction fabrics."

"That's what I assumed, given its good condition. I think I mentioned that I saw an antique quilt using the same block in an exhibit at the Waterford Historical Society last August."

"Yes, I remembered that, which is why I'm calling. Production design wants us to confirm that the pattern definitely would have existed in Sadie's day. I don't know the block name, so I couldn't look it up."

Julia closed her eyes and thought. She could picture the quilt hanging on the Union Hall gallery wall vividly, but her memory of the description offered on the object placard was a bit vague. "I know it was called the Sugar Camp Quilt, but I can't remember the block name."

"Do you remember when it was made?"

"Not off the top of my head, but I brought home an exhibit program." Pressing the phone to her ear with her shoulder, she began opening desk drawers and leafing through papers. "Let me look for it and I'll get back to you. We won't have to cut those scenes if the quilt pattern turns out to be a historical anomaly, will we?"

"That'll be up to the director, but personally I think the scenes are too good to lose. We'll just have to brace ourselves for an onslaught of corrections from sharp-eyed viewers."

"Great. Well, maybe we'll get lucky. I'll do my best to have an answer for you before I swing by in the limo to pick you up for the Emmys."

Lindsay squealed. "I'm sorry," she said, laughing at herself. "I know I should be able to play it cool by now, but I will never *not* be excited to be whisked off to the Emmys in a limo."

"I sincerely hope not," said Julia. The world was already overfull with the bored and the cynical. She hoped Lindsay would always retain her sense of wonder and delight.

Julia was certain she had saved a program, but she also had a vague memory of autographing it for a grateful fan as she and Vinnie left the gallery. When after a good twenty minutes neither she nor her assistant nor her housekeeper could find it, and with her stylist reminding her with increasing urgency of her appointments for hair, makeup, and mani-pedi, Julia abandoned the search. While her stylist paced the length of her study, stealing increasingly frantic glances at her watch, Julia composed a quick email to Summer Sullivan, the exhibit's curator and the youngest founding Elm Creek Quilter. Explaining their hope to avoid historical anachronism, she asked for the date the Sugar Camp Quilt had been made, the name of the block that figured most prominently in it, and the year the block had been invented or its earliest known appearance in existing quilts or in print. Julia closed by asking Summer to give her best to all the Elm Creek Quilters, and almost as a postscript, asked how things were going at Elm Creek Manor now that quilt camp was over for the year. She honestly had no idea how the Elm Creek Quilters filled their hours during the offseason. Quilting and planning for the next year of camp, probably, she mused as she clicked send and put her computer to sleep.

"I'm all yours for the next few hours," she promised her stylist as she rose. Julia knew well that it was as important to look fabulous when losing an award as when she won, perhaps even more so.

But maybe she ought to jot down a quick acceptance speech, just in case.

5

On the way to pick up Lindsay, Julia hastily scribbled a few notes on an index card and tucked it into her sequined clutch just as the limo pulled up in front of the young woman's apartment. Lindsay must have been watching from the lone front window, for she promptly stepped outside and descended the stairs carefully, holding on to the railing for balance. She was so strikingly beautiful, even in a region packed with young, blond starlets, that Julia could only gaze at her admiringly as she approached, graceful even in the uncharacteristically high heels.

"You look lovely," Julia exclaimed when the driver opened the door and helped her inside.

That was an understatement. With her blond hair upswept to reveal her elegant neck and shoulders, Lindsay was absolutely radiant in a vintage Christian Dior gown of rose silk with a draped bodice and full skirt. "Thanks. It's the dress," she said breathlessly as she settled into the limo next to Julia, her eyes bright with nervous excitement. "I got it secondhand at Paper Bag Princess. It cost me a month's pay, but I'll wear it again the next time I'm invited to a fabulous gala."

"You might not be able to. The paparazzi and the press are going to think you're a movie star. I wouldn't be surprised if your photo is everywhere tomorrow."

"Do you really think so?" For a moment Lindsay looked taken aback, but she quickly shook her head. "Doesn't matter. I don't care how many people see me in this tonight. Girls from Minnesota don't buy a couture gown, even secondhand, and wear it only once."

"This girl from Iowa does."

Lindsay's eyes went wide. "You're from Iowa? Really? You?"

"Yes, originally, but don't spread it around." Julia gave her an appraising look as the driver pulled into traffic. "And it isn't just the dress, kid. You are beautiful. I wish your mother were here to see you."

Lindsay thanked her with a smile. "Let's make sure we get a picture together to send to her."

That would be easily done. Donna might even see the photo in her hometown paper days before Lindsay could send her a print. As a nominee, Julia was much in demand on the red carpet, and she took care to keep Lindsay in the frame nearly every time the cameras clicked. Star Jones had replaced Joan and Melissa Rivers as the host of E!'s fashion coverage, and she proved to be infinitely warmer and kinder than the snarky, acerbic mother-and-daughter duo ever had been. Julia was pleased to look on like a fond auntie as Lindsay graciously posed for the photographers, turning this way and that as requested, responding with poise and charm when reporters asked her who she was wearing.

"Have you ever considered stepping in front of the camera yourself?" Julia asked as they entered the Shrine Auditorium. The lobby hummed with expectation as they made their way to the corner where the cohort from *A Patchwork Life* had arranged to meet before taking their seats. "You're a natural."

"Me? No, definitely not." Lindsay paused to consider. "I mean, I majored in theater in college, and I've been acting in plays since middle school, but I never really considered myself an actress. I can't really pretend to be anyone but who I am. If I were going to be on camera professionally, it would be as a journalist."

"Is that so? I had no idea. All this time, I've thought you were an aspiring director."

"I am. I love working on *A Patchwork Life*. I've learned so much, and I'm so grateful to have had this experience. When I think about the films I want to make, though, I'm drawn to documentaries. I don't think I ever told you how much I admire your husband's work. His biography of Frances Perkins was so inspirational, but it was his documentary about the Triangle Shirtwaist Factory fire that made me want to become a filmmaker."

Julia felt her breath catch in her throat, flooded by memories of other awards ceremonies when she had walked the red carpet on Charles's arm, and had beamed and applauded from the audience as he thanked her from the podium after accepting an Oscar or a Peabody. "You're full of surprises tonight," she said, smiling to hide a sudden pang of grief. "Most aspiring directors your age cite Steven Spielberg as their inspiration, not Charles Bryson."

Lindsay shrugged. "Steven Spielberg is pretty great too."

Something about that struck Julia as so comical that she burst out laughing, and in that instant her overwhelming longing for Charles transformed into joy. Even now his work was making a difference in the world by influencing young artists. If only he were there so she could kiss him and tell him how proud she was.

Lindsay's revelations weren't the only surprises of the evening. The next was a fashion faux pas—mildly embarrassing, but it would link Julia to one of Hollywood's biggest stars, so at least some good publicity would come of it. After they met up with their *Patchwork* colleagues, Lindsay went ahead into the theater with Noah and Ellen, while Julia lingered in the lobby with Olivia Muñoz, who played Sadie's perpetually jealous rival, and Nigel, who inexplicably had come alone, and was wittily evasive when she asked why Alistair had not accompanied him after all. When they finally went to claim their seats, Julia stopped short at the top of the front orchestra section, momentarily confused by what at first glance appeared to be her mirror image. A second glance revealed the vision to be Glenn Close, beautifully attired in an Oscar de la Renta gown a shade lighter than the Versace Julia wore, but except for that, and the small differences in the ruffle detailing down the center and the length of the train, it was virtually identical to her own. Julia and Glenn both needed a moment to recover from their surprise, but after that, they had a good laugh and even posed for photos in the aisle, feigning, in turn, horror, outrage, indignation, before smiling with genuine amusement. They did, however, avoid standing next to one another for the rest of the evening, and Julia made a mental note to avoid whatever snarky "who wore it better" reportage would likely appear in the media the next day.

Soon after the ceremony began, in an astonishing upset, Noah took the Emmy for Outstanding Supporting Actor in a Drama Series, turning his first nomination into his first win. When Heather Locklear opened the envelope and read his name, the *Patchwork* cohort leapt to their feet in celebration, hugging Noah and one another and laughing for joy. At the podium Noah admitted that he hadn't expected to win so he hadn't prepared a speech, and he expressed such humility and admiration for his fellow nominees that Julia felt a surge of maternal pride. The audience roared with laughter when he closed by thanking the Academy, holding his award aloft, and saying, "You better believe I'm going to mention this in my college applications." The fresh reminder of Noah's intention to leave the show broke Julia's composure, but she smiled and applauded and disguised her emotion as blinking away tears of happiness.

About two hours later, Julia's decision not to invest much time or effort in composing an acceptance speech turned out to be justified. Her own loss as Outstanding Lead Actress wasn't a surprise, but Jennifer Garner's was. Instead it was Allison Janney who claimed the Emmy, her fourth for her portrayal of press secretary C. J. Cregg in

The West Wing. As Allison made her way to the stage, Julia applauded as loudly as everyone else, imagining the Cross-Country Quilters watching at home and feeling utterly incredulous, indignant, and perhaps outraged on her behalf. "Ethel's going to get free pie tomorrow," she murmured, smiling for the cameras.

"What did you say?" Lindsay asked, bending closer to be heard over the thunderous ovation.

Julia just smiled and shook her head.

Her chance at an individual Emmy had passed, but Julia still held out hope that *A Patchwork Life* would win for Outstanding Drama Series, even though *The West Wing* was highly favored to extend its four-year winning streak. As the night wore on, it occurred to Julia that the series most likely to pull off an upset wouldn't be her own. HBO was having a fantastic night, and had already claimed thirty-one Emmys by the time their category came up, the last of the evening.

As Glenn Close emerged from the wings to announce the winner, Lindsay suddenly clutched Julia's forearm. "Isn't that your dress?" she murmured close to Julia's ear.

"No," Julia murmured back, her gaze fixed on Glenn Close as she approached the podium with the fateful envelope in hand. "Hers is a nude Oscar de la Renta. Mine is a champagne Versace. My train is longer and my shawl shorter."

Lindsay nodded, her grip on Julia's arm tightening as Glenn Close made her scripted remarks. Julia's heart pounded and she found herself holding her breath—only to let it out in a sigh a moment later when *The Sopranos* was declared the winner. She hadn't expected *A Patchwork Life* to win, not after four losses in a row, but a cable network had never won for Outstanding Drama Series. HBO's unprecedented win had caught her—and a significant portion of the audience, from the sound of it—entirely by surprise despite the impressive number of awards it had collected earlier that evening. But Julia quickly remembered to smile and applaud, and her heartbeat soon subsided into its usual rhythm.

Later, at the network's after-party, the first of several Julia intended to make an appearance at that night, she caught up with Ellen, who had been nominated for Outstanding Writing for a Drama Series but had lost to a writer from *The Sopranos*. They commiserated amiably as they sipped themed wine spritzers, their own disappointment tempered by their happiness for Noah.

"HBO won thirty-two Emmys tonight," said Ellen, shaking her head in amazement.

"Is that so?" Julia sipped her drink. "I wasn't counting."

"This was the first time a cable network ever beat one of the Big Four networks for Outstanding Drama Series." Ellen hesitated. "I know you're worried about me going to HBO after *Patchwork* wraps. Maybe it isn't such a risky move after all."

"Maybe not," Julia allowed, "but HBO will still be there in two years, or four. Why jump ship before it comes into the harbor?"

Ellen looked as if she might reply, but instead she shrugged and smiled miserably, glancing away as she sipped her drink.

Julia felt a sting of guilt. "That came out wrong," she said. "What I meant was—"

"No, it's fine," Ellen said quickly. "I'm sure you just—"

"Julia," Nigel's baritone boomed as he swept in and kissed her on the cheek. Noticing Ellen, he brightened and kissed her cheek too. "Ellen, if you'll let me borrow Julia for a moment—"

"Sure, of course, no problem." Ellen waved them away, smiling with what might have been relief.

Nigel thanked her, took Julia's elbow, and steered her off, explaining that a British colleague in town for the ceremony was absolutely dying to meet her. Nodding along, Julia glanced over her shoulder to find Ellen already joining a lively conversation with a few younger members of the cast and crew, including Noah and the handsome piano player from set design, the one who resembled a young Blair Underwood. At that moment, the group burst into joyous laughter, Ellen too. Her feelings couldn't have been hurt that badly, Julia told herself, relieved.

She saw little of Ellen after that. As far as Julia knew, Ellen remained at the network party after Julia whisked Lindsay off on a tour of several others, one hosted by Maury's agency, another by *TV Guide*, and another that she and Lindsay accidentally crashed on their way somewhere else. Julia felt fatigue setting in by one o'clock, but she found a second wind and gamely reveled on until two. Then, pleading exhaustion, she decided to call it a night. "You stay and enjoy yourself," she told Lindsay, raising her voice to be heard over the nightclub's pounding bass, smothering a yawn. "I'll take a cab home and you can have the limo."

But Lindsay wouldn't hear of it. She claimed to be tired too, although her eyes were bright and her cheeks flushed from dancing, and they left the last party together.

Julia barely stayed awake long enough to undress and remove her makeup, and the next day she slept past noon, an indulgence she rarely allowed herself. Groaning as she rose from bed, she made her way to the kitchen, where she drank several chilled glasses of reverse-osmosis filtered spring water to rehydrate. Her personal chef had come by on Saturday and stocked her refrigerator and freezer with a week's worth of fresh, nutritious meals, so lunch was a simple matter of reading the labels, choosing the one that sounded most gentle on the stomach, and heating it up in the microwave.

She skimmed the newspaper as she ate, the open windows of the breakfast nook letting in refreshing breezes and birdsong. Poring over coverage of the previous night's events, she was delighted to see a flattering red carpet photo of herself and Lindsay, whom one paper mistakenly identified as her niece; she set that page aside to send to Donna. Amid the often amusing, occasionally exasperating anecdotes, she was astonished to discover fervid speculation about what she had said as Allison Janney took the stage to accept her award. One expert lip-reader's interpretation, "Ed knows it's going to be a faux pas tomorrow," was widely regarded as the most credible and had sparked a firestorm of questions. Who was Ed? Ed Norton? Edward

James Olmos? Eddie Murphy? Was the faux pas in question Julia's and Glenn's much-too-similar gowns or something else? Why would this Ed person know and why did it matter? Eventually Julia was laughing so hard that she almost choked on her green tea. Wait until she told the Cross-Country Quilters what she had really said. They would laugh until tears streamed down their faces.

After a leisurely lunch came yoga, a relaxing bath, and a meeting with her assistant, so it was not until late afternoon that Julia checked her email and found the reply from Summer Sullivan she had been waiting for.

Date: September 19, 2004
To: Julia Merchaud
From: Summer Sullivan
Subject: Re: Quick Quilt Questions

Hello, Julia! It's so nice to hear from you. I'm flattered that you consider me your "favorite quilt historian/librarian-in-training," but I can't imagine there were many contenders for the title!

I'm happy to report that you don't have to worry about a historical anachronism if you keep Ben's quilt in the show. The Sugar Camp Quilt, which you saw in the exhibit at Union Hall, was made in 1849. The featured block, Delectable Mountains, dates back to the early 1840s, although the source of its name is much older—John Bunyan's famous 1678 Christian allegory, *The Pilgrim's Progress*. So you can reassure your production designer that your prop quilt definitely could have existed in Kansas in Sadie's day.

Thanks for your good wishes, which I'll be sure to pass along to the other Elm Creek Quilters. To answer your question frankly, and just between us, I'm sorry to say that since your last visit, we've encountered some unexpected financial challenges here at Elm Creek Manor. It's surprisingly expensive to run an artists' retreat at a historic nineteenth-century manor in rural Pennsylvania. (Who would've guessed?) Just a few days ago, for example, we found out that the entire roof has to be replaced. You've seen the size of our roof, so you'll understand why we're dreading the contractor's estimate.

But not to worry! We'll persevere and adapt as we always do. Sarah and Sylvia are already brainstorming ideas for new revenue sources, and Matt is launching a new business venture next week to supplement our income during the offseason: Elm Creek Orchards! The estate's apple orchards are thriving, which I'm sure won't surprise you, since you've sampled some of Chef Anna's delicious apple dishes at quilt camp through the years. Now, in addition to selling apples to local grocers and cider mills, we'll be offering self-picked apples directly to customers. Our grand opening is September 25, and we're hoping for—and counting on—huge, happy crowds for our own season premiere.

Congratulations on your most recent Emmy nomination! All of your fans at Elm Creek Manor are pulling for you. Whatever happens, you'll always be our favorite actress/Cross-Country Quilter/quilt camper!

Hugs and Stitches,
Summer

Julia's relief upon learning that the compelling scenes from episode four wouldn't have to be cut because of a historical anomaly turned to dismay by the time she reached the last paragraph. Elm Creek Quilt Camp was the most popular quilters' retreat in the country, possibly the world. How could a company so successful and beloved have tumbled into financial difficulties? It certainly couldn't be due to financial mismanagement. Sylvia was known for her generosity to the quilting community, but from everything Julia had observed, she was also frugal and pragmatic. Sarah, who rarely taught classes anymore in lieu of focusing on the company's day-to-day operations, had earned a business degree at Penn State and was experienced in accountancy and management. The other Elm Creek Quilters were exceptionally creative and resourceful. Julia couldn't imagine any routine business problem that could stymie this particular dream team, and Summer did sound optimistic—but wasn't that Summer's nature? And what if these business problems weren't routine?

Troubled, Julia read the email again more thoroughly, searching for meanings between the lines. If apple orchards were anything like family farms—which she knew more about than most people would ever suspect—Elm Creek Orchards would likely prove to be a labor-intensive venture with low profit margins. The cost to replace the roof of Elm Creek Manor would likely be substantial, and that was most probably only the beginning of the essential maintenance the historic residence required. It pained Julia to imagine Elm Creek Quilt Camp—a place where she had discovered so much joy, friendship, and fulfillment—no longer able to provide that same priceless gift to others. She had assumed it would endure forever.

Obviously, she should send the Elm Creek Quilters a check. Her income from a single episode of *A Patchwork Life* would surely cover the cost of the roof and then some. But, also obviously, Sylvia wouldn't accept such a gift. Summer hadn't mentioned that Elm Creek Quilts was seeking new investors, or Julia would have eagerly seized the opportunity, over her accountant's objections if necessary. But she couldn't just sit back and let Elm Creek Quilts go under, not when she had the resources and the very strong desire to keep it afloat. But what could she do?

The question nagged at her through the afternoon as she answered fan mail and took a call for a post-Emmys interview with a writer from *Harper's Bazaar*. The perfect solution still eluded her as evening approached. She was tempted to email the Cross-Country Quilters and seek their advice, but Summer had said "just between us," and Julia had been burned by untrustworthy acquaintances too many times not to respect a confidence. Nor did she wish to upset her friends with speculation that Elm Creek Quilt Camp might close before their next annual reunion.

"Not on my watch, it won't," Julia declared to her empty kitchen as she opened her refrigerator door to assess the possibilities for dinner. Somehow she'd find a way to help without offending Sylvia's pride. "An anonymous donation?" she mused aloud, reading the labeled containers her personal chef had arranged so neatly. Sylvia's bank could trace a wire transfer, and a grant from the National Endowment for the Humanities would be difficult to fake. She couldn't just anonymously overnight a crate of cash to Elm Creek Manor. Sylvia would consider it her duty to turn it over to the authorities.

She had just decided on a mushroom and asparagus risotto when the phone rang. Leaving the container on the counter, she glanced at the caller ID and picked up eagerly when she saw that it was Nigel. "Hello, Nigel, dearest," she greeted him pertly. "Just waking up? Or just getting home?"

"I've been up for hours, darling. I swam, had a lovely long phone chat with Alistair, and sat for an interview with *GQ*. Do you believe you were robbed last night?"

"What?" The non sequitur threw her for a moment, and she had to think. "No, I kept my purse with me the entire time and it was definitely on my dresser this morning when I woke. Not that I would have lost much. I wasn't carrying anything in my purse but a lipstick, some breath mints, a pen, and an index card with some bullet points for an entirely unnecessary acceptance speech."

"Not robbed of your purse, darling. Robbed of an Emmy."

"No, of course not. I already have five and I'm not greedy. Why do you ask?"

"Because a certain nominee claimed that *he* was robbed because his show didn't win the prize for Outstanding Reality Competition Program. 'Outstanding Reality Program'—do you suppose that's an intentional oxymoron?"

"My, aren't *you* snobbish this evening," Julia remarked, smiling as she pulled up a kitchen stool and settled in for a long, enjoyable chat.

"I happen to know that you disdain reality television as much as I do."

"Fair enough, but I've watched a few episodes of *The Amazing Race*, and it's not bad. It's probably the best of the genre."

"Faint praise indeed."

"I don't mean it to be," Julia protested, laughing. "I rather enjoy the show—the spectacular scenery of all those faraway locales, the interesting tidbits of world cultures. It certainly isn't how *I'd* like to travel, racing around and completing challenges rather than savoring every moment, but as entertainment, it works. It deserved to win the Emmy last night." She paused as a memory rose. "Charles never liked the idea of pitting artists against one another for prizes. He used to say that the work itself was the reward."

"Charles could say such things. He had two Oscars." Nigel sighed. "Well, one must endeavor to be a good sport. What are your plans for the evening?"

"I don't really have any. It looks like I'll have a quiet evening at home."

"I have a better idea. Come with me to Napa."

"Now? That's nearly a seven-hour drive!"

"Santa Barbara, then. Dinner at Tre Lune. The food is excellent and they never recognize us. We can dine like ordinary people."

"They always recognize us, Nigel," Julia said, amused. "They just don't make a fuss."

"Then you have no reason to refuse. Do say yes," he implored. "I'm bored and lonely. Don't make me eat takeaway at my kitchen counter, alone and pathetic."

"When you put it that way . . ." Julia glanced at the container of risotto gathering condensation on the counter. "What sort of friend would I be if I didn't help you escape such a dreadful fate?"

"I'll come by for you in fifteen minutes."

Then she was already late. "See you soon." She hung up and raced off to get ready.

Soon they were driving up the coast, taking Highway 1 to the 101 and on to Santa Barbara, gossiping and bantering all the way. Arriving just as the sun was setting, they had a brief wait at the bar, but soon were seated at a white-draped table for two, perusing menus and sighing with anticipation as delectable aromas from the kitchen wafted their way. Black-and-white photographs of stars from the Golden Age of Hollywood adorned the walls, but otherwise the ambiance was of a classic Italian bistro, reminding Julia fondly of her travels in Tuscany with Charles. As Nigel studied the wine list, vowing to limit himself to a single glass, Julia's gaze lingered on a still of Audrey Hepburn and Humphrey Bogart from *Sabrina*, regarding each other warily as they danced. With a sudden, wistful ache, she wondered if anything she had ever accomplished in her career would merit including her photo on the wall in such company. Probably not, she decided, and returned her attention to the menu.

Julia was savoring a decadent dish of *rigatoni ai tre funghi*, Nigel the *penne al ragù di cinghiale*, when she finally broached the question that had been bothering her since the previous evening. "Where was your favorite plus-one last night?" she asked lightly, sipping her *acqua frizzante*. "If memory serves, you said he was coming in for the ceremony."

"He meant to have done." Nigel offered a melancholy smile and reached for his wineglass. "At the last minute, UNESCO asked him to join a team tasked with identifying and recovering antiquities looted from the Iraq Museum in Baghdad."

Startled, Julia set down her water glass, nearly toppling it. "Alistair is in Baghdad?"

Nigel allowed a small smile. "The *museum* is in Baghdad. Alistair is in Switzerland, where some of the artifacts have been shipped to black-market buyers—allegedly. That's what he's meant to determine.

From there, he expects to be sent on to Jordan or Paris, but he definitely won't be going to Iraq."

"I'm glad he's safe," said Julia, relieved. "This assignment sounds terribly important, but I'm sorry he had to cancel his visit with you."

"Fortunately, I didn't win the Emmy, so he didn't miss my heartbreakingly beautiful acceptance speech."

Julia reached across the table and clasped his hand. "But he missed seeing you. And I know you miss him terribly."

"Hence my desperate, last-minute invitation to dinner, which you so kindly accepted. I wanted to wallow in self-pity, and for that, I require a sympathetic audience."

"You don't wallow."

"Perhaps 'indulging' is a better word for it." He sighed. "To be honest, I could use a distraction. Alistair meant to spend a fortnight here with me before we returned to London together. Now our plans are scrapped and our reunion has been postponed indefinitely."

"I'm so sorry," Julia said. "How about this—I know I'm a poor substitute for Alistair, but I'm free this weekend. Why don't we drive up to Napa after all? We can tour some wineries, visit a spa, go hiking among the redwoods—"

"Thank you, darling," he said, placing his hand over hers, "but it was a bad idea and I never should have asked you. I wouldn't be a very pleasant travel companion. I fear I'd only make you as miserable as I am myself."

"I'm willing to risk it." When he shook his head and reached for his wineglass again, she changed tack. "At least come for dinner at my place Thursday night. Don't worry, I promise I won't do the cooking. We'll watch the new episode of *Patchwork* and congratulate each other for our brilliant performances."

He mulled it over. "That sounds rather nice, actually."

"Then it's a date," she declared, before he could talk himself out of it.

The mood was more hopeful as they finished the meal. Nigel's promised single glass of wine turned into two, followed by limoncello in a chilled cordial glass, so Julia drove Nigel's Jaguar back to her place. She settled him into her guest room, brushing off his apologies and smiling at his vows of eternal devotion. He was snoring before she switched off the light and softly closed the door.

As she went to her own suite and got ready for bed, her mind churned over the impending demise of her series, Elm Creek Quilts in jeopardy, and dear Nigel's profound loneliness. If unhappy tidings came in threes, perhaps that meant she had passed through the worst and the days to come would bring only good things. One could only hope.

She climbed into bed, drew up the soft quilt, and had almost dozed off when insight struck with such force that she gasped, suddenly wide awake.

"Of course," she murmured. "Yes, that's it. That's the answer."

The pieces had been just beyond her fingertips all evening, but now she held them tightly in her grasp, and she knew precisely how to stitch them together.

She knew exactly what to do to help Nigel, Elm Creek Quilts, and herself.

6

When Julia woke, she pulled on a set of her favorite knit loungewear, eased her bedroom door open, and stepped silently into the hallway to avoid disturbing Nigel. To her surprise, the guest room door was ajar and the aroma of fresh-brewed coffee wafted on the air. She expected to find Nigel in the kitchen, rummaging through her refrigerator for a suitable breakfast among her chef's containers, but he wasn't there. Instead she found the coffeepot full and a single place set before her favorite chair. He had evidently visited her garden too. In the center of the table he had artfully arranged an assortment of lemons and oranges in a cut-glass bowl that she had forgotten she owned, and which Nigel must have discovered in a cupboard. Propped up against the bowl was a page torn from the notepad she kept by the phone. "Sorry to bolt, darling," Nigel had written in his rakishly elegant scrawl. "You know I never miss a morning swim if I can help it. Thank you for your hospitality, and for lifting my spirits last night. See you Thursday."

If he felt better this morning, Julia thought as she set the note aside and went to pour herself some coffee, just wait until he spent a week at Elm Creek Manor.

For that was the brilliant idea that had come to her as she was drifting off to sleep the night before. Elm Creek Quilt Camp was the perfect solution for her dilemma—and it would richly benefit her friends and colleagues too. Five years before, her first visit to quilt camp had profoundly changed her life. Not only had she learned to quilt, but she had also formed rich, lasting friendships with her fellow campers, none more so than the Cross-Country Quilters. If her cast and crew could share a similar bonding experience, Julia was absolutely certain that they would happily abandon their other plans and stay with *A Patchwork Life* indefinitely. Hadn't Nigel said he was miserable and needed something to distract him in Alistair's absence? A week devoted to learning the craft and heritage of quilting would keep his hands busy and mind occupied, and expressing himself artistically would relieve his stress. The very generous fee Julia would personally provide for her colleagues' tuition, room, and board would relieve the financial burdens weighing down Elm Creek Quilts. And if Julia's scheme succeeded and the series continued, the entire cast and crew of *Patchwork* would benefit personally, creatively, and financially—she had absolutely no doubt about it.

But first, she had to convince the Elm Creek Quilters to host an exclusive week of quilt camp during the offseason. As far as she knew, they had never done anything of the sort before. It was likely no one had ever asked. The faculty might be reluctant to throw something together on such short notice, but they needed a new roof, and Summer said that Sarah was brainstorming ideas for new revenue sources. Julia was all too happy to deliver her one wrapped up and tied with a bow.

Over a quick breakfast of coffee, half an English muffin, and one of the sweet, juicy oranges Nigel had harvested, Julia ignored the newspaper in lieu of mulling over how best to approach the Elm Creek Quilters with her proposal. After tidying up the kitchen, she hurried to her computer and replied to Summer's email.

Date: September 21, 2004
To: Summer Sullivan
From: Julia Merchaud
Subject: Re: Quick Quilt Questions

Thanks for your help with the Delectable Mountains quilt. I'm so relieved we won't have to cut those scenes. Nigel Crawford broods so marvelously in them. Alas, no sixth Emmy for me, but my young costar Noah McCleod well deserved his, and I'm as proud as it's possible to be!

I'm sorry to hear about the roof and the other challenges. I hope that the estimate wasn't as dreadful as you feared. No matter what, you're all so creative and resilient, and Elm Creek Quilts is so beloved in the quilting word, that I have no doubt you'll triumph in the end. I have some thoughts I'd like to share about how I might help. Would you please call me as soon as you can?

Julia signed off with warm regards and her cell phone number. Knowing she would be tempted to check her email every ten minutes if she didn't get out of the house, she changed into lightweight joggers and a top, meticulously applied sunblock, pulled on her sturdiest trail shoes, and drove to the Solstice Canyon trailhead, where through some miracle she managed to grab the last open parking place in the lot near Dry Canyon. She set out on her favorite route, striding briskly up the paved Solstice Canyon Trail to the waterfall near the ruins of the Roberts Ranch house, where she turned back and descended along the more rugged Rising Sun Trail, a wide dirt path with switchbacks through coastal sage scrub and chaparral and into the much welcome cooling shade of oaks and sycamores. She always took the loop clockwise for the better vistas, and since the morning mists had burned off during her climb, the view of the ocean from the TRW Overlook was especially splendid. She lingered there longer than usual, catching her breath, stretching her calves, feeling the effects of two late nights in a row—and her age, though she hated to admit it. Once she and Charles had been able to dance all night, catch a few hours' sleep, and hike all the next day effortlessly, but Charles was gone and Julia was nearly seventy.

The thought stopped her short. The Emmys had been on Sunday, the nineteenth, which made today the twenty-first, which meant— Goodness. She would be seventy on Thursday. How fortunate that she already knew she wouldn't be spending the entire day alone.

She had finished stretching and was about to begin the last half mile when her cell phone rang. The number was unfamiliar, but she recognized the area code for Elm Creek Valley, so she quickly answered before the call went to voicemail. "Hello?"

"Hello, Julia?"

"Yes, hello, Summer. Thanks for calling me back so soon."

"No problem. I would've called sooner except I was in class."

"Oh? What were you studying today? How to shelve books efficiently? How to restore ancient manuscripts?"

Summer laughed. "Neither, actually. The class is called Pedagogical Theory and Practice for Information Professionals."

"I have no idea what that is."

"That's because it's top secret librarian lore. Hey, I'm sorry the Emmys didn't go your way the other night. If it's any consolation, you looked absolutely gorgeous and not disappointed at all."

"That *is* consoling," Julia admitted, amused. "So, the roofer's estimate. How bad was it?"

"In a word, staggering."

"Oh, dear. Well, maybe I can help keep you on your feet."

"You did say you had some thoughts to share, and I'm very happy to listen." Summer hesitated. "First, though, I told Sylvia that I'd mentioned our financial challenges to you. She wasn't exactly pleased with me."

"Really? Why?"

"She said she's not comfortable 'going hat in hand' to our campers—"

"But that's not what you did. I asked how things were going at Elm Creek Manor, and you simply told me the truth. You never asked for a thing."

"That's what I told Sylvia—very contritely, of course. She chided me a bit for discussing our finances without clearing it with her or Sarah first. And rightly so. It really wasn't my place." Summer sighed. "I should have known better, but I've become so used to asking for donations to Union Hall on behalf of the Waterford Historical Society that I didn't think it through."

"I didn't breathe a word to anyone," Julia assured her, grateful that she had trusted her instincts when tempted to confide in the Cross-Country Quilters. "Nor will I. Promise."

"Good. Thank you. Sylvia also told me explicitly that I'm not to solicit donations, and Elm Creek Quilts isn't taking on new investors at this time. I hope that doesn't preempt whatever help you were going to offer. Because despite everything I just said, Elm Creek Quilts really could use a benefactor—but it can't look like a gift, because Sylvia wouldn't accept it."

"That's fine, actually, because I had something else in mind—a business proposition." Julia took a deep, centering breath and plunged ahead. "After five seasons, several of our longtime cast members have let their quilting skills get a bit rusty. We've also added new cast and crew who've never learned to quilt, but ought to understand the fundamentals, at the very least. What we need are intensive, remedial quilt lessons before we begin filming season six in January."

"January? So signing up for a week when camp resumes in March wouldn't work for you."

"No, that would be too late. Also, given our unusual circumstances, we would need an exclusive session—just our group, no other campers."

"We'd have to schedule something during our offseason, then."

"And instead of your usual wonderfully varied selection of classes, ours should focus only on techniques Sadie Henderson would have used in the eighteen eighties."

"So you're saying no longarm machine quilting workshops?" Summer teased.

"Definitely not. And I'm afraid your very popular Modern Quilting class is out too."

"Right, because historical anomalies are frowned upon by your audience."

"Exactly."

"That's not a problem either. We could easily put together a program of classes in hand quilting, hand appliqué, and hand quilting using both a lap hoop and a frame. Your actors should be comfortable with both setups, just as real quilters of the era would have been."

"Good thinking." Julia blotted perspiration from her forehead, wishing she had remembered to wear a cap. "So what should our next step—"

"Excuse me," a tentative voice spoke behind her. "Are you Julia Merchaud?"

Startled, Julia turned to find two remarkably fit thirtysomething women in black spandex with neon accents regarding her expectantly, hands on their hips, panting slightly from exertion as if they had run the entire ascent. "Yes," she replied guardedly, moving the phone only slightly away from her ear.

"I knew it was you. I'm a huge fan. I love *A Patchwork Life*," the woman on the left gushed. "I mean, I loved *Family Tree* too, but *Patchwork*—" She paced a hand on her heart and shook her head, eyes shining. "It really speaks to me."

"Thank you," said Julia, more warmly than before. "That's kind of you to say."

"Is Nigel Crawford as handsome in person as he is on TV?" the woman on the right asked, her eyes alight with eagerness.

Julia lowered her voice confidentially. "More."

The two women fairly squealed. "I knew it," the woman on the right exclaimed.

"Julia?" Summer asked, her voice faint.

Quickly Julia returned the phone to her ear. "Sorry, I'm still here."

"Could I ask just one more question?" the woman on the left begged. "When are Sadie and Ben going to get together?"

"Are you trying to get me in trouble?" Julia protested, smiling as she lowered her phone again. "Even if I knew, I couldn't tell you."

"But they *are* going to get together?"

"That's two questions, and you know I can't answer either one of them."

The two women groaned comically.

"Um, should I call you back later?" Summer asked.

"Can I ask a question too?" the woman on the right asked, drawing closer.

Julia raised her phone again. "Sorry, Summer. One more minute." To the eager fan, she replied, "I'm so sorry, but as you see, I'm on a call—"

"Oh, this'll be quick. What did Noah McCleod mean at the Emmys when he said that thing about his college applications? He's not leaving the show, is he?"

"Wait, what?" the other woman asked sharply, turning and grabbing her friend's arm. "I didn't watch. What did he say?"

"He said he was going to mention his Emmy on his college applications," the other woman explained, then turned back to Julia. "What did he mean? Is he leaving the show? Is it going to be canceled?"

"It can't be canceled," her friend wailed. "Sadie and Ben haven't gotten married yet."

"But Sunday night at the Emmys—"

"The show hasn't been canceled," Julia broke in hastily. "Our head writer is already working on scripts for our sixth season. *Patchwork* hasn't been canceled. I swear."

The woman on the left heaved a sigh, relieved, but her friend looked skeptical. "Then what was Noah talking about?"

"Well—" Julia shrugged and forced a smile. "Maybe it was a joke. Maybe he's thinking about going to college when we're on hiatus. I really wouldn't make anything of it."

The women exchanged a look. "I guess the show could continue without him," the woman on the left said, her expression doubtful. "You could, like, have Jesse go to college too, and maybe appear in a few episodes now and then."

"Sure, that could work," said Julia, smiling agreeably and backing away as she raised the phone to her ear. "That would be up to our writers, of course. It was lovely meeting you both, and thanks for supporting the show, but—"

"Oh, sure. Sorry to interrupt," the woman on the right said, and her friend quickly chimed in with thanks and apologies. As they hurried off down the trail, Julia turned back to face the ocean view again, but not before she heard one of the women tell her friend, "I can't *wait* to post about this on my blog!"

Julia felt a pang of misgivings. With any luck, the woman only had a dozen readers, all of them family members and neighbors. Quickly she pressed the phone to her ear. "I'm so sorry to keep you waiting."

"No worries," Summer assured her. "Does that happen a lot?"

"Yes, but I'd rather be ambushed by true fans than by the paparazzi. Where were we?"

"You explained what sort of camp experience you needed, and I think you were about to ask what our next step should be. I think it's a fantastic idea, and I'm confident we can provide what you need, so at this point I'd like to bring Sarah into the conversation."

"Not Sylvia?"

"No, not yet. Sarah is the camp director, so she'd be responsible for organizing your session. And if you can persuade her that it's worth doing, then she can help you convince Sylvia. Not that I expect Sylvia to object. Sarah has proposed expanding our quilt camp season into autumn before, but Sylvia has been skeptical that there would be enough interest to justify the effort. A special session for your cast and crew could be just the test we need."

Summer said she would recap their discussion in an email, and include Sarah in the recipients. "Everyone at the manor is preoccupied with the launch of Elm Creek Orchards on Saturday," she added, "but I'll be sure to emphasize that time is of the essence."

By the time Julia finished her hike and drove home, Summer's promised email had already landed in her inbox. She had summarized the plan more eloquently than Julia remembered proposing it, for which Julia self-deprecatingly thanked her in her reply. Sarah replied with a few cautious questions, and in an intermittent back-and-forth over the next twenty-four hours, Sarah and Summer confirmed that they would have the faculty and staff available to host a week of quilt camp for about a dozen of Julia's colleagues in late October or early November. But before they drew up a contract, they asked Julia to join them in a conference call to work out a few essential details.

"Speaking for myself, I'd be absolutely thrilled to welcome you and your friends to Elm Creek Manor to refresh your quilting skills," Sarah assured Julia when they spoke on Wednesday afternoon.

"And for the newbies to learn the basics," Summer chimed in. "If I weren't busy with library school, I'd teach you all myself. It would be so exciting to play a behind-the-scenes role in *A Patchwork Life*."

"I think some of the other Elm Creek Quilters would insist upon teaching at least a few classes," said Sarah. "We have to share the fun."

"Does this mean we have a deal?" asked Julia. "Shall we discuss dates and fees?"

"Well, actually . . ." Sarah hesitated. "Before we proceed, I'd like to have Sylvia's approval. I may be the director of Elm Creek Quilts, but the manor is her home. I wouldn't want to launch something of this scale without her blessing."

"I understand, of course," said Julia, but something in Sarah's tone made her wary. "Do you think she's likely to approve?"

"To be honest, I'm not sure. In the past, when I've suggested expanding our camp season into the fall, she's been . . . reluctant. But things are different now. Given our financial issues, she might welcome the chance to try something new."

"I think she would," said Summer. "After all, it took her a while to warm up to the idea of launching Elm Creek Orchards, but now she's all in."

"That's reassuring," said Julia, though it wasn't entirely so.

"I think it would be best if the proposal came from you, Julia," said Summer. "Your interest in helping your colleagues perform at their best will make a very good impression on her, and she'll definitely appreciate your concern for historical and artistic authenticity."

"Sylvia prefers phone calls to email, but please hold off until after we launch Elm Creek Orchards," said Sarah. "We still have so much to do to prepare, and we're racing at top speed to finish in time for our grand opening Saturday morning."

"Certainly." Julia didn't want to appear impatient, but she couldn't resist asking, "Would Saturday evening be too soon?"

Sarah laughed. "I think Saturday evening would be fine."

They ended the call with promises to talk again soon. Julia had nothing to do but wait until Saturday evening when she could call Sylvia. Then again, evening in Pennsylvania was really only late afternoon in California—which was the sort of calculation only an impatient person would make.

The Cross-Country Quilters' latest block in their Harriet's Journey challenge provided a timely distraction. That week's assignment was called City of Spindles, a reference to the mill town of Lowell, Massachusetts, where Harriet had once lived and worked. Although it was a strikingly pretty block, with four narrow rectangles along the diagonals, four on-point squares between them and one more in the center, and an isosceles right triangle along each side pointing toward the edge, Julia realized early on that it would not be one of her favorites. The foundation paper pieced pattern allowed for sharp points and accurate seams, which Megan and Donna loved, but Julia disliked removing all the paper from the back of the block afterward. No matter how carefully she would peel off the pieces, even resorting to tweezers for especially stubborn scraps, she inevitably would rip open seams that would then need to be resewn. "Just make your own pattern from the illustration and sew it by hand, then," Vinnie encouraged her whenever she grumbled about the technique, but Julia wasn't a fan of making her own templates and patterns either.

Still, with the same discipline she applied to memorizing lines, Julia persisted, and by Thursday afternoon she had completed the five foundation sections and would need only to sew them together to finish her City of Spindles block. She was looking forward to announcing her progress when the Cross-Country Quilters met for their weekly telephone conference call, but just as she was about to dial in on her landline from her sewing room, Nigel called her cell phone.

"You better not be calling to cancel," she teased, then held her breath, anxious for his reply. She hadn't reminded him it was her birthday, and she assumed he had forgotten, but she was counting on their dinner-and-a-show for her celebration, even if she was the only one who knew.

"I never would," he said, scandalized by the very idea. "I merely wanted to ask if I might bring a friend or two along. They're great fans of the show and they'd adore spending time with you."

"I'd love that," said Julia. Nigel's friends were unfailingly witty and fun, and it certainly would feel more like a birthday party with more guests around the table, even if she'd never met them. "The more the merrier."

"Excellent. Don't worry about sending out for dinner either. I'll bring tapas and sangria."

"Your sangria?" she teased. "I'd better get both guest rooms ready."

"A prudent measure," he replied, and hung up.

Smiling to herself, she phoned into the Cross-Country Quilters' conference call, only a minute late. She had barely said hello when her friends burst into a rousing if not entirely in tune chorus of "Happy Birthday." Joyful tears filled her eyes as she thanked them.

"If only we were celebrating at Elm Creek Manor," Donna said wistfully. "All of us together, one of Anna's scrumptious cakes on the table—"

"But no candles on it," Julia interrupted. "Seventy open flames would be a fire hazard."

"Seventy?" Vinnie teased. "That's nothing. You're still a young woman in the prime of life."

"Maybe from your perspective," Grace teased her in return. "But all joking aside, Julia, seventy is quite a milestone. I hope you're doing something special to celebrate."

"I am indeed. I'm spending time with all of you."

"That's it?" Megan protested. "Not that we aren't awesome, but—"

"You should be enjoying a lavish Hollywood soiree with all your celebrity friends," Vinnie finished for her.

"Don't worry, I won't be alone," Julia assured them. "Nigel's coming over for dinner later, he's bringing a couple of friends. It won't be a birthday party, but that's fine with me."

"But I thought—" Donna began, but abruptly fell silent.

"Thought what?" Grace prompted.

"Nothing," Donna said. "Never mind. So, how are you all doing on City of Spindles? I'm finished with mine, except for removing the paper foundation."

They all chimed in to comically boast about their progress or lament the lack of it. Grace had been especially busy at the De Young Museum that week setting up a new exhibit, so she hadn't even begun. Vinnie had finished her block on Tuesday and had resumed working on her latest jelly roll quilt. Megan and Donna, like Julia, were about halfway through, still confident of meeting the deadline. They chatted for a while longer, pinning sections together or removing foundation papers or some other handwork, until Julia noticed the time and realized she'd have to hurry if she hoped to freshen up before Nigel and his friends arrived.

"We shouldn't keep you any longer, then," Donna said hastily. "Talk to you all next week. Take care!" She hung up with a clatter.

"That was abrupt," Vinnie remarked. "Maybe she has something in the oven."

"She's right, though. I really should go," Julia said. "Thank you for the birthday wishes. You're the best friends I could ever wish for."

"We know," said Vinnie cheerily. "Bye now!"

Still smiling, Julia hung up and hurried off to get ready. The evening was cool, relative to late September in California, and she had just finished lighting the fire in the great room when a knock sounded on the door. Smoothing her hair as she hurried to answer, she opened the door—only to gasp at the sight of Nigel not accompanied by two fellows she had never met, but by Ellen, Lindsay, Olivia, Noah, and Chance, plus Ellen's longtime boyfriend and the young starlet from the Disney Channel whom Noah had been dating, off and on, for the past three years. Each one was grinning broadly, clearly pleased with themselves for so dumbfounding her.

"Surprise, Julia, darling," Nigel sang, kissing her on the cheek as he swept past her into the house, his arms full of reusable grocery bags from his favorite Spanish bistro.

Olivia was right behind him, and she kissed Julia's cheek too. "Happy birthday, Julia," she said. "May all your birthday wishes come true." Julia thanked her with a quick, warm embrace. Although they played fierce rivals on the show, Olivia was one of the friendliest people Julia had ever met. She was in her mid-thirties, and once, early in their acquaintance, after Julia had fretted that the age difference between them was so obvious that no one would ever believe Ben would prefer Sadie to Charity, Olivia had refused to accept that. "You're gorgeous, and with you playing her, Sadie is compelling and desirable. Of course Ben prefers her." That staunch defense had endeared her to Julia forever.

"Happy birthday, Julia," Noah said, his arm slung with casual affection over the starlet's shoulders. She echoed his words prettily, wobbling slightly on her platform shoes.

"You remembered my birthday?" Julia asked, her surprise fading as she held open the door wider so they all could troop in.

"Of course. It's the same date as last year," said Ellen, lugging a box of wine bottles and flavored seltzers, appearing slightly wounded by the suggestion that she would not keep track of such an important occasion.

"My mom reminded me a month ago," Lindsay confessed, pausing to clasp Julia's hand and kiss her cheek. "Happy birthday!"

That explained Donna's haste to end the call. Lindsay must have told her that instead of Nigel and two companions, a crowd of unexpected guests were planning to descend on Julia's home.

Soon Nigel was mixing up sangria while Ellen poured seltzers for the teetotalers and the underaged. Julia raced to add a few more place settings to the table while Noah and Chance unpacked the take-out containers and the starlet searched Julia's kitchen drawers for serving utensils. Then they gathered around the table, where they regaled Julia with the birthday song and made amusing toasts in her honor. Over shared small plates of stuffed olives, *gambas al ajillo*, a variety of empanadas, *albóndigas* with mushrooms, *patatas bravas* with lemon aioli, and *berenjenas con miel*, they talked and teased and reminisced, until Julia was full and her face ached from smiling.

This, she thought as she gazed affectionately around the table at her friends and the plus-ones. This was everything and all that mattered. Why would anyone let it slip through their fingers in their eagerness to seize some shiny new trinket?

Afterward, as they headed to the theater room to watch the latest episode of *A Patchwork Life*, Julia's hopes soared at such irrefutable evidence of how much they all adored the show and their castmates. One week at Elm Creek Quilt Camp and they would remember what they had, how precious it was, and why they should hold on to it.

Now everything depended upon convincing Sylvia to give her blessing to their actors' quilting boot camp.

The next morning, Julia asked her assistant to track down the very best florist shop in the Elm Creek Valley, which, according to her trusted sources, was Sweet Briar Floral of Summit Pass, Pennsylvania. Julia ordered an arrangement to be delivered to Elm Creek Manor the following morning, a lovely autumnal bouquet of blue delphiniums, blush and yellow roses, and burgundy smoke bush leaves in a crystal vase. Next, preferring the personal touch of a handwritten note, she addressed an elegant card to "My dear friends at Elm Creek Orchards," saying, "Warm congratulations and all best wishes for your grand opening. Your friend and admirer, Julia Merchaud." She added a postscript, especially for Sylvia: "Please call me tonight to let me know how your premiere went. I'd also like to discuss a small matter of business with you." She sealed the envelope and overnighted it to the florist, having obtained his assurances that he would wait until he received the card and deliver it with the bouquet.

Then all Julia could do was wait.

On Saturday, she still had plenty of birthday emails and phone calls to respond to, as well as her daily self-care routine and a few work-related tasks to complete, but even then she had too much time to fill with clock watching and worst-case-scenario plotting. She was tempted to phone the manor, but Sarah had urged her not to, and it was very likely that the Elm Creek Quilters and resident husbands were preoccupied with managing the vast crowds of apple pluckers wandering happily through the orchards on their grand opening day. Julia hoped they would be much too busy to answer the phone, even if that meant she would have to wait until Sylvia called her.

When her phone finally rang just as she was sitting down to dinner—farro with blistered cherry tomatoes and spinach, courtesy of her personal chef—her heart thumped to see a familiar area code in the caller ID. She took a steadying breath and picked up on the second ring. "Sylvia, darling," Julia greeted her, her voice warm and mellifluous. "How was your grand premiere?"

"Very grand indeed," Sylvia replied, "as befitting that gorgeous bouquet you sent. Thank you, dear, on behalf of us all."

"You're very welcome. So you had a good turnout? Apples were plucked, fun was had?"

"Oh, absolutely. Attendance well exceeded my most optimistic expectations. We had to stay open twenty minutes past closing to ring up all the sales. If this keeps up throughout the harvest, we should earn a very handsome profit."

"That's wonderful. Congratulations." Julia sighed wistfully. "I do wish I could have been there. You make it sound like such fun. Unfortunately, I think the harvest will be over by the time I return to Elm Creek Manor."

"This year's harvest will be, but not to worry. The Zestar and Ginger Gold will be ripe and ready for picking when you and the other Cross-Country Quilters arrive for your annual reunion next August."

"As a matter of fact," Julia remarked, teasing out the phrase, "I'm hoping to return much sooner than that, which brings me to that small matter of business I wanted to discuss with you."

"Now you've piqued my curiosity. What can I do for you?"

"First, the good news. Filming will begin on the sixth season of *A Patchwork Life* early next year."

"Congratulations, Julia," Sylvia said. "That's very good news for all of us. Sarah, Gretchen, and I gather around the television in the parlor for a watch party every week without fail. We very much enjoyed this season's premiere."

"Thank you," Julia replied, pleased. "Actually, I directed that one."

"Well done, dear. And the bad news? It's hard to imagine how there could be any."

"If only that were true," Julia said. "The bad news is that many members of our cast and production crew need to refresh their quilting skills. We've also recently signed on new actors who have never quilted before, and they absolutely must learn before we begin filming."

"And you thought it would be wise to send them to quilt camp?"

"Yes, but I'm afraid we can't wait until your regular season. March would be too late for our production schedule. Our performers need to look like experts on-screen, and that means intensive training—and the sooner they begin learning, the better."

"But if March will be too late, how can Elm Creek Quilts help you?"

"Well, I've heard that you're considering expanding your camp season into the fall."

"Oh, you've heard that, have you?" said Sylvia, amused. "From Sarah or Summer, I assume. It's true we're considering it, but we haven't made a final decision. If we do move ahead, it wouldn't be until next season."

"I had something a bit earlier in mind. What would you say to a practice run in November—and yes, I do mean *this* November? I'm thinking twenty or so guests for a one-week stay. In the mornings, your teachers would offer classes in quilting fundamentals. The afternoons would be devoted to practice sessions, with an instructor or two on hand to offer assistance and advice. We'd want your usual fabulous meal service, of course, but you needn't arrange any evening programs. If we want entertainment, we can provide that for ourselves."

"My goodness," Sylvia murmured.

"So, what do you think?"

"I think . . ." Sylvia paused. "I think it all sounds . . . very intriguing."

"But doable, though? And maybe even fun?"

"Yes, indeed, but this is rather unexpected. I'd need to consult the other Elm Creek Quilters to make sure they'd be willing and able to participate."

"Sarah and Summer are already on board."

"Of course they are," said Sylvia. "If I didn't know better, I'd suspect this was all their idea, and you're only going along with it to send some work our way."

"Not at all," Julia said, perhaps too emphatically. "Summer did tell me about your financial difficulties, but I had already decided that quilting lessons for our cast and crew were long overdue. But while we're on the subject of finances, I should mention what our producer has budgeted for our quilt camp excursion."

Julia herself was said producer, but she left out that detail as she explained what she was prepared to pay for their week of quilt lessons, meals, and accommodations—a figure she was confident would pay for the roof and then some, with plenty left over to invest for future crises. She didn't explain her reasoning to Sylvia, of course. It would sound like a bailout, and Sylvia would probably refuse it.

Even so, Sylvia seemed positively stunned by the grand total. "I—I hardly know what to say," she stammered. "It's very generous of you—"

"It's not generosity," Julia interrupted, before Sylvia decided it was *too* generous. "I'd expect to pay that price anywhere considering the services we require, but I'd much rather work with Elm Creek Quilts. You're the very best at what you do."

"Thank you. I'll be sure to pass along the compliment. As I said, I'll need to discuss it with the others—"

"Of course."

"But I'm sure we can accommodate your group."

"Excellent," Julia exclaimed, pumping a fist, then sinking back into her chair, lightheaded with relief. "When you're all set on your end, call me back and we'll discuss specific dates and whatever paperwork you need us to sign. I'd prefer to pay up front if that works for you. The studio's accounting department could reimburse me later."

That wasn't exactly honest. The studio *could* reimburse her, but they probably wouldn't, which was fine because Julia wasn't planning to ask.

"An up-front payment would work very well for us too. I'm grateful, Julia. This truly is a windfall in our hour of need."

"No, it isn't," Julia countered cheerfully. "It's a job. I'm not mailing you a suitcase full of cash. Trust me, you and your staff are going to earn every penny. I won't name names, but some of my colleagues are terribly clumsy with a needle."

"If you say so, but thank you very much all the same." Sylvia cleared her throat as if quite overcome. "Let's chat again soon. I'll share your proposal with the Elm Creek Quilters tomorrow, and if they're willing—and I'm quite sure they will be—you and I can work out the details."

"Excellent," said Julia warmly. "I look forward to it. Call me anytime."

With Sarah, Summer, and now Sylvia on board, it was all but certain that Julia's *A Patchwork Life* quilt camp would be green-lit soon.

7

The following evening, Sylvia phoned with good news: The Elm Creek Quilters would be delighted to host Julia and her colleagues for an exclusive week of autumn quilt camp. Maggie Flynn, author of the pattern book *My Journey with Harriet*, would teach them how to piece blocks by hand, while expert traditional quilter Gretchen Hartley would join her for lessons about other stages of the quilt-making process. Their instructors would be available for extra tutoring outside of the classroom, and Anna del Maso-Bernstein, the manor's exceptional chef, would prepare her usual excellent cuisine.

After Sylvia and Julia checked their calendars, they chose the second week of November for their session, with a Sunday afternoon arrival and Saturday morning departure, the same schedule followed during the regular camp season. "How many guests should we expect?" Sylvia asked. "Earlier you estimated twenty or so."

Julia quickly tallied up a roster for a best-case scenario. "Let's say about two dozen," she said. "I'll give you a final head count about a week before we arrive, if that works for you."

"It does indeed. I must say, Julia, Elm Creek Manor is buzzing with excitement these days. We've never done anything like this actors' quilt camp before and we're very much looking forward to it."

They wrapped up the call with a promise to chat again soon.

After they hung up, Julia pressed a hand to her chest and inhaled deeply, relieved. So far, so good. Now all she had to do was convince a good many of the cast and crew to interrupt whatever plans they'd made for their hiatus and join her at Elm Creek Quilt Camp. But where to begin?

Mulling it over, she wandered down the hall to her sewing room, where one last segment of her City of Spindles block still needed to be sewn in place. She had just finished the seam when it occurred to her that Lindsay was the obvious person to approach first. Her mother was a Cross-Country Quilter and veteran camper, so Lindsay would have heard innumerable rave reviews of Elm Creek Quilts through the years. She'd find the manor's elegant ambiance and delicious meals appealing, and although she wouldn't ever quilt on-screen, a better understanding of the art form would enhance her work behind the camera.

Tossing the quilt block onto her sewing machine table, Julia picked up the cordless phone and dialed Lindsay's number from memory. "Hey, Julia," Lindsay answered. "What's new?"

"I'm glad you asked. I'm working on something important and I could really use your help."

"Of course. What do you need?"

"I'd rather discuss it in person. Can you do lunch tomorrow?"

"Sure, if you don't mind meeting me in Ojai. I'm directing an episode of *America's Back Roads*."

"As in 'Welcome to *America's Back Roads*, the show that takes you down the road less traveled to the heart of America, to the small towns where old-fashioned values still endure, where life goes on at a slower pace, where friends are friends for life, where the frantic clamor of the city ventures no closer than the evening news'?"

"Yes, that's the show," said Lindsay, amused. "You should do voice-overs."

"I *have* done voice-overs," Julia replied, feigning indignation. "I've narrated entire documentaries. One of them won an Oscar."

"Oh, gosh, I knew that. Sorry."

"I'm just teasing you, kid. I wouldn't expect you to memorize my entire résumé." Julia crossed to the window and gazed out at her garden, softly illuminated by landscape path lanterns and moonlight. "I haven't watched that show in ages. Is Grant Richards still the host? Does he still wear that red-and-black buffalo-plaid jacket?"

"He's still the host, but I think he retired the jacket years ago. Just between us, he's much better-looking on TV than in person, and he smokes like a chimney."

"So I've heard. He did a segment on Elm Creek Quilts about a year before I first attended quilt camp. That's what put it on Maury's radar."

"Really? That would have been a fun episode to direct. My mom's told me so much about Elm Creek Manor. It would be nice to see it in person."

"Maybe you'll have that chance sooner than you think."

"Are you kidding? I wouldn't dream of tagging along on my mom's annual getaway with you Cross-Country Quilters. Anyway, the episode I'm directing has an interesting lineup too. We're visiting a lavender farm, a company that runs off-road jeep tours through the Santa Ynez Mountain range, and an alpaca ranch. I'd invite you to join me on set for lunch, but we don't have craft services or trailers."

Fortunately, though, Lindsay had discovered a charming café near the lavender farm, so they agreed to meet there at noon the next day.

That morning, filled with restless energy, Julia began the new Harriet's Journey block for the week. Cock's Comb was a two-color pattern of squares of triangles that seemed dauntingly complex. If not for Maggie Flynn's clear, reassuring step-by-step instructions, Julia wouldn't have known where to begin. Actually, she realized, smiling to herself, that wasn't true at all. She would have begun by reaching out to the Cross-Country Quilters, her indefatigable, ever-patient quilting tutors.

She sorted through her stash to find the ideal focus fabric to contrast with the ivory tone-on-tone print she had chosen for the background fabric. She decided on a rich, velvety peach, but she had no sooner made her templates than it was time to leave. Ojai was about sixty miles from her home, a drive that could take as little as an hour or as many as two depending upon traffic, an unavoidable factor in every commute in LA. She found it fairly smooth sailing north on Highway 1 up the coast and inland through Oxnard, but when she merged onto the 101 North, she saw a sea of red taillights ahead. Sighing, she consoled herself with the thought that the traffic slowdown would give her time to consider how best to enlist Lindsay in her plot.

Before Julia and Lindsay had met in person, Julia had come to know her through Donna's stories—heartrending confidences full of love and concern shared during their first quilt camp together and in the months that followed. Each of the Cross-Country Quilters had come to Elm Creek Manor burdened by a troubling secret. Julia's was that she had to transform herself into an accomplished quilter in a very short time if she hoped to keep her movie role. Donna's was that she had come to Elm Creek Quilt Camp to avoid meeting the parents of the young man to whom Lindsay had recently and unexpectedly become engaged.

Lindsay was only twenty then, a rising junior at the University of Minnesota Twins Cities with an abundance of loyal friends, excellent grades, and a promising future. She had dated Brandon, a premed senior, for two years before that summer day when she called together her parents and younger sister, Becca, and hesitantly broke the news that Brandon had proposed and she had accepted. He wanted to marry immediately, but she had convinced him to delay until June so they could plan a proper wedding. More shocking yet, he wanted her to withdraw from the university.

"Brandon says I don't really need to finish," she explained, wringing her hands and shifting her weight from foot to foot as if she anticipated her family's objections. "After medical school, he'll earn enough to support both of us."

Dismayed, Donna and her husband, Paul, reminded Lindsay that she was still quite young and shouldn't rush into marriage. They implored her to think of everything she would sacrifice if she left college—her degree, her dream career, time with her friends and all the memories they would make together, her performing arts activities, the exciting internship she had planned for the following year, everything. "Finish college first," Donna pleaded. "There's nothing wrong with a long engagement. If it's meant to be, two years won't make any difference."

But no matter what her family said, Lindsay could not be persuaded.

Brandon's parents lived several hundred miles from Minneapolis, but they were coming to visit the following month. Lindsay invited her parents to join them for dinner while they were in town so the families could become acquainted before the wedding.

Heartbroken, Donna couldn't bear to plunge into a frenzy of wedding plans, so she made the excuse that she would be at quilt camp when Brandon's parents were visiting. She hadn't actually registered yet, but no one else knew that, and the little white lie stung her conscience only a little. Eventually she would have to steel herself and help plan a wedding, but for the moment denial was her only comfort.

Observing the Candlelight ceremony from her window, Julia had heard Donna confess why she had come to Elm Creek Quilt Camp. "As Megan told you, I came to camp to meet my internet friend," she began, but then she fell silent and gazed around the circle as if weighing how much to divulge. "I also came because I'm a coward. My eldest daughter just got engaged to a young man my husband and I don't know very well. I do know my daughter, though, and something tells me her heart isn't in this marriage. It's just an instinct, but I don't think she's happy—and all I ever wanted was for my daughters to be happy, happy and safe." She took a quick, shaky breath and added, "I came to camp because it got me out of meeting her fiancé's parents. I know I'm just delaying the inevitable, but I want to buy my daughter time. It might be only a few weeks, but it might be enough for her to be certain that this is what she really wants."

"Don't underestimate your intuition," another woman cautioned, but in the semidarkness, Julia couldn't tell who had spoken. "Our maternal instincts are there for a reason."

Others nodded and chimed in their agreement, and as Donna passed the candle to the next woman, it seemed to Julia that their words had comforted her. Megan put an arm around Donna's shoulders and whispered something that made her laugh, even as she blinked back tears. Then Grace leaned closer, murmured, and gave Donna a knowing look. As the next camper in the circle began sharing her story, Julia found herself wishing she knew what had passed among the three women. By the time quilt camp ended, Julia had joined the circle of friends, so she too encouraged Donna when she resolved to convince Lindsay that finishing college would be best for her and her marriage in the long run.

In the weeks that followed, Donna's misgivings about the engagement proved prescient. Soon after she returned home, her husband told her that at the dinner with the future in-laws, Brandon had bossed Lindsay around, telling her what entrée to order and advising her to go without dessert so she would look better in the wedding pictures. Brandon's mother had been a meek and silent woman, his father loud and overbearing. Nothing Paul observed eased his or Donna's concerns about the match.

Donna managed to convince Lindsay to return to campus for her junior year, but as the weeks passed, Lindsay seemed increasingly stressed and distracted, and her emails and phone calls became less frequent. When Donna, Paul, or Becca would ask her what was wrong, she would insist that everything was fine, and that she was just really busy. Donna didn't believe it, and she began to think that she was to blame for their estrangement. Resolving to make Brandon feel more welcome, she invited the couple to spend Thanksgiving dinner together as a family. But although Lindsay eagerly accepted the invitation, she canceled only a few days before, making the excuse that she and Brandon both had too much work to do before the end of the semester.

"I feel like she's pulling away from us," Donna wrote to the other Cross-Country Quilters in nearly identical phrasing in her Christmas cards, as they learned when they compared notes. "I suppose this is natural, considering she's going to be married in a few months, but it makes me heartsick."

Vinnie strongly disagreed. "I don't think Lindsay's withdrawal is natural at all," she fretted in an email to Julia, Grace, and Megan. "In my experience, weddings don't wedge families apart, they bring them together."

"In *my* experience, that isn't always true," Julia responded, thinking of her second and third husbands, whose families she had barely known. But she agreed that something didn't seem right.

Nonetheless, Donna looked forward to Christmas, for Lindsay had assured her that she and Brandon would come for the day. Instead, they arrived several hours late, exchanged gifts, and left abruptly after dinner. Brandon claimed that they were planning to have dessert with his family, several hours' drive away, but Becca, suspicious, waited awhile and then phoned their apartment. Lindsay answered, and when she learned it was her sister on the line, she said she couldn't talk and hung up.

As the weeks passed, Donna became increasingly anxious as she heard less and less from her eldest daughter. The Cross-Country Quilters offered all the support and comfort they could across the miles that separated them.

By then, Julia was in Kansas, filming on location for *Prairie Vengeance*. The daily annoyances and insults she and Ellen faced from Stephen Deneford and Rick Rowan were nothing compared to what Donna was going through, but they were bad enough. The latest humiliation had come from Deneford, who decided that Julia's hands looked too aged for the quilting scenes. When the camera zoomed in close enough to follow the movements of her needle, it picked up "every wrinkle and vein," as the camera operator tactlessly put it. When he pulled back far enough for Julia's hands to pass for those of someone Sadie's age, the details of the quilting were lost. Since there was no time to hire a hand model, Deneford's solution was for Julia to wear gloves.

Incredulous, Julia explained that she couldn't quilt with gloves on. "My hands are perfectly appropriate for my character," she added defiantly. "Sadie was a frontier farm wife. She worked with her hands from dawn until dusk in every season."

Because they were running late, Deneford resumed the shoot without asking her to struggle clumsily with gloves, but he warned that if he didn't like the dailies, he'd have to resort to an alternative. Fearing that his alternative would be to replace her in the role altogether, Julia hurried off to her trailer as soon as they finished the scene. She called Donna, her loyal, long-distance quilting tutor, and asked her to be her stunt quilter.

"To be a what?" Donna asked.

"A stunt quilter," Julia repeated. "You'll fill in for me during all my close-up quilting shots, although I'm afraid only your hands will be on film."

That was perfectly fine with Donna, who confessed some anxiety at the thought of memorizing lines. She agreed to accept the role on one condition: that Julia would find a position for Lindsay too, something suited to her education and theater training. She was an aspiring director, so any opportunity to gain experience working on the set of a feature film would do.

"I'm sure we can find something for her," Julia said. "In the meantime, may I take the liberty of making your airline reservations?"

"As long as you reserve two seats."

"I'll do that," Julia promised. "And Donna—it'll be so good to see you again."

It was only after Donna and Lindsay had been on the set of *Prairie Vengeance* for a week that Donna confided to Julia why she had been so eager to spirit her daughter away from Minnesota. In mid-January, one of Lindsay's professors, apparently assuming he was calling Lindsay's campus residence, had left a troubling message on the family's answering machine expressing concern about her accumulating absences. Alarmed, Donna had phoned Lindsay's apartment, but when no one answered, she had decided to check on her, and Becca had insisted on coming along. When they arrived nearly an hour later, Lindsay wouldn't buzz them into the building. "You shouldn't have come," she had said, her voice muffled over the intercom. "Please go away before Brandon gets back."

At those words, Donna had become even more insistent, and eventually she and Becca had convinced Lindsay to let them in. To her horror, Donna had found Lindsay's lower lip split and swollen, her right eye a mass of fresh bruises.

Swiftly, they had gathered Lindsay's most important belongings, hauled them outside to the car, and loaded them into the trunk. As her daughters had climbed into the back seat, Donna had taken the wheel and locked the doors, expecting at any moment to be blinded by the headlights of Brandon's car as he tore around the corner and screeched to a halt behind them, blocking their escape.

Donna had sped off with her daughters before that could happen.

January had passed with bitter cold and heavy snows and no end to Brandon's phone calls and emails. Lindsay flinched whenever the phone rang and refused to read her emails unless Donna or Becca checked first and deleted anything Brandon slipped past her filters. Paul implored Lindsay to press charges against Brandon, but she refused. She arranged a leave of absence from the university, but although she had been all too willing to forgo her education the previous summer, she now seemed to consider her withdrawal as evidence that she had failed her parents and herself.

Yet as the days had passed, Lindsay gradually lost the haunted looked in her eyes, and by the end of February she resumed some of her usual interests and activities. She went out with old high school friends who had remained in town; she visited the public library often to check out books on stagecraft and filmmaking. She rented recordings of stage plays, which she and Donna would watch together and discuss. Each day had brought a new, positive change in Lindsay's behavior, and only rarely had Donna overheard her crying in her room.

Then Julia understood that as beneficial as the job on the set of *Prairie Vengeance* would be to Lindsay's future career, it was even more urgent to put hundreds of miles between her and Brandon. "Lindsay's going to be all right," she assured Donna emphatically. "If you wouldn't mind some advice from someone who's never actually raised a daughter—"

"I would never object to advice from a caring friend."

"Encourage her to get counseling," Julia said. "Gently, of course. It needs to be her decision. But in my opinion she would benefit enormously from talking to someone who can guide her through this crisis of confidence."

Lindsay did seek counseling, and as winter gave way to the first signs of spring, she blossomed. She began as the assistant to an assistant, but before long, after proving herself capable and hardworking, she was promoted to production assistant. Even Stephen Deneford took notice of her, after some subtle hints from Julia. He told Lindsay if she wanted work during the summer, he could get her an internship at the studio.

Lindsay had officially broken off the engagement by then. When filming wrapped on the Kansas set and the cast and crew headed back to Los Angeles to shoot interiors at the studio and outdoor scenes that didn't require snow, Lindsay returned to Minnesota. She arranged to meet Brandon to return his ring, choosing a restaurant near campus favored by professors and students from the medical school. Since losing his temper in front of his colleagues could ruin his professional aspirations, Brandon contented himself with shoving the ring in his pocket and snarling, "Fine. You were never good enough for me, anyway."

Lindsay wasted no more words on him. She rose, walked to her car without looking back, and drove home to visit her father and sister before catching an evening flight to LAX.

Julia had invited Donna and Lindsay to stay with her while they were in Southern California. By day, they worked together at the Culver City back lot or on the outdoor set in Malibu Creek State Park in Calabasas. On weekends Julia escorted them around to the iconic tourist destinations they were most eager to see—the Hollywood sign, the Chinese Theatre, and the Walk of Fame—or to her own favorite scenic places known only to locals. In the evenings they might relax by Julia's pool, or Julia and Donna would work on their challenge quilt blocks while Lindsay read, chatted with her friends on the phone, or watched classic films in the theater room. Lindsay smiled indulgently whenever she came upon Julia and Donna reminiscing fondly about Elm Creek Quilt Camp. "I think you two would move in permanently if you could," she teased, and neither denied it.

Julia was forlorn when shooting wrapped, the film went into post-production, and Donna and Lindsay returned to Minnesota. Except for her housekeeper and gardener, a widow and her son who resided in the guesthouse, Julia had lived alone since her second divorce, and she had forgotten how pleasant companionship could be. Thoughts of her upcoming reunion with the Cross-Country Quilters at Elm Creek Quilt Camp offered some consolation, and she rewarded herself for surviving Deneford and Rowan with a week at Aurora Borealis, her favorite spa. But when she returned home, pampered and refreshed, awaiting her was a curt, cryptic note from Deneford summoning her and Ares to a meeting.

Ellen had been called in too, Julia discovered when she and Ares arrived at the studio two days later, along with the other lead actors, their agents, and an excessive number of assistants. Deneford wasted no time in pleasantries before breaking the bad news: A test audience of men aged eighteen to thirty-five had viewed an early cut, and they didn't like it.

"Since when is our intended audience eighteen-to-thirty-five-year-old men?" asked Ellen, bewildered.

"Excellent question," said Julia.

"Obviously we had hoped for a better response, but I'm confident that the film is salvageable. Sorry, people, but that means we reshoot." Ignoring the groans, Deneford looked to Ellen, slouching unhappily in her chair at the far end of the table. "Is your calendar clear for rewrites?"

"Clear enough," she said. "I'm almost afraid to ask, but what sort of changes did you have in mind?"

"I've decided to ax all the quilting stuff."

Julia started. "I beg your pardon?"

"We're going to lose the quilting." Deneford regarded her, brow furrowed. "Surely you don't have a problem with that. Now you won't have to admit to the world you hired a stunt quilter for your scenes."

"I could live with that," Julia said. "Stephen, do you really think such a drastic change is necessary? Quilting is the metaphor that binds the entire story together."

"Not to mention that it's how Sadie supports her family and saves her farm," Ellen added.

"I had some thoughts about that, too," Deneford said. "Our test audience thought earning money from quilting was, well, a little tame. I decided she'll run a bordello instead."

Deneford's assistant held up his hands as if framing a sign. "Think *Little House on the Prairie* meets *Die Hard* meets *Pretty Woman*."

Ellen blanched. "You're going to make Sadie Henderson a prostitute?"

"At least at first," Deneford said. "Later, when the money starts rolling in, she'll become the madam."

That proved to be too much for Ellen, who couldn't bear to see her great-grandmother's life story so distorted. Julia knew her only options were to cooperate with Deneford or quit, so she followed Ellen out the door.

Afterward, Julia's role was entirely recast and only a few glimpses of Donna's quilting made it to the final cut, but Lindsay's name still appeared in the credits. More important, time and distance had given Lindsay perspective, rekindling her creative aspirations as well as her confidence. In August, when the Cross-Country Quilters reunited at Elm Creek Quilt Camp, Julia was thrilled when Donna announced that Lindsay had decided to return to college. Not only that, she was transferring to the University of Southern California, where she had been accepted into the School of Cinematic Arts.

Lindsay's training at USC included internships on other feature films. After she earned her degree, Julia was all too happy to take her on as a production assistant for *A Patchwork Life*. Before long Lindsay worked her way up to assistant director, which led to other opportunities in television and movies. The gig with *America's Back Roads* was only the most recent, and Julia was certain Lindsay would soar even higher in the years to come.

But that didn't mean it was time to leave *A Patchwork Life* behind.

Julia reached the café five minutes late thanks to the traffic on the 101, but she still arrived before Lindsay. It was such a beautiful day that she asked for a table in the courtyard, where a pergola offered just the right amount of shade. A tall, encircling hedge of bougainvillea reminded Julia fondly of the cornerstone patio at Elm Creek Manor.

She was sipping a cup of honey chamomile tea when Lindsay arrived in a rush. "Sorry I'm late," she said breathlessly, dropping into the chair opposite Julia's. "You know how it is when you plan a day's shoot."

"All too well. You stay on schedule for the first five minutes, but then you're at the mercy of the weather, the performers, technical difficulties—" Julia waved a hand airily. "Believe me, I get it."

"In this case, the interview had just taken a very interesting turn and I couldn't bear to cut him off. Did you order yet?"

"Just the tea so far. But I know what I want."

Lindsay quickly skimmed the menu, and when the server approached, they both ordered salads and a plate of goat cheese and arugula flatbread to share, and Lindsay asked for a cappuccino. "So what's going on?" she asked, lowering her voice confidentially, her smile suggesting concern as well as curiosity. "Why do you need my help?"

"First, the bad news. Nigel, Ellen, Noah, and Chance are all planning to leave the show."

"Oh, so it's official?"

"You mean you knew?"

"Sure. It came up at the full-cast meeting. And Nigel wouldn't have said he was leaving in front of those studio execs at the Christmas party unless he meant it."

"I thought it was a ploy for more money."

"I can see why you might have." Lindsay shook her head. "Wow. Four leads bowing out. It's hard to imagine how the show could continue without them."

Julia studied her. "I thought you'd be more upset. *I'm* upset. Why am I the only one upset?"

"Julia, what do you—" Lindsay fell silent for a moment as the server returned with her cappuccino. "Of course this is sad," she continued when he had walked away. "I'll be sorry to say goodbye to everyone too, but isn't that the nature of this business? We come together, we create something wonderful, and then we move on to something new, each of us better for the time spent in good company."

"You're remarkably philosophical for someone so young," said Julia wryly. "As for me, I don't want the series to end. I've put my heart and soul into it, and trust me when I say the camaraderie we've enjoyed on this set is a rare and precious thing."

"That's a fair point." Lindsay sipped her cappuccino pensively. "What's the good news?"

"What do you mean?"

"You said, 'First, the bad news.' What's the good news?"

"There is no good news, only more bad news. Elm Creek Quilts is in trouble."

Lindsay set down her cup. "Oh, no. Really? What sort of trouble?"

"Financial. From the sound of it, operating expenses are up sharply, revenues are flat, and some major remodeling projects might just push them over the edge."

"Over the edge into bankruptcy?"

"No one used that word, but—"

"But that would be terrible," Lindsay exclaimed. "My mom absolutely loves quilt camp. She'd be heartbroken if they closed—" She drew in a breath sharply. "They aren't going to close, are they?"

"Not if we can help it. I think it's possible to solve both of these problems with the same solution."

Lindsay shook her head, uncomprehending. "I don't see the connection."

The server arrived with their meal, forcing another pause in their conversation. Julia smiled and thanked him, watching from the corner of her eye as Lindsay tried to puzzle it out.

When they were alone again, Julia said, "We take the cast and crew on a road trip to Elm Creek Quilt Camp to refresh our quilting skills, or to learn for the first time, as the case may be. We'll have such a wonderful time together that everyone will want to give *Patchwork* another few seasons. Our fees will give Elm Creek Quilts a much-needed cash infusion, enough for them to fix their roof and set something aside for the next disaster. It'll work. Trust me."

"It's not that I don't trust you," Lindsay said carefully, picking up her fork. "It's just—"

"What?"

"Well, as far as schemes go, this is less *Ocean's Eleven* and more . . . *A Simple Plan*. Not to imply that you're an aspiring criminal mastermind or anything."

"Maybe it isn't a foolproof plan, but I have to try," said Julia, impassioned. "Let's say for the sake of argument that we convince the cast and crew to join us at quilt camp—or rather, to spend a marvelous week at a luxurious nineteenth-century mansion amid the autumnal splendor of rural central Pennsylvania, for a restful yet productive working vacation they'll never forget."

Lindsay laughed. "Wow, Julia. Way to spin it. You should write advertising copy."

"I'll keep my day job, thanks." With Lindsay's help, she just might. "Look, if nothing else, we'll enjoy a wonderful time together and return to the set with improved quilting skills and a greater understanding of quilting heritage, all of which will help us make season six our best yet. If things go as I hope, those who are planning to leave might have second thoughts, which would help the rest of us remain employed a little while longer."

"Employment is good," Lindsay admitted.

"Plus, we'll help Elm Creek Quilts stay in business."

"Also a very good thing." Lindsay toyed with her fork, thinking. "All right. I suppose it wouldn't do any harm, and I can't think of a better plan. If nothing else, we'll be supporting Elm Creek Quilts, and I'll gladly do that, for my mom's sake." She hesitated. "What exactly do you need me to do?"

"You can be the first to sign up for our quilting retreat—well, second, after me—and you can encourage others to join us."

"I'd be happy to spend a week at Elm Creek Manor, but I wish we were going to quilt camp to improve our skills, without any other agenda. I don't like inviting our friends under false pretenses."

"Then don't," said Julia airily as she sprinkled balsamic vinaigrette on her salad. "Invite them for the quilt camp experience alone. I'll be the one with the ulterior motives. Your conscience is clear."

Lindsay eyed her, skeptical, and helped herself to a piece of flatbread. Yet by the time they finished lunch, Lindsay had agreed to attend quilt camp and to recruit other campers from among the production crew. Julia would see to the cast. "And I'll talk to Ellen as well," she added as they were walking to their cars. "She's in production, not in the cast, but we have a history."

They *all* had a history, and if Julia's scheme worked—*when* it worked—they would make more of it together.

8

The next morning, after checking the production schedule to confirm that Ellen would be spending most of the day toiling in the writer's room, Julia drove to the studio and gracefully ambushed her friend in the hallway when the team broke for lunch. "Hey, Julia," Ellen greeted her, surprised. "What brings you in today? If you're here to help us fill in some plot holes, you're right on time."

"Thanks, but for the sake of the show, I'm going to give that a hard pass. Do you have a few minutes to chat?"

"Sure, if you don't mind joining me in the commissary."

"As long as you don't expect me to eat there."

"It's not *that* bad," Ellen said as they headed down the hallway. It was, actually, but Julia let it go in favor of her elevator pitch for Elm Creek Quilt Camp. Ellen listened thoughtfully as they crossed the sunny back lot, entered the cafeteria, and moved through the line, Ellen selecting a salad, bran muffin, and diet ginger ale, Julia taking only a sparkling water. Julia omitted all references to her ulterior motives and the quilt camp's financial struggles. Summer was in enough trouble with Sylvia already without Julia spreading the company's confidential information any further.

"The training would be useful," Ellen mused as they found a table near a sunny window with a view of a cactus and bromeliad garden.

"Some of our actors allow their skills to languish between seasons. Their quilting isn't as precise or fluid as it would have been for women of that era who quilted often."

"And some of our actors have never learned to quilt," Julia reminded her.

"We'd have more flexibility with our camera angles if all of the women could quilt well, especially during our scenes around the quilt frame." Then she shook her head. "I agree it's a great idea, but is a retreat like this in the production budget?"

"Don't worry about that. I've got it covered."

"Out of your own pocket? Julia—"

"I said, don't worry about it," Julia said, laughing lightly. "I'm an executive producer. Securing funding is in my job description. As far as I'm concerned, anything that improves the quality and historical accuracy of the series is money well spent."

"Careful you don't say that too close to the writers' room or everyone will ask for a raise." Ellen glanced at her watch, gave a little start, and quickly dug into her salad. "Yes, I think you should do it. It's wonderful that the Elm Creek Quilters are willing to put on a special session just for you."

"You mean for *us*. You're coming along. When I said cast and crew, I was including our writers."

"I don't know, Julia," said Ellen, wincing. "I tried to learn to quilt when I first read my great-grandmother's diaries. I barely mastered the running stitch, and my quilting stitches were appalling. They were huge, and no two were the same size."

"It couldn't have been that bad, but that was only your first quilt. You would've improved if you'd attempted another. Besides, that was ages ago, and you didn't have the Elm Creek Quilters as your teachers."

"Well, no, I didn't," Ellen acknowledged. "I admit your stories about Elm Creek Manor have intrigued me. How wonderful it must be to take a week each year to escape the daily grind and focus on your creativity and artistic expression in such a beautiful, historic setting. I've been just a tiny bit envious of you."

"Why envy me when you could join me? While the rest of us are quilting, you could wander off to some quiet, comfortable spot and write. The library, maybe. Think of it—bookcases lining the walls, their shelves filled with enticing volumes, a fire crackling on the hearth, autumn sunshine streaming through the tall windows, a cup of mulled cider steaming on the table beside your pen and paper—"

"I write on my computer."

"On the table beside your laptop, creative inspiration all around you," Julia finished. "Just imagine how the experience would enrich your writing. You could learn so much about quilt history and folklore from Sylvia even if you don't sew a single stitch all week."

"It would be nice to have hours of uninterrupted time to work on the outline for season six." Ellen grimaced. "I'm especially concerned about the last episode. A series finale has to accomplish so much that it's almost impossible to satisfy viewers."

"You could run ideas past Sylvia and the other Elm Creek Quilters while you're there. And just think about how much you could accomplish with someone else preparing gourmet meals for you three times a day."

"And cleaning up afterward."

"Plus, you'll have access to a vast library and an expert faculty ready and willing to advise you on all aspects of quilt artistry and history."

Suddenly Ellen drew in a breath, eyes widening. "Wait. That quilt you and your friends are making, your reproductions of that antique sampler—"

"'Harriet's Journey'?"

"Yes, that's it. Will the woman who researched that quilt and wrote the pattern book be there?"

"You mean Maggie Flynn. Yes, she'll be there—in fact, she's teaching the hand-piecing classes."

"I'd love to talk to her about a quilt I want Sadie and Charity to collaborate on in season six, episode five."

"Sadie and Charity, quilting together? But they're practically sworn enemies." Julia gave herself a little shake. Exploring that intriguing tangent would have to wait. "I'm sure Maggie would be delighted to share her expertise."

Nodding, Ellen picked up her fork and poked at her salad, but her thoughts were elsewhere. For a long moment, Julia let her mull it over, sipping her sparkling water with feigned nonchalance and resisting the impulse to beg her to say yes.

Finally, Ellen spoke. "You said it'll be during the second week of November?"

"That's right."

"I might have to move some things around on my calendar, but okay, I'm in."

"Wonderful," Julia exclaimed. "We'll have a fabulous time. Please pass on the invitation to anyone else from the writers' room who should join us."

Ellen's eyebrows rose. "You're brave, but sure, I'll invite them."

"Excellent." Julia leaned forward, resting her arms on the table. "Now, what's this about Sadie and Charity collaborating on a quilt?"

Ellen had only twenty minutes to spare, so she gave Julia a quick sketch of the narrative arcs she hoped to work into the final season. Julia winced at the word "final," but Ellen didn't seem to notice.

Two days later, Julia was working on her Cock's Comb block in anticipation of her weekly conference call with the Cross-Country Quilters when her phone rang. She was going to let the answering machine take it when she glanced at the phone and saw that it was Donna calling. Quickly she picked up. "Hi, Donna," she greeted her. "I wasn't expecting you for another ten minutes."

"I wanted to speak with you privately before everyone else joined in." Donna inhaled deeply. "So. You spoke to Lindsay a few days ago about your series possibly ending."

"I did," Julia confirmed. "She was expecting it. Apparently I'm the only person who missed the meeting *and* neglected to read the email."

"I'm sure Lindsay will be sorry to see the show end, but she never expected it to last forever. Elm Creek Quilts, on the other hand—" Donna's breath caught in her throat. "Lindsay said you told her it's in financial trouble? That it might go bankrupt?"

Julia closed her eyes and muffled a groan. She should have anticipated that Lindsay would share the alarming news with her mother. "Summer didn't say anything about bankruptcy. It's serious, but I don't think it's quite that dire yet."

"'Yet'?"

"It sounds like a short-term cash flow problem. Revenues are down—"

"Of course. It's their offseason."

"Exactly. What's worse, they recently found out that they have to replace the entire roof of the manor."

"Oh my goodness. That's a lot of roof. And you think your actors' quilting boot camp will bail them out?"

"Our fees will pay for the roof and then some. Trust me, I offered them far above the standard summer rate."

"I should hope so. Oh, Julia, I can't imagine what I'd do if Elm Creek Quilt Camp closed."

"If my plan works, you won't need to worry about that. Sarah and company are working on other revenue streams too." Julia told her about Elm Creek Orchards, which was surely just one of several plans the exceptional creative team at Elm Creek Manor had in the works.

"I'm worried that won't be enough," Donna fretted. "Maybe we should start a fundraiser for them. A capital campaign."

"I know your heart is in the right place, but tread carefully," Julia warned. "Sylvia won't accept anything that looks like a handout, and she doesn't want the world to know that Elm Creek Quilts is struggling. She didn't want Summer to tell me, and I really shouldn't have told Lindsay. It can't go any further. If the Elm Creek Quilters decide to go public, that's their choice, but it isn't our story to tell."

"But I can tell the other Cross-Country Quilters, right?"

Julia didn't suppose there was any way she could stop her. "Only if you swear them to secrecy."

When their conference call began a few minutes later, the conversation quickly turned to the plight of Elm Creek Quilts, even though, as they all readily admitted, they had more concerns and speculation than actual facts. They all wanted to do something to help, but they agreed that it would be unwise to launch a fundraiser without Sylvia's blessing. And they couldn't secure that without confessing that Julia had shared with her friends confidential information Summer shouldn't have disclosed in the first place. By the time they wrapped up their weekly call, one truth was abundantly clear: Julia's actors' quilting boot camp absolutely must be a rousing success. If this first effort to expand quilt camp failed, Sylvia might not be willing to risk another bold move to raise funds, regardless of the need.

With a new sense of urgency, Julia emailed Olivia Muñoz first thing the next morning to ask if they could meet for a chat. Then, over a simple breakfast of coffee and a grapefruit with a sprinkling of toasted walnuts, she made a list of other likely willing campers. If the most popular members of the cast and crew agreed to attend, others would be encouraged to come, compelled by the fear of missing out. Julia was debating whether to include special guest stars or focus only on the regulars when her computer pinged, signaling Olivia's reply to her email.

"Hey, Julia!" Olivia had written. "So you'd like to chat today, out of the blue, while we're on hiatus? Sounds ominous! Curiosity officially piqued. Why don't you join me for my Zumba class in Westwood at 10 AM? Or meet me afterward, if you'd rather skip the workout. If neither works for you, let me know what would. Cheers!"

Julia promptly wrote back to say that she'd never done Zumba before but it sounded like fun and ten o'clock would be perfect. By the time she finished her coffee and tidied up, Olivia had written back with the studio's address and a list of a few items she might want to bring along—a water bottle and towel, and a change of clothes and a shower caddy.

Julia packed up her favorite sporty tote, and soon, dressed in close-fitting, stretchy workout attire and appropriate footwear, she was driving east on the Pacific Coast Highway toward LA. Traffic was remarkably reasonable for that hour, so she arrived twenty minutes early. The studio was tucked into a business development with a broad sidewalk winding through a narrow green space, so she passed the time warming up with brisk walking and stretches while keeping an eye out for Olivia. As the hour approached and Olivia still hadn't appeared, Julia entered the studio, purchased a one-day pass, and set off to find the proper room. Either Olivia had arrived even earlier than herself and was holding places for them, or she would rush in at the last minute, in which case Julia should grab spots for them both. It wasn't until Julia entered the room and recognized the enviably fit woman adjusting the sound system that she realized when Olivia had called it *her* Zumba class, she'd meant that she was the instructor.

And an encouraging, engaging, yet formidable instructor she proved to be. Julia had to modify some of the more difficult movements, but she could handle rigorous cardio thanks to her hiking habit, and she had long ago mastered the professional survival skill of learning unfamiliar choreography quickly. She was definitely panting by the time class reached the midpoint, and she was grateful for her towel since she worked up quite a sweat, but she enjoyed herself, and the vigorous workout had allowed her to forget her worries for a while.

Afterward several other students lingered to chat with Olivia, so Julia waited her turn, exchanging smiles and greetings with a few who apparently recognized her, unless they were just being friendly to an obvious newcomer. "You came," Olivia exclaimed, pleased, when Julia could approach. "You did so well today. What did you think of the class?"

"It was so much fun," Julia said, draping her towel over her shoulders. "And you, Olivia, you're amazing! I never knew you were a fitness instructor."

Olivia gave a little laugh as she squatted gracefully and began packing up her gym bag. "I'm a working actor, Julia. I have to have a survival job, and I'd rather do this than wait tables." Rising, she slipped the strap over her shoulder and smiled. "I'd give it all up for a career like yours—starring roles in one series after another, the occasional movie thrown in, awards, acclaim. You're living the dream."

"Only until something wakes me up," Julia said ruefully. When Olivia laughed, she added, "But what about all your voice work? You've been in almost every major animated film released in the past few years, and your series must be in its tenth season by now."

"Ninth, actually," Olivia replied in the gravelly drawl of one of her most popular characters. In her own voice, she added, "I know I'm lucky to have something so consistent in addition to my guest appearances in *Patchwork*. All the rest is gig work, one supporting role here and another over there. I actually just got cast to voice a car in a kid's movie."

"A car?" Julia asked. Students for the next class were beginning to file in, so when Olivia beckoned, Julia followed her to the locker room. "A talking car, like KITT in *Knight Rider*?"

"Not quite. I'm playing a cute Mazda Miata who's a NASCAR fan. It'll make sense when you see the movie."

"Of course," said Julia, although she doubted it.

"Are you up for nutrition afterward?" Olivia asked as she held open the locker room door for her. "They make a fabulous green tea antioxidant smoothie here."

"Sure, sounds great." Julia liked green tea in its standard form, so why not?

Before long they were showered, changed, and poised on stools at the nutrition bar, sipping a surprisingly tasty, vividly green concoction of almond milk, spinach, matcha powder, and a few other healthful ingredients through paper straws. "So, given that you're exceptionally busy," Julia ventured, "how would you feel about spending a week at a quilter's retreat in gorgeous, restful central Pennsylvania to refresh your quilting skills?"

"Sure," said Olivia, shrugging. "When do we leave?"

For a moment, Julia was dumbfounded. "That's it? You don't need the sales pitch?"

"No, I'm in. Although if you don't want your sales pitch rehearsals to go to waste, I'll listen. I'll even give you notes if you like."

"No, that's fine. I might accidentally say something to change your mind. As for when we leave, camp begins on Sunday, November seventh. All expenses paid."

"I'll be there." Then Olivia paused to think. "Although that would mean missing a final interview for a gig. Don't worry. It wouldn't interfere with *Patchwork*—unless I suddenly get promoted to series regular."

"Wouldn't that be fun, to have Sadie and Charity sparring more often?" said Julia. "But as much as I'd love to have you at quilt camp, I couldn't ask you to throw away a shot at a great role."

"I'm not sure how great it is, to be honest. It's for a celebrity edition of *Survivor*."

"*Survivor*?" Julia echoed, aghast. "Isn't that the show where they abandon you in some desolate wilderness and you can't bathe for weeks and you have to eat bugs?"

"That's an apt description, although eating bugs isn't limited to *Survivor*. It's standard repertoire of the reality genre."

"Oh, Olivia, no. If you have to do reality television, do something cultural or artistic, like *The Amazing Race* or *Dancing with the Stars*."

"If I could get cast, I would. But if I have to choose between suffering on *Survivor* or quilting with my *Patchwork* friends, sign me up for quilt camp."

"Consider yourself cast, no audition required." Julia regarded her curiously. "To be honest, I thought I'd have to work a lot harder to convince you."

"It's simple, really. I don't have a clue how to quilt. I barely know how to sew on a button. Charity is never invited to Sadie's quilting bees, and the one time she quilted with her mother in season two, they had to hire a stunt quilter for me. Since then, the writers have never had me even thread a needle on camera. If I learn how to quilt, maybe Charity will appear in some of those quilting bee scenes. I'd definitely like to be prepared if the opportunity arises."

Julia studied her. "Have you been talking to Ellen?"

"No, not recently. Have you?"

"Let's just say that particular opportunity might come along soon."

Olivia's eyebrows rose. "Really?" She sipped her smoothie, thoughtful. "But it would *have* to be soon, wouldn't it, since season six will be our last?"

"Maybe it will be, maybe not. In my opinion, we have another few years of exceptional storytelling in us. I'm not ready to wrap just yet."

"Neither am I," said Olivia. "I need all the gigs I can cobble together. You know who else you should invite? Paige."

"Who?"

"Paige Lyons. She's new to the cast, but she was at your season premiere party, so you must have met her. She plays Anabelle, the beautiful niece of railroad baron Theodore Wedgington."

"Jesse's love interest?" Julia asked. "The girl who looks like a young Elizabeth Taylor? I thought her name was Paula. Or Pamela."

Olivia shook her head, amused. "It's definitely Paige. Quilt camp would give her a chance to get to know the rest of the cast before we begin table reads for season six. She only appeared in that one scene in the season five finale, and I think Noah was the only other actor on set with her that day. And like me, she might want to increase her skill set so she can wrestle her way into more scenes."

"Good idea. I'll reach out to her."

"She'll be *very* happy to hear from you," said Olivia, a note of warning in her voice.

"That's good, isn't it?" asked Julia. "Certainly better than the alternative."

Olivia only smiled cryptically and sipped her smoothie.

Later, back at home, Julia found Paige's contact information among the Evite list for her season premiere party and dashed off a breezy email. "Hello, Paige," she began. "I hope you're enjoying our hiatus and looking forward to our first table read in January. Would you have time for a quick chat sometime soon, just us? Cheers, Julia."

She spent the afternoon pleasantly in her sewing room, finishing up her Harriet's Journey block and listening to classical music on the radio. It didn't occur to her to check her email until she passed by her computer on the way to prepare supper, and she was surprised to see that Paige had responded to her note not quite five minutes after she had sent it. "Hello, Miss Julia!" Paige had written. "It's so awesome to hear from you! TBH I can't wait for our hiatus to be over and for filming *Patchwork Life* Season 6 to begin! I'm visiting family in North Carolina at the moment but I'd be thrilled to talk with you anytime, day or night!" She signed off with her phone number and the postscript, "Call me whenever!"

Julia glanced at the clock, added three hours, and mulled over whether it would be too late to call. Not for someone Paige's age, she decided, and certainly not after an invitation peppered with so many exclamation points.

Julia poured herself a glass of sparkling water, added a slice of lime, pulled up a stool at her kitchen island, and dialed Paige's number. She answered on the first ring. "Hello?" she said breathlessly, barely audible over a wild tumult of fiddle, electric guitar, drums, and a cheering crowd.

"Hi, Paige. It's Julia Merchaud," she said, raising her voice. "Are you at a concert? We could chat another time."

"No! No, I mean, I am at a concert but it's no big deal. Let me just—" There was some scraping and thudding as if the phone had been covered with a hand or tucked into a pocket. Julia waited, and before long the music abruptly faded. "There. Sorry about that. I'm outside now. My brother has a band."

"They sound very good," said Julia generously.

"Oh my gosh, I'll tell him you said so. They're the Smoky Mountain Shredders, Asheville's most popular country bluegrass metal band. They have a CD. I could bring you one."

"That's very kind," said Julia. "Thank you. Listen, I'll make this quick so you can get back to—"

"It's fine, really. Take all the time you need. Did you want to discuss our characters? I can't wait for Anabelle and Sadie to meet. I really hope they like each other. I'm so tired of stories that pit women against each other, fighting over a guy, you know what I mean?"

"Well, Sadie already has that sort of relationship with Charity, over Ben."

"Oh my gosh, Miss Julia, I wasn't thinking of that," Paige blurted, mortified. "I didn't mean to criticize."

"No, that's fine. I didn't write it. To your point, though, I hope our characters have a cordial relationship. I don't want Sadie to be a stereotypical overbearing mother-in-law. Grandmother-in-law. Whatever. The fans would revolt."

"Yes, a grandmother-granddaughter relationship would be wonderful," said Paige warmly. "So refreshing. And it would be a dream come true to have you as a scene partner in stories that celebrate supportive bonds between women."

Julia decided that Paige would fit right in at Elm Creek Quilt Camp. "Let's trust the writers. They almost always get it right. If something feels off at the table read, we can bring it to Ellen. But that's actually not why I wanted to chat." Julia quickly gave her the sales pitch for Elm Creek Quilt Camp, emphasizing what a wonderful opportunity it would be for Paige to get to know some of the cast and crew better, and to improve her quilting skills before filming began.

"I already know how to quilt a bit," Paige said. "My mom's a quilter, and so are both of my grammies. They've been coaching me. They wanted to teach me when I was young, but I couldn't sit still long enough to learn. I always just wanted to be singing and dancing and putting on little plays for my family and the kids from the neighborhood, you know?"

Julia smiled. "I can relate."

"You can? Oh my gosh, that's so awesome. I bet we have a lot in common."

"Well, we could find out if we got better acquainted at quilt camp. Are you in?"

"I'll have to check with my agent to make sure I'm free, but I'd love to come. To be honest it's a little awkward to join such a successful, long-running series so close to the end of its run, and I really want to make the most of the final season."

"Season six might not be the final season."

"Wait, what? My agent said it was, and at the meeting in August, Nigel and Ellen announced they were leaving, and Noah says he's going to college—"

"I think we have more stories to tell," Julia broke in, "especially given the romance between your character and Noah's. There's a lot to explore there."

"That's what I've been saying," Paige exclaimed. "I mean, just to my mom. I wouldn't, you know, complain in public where the tabloids might pick it up and run with it."

"That's very sensible," said Julia. "Keep that up."

"I will, promise. Speaking of Noah," Paige said, too casually, "do you know if he's coming to quilt camp?"

"I haven't asked him yet."

"Oh. I was just wondering."

Julia sensed an opportunity and plunged ahead. "But I'm sure when he finds out you're coming, he'll be more interested."

"Do you really think so?"

"Of course," said Julia, ignoring a tiny pang of conscience. "It seemed to me that you two really hit it off at the premiere party."

Paige drew in a quick breath. "Just between us, I thought we had a moment, but I heard he has a girlfriend."

"I could try to find out. As soon as we hang up, I could call him and say, 'Hey, Noah, I was just chatting with Paige, and she was wondering if—'"

"Don't you dare," Paige protested, laughing.

"Are you sure? It's no trouble."

"I'm very sure," Paige said emphatically. "Okay, Miss Julia. I'm all in for quilt camp. If Noah signs up too, fantastic. I'll see him there. If not, he'll be the one missing out."

"I couldn't agree more," Julia replied.

But the fact was that if she couldn't recruit more campers soon, Julia herself had the most to lose.

9

Even though quilt camp would not begin for another five weeks, something about the turning of the calendar from September to October made the task of enlisting cast and crew seem more urgent than it had just a few days before. Although Julia believed she could be more persuasive in a one-on-one conversation, there simply wasn't enough time to meet with each potential camper individually. So first thing Saturday morning, Julia called Noah to plead her case over the phone rather than arranging to meet for lunch or coffee. She happened to catch him in the middle of a workout with his personal trainer, so she headed to her favorite yoga studio for a long, restorative workout of her own while she waited for him to ring her back.

"What's up, Julia?" he greeted her when he called later that morning.

"Oh, so many exciting things, but there's one in particular that concerns you." She delivered her by now well-practiced sales pitch, adapting it on the fly in ways she hoped would make it more appealing to his demographic.

When she finished, Noah let out a groan that sounded genuinely regretful. "It would be great to hang with everyone, and I wouldn't mind adding quilting to the special skills section of my résumé, but

I'm fully booked pretty much now through Thanksgiving," he told her. "I just started working with a tutor twice a week to prepare for the ACTs, and my parents and I have scheduled a bunch of college tours."

"Any chance you could reschedule those tours?" Julia asked. "If you're planning to visit schools on the East Coast, you could tour a few before quilt camp and a few after. You could save yourself a cross-country flight and enjoy quilt camp too."

She knew it was a big ask, so she wasn't surprised when Noah explained that it wouldn't be possible. Everything had been carefully arranged, and if he pulled out one block, the whole structure would fall apart. "I'm sorry to miss the fun," he said. "Maybe we could do another group trip another time, like to celebrate the series finale."

"That's a fine idea," she said, forcing lightness into her voice. "Maybe we could crash at Nigel's place, and he could show us around London."

"That's brilliant," said Noah, with much more enthusiasm than he had greeted her invitation to quilt camp. "Arrange it for when I'm not in school and I'll be there."

"I'll do that, but I suppose I should check with Nigel and Alistair first."

Noah laughed and agreed, although he confessed that he thought it would be much more hilarious if they all just showed up on his front doorstep unexpectedly. "Hilarious for us," he acknowledged. "Maybe not so much for Nigel and Alistair."

After they hung up, Julia took a cleansing breath and dialed Chance's number, bracing herself for another refusal. She had considered Noah the more likely of the two to sign up, since through the years Noah had occasionally asked questions about the quilting process and had admired particularly striking quilts on the set. Chance, on the other hand, had never expressed the slightest interest in quilts except for their usefulness in keeping him warm on location in wintery Kansas. Sure enough, after playing phone tag for the rest of the weekend, when Julia and Chance finally connected late on Sunday afternoon and she made her most dazzling pitch, Chance's first question was "Is Noah going?"

"No," Julia admitted reluctantly. "He'll be busy preparing for the whole college application rigmarole."

"In that case, I think I'll pass too, but thanks for asking. I should probably stick around here and prepare for my new role."

Julia closed her eyes and muffled a sigh. "Oh, so you landed the part in the supernatural ghost chasers series? That's fantastic, Chance. Congrats."

"I don't actually have the part yet, but I made it through to the final round. My agent says I'll probably be called in for a chemistry read next week. Hopefully I'll have good news not long after that."

"I'm sure you will. I'll congratulate you again when it's official."

After they hung up, Julia pressed a hand to her forehead, inhaled through her nose, and exhaled in a sigh, rolling her shoulders to work the tension out of her back and neck. She wanted to encourage Chance and she honestly believed he had an excellent shot at the part, but it pained her to imagine *A Patchwork Life* without him. Well, perhaps not all was lost. Noah had said he would defer college if the series continued, and perhaps Chance would return for a few episodes if they could work their filming around his new show's schedule. It wouldn't be the same, but it would be something, although even that wouldn't be an option unless she convinced the majority of her castmates to stay.

So much depended upon persuading Nigel, in particular.

For such a dear friend, only a request made in person, preferably over a delicious meal, would suffice. She called him on his cell. "Do you have dinner plans?" she inquired when he picked up just as she thought voicemail would beat him to it.

"I'm insulted," he said, amused. "Do you really imagine me to be so dull and unpopular that I would be available on such short notice?"

"Not at all. I assumed that you'd been invited to a magnificent party somewhere, and I was going to beg you to let me tag along as your plus-one."

"Then you're out of luck, because my only plans were to order takeaway and curl up with a good book. Or a merely acceptable book. I'm currently reading my way through the Harry Potter series."

"I assume you're compelled by your renowned devotion to your craft?"

"Indeed. I'm pleased to report that my character is a lovable rogue, but I can't breathe another word. No doubt I've already said enough to reveal my secret."

"Your secret's safe with me. I haven't read the books."

"Then you probably won't be offended if I observe rather cattily that the author appears to have borrowed heavily from Tolkien."

"If it doesn't bother Tolkien, it doesn't bother me. Would you care to bookmark your page and come over for dinner and a chat instead? My chef has some delectable entrées on offer in my fridge."

"Let's go out instead. It's been ages."

Julia laughed. "It's been, what, two weeks?"

"As I said, ages. Geoffrey's? Moonshadows? Duke's?"

"Moonshadows," Julia replied. "Never Duke's, never again."

"Oh, darling, I'm sorry. I'd forgotten."

"It's really okay. It was years before you and I met. I wouldn't have expected you to remember." Regrettably, the tabloid photos of her second husband necking with a young starlet at a table for two on Duke's oceanfront lanai were indelibly seared into her memory. He had told her he was meeting his agent for drinks, and she had believed him. They had been married only three months.

"Moonshadows it is, then," said Nigel warmly. "Our favorite table at seven?"

"Marvelous. I'll meet you there."

Quickly Julia freshened up, changed into slacks and a long-sleeved top, and tied a light sweater around her shoulders in case she and Nigel decided to stroll on the beach after dinner. After stopping by her office to collect a few favorite snapshots of Elm Creek Manor, she jumped into her car and made her way down the winding hillside road toward Zuma Beach. When she turned onto the PCH, it suddenly occurred to her that she couldn't have chosen a more appropriate setting for such a portentous conversation. Years ago, soon after she and Nigel had first met, they'd had dinner together at that same iconic Malibu beachside restaurant, getting acquainted over drinks and hama hamas on the half shell, shielded from eavesdroppers by the soothing, invigorating crash of waves on the beach below.

After a whirlwind shoot in the fall of 2000, *A Patchwork Life*, the series, debuted its thirteen-episode first season in early January 2001. The premiere garnered warm reviews, and the second episode brought in twice as many viewers as the first. As critical acclaim and ratings soared, the network, pleased with the unexpected success of the modest drama they had acquired on the cheap, promptly ordered two more full seasons and significantly increased the studio's budget. Ellen was absolutely thrilled; her decision to quit the movie had been vindicated, and she would be able to share her great-grandmother's story fully and authentically just as she had hoped. As for Julia, she was relieved and thankful that her decision to accompany Ellen off the movie set had not ended her career, as she had assumed it would, but had instead set her on an entirely new and promising artistic path.

But the show's success and their more generous budget inevitably meant more scrutiny from studio and network executives. Ellen had shouldered the tasks of both head writer and showrunner for the first season, but soon after the second was green-lit, she was replaced as showrunner by a studio executive's nephew or cousin-in-law or whatever, with more advantageous connections than actual experience. With Augustus out of the picture by the end of season one, Ellen and Julia had expected season two to chronicle Sadie's hardships and triumphs as she raised her two orphaned grandsons and struggled to build a homestead, all on her own. The new showrunner, Mitchell, had a different vision: A romance for Sadie would appeal to their two largest demographics, women ages thirty-five and up, while a strong male lead could extend their audience to more men in that same age group and to younger women.

"I just want to tell the best story I can, rather than grafting in certain plot twists or characters to pander to a particular demographic," Ellen lamented to Julia one day as they left a script meeting. "I'd prefer to stay true to my great-grandmother's diaries as much as possible, and she never remarried."

Julia had misgivings of her own. She understood Mitchell's point about romance appealing to certain audiences, although she would argue that the show's appeal already was much broader than he believed. But while she wouldn't object to adding a love subplot, she had been looking forward to portraying Sadie as a strong and independent woman, bravely persevering without depending on a man. Julia could do so much with a role like that. Then again, complex, well-drawn romances between characters over fifty were scarce on television, and she'd enjoy the challenge of proving that there should be more.

"If you write the script, I'm confident it will be excellent," Julia told Ellen. "I know you care deeply about historical accuracy, but maybe it's more important to be true to the *spirit* of your great-grandmother's diaries rather than to the *letter*. Haven't you already taken liberties with the historical record to make Sadie a more believable role for someone of my wisdom and maturity?"

Ellen looked uncertain, but soon thereafter, she agreed to add a love interest for Sadie. "I've learned to choose my battles," she confided to Julia, "and I admit Mitchell has a point." As a compromise, she would develop Sadie and Ben's relationship over several seasons rather than immediately plunging them into the thick of it.

When Julia read Ellen's wonderful script introducing Benjamin Atherton, she marveled at how brilliantly Ellen had risen to a challenge she'd never sought. The tension between Ben and Sadie felt earned and compelled, and their banter was sharp and witty, but never unkind. The scripts for the rest of the season were even more engaging as Ellen developed their relationship. Sometimes Julia laughed aloud as she read; other times she felt a pang of wistfulness to witness Sadie and Ben's steadily growing affection. Sometimes she wanted to give them both a good shake and tell them to stop being so stubborn and just admit they were in love already. "Any story that captivates me this much will enthrall our audience," she told Ellen. "You've outdone yourself. I can't wait to start filming."

"I can't wait to cast Ben," she said, smiling, her cheeks flushed from the warmth of Julia's praise. "I'll want your input at every stage. It's absolutely essential that you feel a connection with whomever we cast. We'll keep searching until we find the perfect person."

Julia promised to attend as many chemistry reads as Ellen and Mitchell wanted, and she didn't regret that promise even when the search dragged on much longer than she expected. A few actors Mitchell called in would have done well in the part, in Julia's opinion, but oddly, the majority didn't suit the character well at all. Once, when Mitchell stepped out for a juice break after observing Julia read with five candidates in a row, Julia made an aside to Ellen—not necessarily a complaint, more of an observation—about the unfocused nature of the search. Glancing toward the door to be sure Mitchell couldn't overhear, Ellen explained that he had insisted upon speaking with the casting agents himself and deciding which of their clients to see without any input from her. "I would have weeded out most of them ahead of time based on their headshots and résumés, but Mitchell wanted to bring them all in," she said. "I guess he has a particular vision for Ben, but I can't quite figure out what that is."

Julia's theory, which she kept to herself, was that Mitchell had never cast a show before and didn't know what he was doing. "Why don't you pick your top five and bring them in next time?" she suggested. "Don't bother running them past Mitchell first. Just put them on the call sheet. With any luck he'll assume we're working from his original list."

Ellen agreed, and the next time they met, if Mitchell wondered why he didn't recall having seen these particular men's headshots before, he didn't mention it. As before, he and Ellen were seated at a table in a conference room, and while there was a chair for Julia too, she rarely had enough time between auditions to sit. Her place was in front of the table, reading lines with each aspiring leading man, performing a scene, or perhaps two, if either Ellen or Mitchell liked what they saw and asked for more. A camera operator filmed each audition for later review, while a production assistant managed the door, clipboard in hand, checking the list, summoning the actors one by one from the hallway, making sure they had the correct photocopied sides of the script, and showing them where to stand.

The first three actors of the morning were quite good, much better suited for the role than any actors Mitchell had invited. But the fourth actor to enter so closely matched how Julia had imagined Ben that for a moment she was struck speechless. As he approached, a slow smile appearing as he saw her waiting and strode toward her, Julia threw a glance to Ellen, eyebrows raised. Ellen replied with a tiny nod, as if to say, *I know, perfect, right?*

Halting in the center of the space before the table, he nodded to Julia, and then to Ellen and Mitchell. "Thanks for coming in," Mitchell said. "Whenever you're ready."

"Thank you. I'm Nigel Crawford, and I'll be reading for the part of Benjamin Atherton," he said in a British baritone so rich and beautiful that Julia nearly swooned.

"Let's begin on the first page, please," said Ellen. While Nigel's attention was on her, Julia quickly fanned herself with her pages, composing herself. "Let's start with Sadie's line, two paragraphs from the top. 'I may not be native to Kansas, but I know an old bushwhacker when I see one.'"

"Got it." Julia turned to Nigel, her eyebrows raised in a question. "Shall we?"

"Ready when you are," he said, smiling.

She nodded and began, ignoring the pleasant fluttering in her stomach she had felt when his warm hazel eyes had held her gaze.

Julia read her first line, but when Nigel replied in a flawless western American accent, she was so surprised she lost her place in the script and had to ask to start over. After that, though, the scene went perfectly. Nigel brought out nuances in the character Julia had not noticed before, adding new facets absent from the other actors' performances. Afterward, Ellen thanked him and asked for another scene, and to Julia's surprise, Mitchell requested a third. "Thanks for coming in," Mitchell told him smoothly when they finished, betraying no more interest in Nigel than he had any other candidate.

Not so Julia and Ellen. "That's him," Julia declared as soon as the production assistant escorted him out. "That's our Ben. He's perfect."

"I couldn't agree more," said Ellen gleefully. "Oh, Julia, the sparks flying between you two—"

"I know, right? If we can capture half of that energy on camera—"

"I captured *all* of it," the camera operator spoke up. "In my opinion that was the best read we've seen yet."

"Yes, he was very good," Mitchell conceded. "But we still have one more actor to see today."

Julia was confident that they had already found their Ben, but, as a survivor of more unhappy auditions than she cared to count, she wouldn't dream of sending away the unfortunate fellow waiting in the hallway without giving him a shot. It wasn't his fault he had such a tough act to follow. As the PA brought him in, Julia reminded herself that he could be even better than Nigel, if given a fair chance. But as soon as he slated, she knew he wouldn't be. He was good, but with Nigel Crawford's performance fresh in their memories, he seemed merely above average.

Julia read a single scene with him. Afterward, Mitchell and Ellen thanked him for coming but requested nothing more. As soon as the door closed behind him, Julia took her seat and clasped her hands together in anticipation. "So are we agreed?" she asked. "Nigel Crawford is our Ben Atherton?"

"Absolutely," said Ellen emphatically, tapping her pencil on the table. "Let's get him signed."

"Hold on." Mitchell raised a hand to check their enthusiasm, then resumed sorting through the pile of more than three dozen headshots and résumés on the table before him. "I want to take a second look at some of the guys we saw last week."

"Okay, that's fair," said Ellen, her voice unperturbed, although she looked taken aback. "That's why we film the auditions."

"And another thing," he said, frowning slightly, his gaze fixed on the actors' photos, "this isn't everyone. At least five actors the agency recommended aren't here."

Julia and Ellen exchanged a glance. "I don't need to see anyone else," said Ellen. "I'm satisfied."

"Same here," said Julia. "Mitchell, is there some reason you don't want to cast Nigel Crawford?"

"To be perfectly honest—" Mitchell winced. "He seems very British, doesn't he?"

"When he slated, maybe," said Julia, bewildered. "His American accent during the scenes was perfect."

"Maybe. But he's not well-known to American audiences." Shaking his head and frowning, Mitchell rose and began gathering up the headshots and résumés. "Let me think about it over the weekend and I'll get back to you."

There wasn't really anything Julia and Ellen could do but accept that he needed more time, so they agreed to call it a day. While Ellen and Mitchell went off to their offices, Julia headed out to the parking lot. She had just unlocked her car door and was tossing her tote on the front passenger seat when she saw Nigel at the bus stop halfway down the block, leaning against the back of a bench, reading.

She hesitated for a moment before approaching him. "Hello," she greeted him from a few paces away, raising her hand in a little wave that felt so artificial and ridiculous that she was glad his gaze remained fixed on his book. "Nigel Crawford, right?"

At that, he glanced up and smiled. "Yes. And you are Miss Julia Merchaud."

"That's right." She inclined her head toward the bus shelter. "Where are you headed? If it's on my way, I'd be happy to take you."

"That's very kind, but I couldn't possibly impose."

"It wouldn't be an imposition. With you along, I can use the diamond lanes and get home faster." When his brow furrowed slightly, she added. "Carpool lanes. High-occupancy-vehicle lanes. They're marked with a diamond."

"Really. I hadn't noticed." He closed his book and straightened. "Too busy admiring the scenery, I suppose."

She glanced up and down the street, all asphalt, adobe, red tile or shaker roofs, and plastic signage, and fixed him with a skeptical look. "This is hardly one of California's most scenic regions."

"Not to one such as yourself, perhaps, accustomed as you surely are to palm trees and sunny skies."

She took another look around, smelled flowers over the car exhaust, glimpsed snow on the Santa Monica peaks in the distance, and decided he made a fair point. "Where are you headed?" she asked again.

His apartment—a rather grim place suitable as a temporary residence only, he told her—turned out to be not far out of her way, so she led him back to her car, quickly grabbing her tote and tossing it into the back seat before he climbed in. They set out for Beverly Hills, but before they reached the 405, they both admitted that they were famished. Julia offered to take him out to dinner at an iconic restaurant on the beach that no overseas visitor seeking a quintessential Southern California experience should miss. When he accepted, she continued on to the PCH instead of turning north.

By the time the hostess was seating them at a table on the long, narrow deck at Moonshadows, they were friends; over drinks and starters, they became confidantes. Julia learned that Nigel had succeeded beyond his wildest expectations in British television and film and on the stage, but, craving new artistic experiences, he had made the jump to Hollywood. His agent had soon found him a modest part in a casino heist picture that had shot on location in Las Vegas, quickly followed by a drama about a corrupt narcotics cop filmed in Los Angeles, but then he had hit a dry spell. He had contemplated returning to Britain when his agent had put him up for the part in *A Patchwork Life*. "I couldn't bear to leave America without doing a single Western," he remarked, sipping his white wine. "This might be my last chance."

She felt a brief pang of disappointment when he explained that he had a longtime partner, Alistair, a gorgeous, brilliant, brooding brunet with doctorates in archaeology and art history. Alistair had encouraged Nigel to audition for *Patchwork*, but left unspoken were misgivings about how long this new role might prolong their separation.

"He would never say so, but I think he'd be relieved if I didn't get the part but returned home instead," Nigel said ruefully as the server set their entrées before them.

"At least you have someone at home who misses you," Julia said. "I haven't known that feeling since my husband died."

"I'm so sorry." Nigel's brow furrowed in concern, and his eyes were kind. "How long has it been?"

"Sometimes it feels like yesterday," she admitted. She told him how she and Charles had met when she had been cast as the voice-over narrator for one of his documentaries, how they had fallen in love over a shared passion for film and art, and how she had lost him suddenly to a heart attack after nearly twenty-nine years of marriage. Her work had sustained her through the aftermath of his death, but it could carry her only so far. Longing to replace what she had lost, she had married again. "Twice remarried, and twice divorced," said

Julia, with a self-deprecating frown. "Impetuous and foolish decisions I deeply regret, although at the time, both times, I thought I was in love. But I'm older and wiser now. Never again."

"Never?" Nigel echoed, eyebrows rising. "Are you so certain?"

"I have my work and my friends. I'm content. Someone truly extraordinary would have to come along for me to risk my heart again."

"Well, as long as you're happy." Nigel raised his glass. "To rewarding work, excellent friends, and a heart open to possibilities."

She hesitated a moment before she lifted her glass and clinked it against his.

Later, when she dropped him off at his apartment, she called to him through the open window, "When you get the role, Alistair should join you here in LA. We have excellent museums and universities. I'm sure he'll have his choice of opportunities."

"I'll tell him you said so," Nigel replied, raising a hand in parting.

On Monday morning, Julia met Ellen and Mitchell at the studio to decide whom to cast as Ben Atherton. Julia and Ellen wanted Nigel, but while Mitchell conceded that Nigel was very good, he wouldn't concur, and he wouldn't explain why.

"Should we review the videos again?" Julia asked, barely keeping her exasperation in check after fifteen minutes of Mitchell's dithering. "Let's run their clips back to back, Nigel Crawford and your favorite. You can even pick two favorites. I won't complain."

"Not possible," said Mitchell. "The actor I want to cast didn't audition. He doesn't need to. Stars of his caliber never do."

"Really?" Ellen threw Julia a dubious look. "Who did you have in mind?"

"And would a star of such high caliber condescend to join our cast?" asked Julia testily.

"I happen to know that he would. His agent reached out to me."

"Whose agent?" asked Ellen warily. "Who are we talking about?"

"Wait for it." Mitchell held up his hands as if framing a shot. "Rick Rowan!"

"What?" Julia exclaimed.

"No. Absolutely not." Ellen shook her head emphatically. "Not if he were the last actor on earth."

"What's the problem?" Mitchell asked, bewildered. "Rick Rowan is a bona fide movie star. *Desert Vengeance* is coming out in May. His popularity will be on the rise just as our season two is premiering."

Julia looked to Ellen and saw her own alarm and disgust reflected in her friend's expression. "Do you know nothing at all about the failed movie adaptation of *A Patchwork Life*?" Julia asked, turning back to Mitchell. "Does *Prairie Vengeance* ring a bell?"

"Never heard of it."

"It was an absolute nightmare," Ellen said flatly. "Rowan was cast as Augustus Henderson. Test screening audiences loathed the movie so much that it went straight to video. And you want to cast him in our series?"

"Well . . ." Mitchell shifted in his chair, uncomfortable. "Every star has a bomb on his résumé, and Rowan is a star. Maybe appearing in *Patchwork* will give him a redemption arc. That could be good publicity."

"I won't work with him." Ellen crossed her arms and sat back in her chair. "We should each get one unassailable veto, and this would be mine."

"What do you have against Nigel Crawford?" Julia asked Mitchell. "And don't give me that 'too British' garbage. He speaks better American than Rick Rowan."

"I just don't find Crawford believable in the role, all right?" said Mitchell, raising his voice. "I mean, come on, he's a fag."

Julia gaped at him. "Excuse me?"

"That's what I've heard."

Ellen fixed him with a level stare. "That word is a slur, Mitchell. Don't use it again."

He threw his hands in the air. "Fine. Whatever. He's a 'homosexual.' The point is, Ben Atherton is supposed to be a tough cattle rancher and Sadie's love interest. How can a homosexual pull that off? Would you really want to kiss him, Julia? I mean, seriously?"

"You do realize that it's *acting*, right?" Julia retorted. "Whoever we cast doesn't actually have to be in love with me. I don't have to be in love with him. But to your point, of course I wouldn't object to kissing him if that's what Ellen writes."

"I can't believe we're even having this conversation," said Ellen. "It's the twenty-first century, Mitchell. You need to get over yourself."

He heaved a sigh. "Okay. Fine. We won't hire Rick Rowan if you can't stand him. We'll find a Rick Rowan *type*. Sure, Crawford had the best audition and he could probably pull off the role, but I don't want to cast a homosexual."

Julia shook her head, incredulous. "That is truly repugnant, Mitchell."

"It's also illegal," said Ellen. "We both heard you say, clearly and unequivocally, that you intend to discriminate against him because of his sexual orientation. That's against the law in California, in case you didn't get the memo."

Mitchell rolled his eyes. "How stupid do you think I am? I'm not going to *tell him* that's why."

"I can't even—" Ellen clasped a hand to her forehead. "I don't even know what to say. I have no words."

"There's no need to explain why you're not casting Nigel Crawford in this role," Julia said, fixing Mitchell with a steely gaze. "Because you *are* going to cast him. If you don't, I'll file a complaint with human resources."

"You wouldn't dare. My father-in-law is a vice president with the studio."

"Father-in-law," Julia exclaimed, slapping her palms on the table. "So *that's* it. I thought it was an uncle who got you this job."

"Your guess was closer than mine," Ellen said. "I figured it was a college roommate's dad. So who won the pool?"

"Edna from wardrobe, I think."

Mitchell looked from Julia to Ellen and back. "What the hell are you talking about?"

Julia waved it off. "Call Nigel Crawford's agent and tell him he has the part, or I go to HR and you'll probably lose this excellent job which you worked *so* hard to earn and at which you *so* excel."

Mitchell reddened and fumed, but after a long moment of opening and closing his mouth as if he had much to say but had forgotten how to say it, he pushed back his chair and stormed from the room. The next day, an email went out from the studio that Nigel Crawford would be joining the cast of *A Patchwork Life* in the role of Benjamin Atherton beginning in the middle of season two.

Several seasons, widespread critical acclaim, immeasurable viewer admiration, and two Emmys later, Nigel had proven himself absolutely perfect for the role. As for Mitchell, although at first Julia had some misgivings about letting him off the hook rather than reporting him, a few months after that meeting, he used the same slur to describe a cinematographer at a studio function. A studio exec overheard him, and as an admirer of the cinematographer's work and someone who recognized a corporate liability when he met one, he promptly took the appropriate measures. Eventually, after due process ran its course, Mitchell was fired. If he remained in the industry after that, Julia never had the misfortune to cross paths with him.

As for Nigel, he proved to be such an essential part of the cast that it was impossible to imagine *A Patchwork Life* without him.

Julia arrived at Moonshadows just before seven o'clock, the sky a deep dusky blue above, a soft rose to the west where the ocean met the sky. She was locking her car door behind her when Nigel pulled into a parking place nearby, so they met in the middle and entered the restaurant together, arm in arm. "This will keep the rumor mill churning," she murmured close to his ear as the hostess led them to their reserved table, with some guests noticing them as they passed but quickly pretending not to, and others openly staring.

They had been friends so long each new conversation felt like a continuation of the last one, as if they had merely paused for breath rather than spending hours or days apart. Over a shared starter they chatted about Nigel's swimming, Julia's quilting, Alistair's enthralling reports from the fine-art black market bust in Switzerland, and industry gossip—who was romantically entangled with whom, who was splitting up, what projects had been green-lit, who had been cast in what. It wasn't until their main courses were served that Julia introduced the topic that had prompted her to invite him to dinner. "It sounds like Alistair is terribly busy," she said sympathetically. "No chance he'll be able to slip away for a visit soon?"

"No chance whatsoever," Nigel replied glumly.

"You said the other day that you needed a distraction," Julia reminded him. "I wish I could arrange a visit with Alistair, but since that's not possible, I've arranged the next best thing."

"Brunch with you, me, Dame Judi Dench, and the Queen at Balmoral Castle?"

"No, although that sounds marvelous. I was thinking a week of quilt camp at Elm Creek Manor."

His eyebrows rose. "The glorious Elm Creek Manor of legend, that renowned, restorative haven of the quilting arts in rustic Pennsylvania? I didn't think it actually existed."

"But I go there every summer!"

"So you say. You definitely disappear for a week, usually in August, and you return rested, rejuvenated, and full of creative inspiration." Nigel savored a bite of his seared snapper in shallot caper sauce. "But this Elm Creek Manor you rhapsodize about—it's too perfect to exist."

Julia retrieved the envelope of snapshots from her purse. "It's real, and I have the photos to prove it." She laid them out on the table between them, and as he admired shots of the front of the manor, the grand front foyer, the bustling classrooms, the verdant orchards, and the view of the wildflower meadow from the verandah, she described their retreat as she envisioned it: time spent with friends far from the worrisome intrusions of everyday life, excellent cuisine, the restful quiet of the countryside, and quilting lessons, in both technique and history.

"Elm Creek Manor does look lovely," Nigel admitted, admiring the photos, "and all teasing aside, your stories through the years have been enchanting."

Julia reached across the table and took his hand. "Then say you'll come. Ellen, Lindsay, Olivia, Paige, and I have already committed, and I'm sure others from the cast and crew will be signing on soon."

"I'd hate to miss all the fun, but what would I do there? Wouldn't expert quilting lessons be wasted on me? My character never quilts in the show."

"Learn for your own creative benefit, then," Julia countered. "You might find that quilting offers you a new way to express yourself artistically. It can be very relaxing and fulfilling."

"Yes, you've said before that you find it rather meditative."

"And if quilting doesn't appeal to you, I know something else that will." She leaned closer, lowering her voice confidentially. "Ellen will be working on scripts for the sixth season, and she promised us glimpses of her work in progress. I expect her to invite us to read pages and workshop scenes in the evenings after our lessons. If you want to influence the direction of Ben's narrative arc, this would be the perfect occasion."

"An intriguing proposition." Nigel sat back and rubbed his jaw, lost in thought, while Julia waited, hardly daring to move rather than interrupt his reverie. "I confess I've been somewhat concerned about how we might wrap up Ben Atherton's story in a manner befitting a thespian of my stature. I hope that doesn't sound dreadfully pompous."

"Not dreadfully," Julia teased.

"It would be wonderful to have a go at another Emmy—"

"Or a second BAFTA."

He offered her a small, knowing smile. "How well you remember my wistful confession about my unfulfilled dream."

"It doesn't have to remain a dream. With the right script and the best supporting cast in the business, you could achieve it."

"Hmm." He studied her, eyes narrowing, a playful smile quirking the corners of his mouth. "You're arranging all of this just for me?"

Julia hesitated. "No," she admitted. "For you, but also for me. Refreshing our quilting skills will definitely benefit the show's production values, but—the truth is, I want us all to spend some quality time together for purely selfish reasons. But this will also benefit Elm Creek Quilts. They could use the revenue right about now, and I want to support them."

"'Purely selfish reasons'?"

"Yes, and I freely admit it. Shall I elaborate?"

"No need, Julia, darling." Nigel smiled fondly. "When you put it that way, how could I refuse?"

10

In the weeks that followed, Julia convinced six actors who played recurring characters to join the company heading to quilt camp, but although twelve guests were better than none, she had hoped to enlist at least twice as many. Fortunately, Ellen and Lindsay came through for her. When Ellen extended the invitation to the writers' room, one of her screenwriters accepted—Jason, a sardonic fellow barely three years out of UC Berkeley and the last person Ellen would have expected to willingly take up needle and thread. "He said that if the experience doesn't inform his season six scripts, he might be able to use it in a novel someday, so it won't go to waste," Ellen explained. "He might have been kidding. I can never tell with him."

Lindsay recruited five members of the crew, including a costume designer, a production assistant, a stunt coordinator, an apprentice prop maker, and an assistant from set design. Julia wasn't sure how quilting classes would benefit the stunt coordinator on the job, but she wasn't about to turn anyone away. Their set designer was perpetually overextended, so she had sent her assistant—Louis Clemence, the handsome pianist from her premiere party—in her place to do technical and historical research.

By the last week of October, Julia had assembled a company of eighteen, including herself. After sending Sylvia the final head count and guest list, she put together a dossier for each camper with a travel itinerary, packing list, and brochures from Elm Creek Quilt Camp describing the manor's amenities. She chartered a flight not only for the sake of comfort, privacy, and convenience, but also because she had promised her colleagues a luxurious retreat experience from the moment they met up at LAX on the morning of November 7.

"This is amazing, Julia," Lindsay said, eyes shining as she prepared to board the gleaming blue-and-white jet. "My mom always flies coach and takes a shuttle from the airport when she goes to quilt camp."

"This must be costing you a fortune," said Ellen in an undertone as she paused on the bottom step to take in the size of the aircraft.

"A small fortune," Julia admitted. She'd pay it a thousand times over to keep *A Patchwork Life* going.

"Quick question," Jason said as he approached, hair tousled as if he'd just rolled out of bed, eyes concealed behind round, blue-tinted glasses. "How's the internet access at this place? Is it wi-fi or Ethernet?"

"Dial-up," Julia replied, but when his jaw dropped in horror, she quickly added, "I'm just kidding. The wi-fi is strongest on the first floor of the new wing, but you can access it in most of the second-floor guest suites. Some of the suites have Ethernet connections, if you'd prefer. Just ask when we check in."

A few members of the production crew boarded next, followed by Paige, her dark hair in a thick French braid, a pastel lavender Fjällräven knapsack on her back. "Hi, Miss Julia," the younger woman greeted her, a bit shyly. "Thanks again for inviting me."

"Thanks for agreeing to come," Julia replied warmly. "I thought you might still be in North Carolina. It would have been a shorter trip to Pennsylvania from there."

"Yeah, it would've been, but I've been back in LA for a couple of weeks. I had some auditions and meetings." Paige shifted her backpack as she glanced up the stairs and behind her, where a few latecomers were joining the queue. "I guess Noah isn't coming?"

She looked so crestfallen that Julia felt a pang of guilt. "No, unfortunately he couldn't join us. He has college application business to attend to."

"Oh, really? That's a legit reason." Paige's cheeks flushed, and she managed to look both relieved and unhappy. "I thought—well, I thought he might be—I don't know, skipping this so he could hang out with his girlfriend."

"Noah?" Julia shook her head. "No, that wouldn't be like him. He takes his work very seriously."

"It's just that I read that he's dating Jayla from *High School Harmony*. There was a photo of them holding hands at a Starbucks, but everyone knows Noah prefers independent local coffee roasters, so I was hoping it was fake."

"Oh, I see. Well, I can't speak to whatever photo you saw, but I do know that Noah and Jayla have been on again, off again for years."

"I guess they're probably on again," said Paige, forlorn.

"May I offer you some advice?"

Paige nodded.

"Apparently you've been reading the tabloids," said Julia wryly. "One thing I've learned the hard way through the years is that it does you absolutely no good to drink from that poisoned well. Sometimes paparazzi and tabloid writers can be cruel with their facts, and sometimes with outright lies. If there's something in those rags that you really ought to know, trust your agent to bring it to your attention. Your time would be better spent reading better things."

"Thanks, Miss Julia," said Paige, managing a small smile. "I'll keep that in mind."

She continued up the stairs, looking a trifle more cheerful than before.

Nigel, who disliked flying and subjected himself to it as

infrequently as possible, was one of the last to board. "Julia, darling, I trust this luxurious country estate has a pool?" he inquired. "You know how I loathe to miss my daily workout."

Julia thought quickly. "It doesn't, but there's a college nearby with an excellent rec center. I can look into getting you some day passes."

Olivia, two steps above, glanced back at them over her shoulder. "I'm happy to lead a Zumba class," she called, smiling winningly as she adjusted her oversized sunglasses. "It's quite a workout, as Julia can attest."

"I'll take you up on that," Julia called back. "Nigel, if we can't get you into a pool, come Zumba with us. It's dancing. You'll love it."

"I might just do that." Satisfied, Nigel nodded and continued up the stairs.

The flight was smooth and comfortable, offering the travelers enough time to read or doze or chat, but not enough to grow bored or restless. On their approach into the Elm Creek Valley regional airport, those with window seats peered outside and outdid one another in dramatic descriptions of what they observed. There were some comical and some genuinely apprehensive wisecracks about the hilly countryside, short runway, and apparent dearth of emergency services, but after the pilot gave them a flawless landing, their qualms were promptly forgotten.

Julia had arranged for a pair of executive shuttles to carry them in comfort from the airport to Elm Creek Manor, and she found herself in the front passenger seat of the lead van with the production crew, Ellen, Lindsay, and Paige. As they sped smoothly along the state highway, Julia occasionally pointed out a significant landmark, but there weren't many, so most of the time passed in conversation or in admiring the landscape of forested, rolling hills surrounding patchwork farms in lush valleys. The muted autumn hues of russet, gold, and brown, with the occasional burst of scarlet or evergreen, seemed a faded memory of a more brilliant display that must have passed a few weeks before, but Julia still found it beautiful.

Eventually they reached the turnoff for the road to Elm Creek Manor, a barely visible curve of brown on the edge of a dense forest. As ever, the familiar sight made Julia's heart beat a little faster in anticipation.

"There," Lindsay cried out from the row behind. "That's the sign! My mom told me to look for it."

A murmur of curiosity and relief rose from the back as the passengers craned their necks to glimpse the solid oak Elm Creek Quilts sign marking the T intersection—four feet wide atop sturdy support beams, angled to be clearly visible to traffic from both directions, with beautifully carved letters that Julia happened to know were freshly painted every March, just before the new camp season began.

The driver turned onto the rough, gravel road, slowing the shuttle as it wound through the dense forest surrounding the Bergstrom estate. Despite some muffled noises of surprise and discomfort from her companions, Julia considered it a true measure of the driver's skill that the ride remained nearly as smooth as on the paved highway, the jolting softened, perhaps, by the light carpet of fallen leaves crunching beneath the wheels. Sunlight filtered through the boughs overhead, the canopy much sparser than Julia had ever seen it in summer. When they approached the familiar fork in the road, she was surprised to discover something new: a wooden sign, similar in design to the older one marking the turnoff. One plank's carved, painted message indicated that the right fork would take visitors to Elm Creek Manor's main entrance. A second plank announced that the left fork led to the manor's rear parking lot and Elm Creek Orchards.

"We're almost there," said Lindsay. "My mom's described this route so many times I feel like I've been here before."

The driver took the right fork, crossing the narrow bridge over Elm Creek. Usually the rushing waters were so clear Julia could glimpse the smooth, round stones at the bottom, but now the creek was thick with fallen leaves sweeping downstream. Soon thereafter they emerged from the forest onto the paved driveway crossing the vast wildflower meadow—and there, at last, the gray stone mansion with its tall, white columns and broad, shaded verandah came into view. Someone behind Julia gasped with delight, someone else sighed contentedly, and others murmured their appreciation. Four people stood on the verandah where the two stone staircases descended in mirror-image arcs to the curved driveway, and as the shuttle drew closer, Julia recognized Sylvia and her husband, Andrew, and Sarah and Matt. By the time the two shuttles pulled up alongside the rearing horse fountain, they were waiting on the sidewalk, Sylvia smiling a gracious welcome, Sarah grinning so broadly Julia half expected her to thrust her fists in the air triumphantly. This autumn edition of quilt camp was as much her victory as it was Julia's.

"Welcome to Elm Creek Manor," Sylvia called as they climbed out of the shuttles, shouldering their backpacks or messenger bags, stretching and moving to work the travel fatigue out of their necks and limbs. As Sarah, Matt, and Andrew assisted the campers with their luggage, Sylvia came to Julia, arms outstretched. "And a special welcome to you, Julia," she said, clasping Julia's hands, "with heartfelt thanks, on behalf of all of the Elm Creek Quilters."

"You keep forgetting that you're the ones doing me a favor," Julia replied, squeezing Sylvia's hands. Although the late afternoon was sunny, the air was cool and brisk, scattering the fallen leaves on the driveway. Julia shivered in her thin cardigan as she dug into her tote for her jacket, grateful that Lindsay had reminded her to pack for a cooler climate.

Her chill did not go unnoticed. "We must get you inside," Sylvia admonished fondly, taking Julia's arm and accompanying her up the nearer staircase. Sarah and Matt were already leading the other guests across the verandah and through the tall double doors into the grand front foyer. A single long table was arranged in the center of the black marble floor, where two Elm Creek Quilters Julia had met on previous visits, Gretchen Hartley and Maggie Flynn, awaited them. As the campers' hosts introduced themselves, the guests received their room assignments and keys, and with Gretchen's husband, Joe, joining Sarah, Matt, and Andrew as luggage wranglers, they were escorted up the grand oak staircase to their suites. Julia was shown to her usual accommodations, the large suite with a four-poster bed covered with a blue-and-red quilt pieced of homespun plaids, and windows overlooking the cornerstone patio.

She had just finished unpacking and was taking in the autumn version of the familiar lovely view from the window when Sylvia knocked on her open door. "Dinner will be served in the banquet hall at six o'clock," she said. "Anna will be treating us to some of her favorite autumnal dishes throughout the week. I trust you and your friends will enjoy them."

"If Anna's cooking, I'm certain we will." Julia was struck by a sudden thought. "What's the latest on the roof? I expected to see construction equipment and pallets of shingles scattered all around. Hasn't the work begun yet? Or are you hiding the mess around back?"

"Thanks to your generosity, the new roof was finished last week. Just a few days ago, Matt and Andrew finished painting the attic, so it will be perfectly sound, dry, and tidy when I begin moving all those trunks and cartons back into storage." Sylvia winced comically and regarded Julia over the tops of her glasses. "That will be quite a chore. I'm very glad you and your friends are visiting so I have a perfect excuse to postpone it."

"Believe me, the pleasure is all mine."

"Not yours alone," said Sylvia, smiling. "Well, I should continue my rounds. Postponing organizing the attic is one thing, postponing dinner quite another. I'll see you downstairs in the banquet hall soon."

As soon as Julia finished unpacking, she too made the rounds to make sure that the company of performers and crew were settling in and had everything they needed. Jason was pleased with the Ethernet connection in his suite near the library and was already typing away on his laptop. Lindsay was strolling the length of the hall, pausing at the railing to gaze up to the third-floor landing and the high coffered ceiling and to take in the view of the grand front foyer from above. Nigel was in the library with Sarah, making arrangements for Andrew to drive him in the Elm Creek Quilts minivan to Waterford College early the next morning for a vigorous swim at the rec center. Olivia and Ellen, whose rooms were on opposite sides of the hallway, were passing from one to another, admiring the views from each other's windows and the cozy quilts on their beds. Paige hurried past clad in black tights and a long-sleeved tech shirt, carrying her running shoes. "I'm going exploring," she called to Julia as she raced down the stairs. "I'll be back in time for dinner."

Assured that everyone was comfortable and happy, Julia returned to her own suite for a quiet, relaxing interlude of yoga before freshening up and dressing for dinner in comfortable slacks and a cashmere sweater. When she left the room, she found nearly everyone else heading down to dinner too, chatting and joking. Julia was gratified to hear them complimenting everything they had seen of the manor so far.

As the company gathered in the banquet hall, Julia was struck by the fond nostalgia she felt whenever she entered the elegant room where she had made so many happy memories in summers past. Several round tables were set with crisp linens and the unique Bergstrom china, softly aglow in the light of the chandeliers and candlelit centerpieces. The curtains were pulled back from the floor-to-ceiling windows on the west wall, where only a faint blur of rose lingered in the deepening blue sky. The grove of elms, maples, and oaks behind the manor was only a silhouette in the darkness, the bridge over Elm Creek and the red barn beyond it not visible at all. Julia knew very well where they were, but her friends would not discover them until the morning.

Sylvia awaited her guests just inside the entrance to the banquet hall, and as she greeted them and invited them to be seated, Julia noticed some changes to the decor since her last visit. The room appeared to have been freshly painted a rich ivory, and beautifully framed enlargements of photos, maps, and other memorabilia from the manor's history were displayed on the walls alongside several lovely antique quilts. Julia wondered if the quilt exhibit Summer had curated at Union Hall for the Waterford Historical Society had inspired Sylvia to create a historical exhibit of her own.

No sooner had they taken their seats than the servers brought out their first course, an arugula salad with apples, pecans, and feta. As the second course was served, a delicious butternut squash soup, Sylvia formally welcomed the company to Elm Creek Manor and introduced the faculty and staff, who were seated at a table of their own. She then offered her guests a history of the estate, which had been founded by her great-grandfather Hans Bergstrom, his wife, Anneke, and his sister, Gerda, immigrants of German and Swedish heritage, in the mid-nineteenth century. The Bergstroms had built the original farmhouse, now the west wing of the manor, in 1858, so noted on the cornerstone near the former front entrance.

From the earliest days the family had grown crops and planted orchards, but Hans Bergstrom's greatest ambition had been to raise horses. "And a family," Sylvia noted with a smile. "Hans and Anneke had six children, including my grandfather, David, the eldest."

As the family grew and prospered, the Bergstroms contributed to civic and social life in the Elm Creek Valley, but as the nation's struggle over slavery intensified, their abolitionist activities demanded great discretion. In the antebellum era, the Bergstrom residence served as a station on the Underground Railroad, a safe haven for enslaved people seeking freedom in the North. The outbreak of the Civil War disrupted the operation of the Underground Railroad, but the Bergstroms and their friends continued to serve the cause of freedom and justice, some by enlisting in the Union Army or the United States Colored Troops, others by working on the home front.

After the war, the Bergstrom horse farm and orchards thrived, reaching the height of its prosperity in the early twentieth century.

"Decades after Elm Creek Farm had become more successful than its immigrant founders could have imagined, my grandfather added the newer, grander wing to the original farmhouse," Sylvia explained. "This includes, on the first floor, this banquet hall, the verandah and the new front entrance, the grand foyer and staircase, and the ballroom. You'll see the ballroom later tonight, and you'll come to know it quite well beginning tomorrow, for that's where we hold our quilting classes. On the second floor, we have a marvelous library, which you're welcome to browse."

"What's on the third floor?" asked Jason.

"More guest rooms and the children's playroom, but unless you'd like to volunteer to babysit Sarah and Matt's toddler twins, you might want to keep your distance." As a ripple of laughter rose from the group, Sylvia smiled, reflective. "I often wonder what my great-grandparents would think of the changes their descendants made to the farm they founded in the Elm Creek Valley in central Pennsylvania so many decades ago. Nothing, I believe, has changed the estate more profoundly than turning it into a retreat for quilters."

"Speaking for the present company," Julia declared, "we're very glad for the changes. I imagine your great-grandparents would be delighted—and very proud of you."

"Hear, hear," Nigel boomed, and everyone broke into applause.

The main course, roasted chicken breast in apple cider reduction with apple-ginger chutney, had been served during Sylvia's talk, and lively conversation resumed as they finished the meal. After a time, when the servers began to clear, Sylvia rose again and raised a hand for their attention. "One of our most beloved traditions at Elm Creek Quilt Camp is to conclude our first evening with a ceremony we call Candlelight," she said. "Ordinarily, we gather outside on the cornerstone patio, but since this is a chilly November night rather than a mild summer evening, please accompany me to the ballroom."

Exchanging glances of curiosity and amusement, the company rose and followed Sylvia through the double doors on the far end of the room into the ballroom. Julia knew it to be a large, elegant room spanning the width of the west wing, but at that moment it was mostly in shadow, the only light coming from a cracking blaze in the large fireplace on the opposite wall. An assortment of eighteen chairs had been arranged in an open circle before it. Between the chairs and the door was a table set up with carafes of coffee, tea, and mulled cider and platters of cranberry oatmeal cookies. Julia accepted a steaming, fragrant mug of cider and seated herself in the middle of the arc of chairs rather than close to either end. She knew what was coming next, and she didn't want to go first.

When everyone had taken their seats, Sylvia moved to the center of the open circle carrying a flickering candle in a spherical crystal holder. There she paused to look around at the faces of her guests. "The primary purpose of the Candlelight ceremony is for you to introduce yourselves to us and to one another," she said. "But our ceremony helps you to know yourselves better too. It helps you focus on your goals and wishes, and helps prepare you for the challenges of the future."

Although Julia had heard Sylvia speak these words before in summers past, she still felt a frisson of anticipation. The familiar phrases seemed like an invitation for the campers to embark on a journey together, one with marvelous opportunities for growth and renewal. If ever there was a time Julia hoped the words would prove prescient, it was this week, with these people.

Sylvia continued by explaining the ceremony. The company would pass the candle around the open circle, and as each person held the candle, they would explain why they had come to Elm Creek Quilt Camp and what they hoped to take away from the experience. "Would anyone care to volunteer to go first?" Sylvia asked, looking first to Paige at one end of the arc, and then to Edna, the costume designer, on the other, just as Julia, safely in the middle, had anticipated.

Paige raised her hand. "I'll go first." Catching the eye of the costume designer, she added, "If that's all right with you?"

"Be my guest," said Edna. "I need time to think of what to say."

"Well, about that." Paige frowned thoughtfully. "Haven't we all come to quilt camp for basically the same reason, and don't we all want to accomplish the same thing? We're all here to learn to quilt or to improve our skills so we can contribute to the show, right?"

A murmur of agreement went up from the circle. Sylvia looked around, eyebrows rising in mild surprise at this unprecedented mutiny. Julia caught Nigel's eye, and his suddenly guarded expression reminded her that they both had ulterior motives Paige wouldn't suspect and they'd rather not disclose.

"If I'm perfectly honest," said Louis, the pianist, "I'm here because the head of our department wanted to send a representative, and I needed the overtime." As laughter rose from the circle, he added, "But I'm glad to be here, and I'll use everything I learn about historical quilting to make your sets better."

"Okay, well, maybe *some* of us have *slightly* different reasons for why we came to quilt camp," said Paige, smiling across the circle at Louis, "but as for what we hope to get out of it, that's pretty much the same for all of us, right? Like Louis said, we all want to help improve the show."

"Then let's omit the second question," said Ellen, shrugging.

"Better yet, let's change it," said Olivia, eyes sparkling with mischief in the firelight. "After we say why we accepted Julia's invitation, let's each reveal something about ourselves no one else here knows."

A murmur of approval met her words, but Julia's heart thudded. If she ever kept anything secret from her colleagues, it was for a good reason.

"Is that allowed?" Lindsay asked Sylvia, uncertain. "We wouldn't want to disrespect your traditions."

"It's quite all right," Sylvia assured her. "You aren't our typical group of campers, and so our typical questions might not suit you as well. By all means, share secrets rather than goals, if you wish—but let's agree that nothing said within this circle shall be divulged outside it."

"Can I use it in my novel if I change the names?" Jason asked.

"No," said Julia and several others emphatically.

"Okay, I'll begin," said Paige, sitting up taller. "I came because I'm a newbie to the cast and I want to get to know you all better before we begin shooting season six. As for something none of you knows about me—well, there are lots of things, but an important one is that I first discovered my love of acting when I was six years old. My parents are hardcore Civil War reenactors, and as soon as I was old enough to stay in character for hours at a time, they put me in a homemade costume and brought me along to their encampment." Smiling, she gave a little bow and, to a round of applause, passed the candleholder to Lindsay on her left.

Lindsay held it thoughtfully. "I came to quilt camp because my mother has been coming here for a week every summer for years. She's told me so much about this wonderful place that I had to see it for myself." She hesitated, and a little sheepishly added, "As for something no one here knows about me, I used to play accordion in a polka band."

"Not so fast," Jason said as Lindsay began to pass the candle. "When was this? What was the name of the band? And most importantly, were you any good?"

"This was years ago, when I was in middle school and high school," said Lindsay, smiling, more proud than embarrassed. "We called ourselves the Silver Pines Polka Dots, and yes, I was very good—good enough to be named Stearns County Polka Princess two years in a row."

To applause and cheers, she passed the candle to the stunt coordinator, Dylan.

"I came to quilt camp because Lindsay asked me," Dylan said when the group quieted down a bit. "I thought, what the heck? What do I know about quilting? What do I need to know? But when Lindsay said we'd be staying at Elm Creek Manor, I had to come. Bergstrom Thoroughbreds may be no more, but those bloodlines run through some of the finest horses in the country to this day." He nodded to Sylvia. "I wanted to pay my respects, and maybe to learn more about the folks behind it."

"Well, that's an answer I've never heard at a Candlelight before," Sylvia remarked, appearing surprised and flattered in equal measure. "I'd be happy to answer any questions you may have."

Dylan nodded in reply and began to pass on the candle, but at the last moment, he caught himself. "Oh, something you all don't know. My middle name is Thomas. I was named after the poet."

"He has a sister named Emily Dickinson," Jason quipped.

Dylan regarded him, puzzled. "How did you know? Have you met my sister?"

"No," Jason said quickly. "I didn't actually think— It was a joke."

"Yeah, I figured. I'm just pulling your chain. My sister's name is Susan."

Everyone burst into laughter, except for Jason, who managed a weak grin.

Around the circle the candle went, hand to hand. Nearly everyone said that they had come to Elm Creek Quilt Camp simply because Julia or Lindsay had invited them and they thought they'd enjoy a unique experience with their work family. "One last hurrah," one of the actors in a recurring role declared happily, but Julia couldn't join in the chorus of agreement that followed. Her eyes met Lindsay's across the circle, and the younger woman offered her a sympathetic, encouraging smile.

The secrets they shared were usually humorous, and often surprising. Louis revealed that he had a Master's of Music in Piano Performance from a conservatory in San Francisco and had performed on three Oscar-winning soundtracks. "Then why are you working in set design?" queried Jason, as everyone else gasped and marveled.

"Do you have any idea how hard it is to make a living as a pianist?" Louis asked.

"But you've won three Oscars," Julia protested.

"I didn't win anything. The composers did."

"Whatever," said Paige, waving a hand. "As far as I'm concerned, you're an Oscar winner."

"Thanks, Paige," he said sincerely, as everyone chimed in with their agreement.

Julia didn't think Nigel would confess anything she didn't already know, but he surprised her. "You've all complimented me on the flawless American accent I use in *Patchwork*," he said in a British accent that seemed rougher and more glottal than his usual speaking voice, "but my Received Pronunciation is equally inauthentic."

"That's the accent you used in *New Kent Road*," Ellen said.

"Not only that, it's my real accent. The one I grew up with. I'm from London, but I'm not from Knightsbridge or Mayfair."

"I can't believe you never told me that," Julia exclaimed.

"I'm sure there are many things you've never told me, darling," he said, reverting to his more familiar accent, as he passed on the candle.

Julia was so flummoxed that the revelations of the next several colleagues barely registered—and then the candle came to her. "Oh, dear," she murmured, studying the flickering light. She had been considering several inconsequential confessions, but after Nigel's revelation, she knew what she ought to say.

"I always tell people that I'm from Riverside," she began hesitantly, noting the several acknowledging nods around the circle. "I let everyone believe I mean the city in California. I'm really from Riverside, Iowa."

Gasps, exclamations, and a smattering of laughter went up from the group.

"Let me guess," said Jason. "Population twelve?"

"More than a thousand, actually," Julia countered.

"Why wouldn't you want anyone to know you're from Iowa?" asked Lindsay, genuinely puzzled.

"Because I have a glamorous image to preserve, of course. When I was first starting out back in the day, it was all about being a golden California girl. Once the studio created that myth, I couldn't very well admit that it was all a creation of their marketing department."

"Did you grow up on a farm?" Olivia asked eagerly, leaning forward. "Did you milk cows and shuck corn? How did you escape?"

"I did grow up on a farm—two hundred acres that had been in the family for three generations. Neither of my brothers wanted to take it over, so when my parents retired, they sold it to a real estate developer. Now it's a subdivision called Stony Acres."

"Oh, how unfortunate," Sylvia murmured from outside the circle.

"As for how I escaped, I got a scholarship to the University of Iowa. My parents wanted me to be a teacher, but I majored in theater instead. Two days after graduation, I caught a bus for Southern California and never looked back."

"Never?" echoed Lindsay, dismayed.

"Well, no, not exactly never. I was being dramatic."

"Occupational hazard," said Nigel.

"Before my parents died, I would visit them twice a year, when I could afford the bus fare. After I was more established, I offered to move them out to California to escape the brutal Iowa winters, but their roots were deeply planted, and they politely refused. My brothers left Riverside long ago." Julia smiled ruefully and passed the candle to her left. "So there really hasn't been any reason to go back."

Hardly anyone she knew lived there anymore, Julia reflected as the next person in the circle cleared her throat and began to speak. She had outgrown her hometown long before she left it.

When the candle completed its circuit, Sylvia returned to the center of the open circle. "This has certainly been a unique Candlelight," she remarked. "I hope you all feel as if you know one another quite a bit better than you did before."

There were murmurs of agreement and thanks, and a few good-natured jokes about accordions, small Midwestern towns, and what other secrets might be lurking in their pasts. Then Sylvia reminded them of the important details they had learned at registration about how the next day would proceed—breakfast, classes, and so on—and she wished them a good night.

"Before we part company," Nigel boomed in the voice Julia knew well, the accent she would always think of as his true one, "I'd like to make a toast."

Everyone obliged him by raising their mugs or glasses, even though most were nearly empty.

Standing, Nigel raised his mug and regarded Julia fondly. "Thank you, Julia, for putting together such an exceptional outing for us so we may prepare for our final season in fine style."

Julia managed a pained smile and nodded graciously.

"May we have a successful week, and leave better friends—and better quilters—than before." He looked around the circle. "Here's to Julia, and here's to us all. We few, we happy few, we merry band of patchwork players!"

"Here's to us," Ellen cried, and a chorus of voices chimed in assent.

"Here's to the Patchwork Players," Julia declared, raising her mug, and this time her smile was unfeigned.

11

Early the next morning, Julia joined Ellen, Lindsay, Paige, and Edna for Olivia's lively Zumba class in the children's playroom on the third floor, which, as Sarah had promised, had a CD player, smooth hardwood floors, and plenty of space to move. After hurrying back to her suite to shower and change, Julia went down to the banquet hall to join a delicious buffet breakfast already in progress. She was pleased to see that everyone seemed to be in excellent spirits, well rested and eager to discover what the first day of class would bring.

As nine o'clock approached, Sylvia and Gretchen opened the double doors on the southern wall and invited the company to follow them into the ballroom, which took up almost the entire first floor of the newer wing of the manor. It looked entirely different by day than it had the night before by firelight, with autumn sunlight streaming through tall, narrow windows topped by semicircular curves lining the south, east, and west walls. A wide, carpeted border encircled a broad parquet dance floor, most of which was subdivided into classrooms by tall, movable partitions. Three crystal chandeliers hung high above from a ceiling covered with a swirling vine pattern of molded plaster. A dais on the far side of the room served as a stage for teachers, lecturers, or performers during the camp season, with a baby grand piano at center stage and a lectern at stage right.

On the wall opposite the dais stood the large fireplace where the company had gathered for Candlelight the previous evening. Since then the hearth had been swept clean and the metal log holder newly filled, no doubt evidence of Matt and Andrew's early morning duties around the estate. The eighteen chairs from the ceremonial circle had been returned to the classrooms, but several armchairs and a love seat had been arranged cozily around the fireplace, and new logs were stacked for a fire, awaiting only the touch of a match.

Sylvia and Gretchen led their guests into one of the larger classrooms and invited everyone to choose a spot at any of the tables arranged in four rows of three. Each place was supplied with a green cutting mat, a pair of scissors, a clear acrylic ruler, a piece of sturdy card stock, and two well-sharpened pencils, one white and the other a standard No. 2. While the students took their places, the teachers went to a counter-height table at the front of the room, where several stacks of folded fabric and other supplies were arranged on top of a green cutting mat. Overhead, a large, rectangular mirror could be tilted to allow students to observe an instructor's work on the tabletop. On an easel beside the table stood a poster-sized illustration of a Nine-Patch quilt in dark, muted hues. Since Julia already knew how to quilt, she took a seat in the back row so the newbies could enjoy the better view up front. Edna, the costume designer, claimed the second chair at Julia's table, likely for the same reason.

When everyone was settled, Sylvia raised a hand for their attention. "Welcome to your first class at Elm Creek Quilt Camp," she said as conversations quieted. She gestured to her companion. "Your instructor today will be Gretchen Hartley, whom you met at registration. I'll be here to assist, so if you have any questions, you may call on either of us at any time." With that, she nodded to Gretchen and made her way to the back of the classroom.

"Good morning and welcome," Gretchen said, clasping her hands together and smiling around at her pupils as if she saw in each of them the potential to become a master quilter, or at least a more confident hobbyist. She was in her late sixties—younger than Julia, although she looked a year or two older—with steel-gray hair cut in a pageboy and a thin frame that seemed whittled down by hard times. Clad in a cable-knit tan cardigan buttoned over an ivory blouse, a long, dark blue corduroy skirt, and sensible shoes, Gretchen seemed perfectly cast in the role of teacher. Julia had taken classes from her before, and she liked her very much for her quiet, thoughtful manner and kindness, through which a core of decency and strength was evident. Though Gretchen was one of the newer members of the faculty, she was one of their most experienced quilters, having taken her first lessons from none other than Sylvia herself as a high school student in Ambridge, Pennsylvania. As far as Julia could tell, Gretchen's knowledge of and love for traditional quilting surpassed those of anyone at Elm Creek Manor, perhaps even Sylvia herself.

"I understand you all want to learn how to quilt as Sadie Henderson would have done back in the day," said Gretchen. "Except for a few necessary modern flourishes—electric lights in the classroom, acrylic rulers, and stainless-steel pins and scissors, for example—we're going to do precisely that as we make a quilt together." She indicated the illustration on the easel. "This quilt, to be precise."

"We're going to make an entire quilt in less than a week?" asked Lindsay, who, having lived with a quilter most of her life, knew exactly how daunting a challenge that could be.

"That's the goal, but we probably won't finish it entirely," Gretchen acknowledged. "We'll definitely piece the top, layer and baste it, and begin quilting. We'll also have you practice binding a quilted top we've already made, so you'll know how to complete your quilt after you return home."

"Quilting bee at Julia's," Olivia sang out, glancing over her shoulder to grin at her.

"Splendid idea," said Nigel.

"Please say yes, Miss Julia," Paige implored. "You throw the best parties."

"Fine, just invite yourselves over," Julia said, feigning exasperation, but she couldn't hold back a smile. "Yes, let's definitely plan on a quilting bee at my place soon after we return home."

"First things first," Gretchen said, amused, and everyone swiveled back around in their chairs to give her their attention. "One of the most important parts of the quilt-making process is choosing a pattern or design. We've taken the liberty of choosing for you—call it a teacher's prerogative. We're going to make Nine-Patch blocks." She held up a simple block of nine small squares arranged in a three-by-three grid, five squares of maroon floral calico in the corners and the center, and four of unbleached muslin in the spaces that remained.

"That doesn't seem terribly difficult," Nigel remarked. "We should all manage quite nicely."

"Speak for yourself, in any accent you like," said the production assistant. "To me, that looks really hard to make."

"It isn't, once you know the basic steps," Gretchen assured her. "Speaking of steps, after you've selected a pattern, you must choose suitable fabrics." She paused to consider. "Actually, sometimes a quilter *first* finds an absolutely wonderful fabric and *then* searches through pattern books to find the perfect block to show it off, but it's usually the other way around."

Julia nodded, thinking of the fabric Donna had chosen for the Cross-Country Quilters' first challenge quilt, a beautiful print of burgundy, loden green, and purple autumn leaves on a rich beige background, exquisitely drawn and highlighted with silver ink. Even Megan, who for some unfathomable reason didn't like the color purple, found it lovely to work with.

"When quilters choose fabrics for a quilt, they usually think first of color and print," Gretchen continued. "However, it's just as important to consider value."

"'Value'?" Paige echoed. "Do you mean like how expensive the fabric is, like, silk versus polyester?"

"No, although you raise an important point," said Gretchen.

"We're going to be using one hundred percent cotton fabric. Most quilters prefer cotton, unless they're making an art piece that calls for a more eclectic mix. You're likely to get better results if you use better-quality cottons, such as those you would find at a quilt shop. Unfortunately, the fabrics available at big box stores are often of a looser weave and lower thread count, and the dyes may be less colorfast. Quilts made from poorer quality fabrics tend to show more wear and tear and fading over time."

Beside Julia, Edna nodded emphatically in assent. She probably ran into the same issues in making costumes.

"Although I do encourage you to use good-quality fabrics, that's not what I mean by value," said Gretchen. "To the quilter, value refers to how dark or light a color is, how much black or white has been added to a hue. It's important to include contrasting values in a quilt so the block pattern can be seen. We describe a fabric's value as dark, medium, or light." She held up a LeMoyne Star block with four star points of pink and four of green against a white background. "In this example, the green fabric reads as dark, the pink as medium, and the white as light. The eight-pointed star is crisp and clear, easily visible." Setting the block on the table, she picked up a second LeMoyne Star block, with what appeared to be star points of light beige and ecru on an ivory background. "In this example, all three fabrics have a light value." She studied the block. "I suppose the ecru is *almost* medium, or medium light. Even so, there's very little contrast, so the eight-pointed star design is difficult to see. From a distance you might miss it entirely."

"What if that's the look you're going for?" asked Jason.

"Then by all means, follow your heart," Gretchen replied, smiling. "You'll find that there are few hard-and-fast rules here at Elm Creek Quilts. Usually when the so-called 'quilt police' insist upon telling us what we can or can't do, we thank them for sharing and then cheerfully ignore them."

"'Quilt police'?" Paige echoed, as the rest of the class grinned or chuckled.

"You know," said Lindsay, "the kind of people who believe that the only *correct* way to do something is *their* way."

"For your Nine-Patch blocks, we'll be using reproduction prints of dark and medium values for the focus fabrics and unbleached muslin for the background," said Gretchen. "Reproduction fabrics are designed by modern manufacturers using palettes and prints from bygone eras, but they're made using modern methods and dyes. A reproduction fabric is often an exact duplicate of a historic print, but it could also be a historically accurate adaptation of a historic print. Reproductions are different from actual vintage fabrics, which can be difficult to source and are often too expensive for your average quilter."

"We use reproduction fabrics all the time in the costume department," Edna remarked. "We couldn't get by without them."

Gretchen nodded, pleased. "Maybe you'll see some of your own favorite prints in our collection." She beckoned to Sylvia, who returned to the front of the room and helped Gretchen distribute the stacks of folded fabrics evenly upon the table. "Please come on up and choose one fat quarter of a focus fabric—the darks and mediums, here—and one fat quarter of unbleached muslin. We'll start with those of you in the front row and work our way back."

"'Fat quarter'?" Olivia echoed as she rose from her front row seat and went forward to browse the stash.

"The cotton fabrics we use are about forty-four inches wide from selvage to selvage. The selvages are the top and bottom edges of the fabric, which are finished during the weaving process to keep the fabric from fraying or unraveling," Sylvia explained. "Fabric is sold by the yard, so when you buy a yard of quilting fabric, you're buying a piece thirty-six by forty-four inches."

"If you divide a yard of fabric into four equal pieces by making three cuts selvage to selvage, you have four strips, each nine inches wide. Quilters call those skinny quarters," said Gretchen. "If instead you divide that yard by making one cut down the middle vertically, and a second horizontally, you would end up with four eighteen-by-twenty-two-inch pieces—fat quarters. Most quilters find that fat quarters are more versatile than skinny quarters because of their shape and size."

By this time, everyone seated in the first two rows had selected their fat quarters, so Julia, Edna, and the other back row students went up front to pick theirs. Julia chose a lovely Prussian blue fabric with a floral vine pattern in white.

"Our next step is to make a template," said Gretchen. "For a twelve-inch Nine-Patch block, we'll need only one template, a three-inch square. To make hers, Sadie Henderson might have used stiff paper or newsprint, or even a piece of thin wood, but we're going to use card stock."

"Another nod to modernity?" asked Olivia.

"Exactly," said Gretchen. "Now, using your pencil, scissors, ruler, and card stock, make a three-inch square. Since this is such a simple shape, we won't be fussy about exactly how you do it, but you should be as precise as you can."

Julia promptly took pencil and ruler in hand, lined up the three-inch marks of a corner of the ruler with a corner of the card stock, traced the ruler's perpendicular edges, and cut out a square. She assumed she would be the first to finish, but Edna had beat her to it, and was already leaning across the aisle to help a bemused Dylan. Gretchen and Sylvia were strolling the aisles, offering assistance and praise where needed. Belatedly realizing that as a fairly experienced quilter, she too could help the newbies, Julia quickly glanced around to see whether anyone was struggling, but Gretchen and Sylvia had everything well in hand. She resolved to be quicker out of the starting gate next time.

"Is everyone ready for the next step?" Gretchen asked, returning to the front of the room. "Very good. Now we'll cut out the five dark and four light squares we'll need for our blocks." Adjusting the overhead mirror so the class could see the top of her worktable in the reflection, Gretchen demonstrated how to use the template to make block pieces. "First, lay your fabric right side down on your cutting board. Next, place your template on the wrong side of the fabric and trace around it carefully, using whichever pencil shows up best."

Gretchen paused to watch while the class dutifully followed her instructions. "Well done," she said when everyone had finished. "Now take your scissors and carefully cut a quarter of an inch around the drawn line."

"Why don't we cut on the line?" asked Paige.

"The drawn line is your sewing line. The extra quarter inch is the seam allowance," Gretchen explained. "If you prefer, rather than estimating, you can use your ruler to mark a quarter-inch line all the way around your template tracing. Then cut out your piece. Just be sure to cut along the outermost line."

Julia preferred the accuracy of that second drawn line, so she took up her ruler and pencil again and drew a cutting line. She had no sooner picked up her scissors when Edna set hers down, already finished cutting her first piece. "You must have a lot of practice estimating seams," Julia said, impressed.

"Decades of it," said Edna. "My problem is that I'm used to working with larger seam allowances—a half inch for most seams so the garment drapes better, a full inch for side seams, and a good three inches for hems. These narrow seam allowances will take some getting used to."

"If they were any bigger," said Julia as she cut out her Prussian blue square, "I imagine it would be difficult to press seams flat in places where several pieces meet, like in the center of a LeMoyne Star."

"I suppose that's true."

"Thank you for that, Edna. You're the expert, but you make me feel so clever."

"Has everyone made their first square?" Gretchen asked as she strolled the aisles, nodding in satisfaction at the chorus of yeses.

"Good. Now I want you to measure your square. Is it precisely three and a half inches square?"

"How precise do you mean?" asked Jason. "Is an eighth of an inch, give or take, good enough?"

"Sorry, but no, it isn't," said Gretchen. "I do mean *precisely* three and a half inches. An error of an eighth of an inch might not seem like anything to fuss about, but such mistakes can accumulate over the width of a block, and over the span of a quilt top. Before you know it, your square is no square at all and your rectangular quilt is a rhombus."

Jason studied his fabric piece. "When you put it like that, I think I need a do-over."

"As do I," Nigel lamented. Glancing over his shoulder at Julia, he said, "You neglected to warn me how difficult this would be."

"Don't blame me," Julia teased. "How was I to know you couldn't draw a square?"

He glowered comically and set himself to the task. After he, Jason, and a handful of others made a second, more accurate square, Gretchen instructed them to use their template to make four more squares from their focus fabric and four from the unbleached muslin, measuring carefully. Julia took her time, joining in the conversations and teasing among the company. When she finished, she arranged her nine perfectly accurate squares in their proper places on the cutting mat and admired them. They would make a very charming Nine-Patch block after she sewed them together.

Gretchen and Sylvia continued to stroll through the classroom, complimenting and encouraging their students. When everyone had finished, Gretchen returned to the front of the room. "Congratulations," she declared, smiling. "You each have all of your pieces, and now you're ready to stitch them together. Let's take a break to stretch our legs, and meet back here in fifteen minutes. Maggie Flynn will be joining us, and she'll teach you how to sew a running stitch."

"I believe we've done quite enough work for one day, don't you?" said Nigel, his baritone booming over the sudden din of conversations and bustling as everyone pushed back their chairs and rose. "Why don't we take the rest of the day off and defer our first sewing lesson until tomorrow morning, when we can confront the challenge afresh?"

"Sounds good to me," said Olivia, lacing her fingers together behind her back and raising them in a stretch. "I want to explore the estate while the sun is shining."

"But it's only midmorning, and we have so much to learn," Julia protested. During the summer, campers enjoyed classes, workshops, and lectures from morning to evening, pausing only for meals and little else. It was unthinkable to call it quits after a single class.

But more of the company were joining the chorus in favor of postponing the next lesson until the next morning. "It's your week to spend as you wish," said Sylvia, looking mildly surprised, but not at all offended. "We're happy to adjust the lesson plans if you wish to have more free time. We should still be able to introduce you to all of the essential steps for making a quilt, but you may have less time to practice them."

Everyone except Julia seemed just fine with that, so, since she already knew how to quilt, she resigned herself to their preferences. Sylvia and Gretchen conferred quietly for a moment before Sylvia announced an alternative schedule for the day so effortlessly that Julia was genuinely impressed, for they couldn't possibly have anticipated such a sudden and dramatic overturning of their plans. Sylvia offered to escort campers on a tour of the manor, and she volunteered Matt to lead a walking tour of the grounds, gardens, and orchards. Andrew would chauffer those with an interest in antiques to Union Hall to view the exhibit of historic quilts Summer Sullivan was curating for the Waterford Historical Society. The second-floor library was open for browsing and reading, and the classroom with all of its sewing machines, tools, and supplies would be available for anyone who wished to experiment on their own. Lunch service would begin at noon and dinner at six, but otherwise, the Patchwork Players were free to relax and enjoy themselves however they pleased.

As the group dispersed, chatting happily like schoolchildren released for recess, Julia tried not to be disappointed that they weren't staying together in a single, merry band of players as she had expected. Her colleagues were enjoying themselves and making memories, and that was what really mattered.

Julia had packed *My Journey with Harriet*, the Harriet's Journey pattern book, and a selection of fat quarters just in case she found some free time to work on her quilt, so she retrieved them from her suite and set up in a classroom outfitted with sewing machines, cutting tables, pressing boards, and irons. The block of the week was Cross and Chains, a striking, two-color pattern with triangle-squares in the corners, a square-on-point in the center, and a Four-Patch set on point along each of the sides. Compared to the squares for Nine-Patch blocks the campers were making, those for Cross and Chains were very small, and measured an odd size of less than three-quarters of an inch. Julia used her leftover card stock to make a template, and before long, she was engrossed in the meditative work of tracing, cutting, pinning, and stitching. She felt so at home at Elm Creek Manor that for minutes at a time, she forgot she wasn't there for her annual summer reunion with the Cross-Country Quilters. She would glance up from her work, ready to share a bit of Hollywood gossip with her friends or to ask about their families, only to find herself in an empty classroom, and rather lonelier for the reminder.

But the distant hum of a sewing machine told her she wasn't entirely alone, so she set her work aside and went in search of her unknown companion. In a nearby classroom, she found Edna singing to herself as she fed large, paired pieces of fabric swiftly beneath the needle of a sewing machine. An iron was plugged in on a nearby ironing board, and brightly colored cotton prints were scattered on a cutting table. The pieces of fabric seemed too large for a standard quilt block, so Julia assumed Edna was whipping together a garment, without any pattern Julia could see.

Julia hesitated at the threshold, wanting to call out a greeting, but reluctant to interrupt an artist at work and maybe cause an irreparable error. She lingered a moment, hoping Edna would glance up, smile, and beckon her inside, but when she didn't, Julia returned to her own classroom. Still, as she took up her needle again, she felt better knowing that her nearest companion was only a few steps away.

She finished two of the Four-Patch segments by noon, when the sound of voices and laughter, and her rumbling tummy, reminded her that her friends and colleagues were gathering in the banquet hall for lunch. Anna had arranged a tempting soup, salad, and sandwich buffet, so Julia helped herself to a deliciously aromatic bowl of brown rice and lentil soup, accompanied by a generous slice of apple cider bread. Throughout the meal, everyone shared stories about how they had spent their free time, from raves about Summer's exhibit of historic quilts to fascinating details from the manor's early years and Sylvia's ancestors, among whom were several courageous abolitionists, suffragists, and veterans. Ellen and Jason had spent the morning writing in the library, while the apprentice prop maker had abandoned Matt's tour to follow the siren call of a band saw to the woodshop Gretchen's husband, Joe, had set up in the old red barn west of the manor, and had spent the morning debating the merits of wooden versus metal planes and whether hand- or machine-cut dovetails were superior. Paige, who shyly claimed the seat beside Julia, had gone for a run and had taken a lengthy call from her agent, who was working on lining up a new project for her as soon as season six of *Patchwork* wrapped.

"Wouldn't you rather have a season seven of our show instead of casting about for something new and unknown?" Julia inquired, sipping her herbal tea.

"Sure, but that's not an option," said Paige, absently tearing a bit of crust off her sandwich.

"Until *Patchwork* is officially canceled, there's still a chance."

"Oh, Miss Julia," said Paige, sympathetic. "It's hard. I get it. But like my mama says, 'Every ending is a new beginning.'"

Julia decided that Paige didn't get it at all—and why should she? She had her whole career, her whole life, still ahead of her. "Maybe for you," Julia said, managing a wan smile.

She was far less sure about herself.

After lunch, the Elm Creek Quilters offered another round of the morning's tours and activities, so Julia joined Nigel, Dylan, Olivia, and a few others for Matt's tour of the estate gardens and orchards. Julia knew the grounds quite well from her previous visits, but she had never seen them in autumn, and never with an expert guide describing the natural and cultivated flora, the landscape architecture, and the organic farming techniques that kept the orchard thriving. It was a cool, crisp day, and Julia found the walk quite invigorating after her rather sedentary morning, but she was happy to return to the cozy warmth of the manor. Chef Anna was keeping a table in the banquet hall well supplied throughout the day with carafes of hot coffee, tea, and apple cider, as well as plates of cookies, so Julia poured herself a cup of tea, carried it back to the classroom she had claimed, and resumed piecing her Cross and Chains block.

She had just begun the last Four-Patch segment when someone began playing scales on the baby grand piano, swift and sure. The dais wasn't visible from her classroom, but when the pianist finished warming up and moved into Beethoven's Piano Concerto no. 3, she knew it must be Louis at the keyboard. His music kept her entertained throughout the afternoon until the moment he abruptly stopped playing. She heard indistinct voices, a brief conversation, followed by a respectable performance of "*Für Elise*" that ended early in a burst of laughter—Louis's, presumably, but also a young woman's. Paige or Lindsay, perhaps? Curious, Julia quietly stole from her classroom and down the partitioned aisle, but by the time she had a clear view of the dais, they had left.

Bemused, Julia returned to the classroom and finished the last

Four-Patch segment just in time to pack up her things, tidy up her workplace, and head upstairs to freshen up before dinner. She hadn't checked her email all day, so she spared a moment to log in. There were newsletters from charities she supported, two queries from her publicist, two chatty additions to the long-running Cross-Country Quilters' email chain, and a message from Maury. "I hope you're enjoying quilt camp," he wrote. "Can we meet early next week after you return home? Lots to discuss, including the two movie scripts on my desk, each with an excellent role for you."

Julia felt a heady rush of excitement. Not one but *two* potential movie roles—Maury was a genius, a magician, a miracle worker. Quickly she opened her calendar; Monday wouldn't work, Tuesday was questionable, but Wednesday afternoon was entirely free. She dashed off a reply and waited a minute or two just in case he responded immediately, but the voices and quick footsteps in the hallway outside her room reminded her that she was expected elsewhere. Maybe she should call Maury after dinner. It was three hours earlier in California, so she wouldn't interrupt his evening plans, and she wasn't sure she could wait an entire week to learn more about these two movies. Was she being offered a role or merely the opportunity to audition? Were they leading roles or supporting? So many questions only Maury could answer. She shouldn't get her hopes up before she spoke with him, but it was hard not to get a bit carried away.

She hurried from the room and down the hall, her steps light—but as she descended the grand oak staircase, her pace slowed, her smile faded, and her hopes drifted downward, no longer in danger of soaring too high. Maury knew that what she wanted most was another season or two of *A Patchwork Life*. Why was he even considering any new parts for her?

Once she would have reveled in the happy dilemma of choosing between several promising new roles, but now was not the time to lose focus. All that mattered was saving her series. Anything else was a perilous distraction.

12

The next morning, Julia woke refreshed after a wonderful night's sleep in the lovely suite she had come to think of as her own. Rising and stretching, she decided that the best way to sustain her good mood was not to give Maury's email another thought. Easier said than done, perhaps, but the day promised to offer an abundance of pleasant distractions.

Although her calf and shoulder muscles ached a bit from the previous day's workout, she nonetheless pulled on her exercise clothes and hurried upstairs to the playroom. Amid the toys, books, and craft supplies, Paige and Lindsay were chatting as they stretched in the space Sarah had cleared, and Olivia was inserting a disc into the CD player. Julia had just taken her place on the floor when Edna arrived with Marisa, the production assistant, a new addition to the class. At the last possible moment, just as Olivia started up the music, Ellen scurried in, downing a cup of coffee.

"Late night writing?" Julia inquired as the warm-up began.

"Late night and into early morning," Ellen admitted, bleary-eyed but cheerful. "I was on a roll and I didn't want to stop."

"I told you Elm Creek Manor would inspire you," Julia teased, but she left it at that. The choreography would soon become too complex for conversation.

Later, after a shower and change of clothes and a quick but tasty breakfast, Julia joined the other Patchwork Players in the classroom. Their block pieces remained where they had left them the previous morning, but new notions had been added to each student's supplies—a small, plastic box of shiny sewing pins; two needles called sharps, inserted in a piece of black felt for safekeeping; a spool of light beige thread, the same hue as unbleached muslin; a thimble; and a seam ripper. Sylvia wasn't there, but Maggie Flynn had joined Gretchen at the front of the classroom.

"Maggie is our resident expert in nineteenth-century sewing and quilting," Gretchen introduced her, smiling fondly at her fellow instructor. "She'll be taking over the class today, and I'll be her assistant. Maggie, take it away."

The class welcomed Maggie with a warm round of applause, which she clearly wasn't expecting, judging by her shy smile. She looked younger than her forty years, with long waves of light brown hair held back by a tortoiseshell barrette, hazel eyes set in a gentle, oval face, and a sprinkling of freckles across her nose and cheeks. "Today I'll teach you how to hand piece a quilt block, just as Sadie Henderson would have done back in the late nineteenth century." She gave their worktables a searching look before nodding, satisfied. "I see you all have your block pieces ready to go, so let's begin."

Demonstrating with two fabric squares of her own, she instructed them to take one of their focus fabric squares and one of unbleached muslin, place them together with the right sides facing, and pin them together on the sewing line. "You can pin the corners first, and then ease the fabric smooth along the width," she said. "Use as many or as few pins as necessary to keep the fabrics secure. If you've measured, drawn, and cut your squares correctly, they should be the exact same size, so the sewing lines should match up perfectly, corner to corner."

"How perfectly do you mean, exactly?" asked Jason. "Is there, you know, an acceptable margin of error?"

"There really shouldn't be any noticeable difference," said Maggie.

"If one of your squares is larger than the other, measure them and see which one is correct."

"Perhaps they're both wrong," Nigel suggested, prompting chuckles and grins from the others.

"No, I'm good," said Jason, setting his ruler aside. "I'll just stretch this one a little and it'll be fine."

Julia was about to caution him not to distort the fabric, but before she could speak, he grasped his muslin square by two corners and tugged fiercely. He looked so pleased with his solution that she let it go. At least he hadn't torn it in half.

"Now that you all have your first two squares properly pinned," Maggie said, looking around the room to make sure, "let's sew them together. First, cut a piece of thread about the distance from your elbow to your fingertips. Anything longer is likely to tangle; anything shorter and you'll have to interrupt your sewing to cut another piece soon."

The students followed her instructions, some with brisk confidence, others more tentatively. When everyone was ready, Maggie told them to tie a knot at the end of the thread.

"What kind of knot?" Jason asked.

"A bowline knot," Dylan quipped. "Or a double overhand stopper."

"I'd rather a half Windsor," said Nigel.

"A simple overhand knot will do," said Maggie, amused. "No need to complicate things. You can double knot it if you want to make it extra secure."

Julia deftly tied a double knot, then removed one of the needles from the felt and threaded it. From the corner of her eye, she saw Edna doing the same.

"Now take one of your needles, slip the other end of the thread through the eye, and pull it through about a third of the way," said Maggie, demonstrating.

"Done and done," Edna said, so quietly that only Julia could hear.

"We're at the head of the class," Julia murmured.

"There's only room for one at the top," Edna retorted, grinning, "and that's going to be me."

"In your dreams."

By then the rest of the class had caught up to them, even those who had never held a needle before.

"Now we'll sew our squares together using a running stitch," said Maggie. "This is a row of small, even stitches along the sewing line that runs through both pieces of fabric without overlapping." She held up two white fabric triangles stitched together with black thread along the longest edge. "Usually we choose a thread that matches the fabric, but in this case, I chose black for contrast so you could see the stitches better."

"It looks like a dashed line," said Paige.

"That's right." Setting aside the example, Maggie picked up her pinned squares in her left hand and her threaded needle in the right. Narrating each step and holding her work so it was readily visible in the overhead mirror, she placed her needle at the very end of her drawn sewing line, pushed the tip through both layers, and slipped it through to the top again, staying on the line and catching only a small bit of fabric. "That is a single running stitch," she said, pulling the thread through until it caught on the knot. "Now you try. Feel free to wear a thimble, if you wish, to protect your fingertip."

"I can't even fit my pinky into this thing," remarked Dylan, the largest person in the company.

"We have a variety of sizes," Gretchen said. "If anyone would like something larger or smaller, raise your hand and I'll come by with the basket."

Julia had brought her favorite thimble from home, so she was all set. Edna had brought an entire sewing case. "Race you," Edna murmured, but before Julia could even pick up her pieces, Edna set hers down on the table, securely stitched together, and folded her hands. "Done."

"Not fair," Julia murmured back, feigning outrage. "You took a head start."

Maggie and Gretchen were strolling the aisles, checking the students' work and offering advice to those who were confused. Returning to the front of the room, Maggie showed her own work again. "Now, since this is the very beginning of our sewing line, we're going to take a backstitch to secure it. First, push the needle back down through the first hole you made, or at least very close to it. Then push the needle back on through to the top again a little further down the sewing line, as if you're making another running stitch." She showed them how it was done, pulling the thread smoothly through the layers and tugging gently to demonstrate that it held fast, but not so tightly that the fabric bunched together as if it were on a drawstring. "You should always backstitch at the beginning and the end of your sewing line. Some hand piecers like to take a backstitch every five or six stitches to keep the thread tension consistent."

Julia had never heard that tip before. She decided to try it as she worked on her Nine-Patch, as an experiment. She didn't hand piece often, but she always enjoyed adding new skills to her repertoire.

"Has everyone made a good, secure backstitch?" Maggie asked, looking around the room, smiling at the mix of tentative nods and loud affirmatives. "Let's make two more running stitches along the drawn sewing line. Keep your stitches small, neat, and even in size."

Julia complied, except that she made four stitches rather than two. Setting her work on the table and folding her hands, she turned to Edna smugly—only to find that Edna was still sewing. "Follow instructions," Julia admonished in a whisper.

"Instructions are for the timid, and fortune favors the bold," Edna replied, but she set down her work and waited for everyone else to catch up.

"Go ahead and finish your seam," Maggie said as she strolled the aisles, inspecting their work. "Carefully remove the pins as you come to them. When you reach the end point of your sewing line, stop, make a backstitch, and tie a secure knot. Take care not to sew into the seam allowance. For some blocks, that makes no difference, but for others it's essential, so let's practice sewing point to point only."

After everyone completed their seam and tied a knot, Maggie instructed them to trim the extra thread, fold the seam allowances toward the darker fabric, and crease the seam flat with a fingernail. Next, they each sewed another focus fabric square to the opposite side of the muslin. "Congrats," Maggie praised them when everyone had finished. "You've made the top row of your Nine-Patch block."

"Huzzah!" Nigel boomed, brandishing his row overhead, evoking laughs and cheers from his friends.

"Now let's repeat all of those steps to make the bottom row," said Maggie, through her own laughter. "When you've finished that, sew two muslin squares to opposite sides of your last focus fabric square to make the center row."

For the rest of the morning, the Patchwork Players worked on their blocks, chatting and teasing, seeking help from their teachers, picking out stitches that didn't fall on the line or were much too big. Edna completed her three rows swiftly—no surprise there—with enviably small, perfectly even stitches. Julia was the next to finish. When Gretchen saw them chatting and realized they were ready for the next step, she directed them to the ironing table to press their rows. "Lift and press with a hot iron," Gretchen said, demonstrating for the class with Julia's top row. "Avoid sliding the iron around, because you might distort the fabric."

When Julia and Edna were finished at the ironing table, they returned their neatly pressed rows to their worktable and joined the Elm Creek Quilters in wandering the aisles, offering help or advice to anyone who needed either. As more of the company finished and proudly or gleefully made their way to the pressing table, Maggie announced that she would teach them the next step after lunch. "Take all the time you need to finish your rows," she told the others reassuringly. "Gretchen and I will be here to help, or just to cheer you on.

If you've finished, you're welcome to spend the rest of the morning as you wish—touring the manor, exploring the grounds, reading in the library, helping Anna in the kitchen, babysitting Sarah's toddler twins—" She broke off, interrupted by the company's groans and laughter. "What?" she asked, feigning bewilderment. "I thought Julia said this was a *working* vacation."

"There's work," said Olivia, indicating her nearly completed center row, "and there's *work*." Grimacing, she tilted her head in the approximate direction of the kitchen.

Tempted by Maggie's offer of time on their own to explore or relax, some of the company who had completed their rows wandered off, and more followed after they too finished, but Julia remained, taking the empty chair at Nigel's table and coaxing him through his last few seams. "My fingers are too big for this tiny needle," he grumbled, but not unhappily.

"A bad workman blames his tools," she teased. "The needle is the standard size for hand piecing, and there's nothing wrong with your fingers that practice won't cure."

Thanks to such encouragement, or perhaps in spite of it, Nigel completed the last seam, tied off the thread, and pressed the three respectable rows, and he wasn't even the last to finish. That honor went to Dylan, who waved them on their way when they offered to stay and keep him company. "You actors might not understand this," he said, "but some folks prefer to work without an audience."

"I can't imagine," Julia said, incredulous, but she smiled at Dylan over her shoulder in parting.

As they left the ballroom, Julia took Nigel's arm. "Where to? The verandah, to admire the view? The kitchen, to spoil the broth with too many cooks?"

"The library," he replied firmly, gesturing toward the grand oak staircase. "I believe that's where Ellen prefers to write. I hope to trick her into revealing what lies ahead for Ben Atherton in season six."

"If tricking her doesn't work, you could try asking."

"No," he mused aloud as they climbed the stairs. "She's too clever to fall for that."

At the top of the stairs, they turned down the hallway, passing two guest suites on the right and the balcony open to the foyer below on their left. Just past the staircase to the third floor, the hall ended at a pair of French doors, which Julia was surprised to see had been left open as if to beckon readers inside. The library was also the business office for Elm Creek Quilts, so it was not available to guests during the summer camp season. In all the years she had attended camp, Julia had been invited into the library only once before, for a private conversation with Sylvia. Even now, knowing the Patchwork Players had been given browsing privileges, when Nigel strode briskly inside, Julia hung back a moment before following cautiously after him, ready to turn back if they interrupted Sylvia and Sarah in the midst of a confidential discussion.

Just like the ballroom directly below, the manor's stately library spanned the entire width of the manor's south wing. Light spilled in through tall diamond-paned windows on the east and west walls, and between the windows stood tall bookcases, shelves bowing slightly under the weight of hundreds of volumes. A fire burning in the large stone fireplace on the south wall made the library warm and snug, but Julia remembered from her previous visit that in summer, gentle cross breezes kept the room comfortably cool on even the sunniest days. On the wall beside the fireplace hung a most unusual Winding Ways quilt comprised of nine panels, nine blocks each, hung side by side so closely that they appeared to be a single, unified whole—or they would have, except that the sections in the two lower corners were absent, with only slender, brushed-nickel rods and brackets to indicate where they belonged. The pieced mosaic of overlapping circles and intertwining curves, the careful balance of dark and light hues, and the unexpected harmony of the disparate fabrics and colors evoked the sense of many winding paths meeting, intersecting, parting, creating the illusion that the separate sections formed a single quilt.

Julia recalled what Sylvia had told her when she had admired the striking artwork: that Sylvia had made the quilt as a gift for the original Elm Creek Quilters, the fabrics and colors of each panel selected especially for its designee. As there were eight founding members and nine panels, Sylvia had dedicated the one in the center to all the Elm Creek Quilters who might join the faculty in the future. "The Winding Ways quilt reflects partings and reunions," Sylvia had explained. "When one of our circle must leave us, she takes her section of the quilt with her as a memento of the loving friends awaiting her return. The empty places on the wall remind those of us left behind that the beauty of our friendship endures, even if great distances separate us. When the absent friend returns to Elm Creek Manor, she returns her panel to its proper place, and the loveliness of the whole is restored."

"What a marvelous tribute to your friendship," Julia had exclaimed at the time. Thanks to the Cross-Country Quilters, she too had been blessed with friends whose affection and loyalty endured regardless of the distances that separated them or the many months that passed between reunions.

Julia's gaze lingered on the quilt a moment longer, but Nigel was scanning the room for Ellen. Two armchairs and footstools sat invitingly before the fireplace, and more chairs and sofas were arranged in a square in the center of the room, but only Jason sat there, furrowing his brow and biting his lower lip as he typed on his laptop. Nor was Ellen seated in the tall leather chair behind the large oak desk that had once belonged to Sylvia's father. That place had been claimed by none other than Sarah McClure herself, her long, reddish-brown hair tucked behind her ears as she glanced between the spreadsheet on her computer and the stack of paperwork on the desktop, entering data with her right hand and holding her toddler daughter firmly on her lap with the other. Caroline was deeply engrossed in a board book, but she looked up to study the newcomers, keenly interested.

"Alas," Nigel grumbled. "My quarry eludes me."

"Hello and welcome," Sarah greeted them, smiling. "Looking for a good read?"

"Yes," said Nigel, peering around the library as if Ellen might suddenly emerge from behind an armchair. "But it isn't here."

When Sarah's eyebrows rose, Julia quickly clarified, "He's searching for Ellen. He hopes to steal a look at what she's written for his character in season six."

"Don't tell her that," Nigel protested. "She might warn Ellen, and I won't get so much as a glimpse of the title page."

Julia rolled her eyes. "Sarah won't tell anyone."

"Dis a good book," Caroline said to Nigel, holdings up hers, arms outstretched, leaning over so far to give him a better look that she would have toppled off her mother's lap except that Sarah instinctively grabbed her with both arms.

"I'm sure it's a delightful story, my dear Miss Caroline," said Nigel earnestly, "but sadly, it isn't what I'm looking for."

Caroline squirmed down from her mother's lap, tucked the book under her arm, and toddled over to Nigel. "Dis a good book too," she said firmly, taking his hand as if to lead him to the sofa, although when he didn't budge, she was limited to tugging on his arm.

"I think she wants you to read to her," Julia said, amused. "Your line is, 'I'd be delighted to read you a story, my dear.'"

"But I wanted to—" Nigel broke off as Caroline nodded solemnly up at him and held out the book, confirming Julia's interpretation. Muffling a sigh, he accepted the offering. "*The Tale of Peter Rabbit*," he noted, glancing at the cover. "A somewhat abridged version of the classic, but a classic nonetheless. Very well. Lead on."

Caroline smiled and led him to the sofa, where she waited for him to be seated before scrambling up beside him.

"If you don't do distinct voices for each character I'll be terribly disappointed," Julia teased.

Nigel gave her a sidelong look, mildly affronted. "As if I would do otherwise." He opened the book and held it so Caroline could easily see the illustrations. "'Once upon a time there were four little Rabbits, and their names were Flopsy, Mopsy, Cotton-tail, and Peter.'"

As Nigel continued reading, Sarah rose from the desk and came to stand beside Julia. "How is camp going so far?" she asked softly. If Caroline heard, she was too entranced by the story to look up. "Are you and your friends enjoying the class?"

"Everything has been absolutely perfect," Julia assured her. "We're all having a wonderful time. I can't thank you enough for accommodating us in the offseason."

"It's my pleasure, believe me," said Sarah. "Your generosity bought us a new roof and then some."

Julia was very glad to hear it. "All I did was to offer a reasonable fee for the expert education, accommodations, and services Elm Creek Quilts offers. You could have charged more and I would have paid it willingly."

Sarah stifled a laugh. "I'll remember that the next time a group of Hollywood stars wants to book a getaway week." Then her smile dimmed. "I've wanted to extend our season into the fall for years, and given our current financial issues, it's almost a necessity. If this trial run is a success, Sylvia may finally give me her blessing."

"So you're saying there's more at stake than whether our merry band of players quilts flawlessly in season six?" Julia inquired, smiling to hide a sudden pang of worry.

Sarah hesitated. "I'm saying that I'm very grateful for this opportunity," she said, choosing her words carefully. "If there's anything more I can do to help you and your colleagues make the most of your visit to Elm Creek Quilt Camp, please let me know."

"I will, but I honestly can't think of a thing I'd ask you to do differently. At the end of the week, you'll hear rave reviews from our entire company, I'm sure of it."

Sarah thanked her with a smile, but there was strain around her eyes that Julia hadn't noticed before.

When Nigel finished the story, Julia invited Sarah and Caroline to join them for lunch. Sarah thanked her but declined, explaining that she and Matt usually ate together in the kitchen with the twins, whose mealtime behavior was still rather unpredictable. "Matt and I don't mind the occasional chaotic meal," she added, swooping Caroline up in her arms, "but it's not something we want to inflict on our guests."

So Julia and Nigel went down to the banquet hall without them, where they served themselves from the tantalizing buffet and parted ways. Nigel had spotted a single unoccupied chair at Ellen's table, and he was determined to claim it, while Julia was determined to spend time with colleagues other than her closest friends. During the regular season, the Elm Creek Quilters always dispersed among the campers rather than sitting at a table reserved for the faculty, the better to create a friendlier, more welcoming, more inclusive atmosphere, or so Donna had said a few years ago, and she had heard it directly from an Elm Creek Quilter. As the organizer of their quilting adventure, Julia felt more like one of the hosts than one of the campers when they weren't in the classroom. If anyone wasn't perfectly content, she wanted to know so she could resolve whatever problems there might be.

She was pleased to see an empty seat at Dylan's table, so she joined him and four other members of the crew. They had been engrossed in conversation as she approached, but it trailed off awkwardly as she sat down. "What did I interrupt?" she asked, glancing around the table in mock alarm. "You're not plotting to nominate me for a Razzie, are you?"

She was rewarded with a few chuckles, but no one rushed to answer. She tasted her salad and waited, eyebrows rising. "It's a union matter," Dylan eventually said. "And you're a producer. You're . . . management."

"Oh, I get it." Julia sipped her iced tea thoughtfully. "Fair enough, but I'm an actor first and foremost, and a proud union member myself. I bet I've walked more picket lines than the rest of you combined. So please, as you were. Carry on."

Dylan laughed, and others smiled, and a few nodded thoughtfully. Tentatively at first, but then with their former enthusiasm, they resumed their friendly argument, with Julia occasionally chiming in with relevant information from her own union. They were so engrossed that they barely noticed the banquet hall emptying, and they might have lingered at the table far longer if Sylvia hadn't come by to remind them that class was about to begin. Quickly, laughing at themselves, they hurried to the classroom and took their seats with not a moment to spare.

"Now that you've made your three rows, let's sew them together," Maggie said. "First, you'll pin carefully along the drawn sewing line and use a running stitch to join the rows together, adding a backstitch at the beginning and the end. So far it sounds familiar, right?"

"Yes, but it can't be that easy," said Olivia. "What's the catch?"

Maggie smiled. "When you reach a seam where you sewed two squares together to make the row, you have to handle it in a certain way. But don't worry. It's easy once you know the technique."

She instructed them to pin their top row to the center row and to begin sewing, but to stop before they reached the first seam. When everyone had caught up, Maggie demonstrated how to abut the opposing seam allowances and sew through them. "If you're sewing by machine, you can just sew right over the seam allowances," she noted, "but a different technique is required for hand sewing."

Slowly and carefully, holding her work so it was visible from the front and from above in the overhead mirror, Maggie sewed the top row to the center row right up to where the seam allowances met, where she made a backstitch. "On my next stitch, I just want to get to the other side of the seam allowance, so I'm not going to sew through both rows," she emphasized. "Slip your needle into the sewing line end point of your focus fabric square and out through the end point of the muslin square." She demonstrated, pulling the thread all the way through and leaving the seam allowance free. "Make another back-stitch to secure it, then continue your running stitch along the sewing line until you reach another one of those seam allowance junctions. Handle that one the same as you did the first." She looked around the room expectantly. "Are you ready to give it a try?"

Most of the class had already begun, following along throughout Maggie's demonstration. Julia deftly sewed through her first seam allowance and was well on her way to the second when Edna finished.

"Show off," Julia teased.

"Jealous?"

"Very."

They laughed together, and Maggie, curious, paused by their table. "You two are making excellent progress," she praised, smiling. "In fact, you're so far ahead that I'm going to ask you to make another Nine-Patch block together."

"Will we get extra credit?" Julia asked.

"Oh, absolutely. You'll each receive an automatic A-plus."

From the row in front of them, Paige turned around in her seat, eyes wide. "We're not seriously being graded for this, are we?"

"No, not at all," Maggie quickly assured her, and Paige turned back around, relieved. "But I really would like you to make another block," Maggie told Julia and Edna, lowering her voice. "We'll need twenty to complete our quilt top, but even with my sample block, we're one block short."

"We're on it," Edna said. Maggie thanked them and brought them another two fat quarters.

The afternoon passed pleasantly as the Patchwork Players finished their Nine-Patch blocks. After everyone finished sewing their top and center rows together, Maggie demonstrated how to attach the bottom row. Even though she had urged them to make sure they were sewing the rows together in the proper order, several students had to pick out stitches, move the bottom row to the correct orientation, and try again. The last step was to press their blocks and hold them up for the rest of the class to admire.

Maggie encouraged them to work at their own pace and to take breaks whenever they wished, whether to stretch their legs with a walk on the verandah or to enjoy a cup of coffee or tea in the banquet hall. Conversation filled the classroom—industry gossip, fond reminiscences about favorite moments from past seasons of *A Patchwork Life*, and wildly exaggerated descriptions of the hazards of filming on location in wintery rural Kansas, for the benefit of the cast and crew who had never enjoyed that dubious pleasure. It was all so convivial and entertaining that nearly everyone lingered until the very last aspiring quilter finished their last seam, and all twenty Nine-Patch blocks were neatly pressed and ready to be sewn into a quilt.

"But not tonight," Gretchen said, smiling. "Tomorrow morning will be soon enough, especially since I've been told that Anna is about to serve dinner."

The company happily returned to the banquet hall, where the conversation and camaraderie proved to be as delightful and satisfying as Anna's delectable cuisine. Afterward, a few left the gathering to spend time on their own, but most returned to the ballroom, where someone had built a fire and the kitchen staff had set up the evening's carafes of coffee, tea, and mulled apple cider and plates of autumn desserts—mini apple tarts, pumpkin cookies, sweet potato petit fours. Paige asked Louis to play the piano for them, so sweetly and persistently that he downed an apple tart in a single bite, brushed off his hands, and took the stage. After entertaining them for twenty minutes with music from classic film scores, he played a dramatic glissando. "Enough of the solo act," he called to his audience. "I need a vocalist." He shaded his eyes with his hand. "Is that you, Paige, raising your hand? Fantastic, thanks for volunteering."

"It wasn't me," Paige called back, shaking her head. "I think it was Miss Julia."

"It definitely wasn't me," Julia said. "Go on, kid. Take the stage."

Lindsay began chanting her name, and as everyone else joined in, Paige blushed furiously and stepped onto the dais to cheers and applause. She and Louis conferred briefly, and as he played the opening measures of "Someone to Watch Over Me," Paige drew a deep, steadying breath and took center stage. She had a sweet, pure, enchanting voice, and as the young pair moved from one jazz standard to another, Julia could not miss the smiles and swift glances they exchanged.

"Is it just me," Nigel murmured to Julia as the delighted audience applauded between songs, "or are there sparks lighting up that stage?"

"It isn't just you," Julia replied thoughtfully. Showmances could be a messy business. Julia had seen more than one successful series go down in flames after a rancorous breakup destroyed the stars' onscreen chemistry, but Louis wasn't an actor so *Patchwork* was in no danger of that. If nothing else, at least Paige wasn't pining over the unavailable Noah anymore.

After Louis and Paige took their bows, Julia herself was cheerfully ordered to take over at the piano. She willingly went, but she dragged Nigel onstage with her, he feigning reluctance so comically that everyone laughed until tears came to their eyes. Nigel would have sung his entire repertoire of baritone show tunes except Julia's hands were tired by the time he finished his fifth piece. As they bowed and left the stage, Louis was persuaded to return to the piano, his audience's cheers and applause so loud that Julia wondered whether Sarah and Matt were struggling to put their toddler twins to bed with all that racket.

But her fleeting concern really was quickly forgotten as she gazed fondly around the room at her friends and colleagues, their faces aglow with happiness and firelight. They were the found family she had always wanted. How could anyone expect her to give up, bow out, and watch them go their separate ways?

13

On Wednesday morning, Julia caught up with Nigel as the company was making their leisurely way from the banquet hall to the ballroom. "You cornered Ellen at dinner last night and again this morning at breakfast," she remarked. "You must be trying to discover the secrets of her scripts in progress, or to influence how she shapes the season's narrative arc, or both."

"Obviously," he replied, casting her a sidelong look.

She nudged him with her shoulder. "Don't leave me in suspense. Have you had any luck? What have you learned?"

"More than I reasonably could have hoped for." He slowed his pace as they approached the classroom so they wouldn't be overheard. "Ellen didn't divulge any major plot twists, but she did promise to give me some Emmy-worthy monologues and a very satisfying character resolution in the finale."

"Really?" Julia gasped, impressed. "Is she giving you a dramatic death scene?"

"She wouldn't say, but hope springs eternal."

"Well, if you do get a death scene, I hope Ben perishes in Sadie's arms." Julia could envision the moment perfectly—Sadie sitting on the prairie grasses, her skirt spread out around her, illuminated by a brilliant sunset in the wide Kansas sky, embracing Ben, who lay on her lap, eyelids fluttering as his life slowly slipped away, both of them exchanging at long last the confessions of love they had withheld until the very end. "That would be glorious for both of us."

"Indeed it would. A finale for the ages."

She almost laughed—but her breath caught in her throat. What was she thinking? She didn't want a finale, glorious or otherwise, in season six. Ellen should file away any such ideas and revisit them in a few years, but it was certainly premature to kill off Ben now. "Did Ellen say anything about her plans for Sadie?"

"Sorry, darling. Not to me, she didn't. But she may divulge something this evening. She finished writing a scene last night and I believe she hopes to workshop it."

Julia would have asked for more details, but they had entered the classroom, and an urgent, whispered conversation would have drawn too much attention.

When everyone had taken their seats, Gretchen welcomed them back to class and announced that they would now begin assembling their completed Nine-Patch blocks into a top. "If you look closely at our diagram," she said, gesturing to the illustration on the easel, "you'll see that our quilt is made up of eleven rows framed by an outer border. But there are two different types of rows: five rows of Nine-Patch blocks, and six narrower rows of sashing between them." She indicated the different rows as she described each type. "Sashing refers to strips of fabric that separate the blocks of a quilt. Cornerstones are squares of fabric that join sashing strips together."

"Both are entirely optional design elements," Maggie added as she walked down one aisle and up the other distributing fat eighths of a dark blue reproduction print, one piece for each table to share. "You can have sashing strips without cornerstones, or you can dispense with sashing altogether and simply sew adjacent blocks to one another with nothing in between."

"Exactly," said Gretchen. "The layout of a quilt is one of many design choices a quilter makes. Sashing can separate complex blocks so each one is more distinct. Sewing adjacent blocks together can create interesting secondary patterns. Whatever you choose, do so with intent, whether it's to create a certain artistic effect or to express a mood or theme."

Julia was pleased to see the other Patchwork Players following along with interest, some of them nodding. Jason appeared to be taking copious notes.

"There's another, more pragmatic reason to add sashing to a quilt," said Gretchen, smiling. "It allows you to increase the size of your quilt without all the work of making additional blocks. And since we've made only twenty blocks for our Nine-Patch quilt, and we have less than a week—" She spread her hands and shrugged. "Adding sashing seems like an especially good idea."

As her classmates nodded or chuckled, Julia studied the diagram thoughtfully. To her, the sashing and cornerstones seemed to be an essential part of the design, not a cheat code for enlarging their quilt. Even so, Gretchen made a fair point.

"This morning we'll begin by cutting sashing strips from your muslin and cornerstones from the dark blue fabric Maggie handed out just now," Gretchen continued. "First, I'd like you to cut three rectangles from your unbleached muslin, each three and a half inches by twelve and a half inches. The actual finished size of our sashing strips is three by twelve inches. Can anyone figure out why we're cutting our rectangles larger?"

"Margin of error?" Jason guessed.

Gretchen shook her head. "Sorry, no, that's not it."

Paige's hand shot into the air. "Seam allowance," she blurted when Gretchen glanced her way. "We're adding a quarter-inch seam allowance to all four sides, so that would add a half inch to the length and width."

"That's exactly right," said Gretchen. "If anyone needs a refresher on how to make a template, let me or Maggie know."

Two people tentatively raised their hands, but everyone else set themselves to work, chatting and bantering, as always. They were still at it when Gretchen addressed the class again. "After you cut your rectangles, cut two three-and-one-half-inch squares from the dark blue," she said, as she strolled the aisles observing their work. "These will be our cornerstones."

"Two squares per piece of fabric?" Olivia asked.

"Two squares per person. We actually won't need that many squares for our layout, but I want everyone to practice making them."

Soon thereafter, when all of the sashing strips and cornerstones were prepared, Gretchen instructed each student to sew a sashing strip to their Nine-Patch block. "It doesn't matter which edge you choose since the blocks are symmetrical," she said, as Maggie demonstrated with her sample block. Edna finished her seam before Julia did, so she sewed a sashing strip to the additional block Maggie had asked them to make.

"Next, table partners should sew their blocks together," Gretchen told them when everyone was ready. "This time it *does* matter which edge you choose. Be sure to sew a Nine-Patch to a sashing strip so that you make an alternating row like the one in the diagram. Whatever you do, avoid sewing a Nine-Patch to a Nine-Patch or a sashing strip to a sashing strip."

"Sounds serious," Jason remarked. "What happens if you *don't* avoid that?"

"The quilt police will arrest you," said Dylan.

"Nothing so dramatic as that," said Gretchen. "You'll just have to pick out the stitches and do it again, correctly."

Fortunately, everyone followed the instructions and did it right the first time, checking their work against the illustration and seeking help if they weren't sure how to proceed. Julia sewed her block to Edna's, while Edna sewed the block they had made together to Maggie's block.

Next, Gretchen told them, the students at two tables would pair up and sew their segments together, taking turns wielding the needle.

Between the two of them, Julia and Edna had enough segments already, which worked out perfectly since there were an odd number of tables. Afterward, each group sewed a single sashing strip to the remaining unsewn edge of the fourth Nine-Patch to create a full, four-block row. As each group finished, they took turns carefully pressing their blocks, then strolled the aisles admiring their friends' work.

When all five Nine-Patch block rows were finished, Gretchen explained how to make the sashing rows in a similar fashion, sewing dark blue cornerstones to a short edge of a sashing strip, then joining those units into pairs and sewing another cornerstone to the end to make six sashing rows.

So the morning passed, with the Patchwork Players sewing and chatting together, sometimes switching seats to join a different conversation or to better encourage or tease a friend. With everyone working together, even with occasional breaks for coffee or tea, to stretch their legs or rest their fingers, they managed to finish sewing and pressing all eleven rows just in time for lunch.

As the enticing aromas of Chef Anna's latest culinary marvels beckoned the company to the banquet hall, Julia fell in step beside Ellen, who was frowning pensively. "Something on your mind?" Julia inquired. "Working through a particularly tangled plot development in a new script? You can always bounce ideas off me."

"Thanks, but that's not it." Ellen halted just inside the doorway. "Even with all eighteen of us working diligently, and with Maggie pitching in her sample block, it took us all morning to make our eleven rows. We'll need the entire afternoon to sew them together, and that's if we keep up our current pace."

"And that's unlikely," said Julia ruefully, massaging her hands. "My fingers are already feeling the strain, and I'm sure I'm not alone. We'll all need to take more frequent rest breaks as the hours go by. Maybe not Edna. She's used to sewing all day long."

"But let's say we do manage to finish by dinnertime. We won't be able to start cutting and attaching the borders until tomorrow morning. Those are long seams, and only one person can sew at a time." Ellen paused to think. "Maybe two people could sew borders to opposite sides, but that would be awkward."

"Awkward, but not impossible."

"True, but even then, I don't see how we'll be able to finish the quilt top, layer and baste it, put it on the frame, and begin quilting before Friday. We will have spent several days on piecing, but only a few hours on quilting, which is the skill we need most for the camera."

Julia felt a stirring of unease. "I don't know what else we could've done. We can't practice quilting until we have a top to quilt."

"We shouldn't have quit work so early on Monday," said Ellen, shaking her head. "I should've spoken up at the time, but everyone was eager to explore, and I wanted to have the afternoon to write—"

"Is something wrong, ladies?" asked Sylvia. Julia had not seen her approach, and both she and Ellen glanced up, startled, to find her regarding them with concern. "You both look rather apprehensive."

"It's nothing serious," Julia quickly assured her, mindful of Sarah's fervent hopes that the week would go perfectly.

"It's a *little* serious," said Ellen, and proceeded to explain.

"We must see what we can do about getting you to the quilting process sooner, without doing anything Sadie couldn't have done," Sylvia mused when Ellen had finished, with Julia chiming in a few details. "You two enjoy a nice, relaxing lunch. In the meantime, I'll consult the other Elm Creek Quilters. We'll come up with a solution."

Ellen hesitated a moment, for it was against her nature to abandon a problem without thoroughly discussing it. Yet when Julia thanked Sylvia for her help and steered Ellen toward the buffet table, she came along willingly. During the meal—Julia and Ellen both chose the pumpkin curry with tofu, served with warm ginger naan—they observed Sylvia conferring with Maggie and Gretchen over by the butler's pantry. They were too far away to be overheard, but they were smiling and nodding as their conversation ended and they went their separate ways. Julia and Ellen agreed that this was an encouraging sign.

They had just finished eating when Sylvia approached their table. "Would you two please join me upstairs for a moment?" she asked. "I believe I have just the thing to speed your sewing along."

Curious, they rose and followed her from the banquet hall and across the foyer. When they reached the grand oak staircase, they let the octogenarian master quilter precede them, setting a comfortable pace up the grand oak staircase and onward to the third floor. Most of the guest suite doors were closed, but one down the south wing hall was open. As they approached, Julia heard two low voices in easy conversation.

"Right this way," Sylvia said, beckoning. Julia and Ellen followed her into the guest suite, but they barely crossed the threshold. The room was haphazardly packed with cartons, trunks, and odd bits of furniture, including an antique treadle sewing machine. Matt and Joe, Gretchen's husband, were attending to it, Matt polishing the gleaming black arm, Joe working the foot pedal slowly up and down, nodding in satisfaction when it moved smoothly and quietly.

"That's beautiful," Ellen exclaimed, glancing about as if she wanted to draw closer but couldn't find a clear path through the clutter. Julia had never seen any room in Elm Creek Manor in such disorder.

"Is that the treadle sewing machine your great-grandmother Anneke brought with her when she immigrated from Germany?" Julia asked, remembering Sylvia's stories about the founding of Elm Creek Farm.

"Oh, goodness, no. Anneke's machine is about one hundred and fifty years old. It doesn't function as it once did, although thanks to Joe's restoration work, it serves as a beautiful decorative table in the parlor." Sylvia rested her hands on her hips and cast a speculative eye over the sewing machine. "Joe and Matt, I must say you've done excellent work with my great-aunts' treadle too. How did the test run go?"

"A perfect seam," Matt replied, holding up a piece of black fabric with three neat parallel rows of stitches down the center in white thread. "Joe had to adjust the tension discs, but now it's good to go."

"Excellent." Sylvia turned to Julia and Ellen. "My great-aunts Lydia and Lucinda acquired this machine around eighteen ninety. They retired it when they purchased an electric version a few decades later, but they kept it in good working order for occasions when they needed a second machine. I realize this is a later model than would have been available to Sadie Henderson during the years you're portraying on your program, but the technology would have been very similar. You're welcome to use it to finish piecing your quilt top, if you aren't absolute sticklers for historical accuracy."

"My great-grandmother actually did own a treadle sewing machine," said Ellen. "It was a Singer, one of her prized possessions. She wrote about it in her diaries."

"Then, since time is of the essence, as far as I'm concerned, the Bergstrom great-aunts' sewing machine passes the stickler test," Julia said. "Also, you never know how training on a treadle might be useful later."

"Are you sure you don't mind us using it, Sylvia?" asked Ellen. "None of us has ever used a treadle, as far as I know, and this beautiful machine is more than a century old. I'd hate to destroy a family heirloom."

"I wouldn't have offered if I feared that you might." Sylvia picked her way through the clutter to join them at the door. "Furthermore, once I teach you how to use it, you'll manage just fine."

"Thank you," Julia said quickly, before Ellen could talk Sylvia out of it. "We're grateful, truly."

"It's my pleasure." Turning to Matt, Sylvia asked him to carry the machine downstairs to the ballroom, where the other Patchwork

Players were likely already taking their seats and preparing for class to resume. Julia and Ellen scrambled into the hallway as the burly caretaker hefted the sewing machine, holding it well above the boxes and trunks as he carried it from the room. The machine didn't appear too heavy for him, but it was rather awkward to hold, so Joe and Ellen preceded Matt down the stairs, the better to guide him or to break his fall if he stumbled. Julia and Sylvia trailed along behind them.

When they reached the second-floor landing, Julia said, "It's none of my business, but every time I've visited during the summer season, all of the guest rooms on the third floor are occupied, and—"

Sylvia gave her a sidelong look, amused. "And you're wondering why that one looks like a pack rat's den, unsuitable for human habitation?"

"Well, yes, although I hope I would've found a more tactful way to put the question."

"If you think that's bad, the two rooms on either side are in a similar state. When we cleared out the attic before the roofers began their work, we had to put all that clutter somewhere. Gretchen, Andrew, and I spent days up there sorting, discarding, and donating things I no longer wished to keep, but we ran out of time. In the end we simply hauled the remaining trunks and boxes into these bedrooms to get them out of the way. We haven't been using them since August, so it was easy to put everything out of sight and out of mind."

"But what happens when your regular season begins in March?"

"We'll need every single one of our suites to be in pristine condition, of course," Sylvia said. "I certainly have my work cut out for me, don't I? That will be my snowbound-in-winter project—opening all those trunks and boxes, discovering what trash or treasure they hold, and deciding what to do with everything."

"You mean you haven't even taken a peek?" Julia asked. "Those trunks and boxes could be full of quilts, or vintage gowns, or fascinating family photographs, or—"

"Gold doubloons?" Sylvia finished for her, eyebrows rising. "That would certainly be welcome."

"Maybe you won't find an entire trunkful of gold coins, but you'll surely find things that are priceless in their own way. How can you put off the search? Aren't you curious?"

"Of course I'm curious, and I have opened several lids and glanced inside, but I'm also exceptionally busy." Sylvia smiled at Julia over the tops of her glasses. "When I do get to work, I'll be sure to let you know if we discover pirate treasure or a long-lost, handwritten draft of President Lincoln's Gettysburg Address."

When Julia and Sylvia caught up with the rest of the group at the foot of the grand staircase, Matt had carefully set down the sewing machine to give his arms a good shakeout. But he soon picked it up again and carried it into the ballroom. Ellen showed him to their classroom, where the Patchwork Players were gathered around their tables in small groups, laying out block rows and pairing them with sashing strips. Maggie and Gretchen were demonstrating how to pin the two different rows together, right sides facing, opposing seams neatly abutted.

Teachers and students alike looked up in surprise when Matt strode in hauling the treadle sewing machine. "Does it work?" Gretchen asked.

"I've been promised that it sews a perfect seam," Sylvia said, directing Matt to place the sewing machine in the nearest corner.

"Is that one of those foot pedal sewing machine things?" Paige asked. "I used one in an off-Broadway production of *Little Women* last year."

"Then you may be the first student to try this one." Smiling, Sylvia turned her gaze to the students' handiwork. "I see your teachers have you pinning rows together. When you're finished, I'll show you how to use this contraption. It's an antique, but it's still very useful and quite capable." She gave a little laugh. "I suppose I can relate."

"Oh, stop," Julia scolded, joining in the chorus of laughter, groans, and protests, which Sylvia cheerfully waved off.

Soon thereafter, when the first group finished pinning, Sylvia called everyone to gather around the sewing machine. She demonstrated how to place the bobbin, thread the needle, and work the treadle at an even, moderate pace while feeding the fabrics beneath the presser foot, carefully removing the pins as they approached the needle rather than sewing over them. Then, as promised, she rose and invited Paige to take over. Paige happily did, and after a tentative start, she sewed half the length of the row before relinquishing her seat to Edna. The expert costumer swiftly finished the seam, deftly backstitching and tying off the loose threads.

For the rest of the afternoon, the Patchwork Players took turns pinning rows, pressing seams, and learning new skills on vintage technology as they assembled their quilt top. When all eleven block and sashing rows were sewn together and pressed, Gretchen showed them how to cut solid fabric borders from a lovely brown reproduction print and properly fit them to the quilt center by measuring the pieced quilt carefully, cutting borders to size on the straight grain, and sewing on the borders, first the sides and then the top and bottom. As far as speed and deluxe features were concerned, the antique treadle was no match for the sleek, computerized sewing machines campers used during the regular season, but hand sewing all of those seams would have taken days, even with several of the company working on different row pairs simultaneously. Thanks to the Bergstrom great-aunts' contribution to the project, their Nine-Patch quilt top was completely assembled and neatly pressed in time for dinner, or nearly so. Anna held back service a half hour so they could finish.

The company was in excellent spirits at dinner, pleased and proud to have met a challenging milestone. Chef Anna had truly outdone herself with a splendid three-course autumn feast—a salad of mixed greens, roasted beets, candied pecans, and crumbled goat cheese with pomegranate seeds and a maple-balsamic vinaigrette; an heirloom carrot and lentil tagine for the vegetarians and herb-crusted roast chicken with root vegetables for the omnivores; and for dessert, a decadent pumpkin cheesecake with gingersnap crust, with whipped cream and a drizzle of caramel for the especially daring. Everything was so delicious that Julia couldn't decide whether it would be cruel to tell the Cross-Country Quilters about it when they spoke the next day. She could well imagine Vinnie lamenting that Julia had not saved her a piece of cheesecake.

"Julia, I have to hand it to you," Olivia called from the next table over. "This is a truly magnificent way to celebrate the beginning of the end of *A Patchwork Life*. Thank you for putting this together for us."

As others chimed in their thanks, Julia held up her hands to silence them. "It doesn't have to be the beginning of the end," she protested, smiling. "Maybe the end of the beginning, but we have so many stories yet to tell."

"If we're being specific," said Jason, pushing his glasses up the bridge of his nose, "we have twenty-four episodes of season six to look forward to."

Julia's heart sank, while all around her, friends and colleagues were nodding and remarking that they actually would have quite a lot of time together after all. She couldn't disagree more. Twenty-four episodes and the time required to film them would pass all too swiftly. Then the show would be over, and there would be no reclaiming it.

Julia sipped her chamomile tea and tried to hold on to the warm, companionable feeling she had carried with her all day. The company lingered longer than usual over their tea and coffee, mingling between the tables, comically bemoaning their tired hands and needle-pricked fingertips. When the waitstaff began to clear the dishes, someone suggested that they withdraw to the ballroom so Louis could treat them to another concert. A chorus of cheerful assent followed and the company began to rise, but Julia glanced the young musician's way just in time to see him wince.

Paige saw it too, and she rushed to his defense. "Louis has been sewing all day too," she reminded them, projecting her voice so they all paused to listen. "His hands are just as tired as ours. It's not fair to ask him to do more."

"Are you volunteering to entertain us instead?" Dylan asked.

"Definitely not," she said, folding her arms. "Trust me, you do *not* want me playing piano. I'm strictly a vocalist."

"Lindsay, did you bring your accordion?" Olivia asked.

"Sure I did," said Lindsay, laughing. "I packed it in my purse. Give me a minute and I'll go upstairs for it."

"I have another idea if music isn't on the agenda tonight," said Ellen tentatively. "I finished writing a scene for the season six premiere yesterday. I'd love to run it by you all, if you'd indulge me with a table read."

"Absolutely," Nigel's resonant voice rang out, easily drowning out any other single reply. "That is how we shall spend the evening. We owe it to Ellen, to the show, and to our craft."

Julia suppressed a smile. One could almost imagine that his intentions were entirely selfless, but who was she to judge? She wasn't exactly pure of heart herself.

The company headed back to the ballroom, where a fire blazed cozily in the hearth and the customary table of warming beverages and cookies awaited them. Julia wasn't at all hungry after the dinner feast, so when she saw several of her colleagues heading for the classrooms and returning with chairs, she quickly joined them. Soon they had arranged eighteen chairs in a respectable imitation of the open circle from the first night's Candlelight ceremony. Everyone found a seat, some sipping from steaming cups, others with a plate of cookies as well.

One chair was empty. "Who's missing?" the production assistant asked.

"Ellen," Lindsay said, just as their head writer hurried in carrying a stack of papers. "Never mind. Here she is."

"Sarah let me use their office printer." Ellen quickly entered the circle and began distributing a few stapled sheets to everyone. "Is the light too dim?" She glanced upward. "I could turn on those chandeliers, if someone can point me toward the switch."

"It's fine," Julia assured her, glad when everyone else chimed in the same. She didn't want to spoil the lovely firelight.

"Okay. Great." Ellen clasped her hands together, gazed expectantly around the circle, and gave a little start when she spotted the last vacant chair. "Oh, I guess that's mine." Quickly she seated herself. "Okay. Um, so this is an early scene from season six, episode one. Jesse and Anabelle are in the post office."

"Where is Ben?" Nigel wondered aloud, leafing through the partial script.

"He's not in this scene," Ellen replied, but she was looking at Paige. "We're picking up exactly where we left them in the season five finale."

"Anabelle overheard Jesse say something disparaging about Theodore Wedgington, and she confronts him," Paige said.

"And he just gapes at her, overcome by her breathtaking beauty," said Olivia, grinning.

Paige's cheeks went pink. "I think he was just surprised that she addressed him before they had been formally introduced."

"No, he really was overcome by her breathtaking beauty. Now, Noah—" Ellen looked around the circle, looked again, and clasped a hand to her forehead. "I forgot. Noah isn't here. I need someone to read for Noah."

"I'll do it," said Jason, shrugging. "How hard can it be?"

Some of the actors gave him a side-eye.

"I should be honored to read any lines from your pen, Ellen," Nigel said grandly. "Or your keyboard, as the case may be."

"Have Louis read the part," said Julia, inspired. "He's the right age. No offense, Nigel."

"None taken. I quite agree."

"Me too," said Paige, brightening. "Louis, say yes."

Louis hesitated, then shook his head. "I don't think so. I'm a pianist, not an actor."

"But you have such a strong, resonant voice," Paige pleaded. "Just read the scene through with me once. If it's utter torture, you never have to do it again."

She was so lovely and sweet, Julia couldn't imagine how Louis could possibly refuse, and he didn't. "Okay, sure. If you insist. But I'm not giving up my day job. Or my night job."

"Let's take it from the top," said Ellen, beaming. "Anabelle, you have the first line."

"On it." Suddenly Paige drew herself up, her eyes flashing fire at Louis. "'I said, sir, how dare you speak such lies about my uncle?'"

Louis blinked at her, stunned

"Your line, Jesse," Ellen murmured.

"What?" Louis gave himself a little shake. "Right. I'm Jesse."

"Should we start over?" asked Paige kindly, herself again.

"From the top," said Ellen, nodding.

Immediately, Paige transformed again into Theodore Wedgington's spirited, indignant niece. "'I said, sir, how dare you speak such lies about my uncle?'"

"'You're Wedgington's niece?'" Louis said, appropriately thunderstruck. Julia suspected he wasn't acting.

"'I am,'" said Paige crisply. "'And who, may I ask, are you, other than an impertinent young man who obviously knows nothing at all about my dear uncle?'"

"Perfect," Ellen murmured, jotting down something in the margin of her manuscript.

Julia caught Nigel's eye across the circle, and they shared a smile. It hadn't been their imagination. Sparks were lighting up the circle as they had the stage the night before.

Julia was happy for them, of course, but also for herself. Surely Paige and Louis would eagerly commit to another few seasons of *A Patchwork Life* if it meant they could continue to work together.

14

Zumba was especially invigorating the next morning, and breakfast was especially lively, with conversation and laughter flying among the tables. Julia's commitment to dining with new acquaintances rather than her closest friends was bearing fruit, for she had unwittingly encouraged everyone else to mingle freely too. Julia was pleased to discover that there were no longer any strangers within the company. After four days of traveling, feasting, working, and relaxing together, they had all become friends.

As she thrilled to observe Elm Creek Quilt Camp working its magic on her unsuspecting colleagues, she was heartened by her friends' occasional, wistful remarks that they were having such a wonderful time together that they would be sorry to part ways when the show ended. "It doesn't have to end," she would remind them, never allowing her smile to falter even when they humored her with a grin or a sigh and a shake of the head.

But although no one had renounced their plans to leave the series, the Patchwork Players seemed much more inclined to stay together than before they had come to Elm Creek Manor. That was a good foundation to build upon, and they still had three days to go.

Sylvia, Maggie, and Gretchen were waiting for the cast and crew when they arrived at their classroom, which had been rearranged in their absence. The treadle sewing machine had been moved into the corner. The supplies and notions that had once graced each student's place had been cleared away. On the back table Julia and Edna had shared, a striking sampler quilt in rich holiday red, green, gold, and cream hues had been neatly folded, the visible side held snuggly within the circle of a quilting hoop. In the center of the room, two of the student tables had been pushed together, side to side rather than end to end, and draped with a clean, white sheet. Gretchen was at the ironing table pressing open a seam that united two long pieces of unbleached muslin. When the students entered, she smiled a welcome, set aside the iron, and unplugged it. Sylvia was picking stray threads from the Nine-Patch quilt top, which was draped upon the instructors' table at the front of the room. Maggie was at another student table near the front, smoothing the wrinkles from a queen-sized piece of fluffy, white batting.

Some of the students found seats at the unoccupied tables, while others strolled about observing their instructors' work until Gretchen beckoned them to gather around the front table, where she had set a tray of pencils, quarter-inch masking tape, a crosshatch stencil, and several clear acrylic rulers of various sizes beside their Nine-Patch quilt top. "Now that you've finished piecing your charming quilt top," she said, "we need to mark the designs our quilting stitches will follow."

"With pencils?" asked Marisa, the production assistant, dubiously.

"Not with a standard Number Two," Gretchen assured her. "These are special fabric pencils that wash out easily. There are dark colors for marking light fabrics, and white and yellow for marking dark fabrics. Some quilters prefer dressmaker's chalk, but I like the fine, precise line you can draw with a well-sharpened pencil." She went on to demonstrate how to mark the quilting designs on the surface, either by using a stencil or by drawing straight lines with a ruler or quarter-inch masking tape as a guide. "You can also put a printed pattern from a book or magazine beneath the fabric and trace it," she added, "but unless you have a light box, that only works with light-colored fabrics."

Returning her pencil to the basket, Gretchen stepped aside and invited the Patchwork Players to take turns marking the quilt top, using her drawn lines as a template for similar sections of the quilt. Since only a few students could work comfortably at a time, they needed the rest of the morning to mark the entire quilt. They broke for lunch and a half hour of free time, which Julia spent in her room answering emails—but leaving unanswered one from Maury, in which he suggested the following Wednesday at two o'clock for their conversation about future projects. She also set out her Cross and Chains block segments in anticipation of her conference call with the Cross-Country Quilters later. She had told her friends that she would join the call in progress and might not be able to stay on the line long, but not even quilt camp could keep her from their weekly gathering across the miles.

Julia returned to the classroom with a few minutes to spare. She was chatting with Nigel, who was both enlivened and wistful after a long-distance conversation with Alistair, when Gretchen raised her hands for attention. At that moment, Paige rushed into the room. "Sorry," she said to the Elm Creek Quilters, breathless, before offering an apologetic glance to the class. "I was on the phone with my agent."

"Did you get the part?" asked Louis.

"Nothing official yet," she said, her smile somehow both radiant and tentative, "but it's looking good."

"Awesome!" Louis said, sweeping her up in a hug while she squealed with laughter. Julia and Nigel exchanged a significant glance, complete with raised eyebrows.

"Now that you've marked your quilt top," Gretchen called above the general din of questions and congratulations, "we'll teach you how to layer and baste it."

"'Baste it'?" echoed Jason, frowning quizzically. "You mean like a turkey?"

Julia, Ellen, and Edna burst out laughing, while Lindsay and the Elm Creek Quilters smiled indulgently. The other students waited expectantly for an answer, as if they had been wondering the same thing.

"What?" said Jason, glancing over his shoulder at Julia and Edna as they smothered their laughter. "What did I say?"

"Not that kind of basting," Gretchen replied kindly. "Basting stitches are large stitches that hold something in place temporarily. You might baste an appliqué to the background fabric so that it stays put while you blind stitch it down. Or you might baste a hem so it stays perfectly even all around while you finish the seam using your sewing machine. But for us, today, basting refers to sewing large stitches through our quilt top, batting, and backing fabric so the three layers don't shift while we're quilting them. Basting stitches are removed afterward, so you don't need to make them small and pretty."

"So they're functional rather than decorative?" Olivia asked.

"That's exactly right," said Sylvia. "Quilting stitches, which you'll learn later this morning, should be both. You can also baste a quilt using safety pins, but we're teaching you thread basting because that's likely the method Sadie Henderson would have chosen."

Meanwhile, Gretchen had gathered up the freshly ironed seamed sheet of unbleached muslin. "This is our quilt backing," she explained, laying it out on the two tables in the center of the room, wrong side up. The nearest students stepped forward to help her smooth it across the surface until nary a wrinkle remained. Next, Maggie brought over the batting and centered it on top of the backing. Then Gretchen and Sylvia picked up the Nine-Patch quilt top by opposite edges and placed it, right side up, upon the batting.

"Many quilters like to call this a quilt sandwich," Sylvia remarked, gesturing to the assembled stack. "I do have one friend who prefers to call it a quilt parfait."

"Quilt parfait," Maggie mused as she retrieved a packet of tapestry needles and a small, rectangular basket containing spools of thread from a supply shelf beneath the instructors' table. "I think I'm going to use that term in my next pattern book."

Beckoning the company to gather around, Maggie chose a spool of bright pink thread from the basket, cut a long strand, and threaded her needle. Next, she demonstrated how to sew large, zigzag stitches through the three layers, end to end across the width of the quilt. "The color of the thread isn't important," she noted as she slipped the tapestry needle through the layers and pulled the pink thread through. "I prefer to use a color that contrasts with my quilt top, because when it's time to remove the basting stitches, they'll be easier to find." Maggie straightened, glanced around, and handed her needle to Marisa, the long, trailing end of the thread still attached to the quilt. "Now it's your turn."

Tentatively, but soon with more confidence, Marisa continued the row of stitches Maggie had begun. "There's room for more people down the length of the quilt," said Gretchen. "Thread a needle and give it a try."

After a bit of playful grappling for the packet of needles, three more aspiring quilters joined in the basting, looking rather liberated by the thought that their stitches needn't be small and precise as long as they held the three layers together until they could be quilted. Julia hung back and let the others precede her, even skipping her turn to let the newbies get more practice. She was having enough fun simply watching her friends delight in mastering a new skill.

When the quilt sandwich was basted, though, Julia stepped forward and carefully helped roll it up to make it easier to carry to the quilting frame, which Gretchen said was elsewhere in the ballroom. "But first," she said, "Maggie is going to demonstrate how to quilt with a lap hoop."

"My understanding from my conversations with Julia is that you want to know how to quilt at a frame," Sylvia said. "I've watched every season of *A Patchwork Life*, and from what I recall, Sadie Henderson and her friends always prefer that method. However, I believe it's worthwhile for you to learn to quilt with a lap hoop too." She gestured to the back table, where Maggie was retrieving the quilt Julia had noticed earlier. "Both in Sadie's era and today, many quilters prefer lap hoops for their portability, the ease of use when one is quilting alone rather than with a group, and their dimensions. A full-sized quilting frame requires more storage space."

Maggie took a seat in a tall chair Gretchen had placed in front of the instructors' table, draped the sampler over her lap, and reached for her sewing basket on the table behind her. "What quilt is that?" Ellen asked, drawing closer for a better look. "It's gorgeous. I love the bright, clear colors, and all the different block patterns are exquisite. Is this a new Harriet's Journey quilt?"

"It is, and it may be my last one for a while," said Maggie. "I call it Harriet's Holiday for the color palette and the Christmas prints. I meant to make another full-sized Harriet's Journey quilt, all one hundred blocks, but I had only finished thirty-six when I signed the contract for my new pattern book, and I really need to get working on quilts for that—"

"You're writing a new pattern book?" Julia exclaimed.

Maggie nodded, smiling. "Yes, a pattern book for the Loyal Union Sampler, one of the quilts on display in Summer Sullivan's exhibit downtown." The campers who had toured the gallery nodded in recognition. "My publisher wants to include photos of other quilts made from the sampler blocks for creative inspiration, so as soon as I finish Harriet's Holiday, I'll get to work on those."

"Oh, how wonderful! May I tell the other Cross-Country Quilters?"

"My mom will be absolutely thrilled," Lindsay said. "Will the book be out in time for Christmas?"

"Not this Christmas," Maggie said apologetically. "I'm still writing the manuscript. It's fine if you tell your friends and family about it, as long as you explain that it's at least a year away."

"It'll be worth the wait, I'm sure," said Julia. "In fact, take your time. I need to finish my Harriet's Journey quilt first, and I'm only on the third row."

"In the meantime, let's perfect our hand quilting." Balancing the quilt and hoop on her lap, Maggie took a needle from the pincushion in her sewing basket and held it up for all to see. "You used a sharp for piecing and a tapestry needle for basting. Now I'll introduce you to a between. They're thicker and sturdier than sharps, which makes them perfect for hand quilting. This is a nine between. The number indicates the size. The higher the number, the smaller the needle. I usually use a twelve, but nine is a good size for a beginner."

Julia preferred a ten, herself.

Maggie cut a length of beige thread about eighteen inches long and slipped one end through the eye of her needle. "I prefer to use a quilter's knot for hand quilting," she said. While the company watched closely, she held the end of the needle and about a half inch of the thread tail between her left thumb and forefinger. With her right hand, she wrapped the thread clockwise around the needle three times to make a coil. Then, shifting her grip, she pinched the coil and the tail end with her left thumb and forefinger, grasped the needle near the point with her right, and gently pulled the needle through the coil, continuing until the entire length of thread was pulled through and only a small, neat, firm knot remained near the end of the thread.

Next, with her right hand beneath the quilt and her left steadying the hoop, Maggie pushed the needle through the backing and batting and out the top, the tip of the needle piercing one of the drawn quilting lines. Grasping the needle with her right hand and slipping her left beneath the hoop, she pulled the thread all the way through, and then gave the thread a careful tug to pop the knot through the back and into the batting, guiding it along with her left hand.

"Do you see how the knot is concealed within the layers?" Maggie asked, carefully turning the hoop over so they could see the back of the quilt, where neither the knot nor a hole in the fabric was visible. "With practice, you'll learn how to tug hard enough to pop the knot through the backing and trap it in the batting without yanking it all the way through the top."

"That's a neat trick," Dylan remarked. "I guess it beats having a bunch of ugly knots on the back of your quilt."

"Exactly." Maggie gave him an approving nod as she turned the quilt back over. "I'm right-handed, so I'll put my thimble on the first finger of my right hand and put my left hand underneath the quilt." Narrating each step, Maggie demonstrated how to sew through all three layers. First, using the finger protected by the thimble, she pushed the needle through the top of the quilt. When the tip of the needle touched her left forefinger on the other side, she pushed the tip of the needle back through the layers to the top. By rocking her right hand back and forth in this manner, she gathered a few stitches on her needle. Then she pulled the needle and the length of thread all the way through to the top, leaving behind four small running stitches in a straight row along the penciled quilting design.

"Well done," Julia declared, and the company burst into applause.

Maggie looked up from her work, so surprised she laughed. "I've never received a standing ovation for a few quilting stitches before. Usually students just nod and murmur." Smiling, she repeated the motions, slowly and carefully. "Don't worry about making your stitches small at first. Instead, focus on making them of equal length, both on the top and on the bottom. The more you practice, the smaller your stitches will become over time."

She quilted an elegant feathered plume in the center of a star block for another few minutes, pausing now and then to ask the students to trade places so that everyone had the opportunity to study the motions of her hands up close. Then she folded Harriet's Holiday into a neat bundle and set it on the instructors' table. "Now it's time to quilt *your* top," she said, rising from her chair and offering the class an encouraging grin. "Sylvia, if you'd like to lead the way?"

Nodding graciously, Sylvia asked Paige and Louis, who were nearest, to pick up the rolled, basted Nine-Patch quilt and then invited everyone to follow her to the quilting frame. Exiting the classroom, they went around the partition walls and headed for the southeast corner of the room, where the quilting frame awaited them. About four feet across and six feet long, the rectangular wooden frame stood on four sturdy legs that raised it to table height. At the corners were various assemblies of knobs and gears with slender rods running the length of the frame between them. Three chairs were arranged on both of the long sides, allowing six quilters to work comfortably at the same time.

Julia noticed several members of the cast and crew nodding in recognition as they studied it. Sadie Henderson kept a frame very much like this one in her farmhouse—or rather, the prop makers had constructed one for the studio set of the interior of Sadie's home.

But at least one of the company was distracted by the larger, more modern piece of equipment a few yards away. "What is *that*?" Louis asked, giving it an appraising look.

"That is a longarm quilting machine," said Gretchen, turning. "It's a bit flashier than the Bergstrom family's wooden frame, isn't it?"

"Maybe a little," said Paige, with a comical shrug.

"It's essentially a large sewing machine with a long throat—the space between the needle enclosed by the base and the horizontal and vertical arms," said Gretchen. "It's mounted on a system of rails that allows you to move the needle over the surface of the quilt rather than feeding the quilt beneath the needle. When you use a longarm, instead of moving the quilt through the sewing machine, you move the sewing machine across the quilt. Instead of basting your quilt sandwich, you place your quilt top, batting, and backing onto different rollers, pull everything taut and smooth, and stitch away."

"Will we have a chance to try it out?" asked Louis.

"Not with your Nine-Patch quilt, you won't," said Maggie, smiling. "A longarm quilting machine would definitely be a historical anomaly in Sadie Henderson's household."

"That pretty Chandelier quilt on the rollers is Sarah's work in progress," said Sylvia. "I'll ask if she's free to demonstrate the longarm after dinner this evening. I can't make any promises, but she may even allow you to make a few practice stitches on her quilt, in the interest of education."

"I'm sure she'd appreciate the help," said Gretchen. "It's nearly finished, but between work and the twins, she hardly has a minute to spare for quilting."

Edna shook her head, sympathetic. "It's hard to imagine anything more tragic than an Elm Creek Quilter who doesn't have time to quilt."

Julia could think of something more tragic—an acclaimed actress on the verge of losing her beloved, award-winning series—but she didn't say so aloud.

"At the moment, though, you have your own quilt to work on," said Gretchen, beckoning them back to the quilt frame.

After the company gathered around, Gretchen and Maggie carefully placed the shorter ends of the quilt sandwich around the rollers along the long sides of the quilt frame. By adjusting the gears, the three layers could be held firmly and smoothly without being stretched to the point of distortion. The middle of the quilt top was visible now, but when they finished quilting that section, they could bring the other parts into view by adjusting the rollers.

"I have a confession to make," said Gretchen. "For this style of frame, we didn't actually need to baste the quilt sandwich first. We could have just placed the backing, batting, and quilt top around the rollers."

"What?" Olivia exclaimed, feigning outrage. "We did all that extra work for nothing?"

"We wanted to teach you how to thread baste in case you needed that for a future episode," Maggie explained, joining in the company's laughter. "Also, if you're not able to complete the quilting before you leave, your quilt sandwich will be much easier to transport if it's basted."

"Fair point," said Olivia, waving a hand to show that all was forgiven.

"Are we ready to quilt now?" asked Lindsay.

"We are indeed." Gretchen looked around the company, her gaze lingering on Julia, Ellen, and Edna. "Why don't we begin with those of you who have quilted by hand before? Please take a seat, and Maggie will provide the needles and thread."

Julia, Ellen, and Edna promptly seated themselves on one side of the frame, and, when none of the other students came forward, Sylvia, Gretchen, and Maggie sat opposite them. Maggie repeated the steps she had shown them in the classroom, with minor adjustments to account for the differences between working with a small lap hoop and a larger, freestanding frame. Julia and the other quilters threaded their own needles and began quilting the sections in front of them, following the drawn lines with their finest stitching. At first Julia tried to match the Elm Creek Quilters' brisk pace, but she soon gave up and proceeded more slowly, focusing on making her stitches small and even.

The rest of the company watched closely, admiring their work. "What do you do when the strand of thread runs out?" asked Paige.

"What happens when you reach the end of the drawn line?" asked Marisa.

"Two excellent questions," said Gretchen, glancing up from her work to smile encouragingly. "I promise to show you when we get there."

Nigel peered over Maggie's shoulder, studying her hands intensely. "Tell me, Maggie," he asked. "Do you feel that the needle is an extension of you, or that you are an extension of the needle?"

She had to pause to think. "Um, the former, I guess?" She gave her head a little shake and resumed quilting. “No one has ever asked me that before.”

“Is that so?” Nigel replied, his brow furrowing. “I can’t imagine a more essential question.”

Soon thereafter, the quilters relinquished their seats so another group could have a turn. Paige, Lindsay, Jason, and Nigel quickly took their places at the quilt frame; Marisa and Dylan joined them a bit more warily. Yet before long all six were quilting steadily along, gaining confidence, chuckling at their mistakes. After a few minutes, Gretchen asked them to secure their needles in the quilt and inspect their own stitches.

“Mine are pretty terrible,” Marisa admitted. “I’ll get the hang of it, I promise.”

“Mine are straight and even, but they’re huge,” said Paige.

Sylvia bent over for a closer look. “Oh, yes. My great-aunt would have called those ‘toenail catchers,’ but they’re quite good for a beginner. Now I’m going to ask all of you to peek beneath the frame and see how your stitches look from the back.”

As the six novice quilters obeyed, Edna nudged Julia and whispered, “We didn’t have to do that.”

“That’s because she thinks we’re the experts, in comparison,” Julia whispered back. “To be honest, I don’t think my stitches would pass a close inspection.”

“I’m sure mine would,” Edna remarked. Julia gave her a playful shove.

“They look the same to me,” Paige called, her voice muffled through the quilt’s layers. “Huge, but equally huge.”

“Good,” said Sylvia. “That’s the ideal—neat, even stitches the same length on the bottom as on the top.”

“My stitches are equally unequal,” said Marisa as she emerged from beneath the frame.

“They’re perfectly acceptable for your first try,” said Sylvia. “Practice makes perfect.”

"Perfect might be too ambitious for me," said Dylan ruefully as he returned to his seat. "I'd settle for better."

"You'll get there," Maggie assured him, "if you stick with it."

The six got back to work, but soon they rose and let six others take their places. Surely and steadily, the quilt transformed beneath their needles as the quilting stitches added dimension to the pieced pattern. But as the afternoon passed, the students relinquished their places more readily, and a few complained about tired arms, aching necks, and sore left forefingers stinging from too many needle pricks.

"Quilters develop a callus there over time, and the needle pricks don't hurt as much," Gretchen said. "Until then, a bit of medical tape or a second thimble can prevent soreness."

"My mom uses a metal thimble for her needle-wielding hand and a leather thimble for the one beneath the quilt," said Lindsay.

Julia, seated at the frame, nearly dropped her needle. "Your mother." Glancing at her watch, she gasped and rose. "Someone can take over for me. I have to make a phone call."

"Is something wrong?" Gretchen inquired.

"No, not at all. I'm just late for my weekly check-in with the Cross-Country Quilters."

"The who?" Julia heard Louis ask as she hurried away. She didn't pause to answer, trusting that Lindsay or Ellen would explain.

She raced upstairs and down the hallway to her suite, pulling her cell phone from her pocket and jabbing the key to speed-dial the group as she shut the door behind her. "I'm here," she said breathlessly as she dropped into the desk chair.

"Nice of you to join us," Vinnie exclaimed cheerily. "How is quilt camp?"

"Oh, it's lovely," Julia replied. "Yet it isn't the same without all of you."

"I'm sure you're having a wonderful time," said Donna. "I know Lindsay is."

"Did she tell you that? I'm so glad."

"So, how's it going?" asked Megan. "Are your work friends becoming expert quilters—or at least, are they learning enough to pass themselves off as experts on camera, with skillful editing?"

"They're all making progress. I'm really quite proud of them."

"What's Elm Creek Manor like at this time of year?" asked Vinnie.

"Cooler, by far. The grounds aren't as lush and green as when we visit in summer, and it's past peak season for fall color, so we missed what was surely a beautiful display." Julia glanced to the windows. "And I may be mistaken, but I believe I see snow flurries."

"Hmm. I think I'll stick to visiting in the summertime, thanks very much," said Grace.

"A flurry, that's nothing," said Donna. "We've had at least an inch of snow on the ground since Halloween."

"Before you let the weather discourage you from attending autumn quilt camp, if the Elm Creek Quilters decide to expand their season," said Julia, "you should know that Anna's autumn recipes are just as delicious as her summer menus."

Her friends moaned wistfully. "What's the best dessert you've had so far?" Vinnie asked eagerly.

"Pumpkin cheesecake with a gingersnap crust, fresh whipped cream and a caramel drizzle optional."

"Oh my goodness, how luscious." Vinnie sighed longingly. "I love you too much to be jealous, but I do wish you could send me a slice in the mail."

"I wish I could too," said Julia. "Even though it's a seasonal recipe, Anna might be willing to make it for you during our next annual visit in August."

"Oh, I bet she would, for my birthday," Vinnie exclaimed. "I'll have to drop a few hints between now and then. Maybe you could drop one for me, since you're there. Don't be too subtle or she might not get it. But don't be too obvious either."

"I'll strike the right balance," Julia promised.

"So, the quilting and the dining are going well, and the manor is lovely even in late autumn," said Grace. "How about your scheme to keep your cast and crew together?"

Julia hesitated. "It's difficult to say," she admitted. "No one who was intending to go has announced that they've changed their minds, but several have said that they'll be sorry to see the series end."

"That's promising," said Donna. "Maybe they're coming around."

"I hope so. I'm running out of time to persuade them."

"Are you going to make a dramatic, heartrending, last-minute speech to win them over?" asked Vinnie eagerly. "Maybe at the Farewell Breakfast, or as you're boarding the plane home? That would be so exciting."

"Well, no, I wasn't planning to," said Julia.

"Sadie would do something like that on your show."

"Yes, but sadly, real life doesn't follow a script."

"I suppose not," Vinnie conceded, "but it's more exciting that way. If you change your mind and *do* make a dramatic speech, would you call me on your cell phone so I can listen in?"

"Sure," said Julia, quite sure that she wouldn't have to fulfill that promise.

The conversation turned to their progress on their Cross and Chains blocks. Grace, Donna, and Vinnie had finished theirs, but Megan had been preoccupied by a very complicated engineering project at work and hadn't even begun, although she intended to first thing Saturday morning. "I imagine you haven't had time to work on your block either, Julia," she said. "You must be busy with your Nine-Patch quilt and all your scheming."

"That's where you're wrong," said Julia. "I actually managed to get a lot done on Monday. I'll be home by Saturday evening, so I'll have all day Sunday to finish the last few seams. That reminds me—Maggie Flynn is working on the manuscript for a pattern book for the Loyal Union Sampler."

Her friends were as thrilled as she had expected them to be, and for the next few minutes, they speculated about when the book might be published, how challenging the quilt would be to make, and whether Maggie might need volunteers to make quilts for the book's photo gallery. "Maybe you could ask her, Julia," said Vinnie.

"Sure," said Julia, laughing. "Speak to Anna, speak to Maggie—anything else?"

"You have homework, Julia," said Grace, amused. "I hope you're taking notes."

They chatted for a while longer, but Julia was eager to return to the quilting frame, so she bade her friends goodbye and hung up, smiling to herself as she took a moment to rearrange her Cross and Chains block segments on the desk. Once she couldn't have imagined finishing a quilt as complex as Harriet's Journey, and now here she was, contemplating another, even more challenging project. It was truly amazing how her friends inspired her to attempt more than she'd ever thought possible.

Pausing for a moment to admire the view outside the window—yes, those were definitely small, icy snow crystals whirling about in the air—she was about to leave the room when her cell phone rang. Shaking her head and smiling fondly, wondering which of the Cross-Country Quilters had apparently forgotten to tell her something too urgent to wait, she took her phone from her pocket and checked the caller ID—

And almost dropped the phone.

Stephen Deneford. Why in the world would he be calling her? They hadn't spoken since she and Ellen had walked out of his office years before, abandoning *Prairie Vengeance* and Julia possibly her career, or so Julia had assumed at the time—incorrectly, thankfully. All communications relating to her contract had gone through Maury, and when she and Deneford crossed paths at industry events, they exchanged a polite nod but nothing more.

She told herself to let the call go to voicemail, but curiosity won out. Taking a deep, steadying breath, she answered. "Hello."

"Julia?"

"Yes?"

"Stephen Deneford here. "

"Oh, hello, Stephen. It's been a while."

"It sure has. Congratulations on your most recent Emmy."

"Thank you," she said graciously, wondering if he was referring to her win two years before, or if he wasn't aware that she'd lost to Allison Janney in September. "To what do I owe this unexpected pleasure? Are you looking to cast the villain in *Arctic Vengeance*, or *Savannah Vengeance*, or one of the other *Vengeance* films? If so, you really ought to speak with Maury."

"Oh, no, no, no. I got out of that franchise as soon as my contract permitted—" He made a harsh sound, something between a laugh and a groan. "And it wasn't soon enough."

"You don't say?" Julia suspected that it hadn't been his decision.

"You're close, though. I am calling about casting a role."

"Is that right?" she asked warily.

"It's a major feature film, a period piece, an adaptation of a gothic novel, *The Mysteries of Udolpho*."

She was impressed, but rather than admit it, she said, truthfully, "Sorry, I haven't read it. Or even heard of it."

"It was the *Twilight* of its day, but its day was seventeen ninety-four. Anyway, I've been searching for my Emily St. Aubert—the beautiful, young, perpetually imperiled heroine—and I think I've found her."

Julia paused, wondering if Ashton Kutcher was lurking somewhere nearby with a camera crew from *Punk'd*. No, she quickly decided. Sylvia would never allow it. "Congratulations," she said carefully. "And the lucky girl is?"

"Paige Lyons, your costar."

"Oh, yes, of course." That made much more sense. "Paige is a lovely, exceptionally talented young woman. She's been an excellent addition to our *Patchwork* cast."

"That's what I was hoping to hear. So, you wouldn't have any qualms about entrusting a lead role in a feature film to her?"

Julia shook her head, perplexed. "Why are you asking me? No offense, Stephen, but we don't know each other well and we didn't exactly part amicably. Did you like her audition? Did you do a chemistry check? If you want some insider information, you must have someone else to ask."

"I don't, actually. I've never worked with Paige, and I don't know anyone who has, aside from you. And you might not believe this, but I trust your opinion." He hesitated. "Look. You were right about *Prairie Vengeance*. I can't blame you for quitting. If I'd kept the original script, I might have had a blockbuster."

"Maybe so," said Julia, a bit taken aback by his candor, although it was certainly gratifying to hear. "It's impossible to say. Maybe the story was better suited for television. I do hope you'll share your newfound insight with Ellen Henderson."

"Who?"

"Ellen Henderson," Julia said, an edge to her voice. "The original screenwriter."

"Oh, right, of course. Yeah, maybe I'll do that. But anyway, about Paige. You've worked with her on a period piece, and you think highly of her. Any red flags?"

"No, of course not," Julia said, annoyed. What a thing to ask. A better question was whether Paige should be wary of red flags from Stephen Deneford, even in this new penitent persona. "In my opinion, since you asked for it, you'd be lucky to get her. But unless you're shooting during our hiatus, you won't be able to."

"What do you mean? I thought *Patchwork* was canceled."

"That's not even remotely true," she said, a trifle sharply. "The series has not been officially canceled, unless it happened within the past few days and no one told me. We begin shooting season six in January, and I hope to have at least one or two more seasons after that. Paige plays a recurring character now, but I would expect her to become a season regular."

"Oh, no, really? That's terrible news." Quickly he added, "Not for you, of course. For me. I really thought I'd found my Emily. Are you sure?"

"As sure as I can be. But like I said, if you can film while we're on hiatus—"

"That wouldn't work." He heaved a sigh. "Well, I'm glad I called, even though you're not telling me what I hoped to hear. Appreciate the insight."

"Stephen, listen," she said, suddenly uneasy. "You should be talking with Paige and her agent, not with me."

"Sure, I'll do that," he said briskly. "Thanks again. Let's do lunch sometime."

"That would be nice," she said, but he had already hung up.

Julia slipped her phone into her pocket, thought for a moment, and took it out again. Her finger poised over the keys as she considered what to do. Obviously she should call him back. She hit redial, then listened as it rang and rang until it finally went to voicemail.

"Hey, Stephen, it's Julia Merchaud," she said. "I may have spoken out of turn. Would you please call me back as soon as you get this message and let me explain? Thanks so much. Take care."

She hung up and put her phone away. Should she follow up with an email, or would that simply make matters worse? No, she should wait for his call. It was fine. It would be fine. When they spoke again, she would emphasize that Paige was a wonderful actor and colleague, and Julia honestly couldn't say for certain that she would be busy with *Patchwork*. Ideally, she would be, but in that case Deneford should adjust his shooting schedule to accommodate her, because casting Paige would be worth it. But that was something for Deneford, Paige, and her agent to work out among themselves. Julia had already interfered too much.

She checked her phone to make sure that it was fully charged and not on silent. It was perfectly fine, of course. Deneford just hadn't called, which made perfect sense, since it had only been a few minutes and he was a busy man.

Deneford would call, she assured herself as she headed back to the classroom. She was worrying needlessly. She'd set him straight, and whatever happened next would be up to Paige.

15

When Julia returned to the ballroom, she found six of her colleagues stitching away at the quilting frame, another four watching over their shoulders, and everyone else gathered around the longarm machine, where Sarah was guiding Louis through the rudimentary steps of free-motion quilting. Paige stood at his side, complimenting him and apparently teasing him too, if his grin was any indication. Reluctant to kill the happy mood by taking Paige aside and telling her about Stephen Deneford's unsettlingly odd phone call, Julia decided to let the matter drop. There was no point in worrying Paige needlessly. If Deneford didn't return Julia's call by the time she left Elm Creek Manor, she'd steel herself, invite him to lunch, and explain the regrettable uncertainty about *Patchwork*'s future. She'd even pick up the check afterward. That should make up for her careless talk.

Taking a cleansing breath, acknowledging her uneasy thoughts, one by one, she deliberately let them go. Then she returned to the company, taking another turn at the quilting frame and even trying her hand at the longarm. Later, after supper, her lingering misgivings were put to rest when everyone gathered by the fireplace to read a new scene Ellen had written for Sadie, Ben, Jesse, and Anabelle. Julia and Nigel jousted as magnificently as ever, while Paige and Louis were riveting in an exchange of sharply comic barbs that suggested an undercurrent of desire between the characters, sure to be explored later in the season.

At the end of the scene, as the performers bowed to their colleagues' applause, Nigel leaned closer to Julia and murmured, "Is it just me, or are they the new us?"

"It's not just you," Julia replied as they returned to their seats. "I see it too. The only difference is that they're younger and they're actually attracted to each other. And Louis isn't an actor, more's the pity."

"That was fantastic," said Ellen, glancing up long enough to beam at Paige and Louis before bending over her script again, swiftly jotting notes in the margins, crossing out passages, circling a paragraph and drawing an arrow to indicate where it should be moved.

"If it was so awesome, why are you changing everything?" teased Paige as she took a seat beside Louis.

"I'm just fine-tuning a few things," said Ellen, but it certainly looked like much more than that to Julia.

"You're actually very good at this, Louis," said Olivia, regarding him speculatively. "Have you ever considered acting?"

"I had the same thought," Nigel declared. "You have a marvelous speaking voice and a compelling presence."

As others chimed in with their agreement, Louis shook his head and raised his hands to fend them off. "No, thanks," he said emphatically, smiling. "Not interested. I only want to be onstage or on camera if I'm at the piano."

"Pity," said Nigel. "Ah, well. More roles for the rest of us."

In reply, Louis threw him a grin and made his way to the piano, where he let loose with a rendition of John Coltrane's "Giant Steps," clearly intending to prove his point that he shouldn't change careers. He graciously entertained them for the rest of the evening, occasionally accompanied by Paige on vocals. They were still at it when Julia, though reluctant to be the first to leave the gathering, nevertheless bade her friends good night and headed off to bed, tired but content.

The next morning, when Paige didn't appear for Zumba class,

Julia and Olivia exchanged a significant look. "She and Louis must have stayed up late making music together," Julia speculated as they toweled off after the workout.

"Oh, I have no doubt they did," Olivia replied archly. "But not at the piano."

Julia gasped as if scandalized. "What are you suggesting?"

"Exactly what you're thinking," Olivia countered, grinning.

Later, when Julia came down to join breakfast already in progress, she noticed that neither Paige nor Louis was there. "Have our Perdita and Florizel put in an appearance this morning?" she asked Nigel in an undertone as she took the seat beside him.

"I haven't seen either of them, neither separately nor together," said Nigel, glancing surreptitiously around the room. "Perhaps their 'bud of love, by winter's ripening breath, may prove a beauteous flower when next' they appear—if you'll pardon the paraphrase of the Bard, and the change of play."

"I don't mind the paraphrase," said Julia, "but let's not liken our friends to Romeo and Juliet. I'll take *A Winter's Tale* and its happy ending any day."

"And yet," murmured Nigel, looking past Julia to the doorway from the foyer, "perhaps, as a tragedy, *Romeo and Juliet* is more fitting after all."

"What do you mean?" asked Julia, turning in her chair to look. She drew in a breath at the sight of Paige and Louis entering the banquet hall, his arm around her shoulders, her face streaked with tears.

Conversations faded as the company became aware of the young woman's distress. "What's the matter, honey?" Edna called.

"She's had some bad news," Louis said as he led Paige to a seat at the nearest table. She sat down woodenly, and when her gaze fell on the napkin at her place, she picked it up and dabbed at her eyes.

"How bad?" asked Jason, brow furrowing. "Is your family okay?"

"Yes," Paige said, nodding, and then shaking her head. "Yes, everybody's fine."

"Even so, a cup of tea wouldn't go amiss," said Nigel, touching Julia's shoulder in passing as he went to fetch Paige a cup.

The gesture roused Julia from her paralysis. "What happened, kiddo?" she asked, hurrying over to take a seat by her side.

"It's—well, I had a call from—" Paige's gaze traveled from Julia to the rest of the company as they gathered around. "I'm sorry, guys. I didn't mean to scare y'all. I'm just—sad. And disappointed. And confused."

"Why?" asked Julia. "What happened?"

"Maybe we can help," said Dylan, folding his arms over his broad chest.

"Don't I wish. I just got off the phone with my agent." Paige took a deep, tremulous breath. "I probably mentioned that she's been trying to line up a new project for me for after *Patchwork* wraps."

Everyone nodded—except for Julia, who froze.

"All week she's been super busy working out the details for this fantastic movie role I really wanted. It's a lead in a big, sweeping, historical epic—lots of drama and romance, gorgeous costumes, on-location shoots in real castles, you know."

"We know," said Olivia, wincing slightly as if bracing herself for the reveal, which they all had guessed by then.

"I totally thought I had the part." Paige shook her head, bewildered. "Then, just this morning, my agent got an email from the director's assistant withdrawing the offer. My agent called the director right away, but all he would say is that he's going in another direction, whatever that's supposed to mean."

A murmur of dismay went up from the company. "That's a dreadful blow, my dear," said Nigel, handing her a cup of tea, which was no doubt well fortified with milk and sugar. "This ill-mannered director will rue the day he squandered the chance to cast you, of that I've no doubt."

"Thank you, Nigel." Paige took a careful sip of the tea. "I just really wanted this part. I *needed* this part. It was going to be my breakthrough role."

"You'll have another chance," Julia said. "We've all been passed over for roles we thought were in our grasp. It's painful and demoralizing, but something else always comes along."

"Julia's right," said Olivia, offering Paige a commiserating smile. "Unfortunately, rejection is a part of the industry. It's never fun, but we all have to learn to deal with it."

"Stiff upper lip, my dear," said Nigel, his baritone rumble kind and consoling. "Julia is right: Something better is certain to come along soon. When that happens, you'll be glad you're not committed to this other picture."

"Maybe," said Paige, clearly dubious. But as her fellow actors chimed in with stories of their own dream roles that got away, and Ellen and Jason threw in tales of beloved scripts that were optioned and never produced, the doubt clouding her expression began to lift.

Julia shared a story of her own, one she had confided to only a small circle of close friends. Nigel and Maury knew, of course, and the Cross-Country Quilters, but very few others. "When I first came to Hollywood right out of college, where I'd been the star of every theater department production, I struggled for about five years, waiting tables, auditioning like mad, and being grateful for every bit part I was given," she said. "Somehow I managed to get an agent, which led to better roles and some critical acclaim, but that breakthrough role still eluded me. Then the day I had longed for finally came. My agent told me I was in the running for the part of Marian Paroo in *The Music Man*."

"But Shirley Jones played Marian," said Jason, puzzled.

Julia gave him a look. "Yes, thank you, Jason. I was there. I remember."

"No spoilers, please," said Paige, her gaze fixed on Julia.

"So, no, I didn't get the part. Shirley Jones was a full-fledged star, after all, and I was not. What can I say? I was crushed. My parents were begging me to come home to Iowa, help run the farm, and settle for community theater."

"Good heavens," said Nigel, appalled. "You never told me you had considered abandoning Hollywood for am-dram."

"That's because I never did. Maury believed in me, and when I told him I would take any respectable job if it meant I could pay my rent before my roommates threw me out, he found me a voice-over role for a documentary about the Triangle Shirtwaist Factory disaster."

"*Threads and Ashes*," said Lindsay.

"Yes, that's right." Julia smiled wistfully, remembering. "I didn't meet the director in person until recording had already begun. One afternoon, when I was reading my lines—headset on, microphone before me—Charles Bryson himself walked into the studio, sat down quietly, and just watched and listened. When we finished for the day, he rose, thanked me politely, and left. When we resumed the next morning, he came in, sat down, and listened again. His presence was rather unnerving. I assumed he didn't like what he was hearing, but he didn't offer any direction or criticism, so I just carried on."

"Little did you know that he had fallen for you," said Ellen, smiling.

"That honestly hadn't occurred to me," Julia admitted. "He was seven years older than I, and he was so much more successful and distinguished that I assumed he was, well, already married and settled. And he was a consummate professional. He didn't ask me out until a full two weeks after production wrapped. By the time we attended the Oscars together the following year, and *Threads and Ashes* won for Best Documentary, I was head over heels in love. Two years after that, we were married, and we lived happily ever after—" Her voice caught in her throat. "For as long as we could."

Paige smiled, and except for the tears lingering on her eyelashes, one would not have known she had been desperately unhappy only moments before. "So you're telling me that by losing this role, I'll get another one that will lead me to true love?"

Julia cleared her throat and managed a smile. "I can't promise that, but one never knows."

As a ripple of laughter passed through the company, Paige laughed too and dried her eyes. "I think you would've been fantastic in *The Music Man*," she said. "They really missed out."

"So did whoever failed to get you on contract for this movie, Paige," declared Olivia, planting a hand on her hip. "Whatever it is, I'll refuse to see it on principle."

"Well, that's the thing," said Paige, shaking her head, still bewildered. "They *did* send my agent a contract. I was supposed to sign it on Monday, after we get back to LA."

Julia gasped, and she was not alone. "They'd already sent you a contract?" asked Ellen. "And they, what, asked your agent to tear it up?"

"That's not the only strange thing," said Louis. "Before her agent called with the bad news, someone had already emailed Paige about arranging a shoot for publicity photos, and the head costumer asked to schedule her first fitting."

Murmurs of surprise rose from the company and significant glances were exchanged. "That's rather odd," Julia managed to say.

"Very," said Olivia, shaking her head. "Still, it doesn't surprise me. We've all heard stories of actors who are fired after the first dailies come in, or who don't find out they've been replaced in a role until their name is missing from the call sheet."

"As a costumer myself," said Edna, frowning, "I'm surprised by that costumer's lazy mistake. We're better than that."

"That's what I'm saying," said Louis. "People other than Paige and her agent believed she had the role. Why would they?"

"Poor communication?" Julia suggested faintly.

Louis shrugged. "Maybe. I don't know. But something isn't right."

"Maybe you should talk to your agent again," Ellen said to Paige. "She might not have any more information to share, but if you think it would make you feel better—"

"Sometimes it's better not to know why you didn't get a role," Julia broke in hastily. "Sometimes it's best to accept the loss and move on."

"That's a fair point," said Nigel. "Why pour salt into a wound?"

Paige wiped her eyes and steeled herself with a deep breath. "I think I could move on more quickly if I understood what happened. I'll call my agent. If I find out what went wrong, I can learn from it and do better next time."

"That's the spirit," Nigel declared, but Julia sensed impending disaster.

"Sorry to interrupt, but is everything all right?"

The company turned to find Gretchen standing in the ballroom doorway, regarding them with concern.

"Oops," said Edna. "What time is it?"

"Quarter past." Gretchen gave them a searching look. "We've never misplaced an entire class before. When not one of our students showed up this morning, we sent out a search party. Well, I sent myself. I'm the search party."

"I'm so sorry," Paige exclaimed, bolting to her feet. "It's my fault. I kept everyone back."

"No harm done," Gretchen assured her, smiling as she beckoned the students to accompany her into the ballroom.

Julia hung back as her colleagues followed Gretchen into the ballroom, murmuring to one another incredulously, shaking their heads, assuring Paige that everything would be all right eventually, somehow. "Wait," Julia called after them feebly, but no one glanced back. She should explain—but what could she say that wouldn't make everything worse?

Perhaps it would be better to wait until everyone had calmed down. Quilting would soothe their tempers, or so Julia hoped.

Hurrying after her friends, she found them not gathered around the quilting frame, as she had expected, but in their familiar classroom. Maggie and Sarah stood at the instructors' table, chatting quietly as Sarah unrolled a bolt of forest-green fabric on the cutting mat. As before, two student tables stood side by side in the center of the room covered in a clean, white sheet, but this time, Sarah's Chandelier quilt was spread out upon it, the top facing up, allowing them to admire the beautiful patterns of stitches etched into the surface. Only the edges remained unfinished, with all three layers of top, batting, and backing still visible.

"Since today is your last full day of camp, we're going to skip ahead and teach you how to bind a quilt," said Gretchen as the students seated themselves at the remaining tables. "Yours is still on the frame, so we'll practice on Sarah's, which, thanks to you, is finally quilted."

"Just in time, too," said Sarah. "There's a queue of Elm Creek Quilters waiting to use the longarm, and I've tested their patience long enough."

"She's kidding," Gretchen added so quickly that the company laughed. "Well, there *is* a queue, but we're not impatient."

"No?" teased Sarah. "I bet you'll have your top for the Christmas boutique on the rollers by lunchtime."

"The first step in finishing a quilt is to remove it carefully from the rollers, the frame, or the hoop," said Maggie, deftly steering the class back on topic. "We'll show you how to remove your Nine-Patch quilt from the frame tomorrow morning, but we'll leave it there for now, so you can continue working on it after our binding lesson."

First, Sarah explained, they would trim the batting and the backing even with the quilt top. "Some quilters prefer to use a ruler and rotary cutter," she noted, taking a gleaming pair of dressmaker's shears in hand, "but we're doing this Sadie Henderson style, with scissors."

"I doubt that my great-grandmother ever had scissors that nice," Ellen observed as Sarah bent over her quilt, smoothed the edge flat with a long acrylic ruler, and carefully trimmed the excess batting and backing until all three layers were even.

After a while, Sarah handed off the scissors to Edna and invited her to take a turn. After a few minutes, Edna inspected her work, nodded in satisfaction, and beckoned Paige to take over. Her violet eyes still puffy from crying, she painstakingly cut along the edge until she reached the corner. Uncertain how to proceed, she glanced questioningly to Sarah, who stepped in to demonstrate how to navigate the right angle. When Paige finished, she offered the scissors to Julia, but Julia declined with a quick smile and a shake of her head. Paige handed them to Louis instead.

The company probably thought that Julia was demurring to give the less experienced quilters more time to practice their new skills. She had done so quite frequently that week. They never would have guessed that she skipped her turn because her nerves were so on edge that her hands trembled, and she didn't trust herself with the scissors. One careless mistake, and she would ruin Sarah's quilt.

When all four sides of the quilt were neatly trimmed, Maggie returned to the instructors' table and explained how to make a bias binding to cover the raw edges of the quilt. As Gretchen and Sarah passed through the aisles distributing sheets of paper, Maggie recited a mathematical formula for calculating the amount of fabric required to create a strip of bias binding of a particular length and width. "You don't need to memorize it," she assured them. "It's on the handout."

"That's a relief," said Olivia. "I haven't had to calculate a math formula since high school."

"This one is easy," Maggie promised, and to prove her point, she measured the length and width of Sarah's Chandelier quilt, plugged the numbers into the formula, and determined the size of a square she needed to cut from the forest-green fabric. After cutting the square to size, she cut it in half along the diagonal, pinned the resulting triangles together along opposing short sides, and sewed a quarter-inch seam. Next, she brought the angled edges together, offset by the width of the bias strip, and stitched them together to form an asymmetric tube. Then, narrating each step, walking the aisles, and pausing at each table so everyone had a chance to see her work up close, she cut on the line to create a narrow strip on the bias, rolling it into a coil as she went along and tucking it beneath her arm to keep it from tangling.

When she finished, Maggie carried the coil to Gretchen at the pressing table. Gretchen folded the long binding strip in half, wrong sides facing inward, and pressed it with a hot iron along its entire length, making a sharp crease. "Doubling over the strip increases its durability," she explained. "That's important because the edges of a quilt experience the most wear and tear."

"Would Sadie Henderson have used an electric iron, though?" asked Jason, tapping his notebook with a pencil.

"No, probably not, considering that she lived on a frontier homestead," Gretchen conceded with a smile. "She probably used a flat iron that she heated up on a cast-iron stove. It probably had a detachable wooden handle to help prevent burns, and possibly a plaster of Paris coating too."

"Often flat irons were sold in sets of two or three irons and one handle, so while one iron was being used, another could be heating on the stove," Maggie added. "If Sadie had lived in the city, though, she might have owned an electric iron, or a model that ran on gas or an alcohol-based fuel."

Jason regarded her, skeptical. "Seriously?"

"Seriously," Maggie replied. "They existed by Sadie's day. As you can imagine, though, they weren't exactly the safest household appliances ever invented. They smelled bad, they were a burn and fire hazard, and they could leak or explode."

"And that is why we're using a modern electric iron today," Gretchen declared cheerfully as she finished pressing the bias strip and rolled it into a loose coil. "Safety first."

"Now we'll sew the binding to the front of the quilt," said Sarah.

"By hand?" asked Paige.

"First on the treadle sewing machine, and later by hand."

Taking the coiled strip from Gretchen, Sarah returned to her Chandelier quilt and began pinning the bias strip to the top, leaving an eight-inch tail of binding at the beginning and matching the open side rather than the crease to the raw edges of the quilt. After that, with Maggie's assistance, she carefully rolled up the quilt and carried it to the treadle, where she demonstrated how to sew the binding strip around the edges of the top of the quilt, removing pins as they approached the throat plate and pausing now and then to pin more of the strip in place. Whenever she reached a corner, she invited the company to come closer to observe how she mitered them. Even Julia paid careful attention, for mitering corners was a task she had not yet mastered, and she was glad to pick up a few new tips.

With the binding firmly attached to the top of the quilt, Sarah gathered it up in her arms and spread it out upon the center tables once more. "The next step is to fold the binding strip over the raw edges of the quilt and sew it to the quilt back," said Gretchen. "Some quilters use a whip stitch, which is faster, but I prefer a blind stitch." She showed them how both stitches were made, pointing out how the blind stitch took more time, but afterward, the stitches were virtually invisible. "Personally, I think that's prettier, and then you don't have to worry about the whip stitches snagging on something that might break the threads."

After demonstrating for a few minutes more, Sarah invited them all to take a turn sewing the binding to the back of the quilt. Dylan volunteered to go first, unexpectedly and so eagerly that everyone laughed from surprise. The usual conversation and teasing and banter broke out as they watched him have a go at it, the needle like a tiny sliver pinched between his broad, weathered fingers. Julia watched Paige surreptitiously as the younger woman took her turn, relieved to see her enjoying herself, the morning's dreadful revelation apparently forgotten for the moment.

The company had finished binding two sides of the Chandelier quilt when delicious aromas began drifting into the ballroom from the banquet hall. At noon, Gretchen praised them for their very good work and announced that after lunch, they would reconvene at the quilting frame. "You can spend the rest of the day quilting the Nine-Patch if you wish, and part of tomorrow morning too," she told them.

"Thanks to this morning's lesson, you'll know how to bind your quilt when you finish it back home."

"You mean at Julia's home," Olivia said, tossing a grin in her direction. "Hope you have a quilting frame, because you're playing hostess again."

"I'll borrow one from the props department," Julia replied.

"I can help with that," said Louis. "I have a key."

"And I have a truck," said Dylan.

"You *are* going to ask permission first, right, Miss Julia?" asked Paige, feigning alarm.

"Of course," said Julia innocently as the company filed out of the classroom. "That was the plan all along."

"And yet a heist would be so much more fun," said Olivia, sighing.

Chef Anna's lunch buffet was another culinary triumph, but Julia barely tasted a morsel. She wasn't seated at Paige's table, but she was close enough to overhear when Paige's cell phone rang. She watched uneasily as Paige quickly rose and hurried into the foyer, the phone pressed to her ear. Louis hurried after her.

It was surely Paige's agent on the line. Julia turned back to her salad and moved it around with her fork, her heart thudding with dread.

When Paige returned, she looked both incredulous and deeply wounded. Louis had his arm around her shoulders as if to bear her up.

"What did your agent say?" asked Ellen. "Did she find out why the director changed his mind?"

"She couldn't get him on the phone," said Paige. "Obviously he didn't want to talk to her. She did hear an awful rumor, though. It's just a rumor, but she says it's from a very credible source."

"What rumor is that?" asked Julia, keeping her voice steady.

Paige inhaled shakily and spread her hands, fresh tears springing into her eyes. "The director spoke to one of the producers of *A Patchwork Life*, and that producer urged him to cast someone else."

"What?" Olivia exclaimed.

"That can't be right," said Ellen, shaking her head. "I can't imagine any of them doing such a thing."

Paige shrugged and sank into a chair, slumping forward and bracing her hands on her knees. "I can't either. I thought they were happy with my performance in the season five finale. Why would they have signed me for season six if they weren't?"

"Actually, I'm the one who signed you for season six," said Ellen. "But Paige, I promise you, none of our producers have ever expressed any dissatisfaction with you in my hearing, not once, not ever."

Paige's bleak expression told them that this was no consolation. "Then why ruin my chance to land this role? They hardly know me. Why interfere?"

"I think a better question is 'Who?'" said Olivia, eyes narrowing.

As the outraged company debated who among the studio executives could have done such a terrible thing, and why, Julia braced herself for their condemnation—until she realized that they had forgotten she was one of the executive producers. She held perfectly still, willing herself into invisibility, as other names were brought up and voices rose in indignation and anger. Then she chanced to look across the circle and her gaze fell on Lindsay, who also stood in silence, regarding her with stunned uncertainty.

Thoroughly wretched, but unwilling to let someone else take the blame for her mistake, Julia waved her hands for their attention. "It wasn't any of them," she said, and when no one looked her way, she raised her voice to be heard over the din. "Listen to me. I said, it wasn't any of them."

The company fell silent and turned to look at her. "How would you know that, Julia darling?" asked Nigel.

She took a deep, steadying breath. "Because it was me."

16

I'm the executive producer who spoke to Stephen Deneford," Julia confessed as her friends and colleagues stared at her, stunned and disbelieving. "But it didn't happen the way Paige's agent said."

"Whatever you said, it obviously wasn't good," said Olivia sharply.

"I just—I said Paige is a lovely person and an extremely talented actor and she's been a wonderful addition to the *Patchwork* cast. Deneford asked me if I'd have any qualms about casting her as a lead in a movie, if there were any red flags he should know about. I told him of course not, and that he'd be lucky to get her." Julia cast a beseeching look around the circle of appalled and angry faces. "I swear that's what I said."

"I don't think so," said Jason, studying her, eyes narrowing. "There must be more to it than that."

"Did you say anything else, Julia?" Nigel prompted, brow furrowing. "Anything Deneford perhaps misinterpreted?"

"Well—" Julia took a deep breath and clasped her hands to try to still their trembling. "I told him that unless he waited until we were on hiatus, Paige wouldn't be available."

"But that's not even true," Louis protested, as Paige stared at Julia, stricken and speechless. "Why would you tell him that?"

"He said he heard that *Patchwork* was canceled. I told him it hadn't been, that nothing was official yet, that we'll begin shooting season six in January, and I expect another season or two to follow. And Paige—" Julia threw her a pleading look, but Paige looked away, shaking her head slowly as if trapped in a bad dream. "Paige will probably become a season regular. We'll need her."

"Oh, Julia," said Nigel. "What have you done?"

"I specifically told Deneford that he should talk to Paige and her agent," Julia hastened to add. "In fact, as soon as we hung up, I realized I had probably spoken out of turn, so I called him back."

"What did he say?" Edna asked.

"He didn't pick up. I left a voicemail."

"Oh, fantastic," said Olivia, folding her arms. "Problem solved."

"Let's all take a breath," Lindsay pleaded, raising her hands for calm. "I'm sure Julia didn't mean for any of this to happen. It can't be too late to fix it."

"It *is* too late," said Paige. They all turned to look at her. "My agent said they already offered the role to someone else."

"I'm so sorry," said Julia. "I truly am."

"You're *sorry*?" Paige fixed her with a look somewhere between astonishment and fury. "Your careless, self-interested comments about what I'm like to work with—as if you'd know—cost me a potentially breakthrough role. I know you don't want *A Patchwork Life* to end, but really, Miss Julia? To sabotage my career to save it? Was it really worth that much to you?"

"You have every right to be upset," said Julia, a tremor in her voice. "I didn't mean to sabotage anything. I'll do whatever I can to make amends, I promise."

Paige regarded her skeptically, tears filling her eyes. "Forgive me if I don't believe a word you say. I trusted you. I admired you." She gestured to the next table over. "Just this morning you sat in that chair and told me a story about how you met your late husband after missing out on a role. I thought you were so kind, encouraging me to find hope in adversity or whatever, but the whole time, you knew it was your fault that I didn't get the part."

Julia found herself with absolutely nothing to say. She couldn't justify what she had done, and her apologies and explanations were offering Paige no comfort. Her friends and colleagues were looking at her as if they didn't recognize her anymore, as if they were reconsidering whether they had ever truly known her. She endured it as long as she could, hoping the words that would make everything right would come to her. When they didn't, she took a deep, shaky breath, bowed her head in acceptance of their judgment, turned, and walked away.

"Julia, wait," Lindsay called after her, but she kept going.

She went upstairs to her suite, where she closed the door and stood in the middle of the room, wondering what to do next. After a long moment, she switched on her computer and emailed the Cross-Country Quilters. "Grace and Megan were right," she typed. "My scheme to keep the cast and crew of *A Patchwork Life* together has failed spectacularly. I should have accepted their decision to leave the show and moved forward with dignity and hope. I think that's how Grace put it. Now I've lost my series and my work family, and I have no one to blame but myself."

She hit send and waited to see if anyone would respond. Then a horrible thought seized her: Perhaps the Cross-Country quilters too would judge her harshly. Quickly she closed her computer. That really would be more than she could bear.

She went to the window and gazed outside at a perfect late-autumn afternoon, reminding her suddenly, intensely, of her Iowa childhood. The corn harvest would have been completed by now, unless it had been an unusually cool summer. She and her mother would have been bringing in the winter squash and root vegetables and putting up preserves. As winter approached, the Merchaud family and their neighbors would have been giving thanks for a bountiful season, unless it had been a bad year, in which case they would have been worrying over how to pay the bills and put food on the table after losing the crops to drought, floods, or pests.

It was little wonder Julia had longed to escape into the world of the theater, where she could be anyone, doing and saying things she would never dare in ordinary life, and be applauded for it. At first her parents had found her passion for acting puzzling, but as long as she did her chores and kept her grades up, they had allowed her to participate in her high school drama club. It was a good way for Julia to get involved and make friends, and they were proud, in their understated way, when their own friends and neighbors praised their talented daughter. When Julia announced her intention to major in theater in college, they insisted that she add a second major in education. They dutifully attended most of her college shows, reassuring each other that she would come to her senses eventually and focus on earning her teaching credentials, if they kept praying for it.

That didn't happen, of course, but although they were obviously disappointed, Julia had assumed that they still tuned in to her television shows every week. Then, years later, while they were washing dishes after Thanksgiving dinner, one of her sisters-in-law let slip that her mother had stopped watching *Family Tree* after an episode in which Julia's character's eldest son cheated on his wife. "She said the stories had gotten 'too racy,'" her sister-in-law confided, giggling, until she saw Julia's expression and fell into an embarrassed silence.

Her parents had never visited her in California. Even after her career took off and she had been able to afford to charter a private jet for them, they had politely declined her invitations. They had always welcomed her home, though, and they had adored Charles. Surely that meant Julia hadn't been a complete disappointment, although—

She gave her head a shake to clear it. How odd to be brooding about the past when the problems of that very day were more than enough to deal with.

Throwing on the warmest coat she had packed, really no more than a heavy jacket, Julia put on her hiking shoes, quietly opened her door, and peered into the hallway. Only after confirming no one was around did she leave her room. As she descended the grand oak staircase, she heard distant voices from the ballroom, but thankfully, no one was in sight.

Crossing the foyer, she entered the west wing, but instead of turning left toward the kitchen, she continued straight ahead, past the parlor and the guest rooms to the corridor's end at the side door, which had been the main entrance to the original farmhouse a century ago and now led to the cornerstone patio. The leaves had fallen from the lilac hedges, and not even the smallest green shoot remained of the perennials that had bloomed so lushly throughout the spring and summer, but the barrenness made the large, gray cornerstone with its engraved "Bergstrom 1858" more prominent, the better to evoke the manor's storied history.

Julia passed through the shrubbery arch and stepped onto a gravel path that meandered through a dense grove of elm, sugar maple, and evergreen. A few yellow-gold and burnt-orange leaves clung to the boughs overhead, but most were scattered upon the ground and crunched underfoot in the dappled sunlight that filtered through the branches.

Eventually the path led Julia to the north gardens. In the center of an oval clearing, which was paved in the same gray stone as the cornerstone patio, stood a black marble fountain of a mare prancing with two foals, reminiscent of the rearing stallion in the center of the circular driveway in front of the manor. The water was turned off, and likely had been since before the first frost, but in summer the sound of the water was lovely, and a light spray caught on a whimsical breeze could be quite refreshing. Four large planters were spaced evenly around the fountain, the lower halves of their walls two feet wider than at the top, forming smooth, polished seats where visitors could rest and admire the chrysanthemums, sedum, purple coneflowers, and black-eyed Susans that had bloomed in season amid decorative grasses. On the other side of the fountain was a gazebo, and through its white wooden posts and gingerbread molding, Julia glimpsed terraces cut into the slope of a gentle hill, filled with rosebushes, English ivy, maiden grass, and asters, or rather, what remained of them.

How lush and fragrant and lovely the north gardens had been when Julia and the Cross-Country Quilters had visited them during their summertime reunion at the manor a few months before. Now, in the second week of November, only the English ivy remained as verdant and green as Julia remembered. The rosebushes had been pruned back. The brown grasses rustled tiredly in the breeze, as if resigned to the likelihood that the first significant snowfall would flatten them. Some dried, browned flowers remained of the sedum, black-eyed Susans, and chrysanthemums, their charming, bright colors only a memory. The purple coneflowers too had faded, but browned cones remained atop the stalks, perhaps left by the gardeners to feed the birds.

Shivering, Julia pulled on her hood and tucked her hands into her pockets. How surreal and incomprehensible it was that Elm Creek Manor, the setting of countless joyous memories, had become the scene of so much self-inflicted misery. Worse yet, she had hurt people for whom she cared deeply. Paige, of course. The other Patchwork Players, who would no doubt feel deceived and manipulated once they compared notes about Julia's invitations and questionable motives. Sarah and the other Elm Creek Quilters, who were counting on the success of this unprecedented week of autumn quilt camp to convince Sylvia to expand their season and help resolve their urgent financial issues.

Julia took a deep, shaky breath. If nothing else, the generous fee she'd offered for the actors' quilting boot camp had paid for the manor's new roof, with enough left to tide the Elm Creek Quilters over until camp resumed in the spring. That was a narrow silver lining on a very gray cloud, but she'd take it.

A gust of wind sent dried leaves scuttering across the gray stone pavers, and if her eyes weren't deceiving her, a few minuscule ice crystals were swirling in the air. Her coat was no match for such weather, so she retraced her steps and returned to the manor, only to find that the cornerstone patio door had locked automatically behind her. She considered her options. She could enter through the front door and risk an encounter with her disgruntled and justifiably outraged colleagues as she passed the ballroom, or she could slip in the back way unobserved, and perhaps stop by the kitchen in passing and beg a warming cup of tea from kindhearted Chef Anna.

"Right," said Julia aloud, shivering as an ice crystal slipped down the collar of her jacket. "The back door it is."

The gravel path didn't extend from the cornerstone patio to the rear of the manor, so Julia trudged through the grass, brushing graupel from her sleeves and longing for the warm gloves she'd left behind in her suite. To her relief, she found the back door unlocked, and she quietly crossed the threshold into the small, rear foyer. She wiped her feet on the mat, removed her coat, and ran a hand through her hair before continuing toward the kitchen, beckoned onward by delicious aromas and warmth and the sound of cheerful voices.

The kitchen was the nineteenth-century manor's most modernized space, with state-of-the-art appliances, marble counters, efficient workstations, a central island, spacious cabinets, and a walk-in pantry on the other side of the room. Closer to the doorway where Julia lingered, eight cozy booths lined the walls, offering a welcoming gathering place for faculty and campers alike to catch up with friends over a cup of tea and a snack any time of day, although the Patchwork Players apparently hadn't discovered it. On the wall above the nearest booth hung a bright, cheerful quilt Sylvia and Anna had made together, a charming appliqué still life of fruits and vegetables framed by blocks with a culinary theme: Broken Dishes, Cut Glass Dish, Honeybee, and Corn and Beans. As far as Julia knew, the kitchen's only remaining artifact from the manor's early years was the dark walnut refectory table and benches arranged between the booths and the cooking area.

Anna and her two assistants were so engrossed in their work that Julia decided to forgo her tea rather than get in the way. Just as she turned to go, Anna called out, "Hi, Julia. Do you need something?"

Julia turned back around, managing a smile. "I'd love a cup of chamomile tea, whenever you have a moment."

"Sure," Anna gestured toward the booths. "Sit anywhere you like. I'll bring it to you."

Julia thanked her and settled into the farthest booth from the doorway and windows. Setting her coat on the seat beside her, she retrieved her phone from the pocket and was a bit startled to discover that she had five missed messages. Each of the other Cross-Country Quilters had called, Donna twice, no doubt in response to Julia's forlorn email. Sighing, she set the phone on the table, covered her face with her hands, and rubbed her temples. When she picked up her phone again, she considered which friend to call back first, and dialed her therapist instead.

Her therapist was with a client, but she called back five minutes later, only moments after Anna brought Julia a cup of tea and a pumpkin scone. Julia and her therapist had barely exchanged hellos before out tumbled the whole sordid story—quietly enough, or so Julia hoped, that Anna and her staff would not be disturbed. Her therapist occasionally prompted her with questions, and sometimes Julia would pause to think deeply before answering. Eventually Julia felt, if not *better* about her predicament, at least more capable of coping with it until they could meet in person the following week. In the meantime, her therapist assigned her some journaling exercises and encouraged her to think less about why she had not been honest with her friends—that was fairly obvious—and more about how she had not been honest with herself.

After they hung up, Julia carried her dishes to the counter and thanked Anna for her hospitality. "If it wouldn't be too much trouble," she said apologetically, for she could see how busy Anna was, "I'd be grateful if I could have my dinner brought to my room this evening, please."

"Of course," said Anna, regarding her with concern. "I don't mean to pry, but are you all right?"

"Hard to say," Julia replied, managing a grim smile. "I'm working on it."

On her way upstairs, she saw that the lights were on in the ballroom, suggesting that the rest of the company had not abandoned the Nine-Patch quilt or lost interest in improving their skills before shooting began. It was a heartening thought, but not enough to compel her to join them. She made it to her suite undetected, and since her phone was nearly out of charge and she was too weary to talk anyway, she composed a single email in reply to the very long thread that her woeful lament to the Cross-Country Quilters had provoked. Her friends were worried about her, concerned and sympathetic, and not one of them said that they had warned her, or that she should have known better. They knew she was painfully aware of that already.

Dinner in her suite was tasty and comforting, but lonely. She was nearly finished when someone knocked on her door and called her name. Recognizing Lindsay's voice, she was tempted to answer, but dread quickly overcame her longing for companionship. Eventually Lindsay went away, so Julia finished her meal, packed for the trip home, and went to bed early.

The next morning, Julia woke before her alarm with a knot of apprehension in her stomach. After some deep breathing, she rose and did yoga in her room rather than crash the Zumba party. She showered and dressed, and since it was still rather early for the rest of the company to drag themselves out of bed, she steeled herself, put her shoulders back, and went downstairs to breakfast, though she had little appetite. She had hoped to be the first to arrive, but Edna and Marisa were seated together, quietly chatting over waffles and coffee, while Dylan and Jason were loading their plates at the buffet. Edna and Marisa fell silent at the sight of her, but they returned her tight smile and nod with slow nods of their own.

"Good morning," she said to the men as she joined them at the buffet.

"Good morning," Dylan replied politely.

"It is for some of us," said Jason, taking a second waffle and moving off, all without looking at her.

It was going to be quite a day.

As Julia and her therapist had discussed, she chose a nutritious breakfast, poured herself a cup of herbal tea, and took a seat at an empty table, not at the direct center, but not isolated on the fringes either. She ate slowly, contemplatively, and as others filtered into the room and glanced her way, she made eye contact and nodded in greeting, and was usually offered a nod or a brief wave in reply. No one sat with her, but she had expected that. She ate enough to get through the morning and left the banquet hall before most of the company had arrived, so not everyone was given the opportunity to shun her.

Her therapist would have asked her to reframe that thought, but Julia gave herself a pass.

Usually Elm Creek Quilt Camp ended with a Farewell Breakfast and show-and-tell on the cornerstone patio, but the morning was blustery, overcast, and cold, and Julia couldn't imagine that anyone was in the mood for sitting outside in a circle and fondly reminiscing about the magical week they had spent together. The long flight to LAX would give them ample time together, whether they wanted it or not.

Not long after Julia returned to her suite, Sylvia and Andrew knocked on her door. While Andrew collected her luggage, Sylvia peered at her inquisitively over the rims of her glasses. "I trust you slept well, Julia, dear?"

"Yes, thank you." Julia inhaled deeply and exhaled shakily. "No, if I'm being honest, I didn't. I had too much on my mind."

"So I understand."

Though Sylvia's expression was sympathetic, Julia felt a rush of embarrassment. "Word travels fast in Elm Creek Manor."

"Sometimes it does. Sometimes secrets remain so for decades." A pained frown appeared on Sylvia's face for a moment but quickly vanished. "That's rarely a good thing. You were right to tell the truth as soon as you did."

"I wish I could take it all back," Julia blurted, then shook her head. "I don't mean my confession. I had to come clean. I mean blathering on to that director about Paige and the series. I just—wasn't thinking. Or if I *was* thinking, I was thinking only of myself."

"We've all said things we later regret."

"Yes, but not all of us say things that ruin a young woman's career."

"I doubt very much that you've done that. No offense, dear. I'm sure you have influence in the show business world, but probably not *that* much." Sylvia reached out to clasp her hand. "You'll find a way to make amends."

Julia could only hope so.

With Andrew leading the way and Sylvia by her side, Julia joined her colleagues on the front verandah to await the chartered shuttles to the airport. She wore her sunglasses despite the gloomy skies and clutched her tote to her side, shivering in the cold in her inadequate jacket, offering nods and murmuring good morning to anyone who came near and made eye contact. Sylvia remained by her side for a little while, but eventually she had to move on to bid farewell to her other guests. No one else spoke to Julia or offered anything more than the barest acknowledgment of her greetings. Paige kept her distance and avoided looking in her direction so vigorously that Julia might have been amused in any other circumstances.

"Did you try the cranberry scones?"

Julia gave a start and looked to her left. Edna was peering at her over the rims of her glasses. "Sorry, what?"

"Did you try the cranberry scones?" Edna repeated slowly. "At breakfast. They were excellent."

"Oh. No. No, I didn't. I had yogurt and fruit, and one of the mini bran muffins."

"Your loss. They were fantastic." Edna grinned and patted her purse. "I packed a half dozen for the trip home. Want one?"

In spite of herself, Julia laughed, though it got caught in her throat and came out like a strangled cough. "Thanks, but I'm still pretty full from breakfast."

"Well, if you get hungry on the plane, all you have to do is ask. You know, you left breakfast so early that you missed Sylvia's farewell speech. It was really quite inspiring. I might come back next summer and see what regular quilt camp is all about."

"You really should," Julia replied, forgetting herself for a moment. "If you have any questions—"

But the shuttles had appeared in the distance, emerging from the forest, and Edna was already moving toward the nearest staircase, eager to get into a van and out of the cold.

Julia hung back to allow everyone else to claim their seats first, hoping some of her colleagues would choose both front passenger seats so she could sit among them, the better to be drawn into a conversation. Perhaps Edna had broken the ice, and the others' frostiness would soon thaw. But the front passenger seat of the lead van had been left unoccupied, perhaps because Julia had claimed it on the inbound trip and the company assumed she wanted it back.

She settled into it, resigned. As they drove off, she watched in the rearview mirror as Elm Creek Manor receded behind them until the forest concealed it from view. She longed to return next summer, in much happier circumstances.

On the way to the airport, the conversation in the two back rows seemed quiet but pleasant, with some subdued laughter and teasing mixed in. Julia was glad to hear it. Paige was in the other van, or the entire long drive might have passed in stony silence. Later, aboard the plane, it would be far more difficult to avoid each other, but Julia made it easier by boarding first and settling down in an aisle seat in the last row.

She had just buckled her seat belt when Nigel came down the aisle. Too embarrassed to make eye contact, she pretended to study her watch, assuming he was heading to the galley. Instead, he halted in the aisle beside her. "May I?" he inquired, indicating the empty seat to her right. "I prefer the window."

She glanced up, and for a moment she didn't know what to say. "You have plenty of window seats to choose from," she pointed out, gesturing to the one in the row ahead of her and the one across the aisle.

"Yes, but that's the only window seat next to you."

Her throat constricting, Julia could only nod, unbuckle her seat belt, and rise, stepping into the aisle to let him pass. After they had taken their seats, Nigel offered her a kind, encouraging smile before closing his eyes and settling back for the journey. He was asleep before takeoff, but she was grateful for his company all the same.

As soon as the jet was in the air, Julia too reclined her seat, put on her sleeping mask, and pretended to doze until at last, she drifted off—

Until she woke with a jolt as her stomach dropped. Alarmed, she fumbled to remove the mask and looked around wildly, clutching her armrests, heart thudding. Nigel was idly paging through a Harry Potter novel, and in front of them, the other passengers were sitting comfortably in their seats, chatting or reading or dozing. To her left, Lindsay was watching her sympathetically from across the aisle. "We're passing over the Rockies," she explained. "The pilot warned us that we might encounter some turbulence."

"Some turbulence," Julia echoed, pressing a hand to her chest and inhaling deeply to steady her pulse. "That felt like a minute of free fall."

Lindsay allowed a smile. "Ten seconds, maybe."

"It felt like sixty." Julia realized she was cringing in her seat and made herself straighten, shoulders back, chin up. "Did I ever mention how much I dislike roller coasters?"

"You have." Lindsay leaned upon her right armrest, coming as close as she could with her safety belt fastened. "Listen, Julia. I know today was rough. Paige is hurt and she's not really receptive to apologies at the moment. As for the others . . ." She hesitated. "Well, either they don't want to take sides, or—"

"They've chosen Paige's."

Lindsay nodded.

"I can't blame them," Julia admitted. "She's the wronged heroine, and I'm the villain."

"You're not a villain. You've apologized, and I believe you when you say you're going to make amends." Lindsay gestured to their colleagues, all of whom were seated closer to the front of the plane. "Paige will forgive you, and everyone else will come around. Just give them time."

Julia managed a smile to thank her for the encouragement, but she couldn't wait and hope that their anger would fade with time. As Sylvia had suggested, Julia needed to make amends. And the sooner she fixed things for Paige, the sooner she would be forgiven, and the company would come together in friendship once more.

If only she knew what to do.

At last the plane touched down at LAX. Slipping on her sunglasses and shouldering her tote, Julia waited for everyone else to disembark before following Lindsay up the aisle to the exit and down the stairs. The company chatted amiably as they waited on the tarmac for their luggage to be unloaded. Julia spotted her driver waiting with the car nearby, next to a second black sedan that promptly carried Nigel off, but before she could offer anyone a ride home, the steward approached her with a clipboard full of forms and checklists she was required to fill out and sign. She hadn't yet finished when the luggage arrived, but she glanced up long enough to see her colleagues gathering their belongings and bidding one another goodbye, some with hugs and promises to get together soon. Lindsay caught her eye, smiled, and waved, but no one else spared her a glance. Turning away, closing her eyes and counting silently to ten, Julia fought back tears of disappointment and plowed doggedly through the paperwork. She had hoped that some of her traveling companions, mindful of their long professional relationship, would thank her for arranging their week of quilt camp. Until that last awful day, they'd all had a wonderful time.

Maybe in the light of all that had happened, she was the only one who remembered that.

While Julia was occupied, her driver had located her suitcase and stowed it in the trunk, so as soon as she signed the last form, she thanked the steward, returned the clipboard and pen, and headed for her car. The driver opened her door and she was just about to climb wearily in when a member of the ground crew approached, calling her name, moving as quickly as he could while encumbered by the blue duffel bag slung over one shoulder.

"Yes?" Julia asked politely, though she was eager to depart. The wind was whipping her hair around and into her eyes, and she desperately wanted a cup of herbal tea and a soothing bath.

"Someone forgot their bag," the man said, giving it a pat. "There's no tag, but it's definitely one of your party's. We loaded it in Pennsylvania."

"I don't recognize it," said Julia, looking it over. "Not that I would." She paused, considering. Maybe she'd recognize the clothing inside it, and could get it to the owner before they left the airport. Or she could drop it off at their home. If that failed, she'd email the group—if they hadn't all blocked her address already.

Reframe, she reminded herself. Stooping over, she unzipped the bag and peered inside.

It was the Nine-Patch quilt, carefully removed from the frame and neatly folded. She had forgotten all about it.

And no one else had wanted it.

"I guess this is mine," she said evenly, zipping the bag shut and rising. "Thank you." She nodded to her driver, who waited for her to be seated before closing her door and stowing the duffel in the trunk.

No one had wanted to take the quilt home, a cherished memento of an extraordinary week. But what else should she have expected, given the way their time together had ended? And that was all her fault.

Julia knew that nothing else mattered—not saving her show, not prolonging her career—but to fix what she had broken and to earn back her friends' trust. Their friendship had been a marvelous patchwork of shared experiences and longtime collaboration, but she had torn the seams, and she must be the one to stitch them back together.

17

When Julia arrived home on Saturday evening, she was too exhausted to do more than the most essential unpacking before retiring to her bath for a long, soothing soak, a cup of herbal tea at hand and cool cucumber slices on her closed eyelids. When the water cooled, she toweled off, applied a rich moisturizing lotion, and slipped into her favorite silk pajamas. She contemplated the blue duffel bag for a long moment before stowing it in the closet of her sewing room. Then she climbed into bed, heavy-hearted but relieved to be home, hoping that wisdom would fill her as she slept and answers would come with the sunrise.

That didn't happen, unfortunately, but Julia did wake feeling less anxious and more confident that she would find a way out of her predicament. She lay in bed, eyes closed, breathing deeply, envisioning Paige beaming with joy when she learned that her career was back on course. Ideally, Julia would convince Stephen Deneford to give Paige the role of Emily St. Aubert, which she had already been offered and for which a contract had already been approved. If he had given the role to someone else, he could cast Paige in an equivalent role in a similarly prestigious movie. Deneford always had multiple projects going on at once, but if none of his own films had the perfect role, he had connections throughout the industry. He could come up with something for Paige, and he must, if Julia ever hoped to redeem herself in the eyes of her friends and colleagues.

But that was Julia's problem, not Deneford's.

That being the case, Julia wasn't sure how to get him to do what she wanted. They didn't particularly like each other, and she didn't have any leverage over him. Muffling a groan, she threw back the quilt and climbed out of bed. She'd figure out how to craft the perfect persuasive argument later. First, she had to land the meeting.

By midmorning Deneford still hadn't responded to her emails or voicemails, so she called again and left another message and sent another email. Although it was Sunday, Deneford had too many deals pending to stay offline for long. Eventually, she hoped, he'd realize that she was determined to speak with him and he'd reply just to get it over with.

She worked on her Cross and Chains block to pass the time, but when she found herself checking for voicemails and refreshing her email inbox almost as frequently as she finished a seam, she abandoned her sewing and changed into hiking clothes. She was halfway up the Solstice Canyon Trail, silently composing and revising dialogue between herself and Deneford, when she abruptly halted. She was going about this all wrong. Had she learned nothing from this debacle? She was essentially planning to manipulate Deneford into giving her what she wanted, to be as disingenuous with him as she had been with the Patchwork Players at quilt camp. What she ought to do now, what she should have done then, was to be honest and straightforward. If she offered Deneford unmistakable proof that Paige would be brilliant, then he would see for himself that he should cast her in a breakthrough role. It would benefit them both—and Julia too.

She scarcely noticed the beautiful scenery as she finished her hike, thoughts racing with potential next steps and pitfalls to avoid, confidence increasing with each quarter mile. And yet the bruises of her recent failures were too fresh for her not to seek the counsel of wise friends. As soon as she returned home, she got the Cross-Country Quilters on a conference call—a bit of a scramble considering none of them were expecting it—and quickly explained what she intended to do.

"I like this plan much better than your last one," said Megan. "It's refreshingly free of subterfuge."

"Thanks," said Julia dryly.

"Well, I for one like a little subterfuge now and then," said Vinnie cheerfully. "But I'm with Megan. In this case, the straightforward approach would be best. Just give the man the facts about how Paige is absolutely wonderful, and he'll make the right decision."

"I hope you're right," said Julia, "because that's all I've got."

"I have a caveat, but it's a big one," said Grace. "Casting decisions are subjective, aren't they? It's not simply a matter of presenting facts or evidence. You have to engage the emotions as well."

"No worries," said Julia, although she had a few herself. "The evidence I'm talking about will definitely touch the heart."

"If he has a heart," said Donna, an edge to her voice. "Remember, I met that guy on the set of *Prairie Vengeance*. I saw how dismissively and disrespectfully he treated you and Ellen. He didn't seem to care much about anyone's feelings back then."

"But he does care about making a good movie." Julia shook her head. "I can't believe I'm defending Stephen Deneford, after all he put us through."

"Maybe he's learned from his mistakes," said Vinnie. "Maybe he'll be glad for the chance to make amends."

"If that's true," said Julia, "then we have something in common."

Her friends wished her luck, and after they hung up, Julia knew exactly what to do next. She phoned *Patchwork*'s lead editor, apologized for calling on a Sunday, and asked her to put together a video of clips from Paige's brief appearance in the season five finale. "Think of it as an audition reel," she said, "for a director who's particularly hard to impress."

Julia heard the scratch of a pencil on paper. "Got it," the editor said. "Anything else?"

"If I could have it by tomorrow noon, that would be fantastic."

"No problem. I'm on it. Paige is a sweetheart. I'm happy to help."

"Even so, I know this is a big ask, especially on such short notice. I owe you one."

"No, you don't," the editor said, surprised. "I owed you one. After this, we'll be even. Not that I keep score among friends."

Julia felt tears spring to her eyes. Someone in the *Patchwork* family still considered her a friend. Then again, that might mean only that the story of her betrayal hadn't traveled very far yet. "What favor did you owe me?"

"You don't remember career day at Los Cerritos Middle School? You made my niece's day—no, her year. Her students were so impressed to have a genuine TV and movie star in their classroom."

"Oh, right, that." Julia had entirely forgotten. She did more appearances than she could reasonably keep track of, which was one reason why she employed an assistant. "That was, what, ten years ago? You don't owe me a thing. I did it for the kids."

"If you say so. As it is, I'm now my niece's favorite aunt, so your Oscar-worthy highlight reel will be ready first thing tomorrow morning. I'll messenger it over."

Julia thanked her, and after they hung up, she checked her messages again, as she did throughout the day. She finished her Cross and Chains block, answered scores of neglected emails, wrote a heartfelt thank-you letter to accompany the gift basket she planned to send to the Elm Creek Quilters—all without a single word from Deneford.

And time was of the essence. If Deneford hadn't yet given the role of Emily St. Aubert to another lovely ingenue, he surely would soon.

The next morning, Julia checked her messages, and did some deep breathing exercises to help deal with the frustration of feeling ignored. A few minutes after eight o'clock a messenger dropped off the DVD with Paige's highlight reel, and watching it distracted her for a little while. She held out until ten o'clock before she gave in and phoned Deneford's office yet again.

The young man who answered greeted her with polished cordiality. "Mr. Deneford said we might be hearing from you," he said after she identified herself, sounding thoroughly pleased by his boss's prescience. "He's not available to take your call today, but he'd be happy to schedule that lunch you requested."

"Wonderful," said Julia. "How soon can we arrange that?"

"Let me check his calendar." The assistant hummed thoughtfully. "I see here that Mr. Deneford has availability at noon on the thirtieth. That's a Tuesday. Would that work for you?"

"But that's two weeks from tomorrow. This is urgent."

"I'm so sorry, but that's the earliest he could do lunch."

"Okay. How soon could he give me a half hour in his office?"

"Let's see." A soft, rapid clicking of a keyboard followed. "Hmm. Same day, nine o'clock in the morning. Is that any better?"

"Not by much, no." Julia thought quickly. "Very well. Put me down for lunch at noon on the thirtieth, but please contact me immediately if his schedule clears and we can meet any earlier."

"Will do, Miss Merchaud. I'm jotting it down on a sticky note as we speak."

"Thank you," Julia said. "I appreciate your help." And she meant it too. Deneford was obviously dodging her, but that wasn't his assistant's fault.

The Cross-Country Quilters had asked her to keep them posted, so she sent a group email lamenting her lack of progress. "That sounds so frustrating," Megan replied within a minute. "Can you go over his head?"

"Not really," Julia typed, but then she paused, thought for a moment, and tapped the delete key until the words were gone. "Maybe," she wrote instead, hope kindling. She sent off the email and reached for her Rolodex.

She hadn't spoken to Stephen Deneford's mother in months, not since their paths crossed at a Make-A-Wish Foundation fundraiser in May, but Lillian had a delightful sense of humor and a strong sense of justice, and Julia always enjoyed their conversations. Julia could only assume that Stephen took after his father. Lillian wasn't one for email, so Julia phoned instead, muffling a sigh of relief when Lillian greeted her warmly, as if they were longtime friends who had spoken only days before.

"I have a very important personal favor to ask of you," Julia confessed after they had spent a few moments catching up. "In return for hearing my pitch, I have something exclusive to offer you that any dedicated fan of *A Patchwork Life* would covet dearly."

"Is that so?" Lillian replied, intrigued. "I'll be the envy of my friends, and I do so enjoy that. Tell me more."

"I'd prefer to discuss it in person. There's something I'd like to show you too, and my home is the best place for that. Would you join me for lunch tomorrow at noon?"

"How mysterious. Are you saying this is so top secret that it can't even leave your house?"

"Something like that, yes."

"Then count me in."

"Fantastic! Would you like me to send a car for you?"

"No need. Stephen gave me the most adorable Aston Martin for my seventy-fifth birthday, and I drive it whenever I have the chance. See you tomorrow, dear."

Julia had less than twenty-four hours to prepare, and she made the most of every minute. She arranged for her personal chef to prepare an excellent lunch, for the housecleaners to whisk away every mote of dust, and for her favorite florist to deliver understated yet elegant arrangements to adorn the great room and dining room. All the while, she held out hope that Deneford wouldn't hasten to cast someone else in the role that would have gone to Paige if not for Julia's interference, but she knew time wasn't on her side.

The next day, when every last detail was arranged and Lillian was due to arrive at any moment, Julia paced by the front door, breathing in through her nose for a three count and out through her mouth, practicing the familiar rituals that always gave her confidence before she stepped onstage. When she heard the smooth, low growl of a high-performance engine coming up her driveway, she opened the door in time to glimpse a sleek, slate-blue coupe slowing as it approached the porte cochere and disappeared around the corner of the house. Julia hurried outside to meet her guest halfway up the front walk.

Moments later, Lillian came into view, petite and thin, yet ineffably commanding, her silver-white hair swept up in a short, layered, textured bob with a blunt fringe, her blue eyes concealed behind enormous mirrored sunglasses. She wore a light rust pantsuit, impeccably tailored, over an ivory blouse with a lavaliere at the neck. An oversized leopard-print tote dangled from her left elbow, and with her right hand she offered Julia a jaunty wave as she approached.

"Thank you so much for coming," Julia said, welcoming her with air-kisses to both cheeks.

"Nothing could have kept me away," Lillian declared.

Soon they were seated at a cozy table on Julia's shaded lanai, chatting like old friends as they enjoyed a delicious farro salad with roasted beets and arugula, followed by grilled salmon fillets with a sweet-and-tangy maple Dijon glaze, served over a bed of quinoa and roasted brussels sprouts. Soon thereafter, over a dessert of coffee and delicate chai-spiced pizzelles, Lillian fixed Julia with a look of amused expectation. "I know I'm excellent company, but that's not why you've treated me to this marvelous lunch. What's on your mind? You mentioned a favor."

"Yes, I did." Julia took a fortifying sip of coffee. "I'm sure you know that Stephen and I aren't exactly on the best of terms."

"Oh, yes. I'm well aware. He's nursed a grudge ever since you and the screenwriter walked off the set of his perfectly dreadful movie."

She sighed fondly, shaking her head. "I'm sure he had it coming. I love my son very much, but I admit sometimes he can be a rascal."

That wasn't the word Julia and Ellen had used when they'd groused about him behind his back. "If he's holding a grudge, then I need your help more than I realized. It's urgent that I meet with Stephen as soon as possible. I've reached out, but he won't reply to my messages."

"How impolite of him," Lillian remarked. "Of course, he *is* a very busy man."

"Yes, I appreciate that. He did have his assistant put me on his calendar for two weeks from today, but this can't wait. A young actress's career may depend on it."

Lillian's eyebrows rose. "So this favor isn't for yourself?"

"No, it's on behalf of one of my very talented costars, Paige Lyons." Quickly Julia added, "She doesn't know that I'm doing this."

"Is that so? Then I won't mention it, should we ever meet."

"You'll meet her soon, and trust me, you'll adore her." Julia reached into the tote bag she had set beside her chair before Lillian arrived and removed a flat, rectangular box tied with a ribbon in alternating stripes of wine and silver blue, the colors of Pi Beta Phi. "This is a gift offered in sincere friendship, to thank you for hearing me out."

An amused smile played at the corners of Lillian's mouth as she accepted the box. "Not a quid pro quo?"

"Not at all. If Paige's talent doesn't convince you to get me that meeting, I shouldn't have it."

"Hmm." Lillian set the box on the table before her, untied the ribbon, and lifted the lid, revealing a thin, gently used stack of papers bound by three brass brads. "*A Patchwork Life*, season five, episode twenty-four—" She gasped, eyes widening with delight. "Is this what I think it is?"

"It's my personal copy of the script for our season five finale, including my handwritten notes and edits. Don't read it until June if you don't like spoilers."

Lillian removed the script from the box and turned the first few pages carefully. "I usually don't, but in this case I'll make an exception. Oh, this is marvelous. Every *Patchwork* fan in the country would love this." She paused, thinking. "You know, Julia, with your permission, I'd love to contribute this to the silent auction for the Big Brothers Big Sisters fundraiser next year. I'll read it first, of course. One more read wouldn't reduce its value."

"I love that idea," Julia declared. "It's a gift, so you're free to do what you like with it. All I ask is that you hold off until after the episode airs. I could get in a lot of trouble if this leaks to the media."

"Not a problem. The gala is in October. I'd love for you to attend too, since your script will be a featured auction item."

"I might just purchase a table and bring my castmates along." With a pang, Julia remembered that they were all rather angry with her and might refuse her invitation—unless her plan succeeded, in which case she would be forgiven, and all would be well. "A fun fact about that episode: It introduces a new character, a beautiful, spirited young woman named Anabelle Wedgington."

"Any relation to Theodore Wedgington?"

"Anabelle is his niece, newly arrived from Boston. She adores her uncle and is utterly oblivious to his villainous ways."

Lillian clapped her hands, delighted. "I trust she'll figure it out soon."

"Not too soon, I hope. That would ruin so many exciting potential plot complications." Julia lowered her voice confidentially, although they were entirely alone, unless they were being observed by paparazzi with telephoto lenses. "Anabelle and Jesse are going to fall in love."

"No!"

"Yes."

"That's wonderful! It broke my heart when that Ida Mae spurned Jesse to marry that wealthy banker from Cleveland. Whose bright idea was that?"

"Don't blame the writers," said Julia. "The actress who played Ida

Mae left to do another series. But it's all for the best, because Paige Lyons is absolutely wonderful as Anabelle, as you're about to see."

Rising, Julia invited Lillian to accompany her to the theater, where she had queued up the DVD the editor had sent over that morning. Without giving away too many of the season's plot twists, Julia set the scene as she showed Lillian to the best seat in the house. Then she dimmed the lights, settled into her own seat, and pressed play.

Paige's performance spoke for itself, more eloquently than Julia's praise could have done. She watched from the corner of her eye as Lillian became happily engrossed in her exclusive advanced screening. It occurred to Julia that she probably should have asked Lillian to sign a nondisclosure agreement first, but it was too late for that, and anyway, Lillian didn't seem like the type to run to the tabloids.

When the brief film ended, Lillian applauded. "That actress is marvelous," she exclaimed as Julia turned on the house lights with the remote. "So talented, and so lovely! She resembles a young Elizabeth Taylor."

"That's exactly what I thought."

"I can't wait to see what she does in season six." Then Lillian peered at her quizzically. "But what do she and your series have to do with my son?"

"Stephen had offered Paige a lead in an upcoming movie. It had the potential to be a breakthrough role for her."

"Well, good for Stephen. I'm glad he recognized her star quality."

"He *had* offered Paige the role," Julia emphasized, a flush rising in her cheeks. "Then, unfortunately, he asked for my input. Who knows why, but I wish he hadn't. I said something stupid and careless about her not being available because she'd be working on *Patchwork* season seven, when that was only wishful thinking on my part."

"There won't be a seventh season?"

"It's not officially canceled yet, but—" Julia shook her head and managed a forlorn smile.

"Oh, Julia." Lillian patted her arm, sympathetic. "I'm so sorry."

"I am too. I was in denial for quite a while, and I made some regrettable choices because of it. That includes what I said to Stephen."

"He withdrew Paige's offer?"

"He did. I urged him to speak with Paige's agent before he made a decision, but he just—" Exasperated, Julia waved a hand dismissively, but then she caught herself. "Sorry. I don't mean to insult your son."

"No, it's quite all right. I know exactly what you mean." Lillian rested her chin on her hand, thinking. "Did he already give Paige's role to someone else?"

"I have no idea."

"Of course you wouldn't; he won't speak to you." Mouth pursed, Lillian rose. "He *will* speak to *me*. Care to take a little trip?"

"Sure." Julia scrambled to her feet. "Where?"

"To Stephen's office, of course." Lillian smiled brightly. "I'll drive."

Julia took a moment to grab the DVD, toss it into her handbag, and run a brush through her hair, but soon they were in Lillian's magnificent Aston Martin, speeding down the mountainside to the PCH. Less than an hour later they arrived at the studio, where the security guard deferentially waved Lillian through the entrance without asking for ID.

"Let me do the talking," Lillian said as she parked her car outside Deneford's bungalow. "At least to get you into his office. Then you're on your own."

Julia nodded and followed her inside, where Lillian paused at the front desk to chat with the receptionist about their dogs, the receptionist's children, and their plans for Thanksgiving. Julia plastered on a pleasant smile and feigned interest, trying not to fidget impatiently as the minutes ticked by. Finally Lillian pointed to the inner door and asked, "Is he in? I need a minute."

"He has a meeting in fifteen," the receptionist replied, giving Julia a quick side-eye, "but he's always in for you."

Lillian thanked her and swept toward the office door, rapping twice but not waiting for a response before opening it. "Hello, dear," she sang, striding into her son's office and beckoning Julia to follow.

"Mom," Deneford said with a start, nearly dropping the phone pressed to his ear. "I'll have to call you back," he murmured into the receiver and hung up. "Lovely to see you." He rose and came around his desk to kiss her on the cheek. "And you brought a friend," he said, escorting his mother to a comfortable chair and taking the one beside her. Julia, left to fend for herself, settled gracefully onto the sofa opposite them.

"I did indeed," Lillian replied, smiling. "Something must be wrong with your phone or your computer, Stevie, because my dear friend Julia has left you several messages to which you haven't replied. I know you aren't simply ignoring her, because I brought you up better than that."

Deneford spread his hands and shrugged, chagrined. "I've been swamped," he said. "No offense intended."

"None taken," Julia assured him.

"Stevie, I understand you're considering Paige Lyons for a role in one of your upcoming films," said Lillian. "I'm so thrilled to hear that. I've seen some of her work, and she's definitely someone to watch."

"You've seen her work? I mean, there isn't much of it."

"And yet I have, enough to know that she shows great talent and presence. That's why I'm puzzled. I also heard that you rescinded your offer. I hope I misunderstood."

"No, actually, that's true." Deneford gestured to Julia, his voice amiable, but his look unmistakably annoyed. "It was Julia herself who told me Paige wasn't available."

"I spoke out of turn," Julia said evenly. "I tried to tell you that."

"I don't think so," said Deneford, shaking his head. "This frantic backpedaling is actually kind of suspicious."

"Oh, Stevie, just stop," said Lillian, exasperated. "Haven't you ever misspoken? You don't need to answer that because I know you have. There's that story you love to tell about how you bought your first eight-millimeter camera with money you saved from your paper route—"

"Mom," he interjected sharply.

"That story isn't true?" Julia asked, looking from Lillian to Deneford and back. "I read that in an interview you did with *Time* magazine."

Lillian waved a hand dismissively. "*Time*, *60 Minutes*, *GQ*—he's shared that story far and wide. That doesn't make it true."

"Mom, please."

"I gave him that camera for his birthday," Lillian told Julia, shaking her head and regarding her son with fond amusement. "As for the thirty thousand dollars he allegedly saved up from his job at RadioShack to fund his first feature film—"

"Mom—"

"Five thousand of that was his savings," Lillian continued. "The rest I gave him. I sold my car and started taking the bus to work."

"You're kidding," said Julia, astounded. "His entire origin story is a lie?"

"Everyone embellishes," Deneford countered, face reddening. Turning to his mother, he added, contritely, "I bought you another car as soon as I could afford it."

"Yes, you did, dear." Lillian patted his hand, beaming. "Several, in fact. Your most recent gift is my favorite. As I've always told you, I was happy to invest in your future. I wanted you to fulfill your dreams." She gestured expansively, as if to take in his office, the studio, perhaps the entire film industry. "And hasn't it paid off splendidly?" Her smile faded. "But you *have* misspoken, deliberately and repeatedly. You of all people should be generous and understanding when someone else does the same."

Deneford heaved a sigh. "Okay, Mom. Maybe you're right."

"Oh, I'm definitely right," said Lillian. "You know what would make me very happy, dear?"

He hesitated. "What?" he asked grudgingly.

"If you would listen carefully as my good friend Julia corrects whatever misunderstanding there may be regarding Paige Lyons—who, in my opinion, is a promising young actress with a brilliant career ahead of her." Rising, Lillian slipped on her sunglasses and looped the handles of her tote over the crook of her elbow. "I'll see myself out. Julia, after you two chat, I'll meet you outside by the car."

With a final pointed look for her son and an encouraging smile for Julia, she swept from the office and left them to it.

18

Deneford heaved a sigh, resigned. "I'll give you five minutes."

"I'll need at least fifteen."

"You have five."

"And when I walk out of here and meet your mother at her car after only five minutes—"

"Fine, fifteen." Deneford sat back in his chair and steepled his fingers. "Just get on with it."

"First of all, thank you for hearing me out," Julia said, with a small, wry smile to show that she understood it was under duress. "Let me be perfectly clear: Paige Lyons is an exceptionally talented young actor with tremendous potential. She's dedicated to her craft, well-liked by her colleagues, reliable, and a pleasure to work with. That's why I didn't want her to leave our show."

Deneford studied her. "Fair enough."

"It was selfish of me to interfere when you offered her such a wonderful opportunity." Julia drew in a deep, shaky breath. "All the more so because the sixth season of *A Patchwork Life* will be our last. At the moment, Paige is available to appear in your film. You should cast her while you still can, because if you don't, some other, more perceptive director will, and they, not you, will take credit for giving her the breakthrough role that launches her as Hollywood's newest, brightest star."

"I did intend to cast her," he pointed out. "You convinced me not to."

"I shouldn't have." Julia took the DVD from her tote and went to the flat-screen television in the media cabinet on the opposite side of the room. "This will remind you why you should have followed your instincts."

Inserting the DVD into the player, she pressed play and crossed the room to turn out the lights. She remained by the switch while the reel played, watching Deneford closely for any reaction, but he kept his expression carefully neutral.

When the film ended, she turned on the lights and returned to her seat. "Well?" she prompted, concealing her sudden anxiety. She had hoped for a spontaneous expression of enthusiasm while he watched, or at least a smile.

"She's very talented," he allowed. "That's why she was my first choice for Emily."

"Have you given the role to anyone else?"

"Not yet. We haven't drawn up a contract, but we're nearly there."

"Then why not cast Paige as you originally planned?" said Julia, impassioned. "Come on. Give her the part. I'll even sweeten the deal. I'd be happy to throw in a bottle of wine from Charles's cellar—he was quite the sommelier, as you well know—or my Louisa Matthíasdóttir landscape. I know you admire her work."

"I do. And that's a tempting offer."

"Then what'll it be? Wine or art? Or both?"

"Neither." A slow grin was spreading over his face. "I have something better in mind."

Julia studied him, vaguely uneasy. "I can't imagine what."

"No, really, this is a great idea. You'll love it."

That did nothing to inspire confidence, but Julia reminded herself that she had promised Paige she'd do whatever it took to fix her mistake. "Fine. Let's hear it."

"This might surprise you, but I want to offer you a role."

"Wow. Yes, I *am* surprised," Julia admitted. "Who would I play? Emily's elderly grandmother? A crotchety old housekeeper?"

"No, no, no. I'm not talking about my movie." He chuckled at the very idea. "I want you to be in my nephew's new TV series."

"Oh. I see." Julia braced herself for the worst. "Is it a decent role, at least?"

"It's an ensemble cast, but you'd have a standout part." He held up his hands as if framing a shot. "*Celebrity Jury*, a new reality series in which twelve of America's most popular stars determine the fate of plaintiffs and defendants embroiled in the quirkiest cases ever brought before the court."

"A reality show?" Julia exclaimed, dismayed. "I loathe reality television—except for *The Amazing Race*. Could you cast me in *The Amazing Race* instead? I'm sure I could convince Nigel to be my partner."

"My nephew isn't directing *The Amazing Race*."

"But *Celebrity Jury*, really?" Julia protested. "This sounds terribly irresponsible. How could you allow a dozen celebrities to decide whether someone goes to prison, or worse? That's not entertainment. That's a travesty of the judicial system."

"What are you talking about? Celebrities serve on juries all the time. Oprah Winfrey was on the jury for a murder case in Chicago back in August. If Oprah can do her civic duty, so can you." Deneford waved a hand, dismissive. "Anyway, you wouldn't be hearing criminal cases. It would be small claims court stuff, civil cases. The plaintiffs and defendants would have to apply to be on the show, they'd be thoroughly vetted, and they'd have to agree to abide by the jury's decision."

"I don't know, Stephen. It sounds so vulgar."

"Final offer," he said emphatically. "I agree to cast Paige as Emily

St. Aubert if you accept a part, at scale, in *Celebrity Jury*, a new, low-budget reality television series to be directed by my nephew."

"'Low-budget'?" Julia echoed. "The more you say, the worse it sounds. Will they at least validate parking?"

"For you, I'm sure something can be arranged."

Julia groaned and clasped a hand to her forehead. This was for Paige, she reminded herself, and to redeem herself in the eyes of her friends and colleagues. "That's your final offer?"

"Final offer."

"Then I accept." Before he could celebrate, she held up a hand. "I have two conditions. First, I'll do one season and one season only. Second, you may tell Paige that we spoke—she'll probably ask why you changed your mind and I don't want to lie to her—but you mustn't breathe a word about our arrangement. Not to Paige, not to her agent, not to anyone."

"Fine," he said, shrugging. "I'll say you put in a good word for her, but she was cast solely on the basis of her talent."

"Good. That's our story and we're sticking to it." Suddenly Julia thought of something else. "I'll allow one exception to the confidentiality rule. You may tell your mother, if you swear her to secrecy."

"Are you kidding? My mother would never allow me to extort you like this." Quickly he added, "You're not allowed to tell her either."

"If you insist, but she'll probably figure it out on her own when I suddenly appear on your nephew's show." Julia sighed. Reality television—what a dreadful penance.

"Maybe so, but don't give her any hints." Deneford rose and extended his hand. "I'm glad we worked this out. I'll break the good news to my nephew, and I'll send a contract over to Maury this afternoon."

Julia stood too. "But first, the moment I leave your office, you'll contact Paige's agent."

"Sure, of course."

Satisfied, Julia shook his hand. Maybe *Celebrity Jury* wouldn't be as awful as she feared, she told herself as she left Deneford's office. Even if it was, it would only be for one season.

Soon thereafter, Lillian regarded Julia speculatively as she approached the car. "You look happy," she remarked as they each opened their doors and climbed inside.

"Paige has the part," Julia said as she buckled her seat belt and settled back, smiling in satisfaction.

"That's wonderful! Congratulations to all three of you. I'm glad common sense surpassed ego."

"I'm so grateful to you for getting me through the door," Julia said as Lillian pulled out of the parking lot and headed toward the front gates. "'Thank you' doesn't even begin to cover it."

"Knowing that I'll get to see our favorite ingenue in a major motion picture is all the thanks I need." Lillian gave Julia a quick, sidelong glance before returning her eyes to the road. "What will I be seeing *you* in next, I wonder."

"There's the rest of season five of *A Patchwork Life* and then all of season six." Julia couldn't bear to add that after *Patchwork*, she'd be joining a reality show she fervently hoped wouldn't be an unmitigated disaster. After *Celebrity Jury* wrapped, though, she couldn't imagine what she might do next.

Then she remembered: Maury already had some ideas.

As soon as Lillian dropped her off at home, Julia emailed her agent and belatedly confirmed the meeting he had proposed via email the week before. The next day, she went to Maury's office and listened with an open mind as he pitched the two movie roles he had mentioned. To her pleasant surprise, both were intriguing parts in feature films with excellent directors and other acclaimed stars attached. She would need more time to study the scripts before making a decision, but it was comforting to know that the end of her beloved series wouldn't be the calamity she had feared.

When the Cross-Country Quilters phoned in for their weekly

conference call the following evening, Julia admitted that she had sewn only a few seams for that week's Harriet's Journey block, Cross Plains, a pattern that would have been relatively easy to sew, despite its sixty pieces, if only the block were twelve inches square rather than six. They were thrilled to hear that Paige would be starring in Deneford's movie after all, and they assured her that *Celebrity Jury* probably wouldn't be as bad as she feared.

"Maybe not," Julia said. "Oh, I just thought of a third condition I'll have to give Deneford before I sign a contract. His nephew will have to work around my schedule for the movie, once I decide which role to accept."

"Follow your heart," Donna advised.

"Hear, hear," Vinnie chimed in. "That policy has always served me well."

"It's good to see you looking to the future, Julia," said Grace warmly. "You really do have so much to look forward to."

Julia truly hoped that Grace was right, but she knew she would move forward with greater confidence and a lighter heart if she reconciled with the Patchwork Players.

On Friday morning, after the trades broke the news that newcomer Paige Lyons would be starring as Emily St. Aubert in Stephen Deneford's much-anticipated adaptation of *The Mysteries of Udolpho*, Julia sent a group email to the Patchwork Players, as well as others from the cast and crew who had not attended quilt camp with them. "Our Nine-Patch quilt isn't yet finished," she noted. "If you all agree, I'd like us to finish it together. We could autograph our blocks and donate the quilt to the Big Brothers Big Sisters of Greater Los Angeles. I'm sure it would be a popular item in the silent auction at their annual fundraiser." She invited everyone to gather on Sunday at her place, where she would set up a quilt frame, provide all the necessary sewing supplies, and serve an autumnal buffet lunch. "Please reply to RSVP," she concluded. "Hope to see you all soon."

She hit send and waited a few moments, then put the computer to sleep and left the room without looking back. Her time would be much better spent working on her Cross Plains block rather than staring morosely at the computer screen, refreshing her inbox every two minutes in hope and dread of her colleagues' replies.

After an hour of pinning and sewing ridiculously small triangles and squares together, curiosity won out and she returned to check her email. To her relief, Ellen, Lindsay, Nigel, and Edna had already replied to say that they would attend. They had, in fact, replied to all, so that everyone else would understand that they were no longer subjecting Julia to the cut direct, casting her out of society.

"Don't be so dramatic," she muttered.

She was just about to return to her sewing room when her computer pinged, alerting her to a new email from Ellen. "I thought you should know that Paige told the other campers that her agent said you marched into Deneford's office and refused to leave until he agreed to cast her," she wrote. "That must have been fun. I wish I'd been there to see it. I think it's safe to say that all is forgiven."

Julia fervently wanted to believe it, but until she heard from Paige, she couldn't be sure.

She worked on her Cross Plains block throughout the afternoon, pausing occasionally to rest her fingers, to stretch, to discuss her next week's schedule with her assistant, and to take a few phone calls from Maury. Dinner would be a solitary affair, delicious and healthy, thanks to her personal chef, but quiet and lonely compared to the convivial meals she had enjoyed among friends in the banquet hall of Elm Creek Manor.

On her way to the fridge to inspect her options, she paused once more to check her email. Her heart thudded when she discovered that Paige had replied.

Taking a deep, steadying breath, Julia opened the email.

"I wouldn't miss it!" Paige had written. "Don't know about y'all but I need to practice quilting before we start filming. Should I bring anything for the buffet?"

Then, as if Paige's acceptance had given everyone else permission, nearly all the other cast and crew had replied, most to say that they were coming, some to send their regrets and to demand that the attendees share photos and recaps afterward.

Overwhelmed with relief, Julia responded to say that they needn't provide anything for the buffet, but if they had any favorite sewing tools, they should bring them along.

Then she sprang into action, mindful that it was almost end-of-business on a Friday and she had not a moment to lose.

She called her personal chef, who also ran a professional event catering business. After insisting upon paying a premium for the short notice, she arranged for a seasonal buffet that would make Chef Anna proud. Next she called her local quilt shop, and when she explained that she needed a state-of-the-art quilt frame, they gave her the contact information for their preferred distributer. She phoned the company, but when she identified herself, the man who answered the phone thought it was a prank and promptly hung up. She sighed and dialed again. This time she kept the fellow on the line long enough to convince him that yes, she was *that* Julia Merchaud, and yes, she needed a quilt frame for the real cast and crew of *A Patchwork Life*, because yes, they actually were quilters, ranging from novice to experienced.

"I can have our best model delivered to your residence tomorrow afternoon," he assured her, sounding a bit starstruck. "No charge."

"No charge for delivery? That's generous."

"No, Miss Merchaud. I mean it's all on the house."

"Don't be silly," Julia exclaimed. "That's a terrible business model. You have to let me pay you."

But he wouldn't hear of it. Eventually they agreed that she would write a letter praising the frame—as long as she genuinely could recommend it—which the company could use in a new advertising campaign. Maury wouldn't approve of the arrangement, what with no contract and only the vaguest of terms, but Julia would sort that out later. The important thing was that she would have a quilting frame and friends gathered around it in her great room in less than forty-eight hours.

The frame was delivered and assembled on Saturday afternoon. The following morning, when she was as ready as she would ever be, Julia paced in her great room, half expecting that no one would show up. Ellen had told her that all was forgiven, she reminded herself. Her friends had said they would be there. She just needed to have faith in them, and in herself.

The doorbell rang.

She flew to answer it. "Julia, my dear, you look lovely this morning," Nigel purred, kissing her on both cheeks and showing off a bag filled with fixings for mimosas. Other friends were already coming up the front walk—Ellen and Lindsay, chatting happily; Dylan and a woman with waist-length, gray-streaked blond hair, presumably his wife; Noah and the pretty starlet from the Disney Channel, whose name Julia could never remember; and all the others. Julia urged them all inside, to help themselves to food and drink, or to slip on a thimble, thread a needle, and stitch to their heart's content. The Patchwork Players could teach those who had not come along on their journey, creating a bit of Elm Creek Quilt Camp in the hills of Malibu.

Last to arrive were Paige and Louis, walking hand in hand.

Julia welcomed them warmly, tentatively. After Paige murmured for Louis to precede her inside, she lingered on the doorstep, her gaze fixed on Julia's.

"I'm so sorry," Julia told her simply. "I regret every moment of anxiety and hurt I caused you."

"I'm sure you didn't mean any harm," said Paige. "And whatever you said to Stephen Deneford, you more than made up for it. Would you believe he actually increased his offer? He said his mother wouldn't forgive him if he let me get away."

"Is that so? In that case, I think that's what did the trick, rather than anything I said."

"We both know that's not true," said Paige, offering a small smile. "I do get it, you know? You wanted to believe that the show would go on forever. I might have done the same in your place."

"If you ever are in my place," said Julia ruefully, "I trust you'll learn from my mistakes and make better choices."

"Oh, I definitely will," Paige said, eyes wide, nodding for emphasis. Julia watched her for a moment, uncertain, until Paige burst out laughing. "I'm teasing, Miss Julia," she said, giving Julia's arm a playful squeeze. "Since we're going to be working together, I should warn you that I do that a lot."

"I look forward to it," said Julia sincerely. She gestured to the open doorway. "Come on inside. You're very welcome here."

They heard laughter, conversation, and piano music from the foyer, but when they entered together, a hush fell over the room.

"Hey, y'all," said Paige, planting a hand on her hip. "Why are you looking at us like you're holding your breath for the next dramatic plot twist?"

"Because that's exactly what we're doing," said Olivia as she accepted a mimosa from Nigel.

"We've been on pins and needles waiting to see if you'd patch things up," said Jason, grinning. When a chorus of laughter and groans rose from the group, he looked around, feigning indignation. "What? Since when does this crowd object to sewing puns? Just so you know, I'm going to put that line in a season six script."

"No, you won't," countered Ellen firmly, evoking more laughter.

"All's well that ends well," Nigel declared, raising his glass in a toast. "'The web of our life is of a mingled yarn, good and ill together: our virtues would be proud, if our faults whipped them not; and our crimes would despair, if they were not cherished by our virtues.'"

"I don't understand what that means, but I love the way you say it," said Edna, raising her glass.

Julia's heart was full as she joined in the laughter. "Here's to our *Patchwork* family," she said, taking a cup of coffee from a passing server and holding it high. "If all the world's a stage, there's no ensemble I'd rather share it with than all of you. What was it Nigel said so eloquently on our first night at Elm Creek Manor?"

"That's a difficult question," said Nigel, brow furrowing. "Everything I say is eloquent."

"I remember," said Paige. "'We few, we happy few—'"

"'We merry band of Patchwork Players!'" they all joined in, finishing the scene together.

CLOSING CREDITS

Author	JENNIFER CHIAVERINI
Agent	MARIA MASSIE
Editor	RACHEL KAHAN
Copyeditor	KAREN RICHARDSON
Publicists	EMI BATTAGLIA
	MARTIN WILSON
Marketing	KELSEY MANNING
	TAYLOR TURKINGTON
Cover Design	ELSIE LYONS
Page Design	NANCY SINGER
Accounting	SOPHIE WEILER
Assistant to Ms. Chiaverini	GERALDINE NEIDENBACH
Assistant to Ms. Kahan	ALEXANDRA BESSETTE
Wardrobe Supervisor	STEFF LINCECUM
Chief Engineer	MARTIN CHIAVERINI
Acting Consultant	NICK CHIAVERINI
Photography	MICHAEL CHIAVERINI

The author wishes to thank her family, especially her husband, Marty; her sons, Nick and Michael; and her mother, Geraldine, for their enduring love, steadfast support, and tireless encouragement.

An Elm Creek Quilts Production

ABOUT THE AUTHOR

Jennifer Chiaverini is the *New York Times* bestselling author of thirty-seven novels, including critically acclaimed historical fiction and the beloved Elm Creek Quilts series. She graduated from the University of Notre Dame and earned her MA from the University of Chicago. In 2020, she was awarded an Outstanding Achievement Award from the Wisconsin Library Association for her novel *Resistance Women*, and in 2023, the WLA awarded her the honor of Notable Wisconsin Author for her significant contributions to the state's literary heritage. She, her husband, and their two sons call Madison, Wisconsin, home.